SHADOW OPS

Richard Skye faced the trio. Laika was startled once more to see how short the man was. "I doubt if Mr. Kristal will be plying his pseudo-psychic wares before many national audiences after this. I'm very pleased. All in all, this was an excellent, if noncritical, case for you three to get acquainted over and, shall we say, cut your psychic teeth on before you move on to . . . greater mysteries. And you acquitted yourselves admirably. In fact, I'm so pleased that I'm sending you under the very deepest cover so that you can continue to do just this kind of work.

"As of today, you three no longer exist. You will be shadow operatives performing shadow operations." Skye smiled at them. "Ironic, isn't it? Shadows . . . bringing other shadows to light."

THE
SEARCHERS

— BOOK ONE —
CITY OF IRON

CHET WILLIAMSON

AVON BOOKS ◆ NEW YORK

AVON BOOKS, INC.
1350 Avenue of the Americas
New York, New York 10019

Copyright © 1998 by Chet Williamson
Inside cover author photo by Ron Bowman
Published by arrangement with the author
Visit our website at **http://www.AvonBooks.com**
Library of Congress Catalog Card Number: 98-92449
ISBN: 0-380-79187-0

First Avon Books Printing: August 1998

AVON TRADEMARK REG. U.S. PAT. OFF. AND IN OTHER COUNTRIES, MARCA REGISTRADA, HECHO EN U.S.A.

Printed in the U.S.A.

WCD   10 9 8 7 6 5 4 3 2 1

For Andrew,
warrior–poet
who exposes the secrets
and brings light to the shadows

ACKNOWLEDGMENTS

The author would like to thank the following people for their assistance in the writing of this book: Barbara Strong Ellis, T. Liam McDonald, Thomas F. Monteleone, and Andrew Vachss. I would also like to thank my agent, Jimmy Vines, and especially my editor, Stephen S. Power.

Pilate saith unto him, What is truth?

—JOHN 18:38

I will teach you. When the time of dissolution arrives, the first power of darkness will come upon you. Do not be afraid, and say, "Behold! The time has come!"

—*THE DIALOGUE OF THE SAVIOR*, VS. 122

Chapter 1

The man looked up into the night sky and saw only a dizzying blur of whiteness. Individually the snowflakes were so light and airy that a single breath made them vanish, but together they had an immense power. Like The Twelve, he thought.

The plane that was to take him to the meeting was only a dark shadow in the sea of white that swirled in the lights of the tiny airport. A smaller shadow detached itself from the mass and walked toward him. "Sorry, Mr. McAndrews, " the pilot shouted over the roar of the wind. "There's no way, sir."

The man the pilot called McAndrews, but whose real name was Mackay, did not speak loudly, but he knew the pilot would hear nonetheless. His voice, low and resonant, held the trace of a Scottish brogue. "I have no choice," he said. "I must leave. Tonight."

The pilot shook his head, giving the man a smile that indicated both sympathy for his plight and disdain for the man's irrational insistence. "Not tonight," he said. "And probably not tomorrow. It's supposed to keep on like this for the next thirty-six hours. Man, you couldn't fire a rocket through this stuff," and he waved his hand in the snowy air.

"I *must* leave," Mackay repeated. "My meeting is tomorrow evening."

"You're out of luck, then," the pilot said, giving his "Sorry, you idiot" smile once more. "Roads are bad and

1

gettin' worse. You'd never get to New York State by to-morrow night.''

"As I said, I have no choice. You're not willing to fly me? I'll pay you handsomely."

The pilot shook his head firmly. "You'd have to pay my widow," he said. "No way, sir."

"Then are you willing to sell your plane?"

"Sell my—?" The pilot barked a laugh.

"I'm a businessman. And I have . . . an extremely impor-tant agenda. It would be more than worth my while."

"And *you'd* fly it?"

"I can fly."

"Not in this. Besides, nobody's gonna get clearance for takeoff tonight."

In his many years of life, Mackay had learned when dis-cussion became futile. He glanced back toward the small terminal building and saw only the haze that its lights cast through the storm. No one there could see him or the pilot.

His gloved hands slid from the warmth of his topcoat pockets, and he grasped the pilot by the shoulder and pulled him close. The heel of his other hand sharply met the pilot's temple. The pilot gave a short groan and went slack in the man's arms.

Mackay lowered him to the snow-covered tarmac, rolled him onto his back, and pulled the hood of the pilot's insu-lated jacket up around the unconscious man's face. He'd be all right for the few minutes it would take for Mackay to get the plane in the air.

Mackay went through the pilot's pockets until he found the key to the plane. Then he picked up his valise and walked to the Cherokee. The light single-engine plane would not have been Mackay's first choice to fly in a storm like this, but he had taken greater risks in his life. As he stepped onto the wing and opened the door, he knew that God would continue to be with him. Just the same, he was glad to see that a chute was lying on the small backseat. Best to stack the deck in the Lord's favor.

He had no choice but to fly instruments-only, as he

wheeled the plane onto the runway and opened the throttle. A voice began jabbering at him from the radio, so he shut it off and concentrated on getting the small plane aloft.

It rose some, but then the wind pushed it down. He kept his eyes fixed on the artificial horizon and pulled back slowly, struggling to keep it level. Then he was up, coursing through a storm that tossed his plane about like a feather, making him think of the hurricane that had struck the schooner that had first taken him to America.

When he felt confident enough to free a hand, he turned the radio back on and informed the tower that the pilot was lying out on the runway, and that they had better find him before he was buried by the falling snow and froze to death. Profanity rattled back at him, and he switched the radio off again and watched his instruments closely.

He had just crossed into Wisconsin airspace when he felt the plane stall. The altimeter spun backward, slowly at first, then more rapidly, bleeding off altitude as the craft dropped into a full dive.

A glance out the window showed him the reason. Rime ice coated the edge of the wings. He pulled back on the stick, but there was no response.

He reached into the backseat, grabbed the chute, and wrestled it on in the tight quarters, pulling the straps tight. Then he wrapped his fingers around the handle of his valise and hugged it to him. With his left hand he pulled back on the door handle and tried to kick it open, but the hinge was toward the front of the plane, and the pressure blew the door shut instantly.

Now he pushed against it with his shoulder, pressing against the air rushing up from below. At last there was room to get his head and shoulders through, and the cold air whipped at him, tearing off his hat and whirling it away into the night. He tightened his grip on the valise.

Mackay knew he would have to jump fast so that the door would not slam shut on him. He pressed his feet against the instrument panel, took a deep breath, and launched himself into the storm.

The door slapped shut, nearly crushing his right foot, and pain tore through him for a red second. Then he was lost in darkness, and the storm screamed victory in his ears, and the only thought that came to his mind as he yanked at the ripcord was that this would be the first meeting of The Twelve that he had missed in a hundred and twenty years.

The following evening, twenty minutes before midnight, eleven men performed various tasks in a remote lodge in the heart of the Adirondack Mountains. In the small kitchen, a man named Ferguson placed a loaf of bread on a silver plate. Though he knew that vanity was a sin, he admired it for a moment.

It had risen beautifully, and the top was crisp and golden brown, the sides a buttery yellow. A delicious yeasty smell rose with the steam and made Ferguson think of a priest's censer and burning incense. Both this bread and the incense, after all, were intended for the worship of God.

Campbell scurried into the kitchen and looked at the door that led outside, then at Ferguson. "No Mackay yet," he said, then went back into the main room. Ferguson didn't even think of asking if they would wait. On the few rare occasions when one of their party was absent, they had never waited, and they never would. When midnight came, the meeting would begin. That was as sure as the sun rising in the east.

Ferguson stepped to the window and looked out at the road that led to the nearest town, twenty miles away. It lay empty in the clear, cold moonlight. Mackay still had twenty minutes, and Ferguson would be surprised if he didn't show up. Ferguson smiled to himself. They were all fanatical about attending, sure enough, and Mackay was the most single-minded of the lot. If he were alive, he would make it. Mackay would come.

Wallace came into the kitchen. He had finished setting all the glasses and now took the decanter of wine from the kitchen table. "Still no Mackay," he said, and Ferguson nodded as Wallace returned to the main room.

Ferguson whispered a quiet prayer that Mackay had not died. It seldom happened, but it happened nonetheless. Grant had been crossing to the meeting on the *Lusitania* when it was sunk, and Macallan had been murdered by slaves of The One back in 1944. But for the most part, The Twelve knew how to take care of themselves. Those were the lessons that longevity taught, and the lives that faith preserved.

He glanced at his watch and saw that he had been daydreaming longer than he'd thought. That was the problem with constant youth—it made time itself seem unimportant. But tonight time had reasserted its authority once more. Ferguson took the bread knife and placed it on the silver plate next to the loaf. Then he bore it into the meeting place.

All but Mackay were there. Kerr was at the head of the table, going through the mission sheets, both those that would be reported upon, and those that would be assigned this night. Wallace was standing with Campbell, and both were eyeing the table, seeking for some imperfection in their settings but finding none.

Ferguson excused himself, and Murray and Ramsay stepped aside with a murmur of admiration at the artistry of Ferguson's baking. He set the loaf on the table at Kerr's right hand, and the taciturn elder's gaze remained on it long enough for Ferguson to sense his approval.

Then Ferguson went to his place, the second chair on Kerr's left, glanced at his watch, and picked up his portfolio of papers. Seven minutes. That was enough time to pretend to refresh his memory on the past year's missions. In actuality, everything that had happened was so deeply engraved upon his mind that he needed no review. But they continued to pretend, even after all these years, that what they did was more efficacious when committed to paper.

Ferguson looked over his reports with no little amusement. How absurd it all seemed, the ways in which humans deluded themselves and others, the methods they used to express their hatreds and insanities. The Twelve immersed themselves in such excreta like men cleaning out sewers. Ferguson sometimes felt that he had seen as much madness and human vileness in his time as God Himself, though he knew that was not true: God saw all.

Still, they had to follow every lead, track down every clue, trace every crumb of human barbarity on the off chance that The One had inspired it. And if He had, then it was up to them to end it.

"It's time," Kerr said, just loud enough to be heard by the others. Each went to his given seat, and Ferguson sat between Ramsay and Stewart. From across the table, young Gordon smiled at him, and Ferguson smiled back. Best to smile now, for the reports to come would bring no merriment.

"A year has passed," said Kerr, "since we met near Brisbane. So it is time once more to report on our various missions undertaken since that time. As you can see, our brother, Andrew Mackay, is not present. We have discovered that he . . . commandeered a small plane last night but has not been seen since. You all know what the charter says about such occurrences. If Sir Andrew does not appear within eight weeks, he will be considered as passed over, and we will gather to choose a replacement. I pray that is not the case and urge all of you to do likewise so that our brother might be restored to us.

"Now we shall give our individual reports, which will be followed by assignments of new missions. Sir Angus?"

Even after all these years, Kerr's deep faith in their traditional rules of order had not been compromised. The assembly always found this reassuring. Angus Reid, at Kerr's immediate right, stood up, holding his papers in his hands, but he did not look down at them. Instead he fixed his blue eyes on the rest of the company and told the stories of the year that had passed. He spoke of a madman in Savannah who had ripped apart two women and three men. When Reid had finally found him, the man had been torturing a child he had kidnapped. "Though I interrogated him at length," Reid said, "he spoke of nothing that would lead me to conclude that any of what he did was at the behest of The One."

Everyone around the table nodded. Their skills were such

that they knew the man could have held back nothing during Reid's interrogation. Reid shook his head sadly. "Despite my best efforts, the child died." None of them had to ask what Reid had done to the madman. Ferguson hoped Reid had shown no mercy, and that the madman's death had been hard.

Reid then spoke of a dozen other matters, not all of them violent. He talked of a man who had been supposed to possess strange healing powers, but did not; of satanic symbols appearing in holy places as if by magic, until Reid had found the clever and amoral college pranksters who had done it for a lark and stopped them; of bursts of lights that were supposed to have appeared mysteriously in the sky over a small Nebraska town, but were due to hoaxers with a searchlight.

At last he finished and looked at Kerr, who spoke the words they all knew: "And did you, then, find any event to be caused in any way by The One?"

Reid gave the expected answer: "No, and I thank God for the binding."

Ramsay was next, and his report was along the same lines: killings, mutilations, stories of supposed vampires and ghosts, and unexplained lights and other phenomena. Kerr's question was once again answered in the same way.

So it went, down the table, until young Cameron at the end spoke. "There was an occurrence," he said, "on an airplane early in the year—March seventeenth. It was Pan Am Flight 504, from New York to London, and a man in first class went berserk." Ferguson and the others nodded. They were kept well apprised of each other's missions. "He had had only a single glass of wine when he took the bottle, shattered it, and rammed the broken glass into the face of the person in the next seat. It took five people to subdue him.

"I was able, several weeks later, to question him privately. He claimed to have no knowledge of what he had done, no awareness whatsoever. He was telling me the truth." Ferguson believed Cameron implicitly. They all had the ability to ferret out lies. "I believe," Cameron went on, "that The One was directly responsible."

No one asked, "How so?" Their years had taught them patience and economy of language.

"The flight taking Him to his new destination on March seventeenth passed within a mile and a half of the path of Flight 504. Although it's impossible to be certain, it seems the event occurred at the time of that close conjunction."

Stewart said what they were all thinking: "The first time He was ever transported by air."

"Correct." Kerr nodded. "And the last. Too dangerous. Seems the safest place in the world up there, but let the guard down and the bolt is shot." He didn't congratulate Cameron on his findings; they were not in the market for self-congratulation. "This will be reported to the Council," Kerr said. "I have no doubt but that they will change their procedures."

Cameron sat down as Kerr stood and picked up a stack of dossiers. "It has been a relatively calm year, brothers, although with the activity of the past two decades, the Council has been concerned that His power is growing. Constant vigilance, I need not remind you, is still required on our part. We must not allow ourselves to be lulled into a false sense of security. And if perchance His power *is* waning, ours is not to celebrate that, but rather to ensure its perpetuity.

"So here are the missions for the coming year. Nearly all are located in the United States and Canada, since this is where The One's influence would be felt most readily since His relocation."

Kerr passed out the dossiers. None opened his, but each set it beside his silver plate.

"Now," said Kerr, "let us share the bread and wine." He leaned over the silver plate with the golden loaf of bread, broke off a small piece, and placed it into his mouth. Then he passed it to his right. The plate ran down the length of the table and then up again, and by the time it returned to Kerr, only a small piece was left. Kerr made the sign of the cross on his breast and spoke some words in Latin. The others responded in the same language.

Then Kerr slowly opened an intricately carved wooden

box lined with velvet. From it he took a crude wooden cup whose lack of decoration contrasted sharply with the ornamentation of the box. The cup's surface was black with age, though it gleamed as though polished by the oil of countless hands over the centuries.

Kerr lifted the wine decanter and opened it. He poured the ruby liquid into the dark interior of the vessel until it reached nearly the brim. Then he set the decanter down and lifted the cup. He spoke again in Latin, and the others responded. Then he brought the wine to his lips.

But instead of tilting the cup back to drink fully, Kerr suddenly stiffened. The cup slipped through his fingers and clattered onto the table, spilling the wine in a dark red wound across the surface of the white tablecloth. Kerr's eyes went wide, his lips pressed back from his teeth in a snarl of pain, and his hands clutched his stomach.

He gasped for air as his face purpled, and he fell, his chin striking the surface of the table, his head lolling as he slipped to the floor.

Ferguson would have run to help Kerr, but by then the pain had hit him as well. A fire blazed in his stomach, and his only thought, irrational as it was, was that if he could but tear through his flesh he might be able to extinguish it.

Between then and the moment he died, never once did he, nor did any of the ten other agonized men, think of poison. They thought only of the excruciating pain, how they wanted to stop it, and finally, how they wanted to be dead. Their mission, their enemies, their god, all were obliterated from their minds. All that remained was pure agony.

In less than two minutes after Kerr had dropped the cup, the assembly was dead. They lay on the floor, across the table, or with limbs askew where they had fallen against their chairs. Each face was frozen in a rictus of torment. Every finger was hooked and clawed. Some had actually ripped through a coat or shirt and the flesh beneath. The smell of urine and feces, spilled wine and death, hung heavily in the air.

All was silent for a very long time. Had there been any

living thing left inside the lodge, it would have heard only the wind wheezing outside, and the windows rattling. But if anyone had been left alive to see, he might have noticed, an hour after the last of the men had stopped twitching, a white face at the window.

Chapter 2

When the assassin looked through the pane, the expression on his gaunt face was one of incredulity, as though he could not believe that the men inside were truly dead. Then it relaxed as his finger thoughtfully traced a long, thin scar down his right sideburn to his chin. "Eternal life, my ass . . ." he whispered, and gave a soft chuckle.

He tried to count the bodies but could see only eight. The other four, he suspected, were hidden behind the table, where they must have fallen. He didn't go into the lodge. He'd been told to make sure they were all dead and then report back, and that was all he was going to do.

It had been touch-and-go, and he had been afraid he wouldn't get a chance to juice the flour at the grocery store in Malone. But the guy who'd bought it had turned at just the right moment, and he'd been able to push the cyanide capsule right through the plastic grocery bag and into the flour sack. Amazing crap the labs turned out, the plastic and paper sealing behind the capsule as sweet as anything. Then the capsule broke down to let the motion of the man carrying the flour scatter it throughout the bag. God bless the USA.

He walked around to the window at the other side and peered in, looking for the four missing bodies. Yeah, there they were . . . one, two, three. . . .

Three? He carefully looked again but came to the same conclusions: only eleven men lay dead inside the lodge. Then there must be another one somewhere.

11

The assassin drew an Ingram from under his nylon parka and went around to the back door. His footsteps crunching in the snow sounded painfully loud to him, and he could feel the sweat pooling in his armpits. He liked wet work best when there was little or no risk to him. His victims looked a whole lot better at the end of a telescopic sight. These sonsabitches were warriors who made the assassin look like a goddamned beginner. He had thought of them as occidental samurai.

Yet he had killed them, all of them, except for one stubborn bastard.

The assassin turned the knob of the back door but found it locked. He took a deep breath, pulled back his foot, and kicked hard where the lock met the jamb. The frame splintered with a sharp crack, and he hurled himself through, falling prone on the floor, his weapon aimed at whatever might be there.

But there was nothing. The kitchen was empty. He stood up and went into the main room, but found only the bodies. Wrinkling his nose at the sour smell, he explored the other rooms, the muzzle of his weapon nervously preceding him. No one was there.

Back in the main room, the assassin looked at the papers, the dossiers, the spilled wine, the wooden cup that lay overturned on the table. He didn't notice the twelfth portfolio, Mackay's, under Kerr's, where Kerr had left it when the man hadn't arrived.

The hell with it, he thought. He had been told to kill them, that was all. Nothing had been said about bringing back any souvenirs.

But when he was halfway to the front door, he stopped and looked back. The bread, the wine, the men around the table . . . it made him think of something, something religious he had learned about when he was a kid.

The Last Supper. There was a picture of it on his grandma's bedroom wall, with Jesus and his disciples, and the bread and the wine. This was a last supper, sure enough. This bunch would never eat and drink together again.

The assassin glanced at his wristwatch and realized he would have to hustle if he was going to be at the pickup point in time. He went through the door, pulled it shut behind him, and started running down the lane in the moonlight, looking apprehensively about him.

After all, that twelfth man was still alive somewhere.

Fifteen hours later, in bright afternoon sunshine, Andrew Mackay drove down the snow-packed lane toward the lodge. He was cut and bruised and battered, and a cane was propped on the passenger seat of his Jeep.

Three miles east of Eau Claire, Wisconsin, he had bailed out of his plane. It had crashed several miles away in a heavy patch of woods and had not yet been discovered. After he'd landed heavily in a cornfield, he had made his way to a road, where he had flagged down a snowplow driver. In Eau Claire, he'd paid cash for a four-wheel drive utility vehicle and begun the slow trip back to St. Paul, where he'd taken a train east.

The traveling had been slow everywhere, for the storm that was moving steadily west had already blanketed the States all the way back to Connecticut. It was not until the morning after the meeting of The Twelve that Mackay had finally arrived in New York's Penn Station. There he had taken a train to Plattsburgh, where he'd bought a Jeep with cash and driven to the lodge.

Mackay knew, as he came up the long drive, that something was wrong. Their cars were still there, but they would not have waited for him. After the reports were given, the new missions distributed, and the bread and wine shared, The Twelve would have left immediately.

The first thing he suspected was some crisis that had made his brothers remain and plan through last night and today. But as he drew closer, there seemed to be no sign of life within. He could see that the interior was lit, but he could sense no movement.

He parked and took a pistol from beneath the seat, then shrugged off his topcoat to improve his mobility. He left his cane in the Jeep. He could walk without it, though the pain was greater. But if what he now feared had come true, his pain was as nothing.

He could smell death through the closed door. Neither the crisp air of the mountains nor the thick snow melting in the afternoon sun could disguise it. He knew that no one was alive in the lodge, and he lowered his weapon as he opened the door.

They were all there, all dead; and as he walked around the table, he didn't know if he grieved more for the loss of his brothers or the threat to the world. But his eyes remained dry, for he had lost so many people he'd loved over the centuries that his tears had dried up long ago.

Still, it was harrowing to see those with whom he had worked for so many years cut down. Kerr, Douglas, Murray . . . all of them, the only people he'd ever been able to safely call friend. Had it not been for the storm that had nearly killed him, he would be lying here, too.

But there would be time enough for grief . . . and for vengeance. Now he had to determine what had happened, and how.

He immediately surmised that poison had been the culprit, and from the contortions of the bodies he suspected cyanide. He first thought of gas, since they all seemed to have died within minutes, but dismissed that theory when he examined the bodies more closely. The dried froth on the lips and the corpses' hands clawing at their stomachs told him the poison had been ingested.

The level of wine in the decanter was where Mackay would have expected it to be if the wooden cup had been filled, but from the amount of dried wine on the tablecloth, he knew that they had not yet drunk when they were stricken. It had to be the bread, then.

He picked up the remaining piece and sniffed it, but smelled only the spilled wine that had saturated it. Ferguson must have baked it, as he usually did.

Mackay went into the kitchen and saw the broken door, immediately realizing that someone had kicked it in. He pushed it shut, and the room felt warmer. Then he began investigating the baking materials.

He found nothing in the box of baking soda, but when he poured the flour out onto the sideboard, he saw several very small white flakes of what might have been a gelatin residue. When he examined the flour bag, he discovered a small puckered area on its surface. If he hadn't been looking closely for it, he never would have found it.

He smiled grimly. It was a concept so simple that it indicated extremely high-tech equipment, something no cult had access to. It must have come from higher up, a government job. But whose government? And why? Mackay would have to find out before he could take care of those responsible.

But for now there was work to be done, and quickly. Kerr had made the arrangements for the lodge, so Mackay did not know how soon anyone would come out to learn why the eleven men had neither left nor returned to town.

He limped into the main room and gathered all the papers, many stained with wine, that lay on the table. Together they made a stack nearly a foot high. He also removed all the cash from the pockets of his dead brothers, but did not bother looking for any personal identification. Like Mackay, they carried none.

He took the papers and money to the Jeep, then returned to the lodge, where he picked up the overturned wooden cup, wiped it as clean as possible with the end of the tablecloth, and replaced it in its box.

After he had stowed the box safely in the Jeep, he carefully searched the basement of the lodge and found an empty can that had once stored kerosene, and an old garden hose. He cut off a length of hose with a pair of rusted shears and took it and the can outside, where he siphoned gasoline from a car. Back inside, he splashed the gas over the bodies, up the sides of the walls, and all over the floor, repeating the siphoning until the room was saturated.

From his valise he took a battery-powered fuse box and a small charge of white phosphorous, set it on the floor beneath the table, rose, and for the last time looked at his brothers.

"Rest well," he said softly. "God knows you've worked hard enough for Him."

Then he went outside, where he wiped all of the smooth surfaces of the cars, inside and out. When he felt he had obliterated all the prints and picked up any trace evidence from the seats, floors, and trunk interiors, he climbed into his Jeep and drove down the road several hundred yards. He stopped, pushed a remote button, and watched as the door and windows of the lodge burst outward from the instantaneous heat. There was no sound of an explosion, only a low, rolling rush of air and the sound of broken glass. The splintering shards sparkled like huge snowflakes in the setting sun, flames chasing them from their casements.

Sir Andrew Mackay watched the pyre as it consumed the earthly shells of his brothers, and prayed hard and long. Then he drove on. There was much to tell, and much to learn.

And there was vengeance to take.

Chapter 3

"**V**engeance, death, love, jealousy, deceit, mystery, precision, order, chaos—they're all there, Adam, you don't hear them?"

The voice, thickly accented with the heavy tones of Scandinavia, could barely be heard over the sound of Davitt Moroney's harpsichord, which filled the studio with Bach's *The Art of Fugue*. Adam Guaraldi shouted back, "I hear a dozen cats pissing on a tin roof, that's what I hear!"

Peder Holberg sighed in mock exasperation and waved a hand toward the CD player. "Turn it down, then," he said. "Go ahead, I can receive inspiration at a lower volume, it's all right."

The two men, both stripped to the waist and wearing gym trunks, were working in Holberg's studio. Large iron structures dominated the room, some completed, others in progress. A bare wooden floor showed hundreds of burn marks, and various lengths of iron, both hollow pipe and solid rods, lay in heavy metal troughs along the high walls.

Holberg climbed down from the stepladder on which he had been working and took two plastic bottles of Evian from a minifridge, tossing one to Guaraldi. "That was very good, by the way," he told him. "Cats pissing on a tin roof."

"Not original," Guaraldi answered, twisting open the bottle and taking a long swig. "Beecham, I think."

"Well, this Beecham didn't know what he was talking about. Or anyway, he didn't use it like I use it. It's the sound

17

of metal, you know? I like to hear it when I work. The sound of metal while I *work* in metal, yes?"

"Yes, yes, whatever you say, Peder—you know best." Pretending irritation, Guaraldi grabbed a towel and began wiping the sweat from Holberg's well-muscled shoulders.

After a few moments Holberg stopped him. "Ah, ah— that feels *too* good, and I have yet work to do." He looked up at the construction of black iron towering over them, a nightmare orchard of iron, branches projecting outward from vertical trunks, some smoothly curving down, some jutting up like spears. Several curved skyward, pronged at the end like satanic phalluses. "You know what I need?" Holberg mused.

"I have a hunch."

"Later, baby. Now I need you to cut more of those feathers." He pointed to a series of small curled and twisted iron pieces that ran the length of one of the trunks. "You do for me?"

"Whatever," Guaraldi said, shrugging. He tossed back the rest of the Evian and went to a trough. "Shit . . . we're out of three-quarter."

"So, you go get some, huh?"

"Peder, that's thirty blocks downtown—you know what the traffic is like right now?"

"So walk, do you good. Go on, Adam, I really need this now."

"Oh, hell . . ." Guaraldi said, but he picked up his blue chambray shirt from a wall hook and put it on. Then he slipped on a pair of jeans and a down-filled jacket. Holberg draped a scarf around his neck and gave him a short kiss on the cheek. Guaraldi looked at him suspiciously. "You gonna be here when I get back?"

For a moment Holberg looked uncomfortable, but then he smiled. "Of course."

"Wouldn't be the first time you disappeared. I can't leave you alone anymore."

"Baby, you could *never* leave me alone. Now go, yes?"

*   *   *

Guaraldi had been right: the streets of Manhattan were in what looked like a state of permanent stasis, so he began to walk briskly down the street, enjoying the sight of his breath puffing out in front of him. He was glad to get out of the warm studio. Peder liked it that way, keeping it heated to at least eighty degrees. The acetylene torches they used made it even hotter. "If you had lived in Norway all your life," he had told Guaraldi when he'd complained, "you'd like to feel like a hothouse flower, too!"

He just hoped he wouldn't disappear again. Guaraldi had been with Peder for nearly two years, first as an assistant, doing the basic cutting for Peder's assembly, and then as his companion. Guaraldi loved the lifestyle the relationship had allowed him to enjoy, but he also loved Peder, a feeling he feared was not entirely mutual. Peder's brief disappearances over the past few months had only added to his suspicions.

Often Guaraldi had awakened in the middle of the night only to find that Peder was neither in the apartment nor working in the studio that adjoined it. At other times the disappearances took place in broad daylight. Once he and Peder had been shopping at Barney's, and when Guaraldi turned back from the neckties he'd been looking at, Peder had vanished.

At last he'd found a clerk who'd seen Peder walk out of the store, but Guaraldi couldn't find him on the street, and Peder had not returned until the following morning, tired and haggard looking. As before, he'd sworn to Guaraldi that he didn't know where he'd been, that in fact he remembered nothing since he'd been with Guaraldi in Barney's.

At first Guaraldi hadn't believed him. How could you lose up to twelve hours of your life and not know what had happened to them? He had thought it was a lame excuse to cover up a liaison with another lover, and it infuriated him; he'd been faithful to Peder ever since they'd been together.

But he'd finally concluded that Peder's concern and confusion were too sincere to be feigned. Besides, Peder had never lied to him before, and there was no reason for him to start now. As frightening as it was to consider, it seemed

Peder really was undergoing experiences he couldn't remember.

Guaraldi had tried to follow him several times, but Peder had always lost him. Once, when Guaraldi had actually accosted him as he was walking out into the street at three in the morning, Peder had acted as though he'd just woken up from a dream, and been astounded to find himself outside at such a time. He'd never walked in his sleep before, Peder claimed, at least that he could remember.

Ever since his arrival in America and his quick success, Peder Holberg had had a certain mystique about him. It was true that he was eccentric in both his work and his private life, and he made what Guaraldi felt was a huge mistake with the art press when, in an interview with *Art and Artist*, he had mentioned his mysterious blackouts:

PH: There are times, you see, when I don't know what I'm doing.
AA: In the sense, then, that you're a conduit for an inner artistic voice?
PH: No, no, I disappear for hours at a time—don't know where I go, what I do.
AA: Do you mean, as though you are in a fugue state?

That was the first Guaraldi had ever heard the term, and from Peder's blank look, he was sure *he'd* never heard of it either. To the interviewer's annoyance, Guaraldi had jumped in and changed the subject. Peder was wise enough to sense he should speak about it no further, and would not.

But after the interview appeared, the topic, touched upon only briefly, was the talk of the New York art circle. Many of its members and hangers-on already considered Peder somewhat disturbed, for his work frequently represented crucifixions, impalements, and other unpleasantries. And now it was even whispered that Peder Holberg, during his pretended blackouts, attended orgies, black masses, and even ritual killings.

It was utter bullshit, Guaraldi knew. In his personal life,

Peder was no more violent than a newborn kitten. But Guaraldi would have given much to know where his lover went during those dark hours.

At the supply house, Guaraldi bought a dozen of the small iron pieces Peder wanted, and ordered a delivery of another gross for the next day. By then the uptown traffic had slackened surprisingly, so Guaraldi hailed a cab to transport his burden.

It was 4:30 by the time he arrived back at the studio. He fumbled with the keys, juggling the armful of iron, and kicked the heavy door open. "I'm back!" he called as he went in.

There was no answer. He looked everywhere in the studio, and through all the rooms of the apartment they shared, but Peder Holberg was gone.

When Adam Guaraldi went downtown to fetch the iron pieces Peder Holberg required, Holberg worked for a few minutes more. But then his movements slowed, as though he were a machine winding down. His features relaxed, his expression grew dull, and he stared straight ahead of him.

Then he went through the door to his apartment, where he changed his clothes, dressing warmly. He went out into the street and walked to the subway, glancing behind him frequently and mechanically. When the IRT Lexington Avenue local pulled in, he got on and took it north to the end of the line, just over the Third Avenue bridge in the Bronx. As he rode, he stared ahead fixedly, not even looking up when three men stopped in front of him and demanded money.

"He's a tough guy, ain't he?" said one. "Hey, tough guy, I'm talkin' to you." The man reached a hand out toward Holberg, but the appearance of a transit authority cop prevented any trouble.

Holberg walked off the train unharmed, and wound his way through the maze of streets until he was standing in front of a massive building—one story, it seemed, but a thirty-five-foot-high story—whose few windows were boarded up. There was a large door in the center of the wider wall, and a smaller door around the corner. It was to this door that

Holberg went. He took a ring with several keys out of his coat pocket and proceeded to unlock the two locks. Then he pushed the door open and entered. Only when the door was closed and locked behind him did he walk across a small anteroom in the darkness and flick a switch that turned on the dozens of overhead lights in the huge room.

The place smelled of rust and mildew. Red puddles dotted the wide wooden floor, and the cement walls oozed moisture. In and among the puddles lay various lengths of iron rods. At one end of the huge warehouse sat a dozen large tanks of acetylene, and several acetylene torches.

In the center of the floor, taking up nearly the entire warehouse, was an iron sculpture, thirty yards wide and fifty long. In some places it nearly touched the three-story-high ceiling, and in others it hugged the floor, dipping down into the scattered puddles and through the floor, as though descending into the earth.

The red scale of rust was creeping up the bottom of the rods, but Peder Holberg ignored what would have driven him into paroxysms of rage in his studio. He shed his coat, letting it fall onto the dirty floor, then took an acetylene torch and ignited it so that it spat a blue–white tongue of fire. Then he raised his head, as if listening.

He grabbed a two-foot length of iron and climbed one of half a dozen sets of portable stairs that provided access to the higher reaches of the structure. He worked dumbly, obediently, fusing metal to metal, descending from time to time to go to a long table and scribble lines and numbers on large sheets of paper, writing down the design whose lines and spaces were whispered to him—not into his ears, but into his brain.

Far back in that brain there was enough left of the consciousness of Peder Holberg to ask the question, "What am I doing?"

And that brain felt terror at this intrusion. As the man worked on, the mind screamed, "Why?"

There was no answer but commands.

* * *

The intelligence that gave those commands was not far away. As he spoke to Holberg he dreamed of light, recalling, eons ago, the fires of the Andromeda Galaxy as he drifted through it, or the cradles where stars were born, statues of flame hundreds of light-years high; the subtle glow of what they called the Pleiades, the light of its stars scattered by the gases around them.

He thought of freedom, the vastness of space, the day when he had first looked down and seen the face of Earth.

With one part of his mind he relived the agony, and with the other, greater part he guided the hands of the man, using the light of the flame to burn open his prison of darkness.

Chapter 4

*L*aika Harris shifted in her seat, trying to get comfortable. It was no small trick. 757s were cramped during the shortest flights, and a six-hour trek across the ocean was miserable, especially for a woman whose 5'10", much of it long brown legs, exceeded the comfort level prescribed by whatever boneheads had designed the seats. It would have been nice if the Company had sprung for first class on overseas flights, but the lower-costs bug had bitten every government agency, and the CIA wasn't immune.

She bent her knees, trying to wriggle her feet back underneath her seat for a while. Achieving a brief respite from paralysis, she adjusted her own headphones, not the cheesy foam and plastic jobs British Air provided gratis, and tried to lose herself in the Solti *Traviata* playing on her Discman. She wanted to hear it a few more times before making up her mind whether Gheorghiu deserved all the plaudits she was getting or was just another pretty face. From what she'd heard, Laika agreed with the deserving faction, but she wanted to make sure she wasn't getting suckered the way she had with Te Kanawa.

The first disc ended, and she took it out, catching a glimpse of her reflection in its silvered surface. She looked tired, she thought. Her eyes, looking back at her from skin the color of coffee with cream, were slightly puffy, and she thought if she had any sense she would try and get some sleep. But her mind was too full.

She looked at the sleeping woman in the next seat, and then, unobserved, continued to look at her own face. The angle made her chin look too full, and she brought up her head and the silver disc and looked at herself straight on.

That was better. Her face looked thin again—a model's face, with high cheekbones and big eyes, full lips, and a thin, straight nose that spoke of the white blood in her veins. "There's a white boy in the woodpile in *yo'* background, baby," James had told her, and he was right. Her maternal grandfather had been a white man, but not her grandma's husband.

Laika loaded the second disc and tried to shake off the past. But it was hard to concentrate on Verdi's music when she had so many other things to think about. If it had been just her mission on her mind, it wouldn't have been so bad. After all, her mission was what was supposed to preoccupy her time and attention. And God knew there were enough questions about this one.

First, why the hell was she flying to Glasgow? She had never had an assignment in Scotland before. There had been rumors that some of the Scottish nationalists were starting to consider violence as a tactic, but most of those had been planted by Tories, to turn public opinion against the nationals. Besides, that was England's problem, not America's.

And as far as she knew, there were no undercover activities being carried out in Scotland by America's enemies. Drugs, yes. More than a few South American and Middle Eastern cartels had a finger in the active heroin trade that was a part of every large city, Edinburgh and Glasgow included, she was sure. But bringing in the CIA on something like that didn't make any sense. Besides, she had little experience in drug operations.

Laika Harris's specialty was running covert ops. In the ten years she had been with the Company, she had handled operations in Turkey, Morocco, and, most recently, Thailand. There she had infiltrated a Chinese spy cell with three other operatives, sending back briefings to her superiors until the cover of one of the three was blown. Laika had had to kill two people then, but she'd had the comfort of knowing that they'd have killed her if they'd had the chance.

The operation had been aborted and she'd returned to the United States for a commendation and two months of R&R. She needed it. She had found Thailand a beautiful country, and most of the people kind and hospitable, but there had been exceptions.

Most obvious, of course, were the people who had wanted her dead once they'd discovered who she was. But that was to be expected anywhere there were enemies. What bothered her most about Thailand, and what would not let her go, was the market in flesh that flourished there.

Whores were everywhere and AIDS was endemic, but what had horrified Laika was the trade in children. Prostituted children were a viable commodity, readily available to those who knew where to look, and a great many did. Child molesters from Japan, Germany, the States—hell, all over the world—flocked to Bangkok to satisfy their dark and unholy tastes, and as far as Laika could see, the government did little to stop it.

It saddened and appalled her, and when she got back to the United States, she learned that a boycott of Thai goods was under way to force the government to take more stringent steps toward stamping out the problem. She had seen several people wearing "Don't Buy Thai—Ask Me Why!" T-shirts, and would have worn one herself but for her need to remain as invisible as possible. Still, she supported the boycott and told as many people as she could about it.

Most had been sympathetic, but some, like James, had been cynical. She'd told him that she'd been in Thailand opening up a branch office of the fictitious import–export company that was her cover. That much had been a lie, but the stories of the children had been true. "Listen, baby," he had said, when she'd finished, "they gonna be whores sooner or later, right? So what's the difference if it's sooner?"

"The difference is that they have no choice, James. And they have no childhood."

"So you think kids growin' up in this country in the projects have a childhood? You make me laugh—*I* didn't have no *childhood*." He said the word with a sneer.

"No, but you had a *choice*," Laika answered. They had been having breakfast in her apartment after spending the night together for the first time since her return from Thailand. "And you chose to make something of yourself. You think *that* would've happened if you'd had to turn tricks when you were ten?"

"Shit, I sold dope when I was ten."

"Selling dope didn't give you AIDS," Laika shot back.

James gave a hiss of disgust, and Laika knew the wiser path would be to change the subject. But she was not used to backing off in the rest of her life, and she didn't back off from James.

"You don't know whut the hell you talkin' 'bout, bitch," he growled.

"Why do you always do that?" she asked quietly.

"Do whut?"

"Whenever you get angry, you start talking like Dolemite, calling me a bitch. You know I hate that."

"You act like a bitch, thass whut I call you!" He slammed his coffee mug back onto the table, making the liquid slop over the sides.

"James," she said in a low, dangerous voice, "you graduated from City College, you've been with a brokerage firm for the past eight years. I've been to parties where you've conversed pleasantly and intelligently. Now why, whenever we disagree, do you act and talk like some stupid ghetto bully?"

He stood up and slapped her. It was so unexpected, so totally shocking, that she didn't react at all. She only stood there, with her cheek reddening, feeling hot blood rising in her face, and looked at him. "Donchu *ever* diss me, bitch!" he yelled. "You diss me and I'll whup you, you won't siddown for a *week!* You get that?"

She swallowed hard, trying to hold back the anger, knowing that if she wanted to, she could kill him in a matter of seconds, or at least incapacitate him so that he'd never dare raise a hand to her again.

But she didn't. She only stood there, her hand to her aching cheek, feeling herself shake worse than she ever had in her life.

"You *get* that?" James asked again.

"Yes," she said softly. "I got that."

She did not know, then or now, why she'd put up with it. Maybe, she thought, she felt sorry for James Winston. He'd had a rough childhood, but hard work had bought him an easier adulthood. He was well-off enough to have a nice apartment on the East Side and drive a vintage Jag that he kept garaged most of the time. When she'd first met him, he'd seemed cultured and polite, a younger version of Harry Belafonte, and his voice betrayed little of his inner city upbringing.

But there was still a lot of anger in him, and that blow, the first of many that would ultimately separate them, had brought it out for her to see in all its nakedness. James was a black man angry at a white world that in his view had given him everything he had—as long as he played according to its rules and gave up the one thing most precious to him: his black soul. In retrospect, she knew she should have seen the change coming. His bitter comments had been increasing, and his temper would flare more and more frequently.

After he'd hit her that first time, he treated her differently. He went to her place whenever he felt like having sex, and the preambles grew more perfunctory. He showed little concern for her needs, and when she expressed her discontent, he called her more names and hit her again. Somehow, and for some reason she could not name, she endured it, asking herself as she did, "Why am I letting this man do this to me?" but having no answer. The marks were not permanent, and he never drew blood, but they scarred her just the same.

Laika Harris had not grown up with violence, though her profession had taught her its intricate practicalities. Her father and mother had never so much as raised their voices to each other, and had loved each other and Laika and her brother with a quiet steadfastness befitting a minister and his wife. Her father was dead, but she went to Maryland when she could to visit her mother. She had never told her mother about James Winston.

The crisis finally came two days before Laika received news of her assignment. Looking back, even to such a short time before, she couldn't remember what had caused the argument. They were in her kitchen, and she was standing at the stove, cooking a pesto soup for James. He said something that annoyed her, she answered back, and before she knew what had happened, he had yanked a meat knife from its wooden storage block, grabbed her across her chest from behind, and held the knife to her throat.

"God *damn* you, don't you sass me, bitch!" he cried, pressing the sharp edge against her skin so that she could feel its coldness.

What she did then was automatic. It was a movement that she had practiced thousands of times and executed several times before, and it worked more smoothly than ever, because of James's unpreparedness and lack of combat skills. Easily pushing his knife hand away, she crouched and did a spin kick that took his legs out from under him. Then, instead of following up with a knife hand as he fell, she grabbed the handle of the steaming pot of soup and brought it down across his head.

He howled as the scalding soup splashed across his face, and curled into a ball on the kitchen floor, desperately trying to claw the heat away from his blistering skin. With a sneer, Laika grabbed a wet dishrag from the drainer and tossed it into his face.

James pressed it against his flesh, his cries reduced to breathy whining. Laika knelt beside him and roughly pulled the rag away. His face was red, and there was a cut on his cheek where the pan had struck him, but she knew there would be no permanent damage.

When he saw her face, a look of rage swept over him, and his mouth opened painfully. "You b—" he began to say, but Laika whipped the fallen knife off the floor so that its blade was only inches from his eyes.

"Don't you ever call me that again," she said in a low, dangerous voice. "Don't ever touch me again. Don't ever let me see you again. I'm through pitying you, you sad little bastard. Now get out of here."

He saw the killer in her eyes, and she knew he was afraid. Sliding away from her, he pushed himself to his feet and she straightened up as well. He backed away toward the short hall that led to the apartment door, and she followed him all the way, the knife hanging at her side, as though she were too tired to threaten him with it.

James turned his back on her just long enough to fumble with the locks and get the door open. Then he stepped through it and turned back. "This ain't over," he said, and his voice showed the physical pain the words caused him.

"You're wrong," Laika said. "It's over like it never was." She smiled. "I don't even remember your name."

"Well, you'll know it . . . you'll have cause to know it, you . . . you *bitch!*"

He backed away several steps as he said the word, and his fear made her laugh. She said nothing more and did not even look at him as she closed the door in his face.

For the next two days she felt wonderfully free. She did not see James Winston anywhere and lost herself in a shopping trip to Tower Records, where she bought two hundred dollars' worth of new opera recordings.

One evening on a whim she went to the Met, and landed a single ticket for the new production of *Fedora*. In truth, she preferred opera on CD and videotape to the real thing, since she always found the audience too distracting. On her most recent visit to the Met, she had been seated in the Family Circle, and during Senta's dream in *Der Fliegende Hollander*, had begun to hear a slight *tic . . . tic . . . tic . . .* behind her. When she'd finally glanced around, she'd seen that the woman sitting behind her was actually clipping her nails.

Her opera orgy was suspended the next day, however, when a Federal Express delivery from Blair Exporting arrived. In it was a next-day ticket to Glasgow (tourist class, of course) and a sealed dossier that was to be opened an hour before the plane descended into Scotland.

She shook her head at the directive. That was Richard Skye, all right. Her superior loved the cloak-and-dagger stuff, even at times like this, when it wasn't necessary. What difference did it make whether she read the dossier now or tomorrow? But she would follow directions implicitly. She always had.

So she had packed, had called her mother to tell her she would be away for a time, and the next day had taken a cab to JFK. Now, five hours later, here she was, the dossier in her lap, her seatmate still asleep.

Time, she thought, slitting open the seal with a short but sharp fingernail. Let's see how I can help to preserve America's national security in Scotland.

Her assignment was the last thing she'd have expected. The directive was typically terse, though the supplemental briefing papers told her more than she would ever want to know about Helmut Kristal, the subject of her mission.

She had heard of Kristal, read about him several months before in a copy of *People* she had picked up out of boredom on another plane. Though he had not yet visited America, the self-proclaimed psychic was all the rage in Europe. Laika hadn't paid much attention to the article. She had no time for psychics or any of what she considered New Age mumbo jumbo. Most of it was so transparent as to be laughable.

The goal of the assignment was to expose Helmut Kristal as a hoax. There was no reason given, only the information that in three days Kristal would be demonstrating what he claimed to be the greatest accomplishment of his career in the small town of Drumnadrochit, Scotland. There he intended, for one time and one time only, to show conclusively to believers and debunkers alike that he was beyond any doubt capable of receiving images through mind waves alone.

"Sure," Laika whispered. "And I'm the Queen of Ruritania.'' Her seatmate stirred in her sleep, and Laika turned her attention back to the directive.

She and her two associates, whom she would meet when she landed, were to prove to all present that Kristal was a fake—and furthermore they were to do this without calling any attention to themselves. Gravy, Laika thought, as she read through the rest of the material. And maybe, after we're done, Skye would like us to disprove astrology, tarot cards, and palm reading too. . . .

She would learn that she was a lot closer to the truth than she thought.

Chapter 5

*T*he Glasgow airport was relatively small, and her identity cards and papers got her through British customs with no delay. In her dossier were six hundred Scottish pounds, so there was no need to exchange money at the booths.

The waiting shuttle took her to the car rental office near the airport, where she picked up the small blue Peugeot diesel that had been reserved for her. Stick shift, too, she noted with dismay. More savings for the taxpayers, and an additional traffic headache for her. Driving on the left was tricky enough without adding a left-hand shift to the equation.

She headed east on the M8 toward Glasgow, dreading the traffic circles to come, but remembering that after a day or two she always got used to the driving. Hell, she had once torn through the streets of London shooting a riot gun through her shattered back window at the car chasing her and lived to tell about it.

Using the map from the dossier, she made her way easily enough to St. Vincent Crescent, a dead-end street with a picturesque block of townhouses on one side and a lawn bowling club on the other. She parked in front of number 153, the address of the safe house in which she would be staying that night. The Company often used bed-and-breakfasts to house agents rather than hotels. They left no paper trails, and an entire house could be taken for the necessary nights, ensuring no other curious tenants.

That was probably what had occurred here at Kenley

House, as the brass plaque mounted by the front door proclaimed it. Laika suspected she would meet at least one of her new colleagues here, and no one else except the hostess, who opened the door to her knock.

"Miss Jackson?" the woman said, using Laika's cover name. Laika nodded and smiled, and the round-faced and middle-aged woman went on cheerily, "I'm Mrs. Danvers. Your room's all ready, and Mr. Anderson has already arrived." Anderson was Stein's cover name.

"Anyone else?" Laika inquired.

"Oh no, you're my only two guests tonight," Mrs. Danvers replied, taking one of Laika's bags and leading her up the wide stairs.

Laika's room was airy and spacious, with a large double bed against one wall, and she was glad to see that the toilet facilities were *en suite*. "If you need anything, dear, just let me know," Mrs. Danvers said. "I'll bring up a continental breakfast in the morning. What time would you like it?"

Laika told her and found out where Stein/Anderson's room was. When the woman had gone back downstairs, Laika knocked on his door.

"Who's there?" said a voice from inside. It sounded soft and tentative.

"Miss Jackson. Do you have any extra sugar?"

The door opened, and Laika saw a man in his mid-forties dressed in a pullover sweater and khakis. His blond hair was brushed straight back and was thinning slightly on top. Pale blue eyes looked down at her through aviator-style glasses. Despite his height, he seemed stooped, as though he were tired or depressed, laden with years.

Still, his face was unlined, save for crow's-feet at the corners of his eyes. They deepened as he attempted a smile. "No," he said, "but I have some saccharin." Then he cocked his head at her. "Okay? I'm who you think I am, you're who I think you are, right? Come on in, Ms. Harris."

She entered his room, which was slightly smaller than hers. He gestured her to a high-backed, cane chair by the window, and, when she was seated, sat on the bed near her. "Call me Laika," she said.

"All right. And I'm Joseph Stein."

"Joe?"

"I prefer Joseph." He looked at her with a hint of curiosity. "Laika . . . how did you get into the Company with a Russian name?"

"My father wasn't a fellow traveler," she said smiling. "He was a would-be *space* traveler. My brother was named Alan Shepard Harris, but since Dad couldn't name me after any astronauts, he used the name of the only female in space he knew of."

"The space dog," Stein said. "Still, it's a nice name."

The compliment did not flow easily, and Laika heard no sincerity in it. Stein seemed to be lacking in the warmth department. "Thanks," she said.

"It could have been worse. He could have named you Thea von Harbou Harris." Her look told him she didn't get the allusion. "The woman who wrote *Frau im Monde? The Girl in the Moon.* It was an early German science fiction film."

"Ah." She nodded. Wonderful. A sci-fi geek. "So. You've read the dossier?"

"I have."

"Your thoughts?"

"Well, I don't know what exposing a fraud has to do with preserving our national security, but ours is not to reason why." He fixed her with a piercing gaze. "Are you hungry?"

The question took her by surprise. "Well . . . yes, actually."

"Let's get something to eat then. This jet lag's been playing havoc with my appetite, and we can talk over dinner."

They ran into Mrs. Danvers on the stairs, and she directed them to a restaurant several blocks away. "It's in a hotel," she told them, "but the food's quite good anyway."

If it was so good, Laika thought twenty minutes later, why weren't there more people there? Still, with so few diners about, they could talk freely. She ordered venison, Stein ordered salmon. He also had a dram of a local single malt, but she stuck with mineral water, feeling too jet-lagged for alcohol.

Although Laika knew something about Stein from his dossier, she tried to break the ice by asking him about his particular area of expertise in the Company. The shadow of a smile touched his long face. "Sitting at desks. It's what I've been doing for the past twelve years."

"Interpretation?"

He nodded and sipped his drink. "The folks in the field gather it, and I try and figure out how it all fits together and makes sense." Then it hit her. *Stein.* She had heard of him before. When gathered intelligence seemed contradictory, she had overheard her superiors say, "Let's run it past Stein." She hadn't known who Stein was, but now she assumed that this was the puzzle man himself.

"I haven't been in the field in years," Stein said, his gaze on the sporting print behind Laika's head. "Tried to stay in shape, though. Never know what the Company is going to want next."

"Why did they bring you out on this one?"

"Because of my hobby . . . well, one of them. I follow debunking, you see . . . exposing fakes. I've often said my only bible is *The Skeptical Inquirer*, and my only god is James Randi. You've heard of him?"

Laika nodded. She had seen Randi on TV several times, and had admired the way he had exposed fake psychics. "Have you ever seen this Kristal work?"

"Not in person, no, but on videotapes. He does pretty much the same old tricks that most of them do. But he's fooled a lot of scientists, and he couches everything in so much esoteric bullshit that he's attracted more followers than Geller in his prime. I've got to admit, though, he's got style. He does the compass trick nearly nude."

"Compass trick?"

"Yeah. It's ancient. You use your so-called powers to make the compass needle deflect from the north."

"All you'd need would be a hidden magnet or some magnetic metal."

"Right you are. Mentalists used to hide it in their clothes. The skillful ones could palm it. But Kristal does the trick in a pair of gym shorts—*after* several male audience members examine him naked and check out the shorts."

"Something in his mouth?"

"No, they look in there, too. Even up his . . . between his buttocks."

Laika smiled. "How does he do it, then?"

Stein smiled, too. She could see he was warming to the subject. "You tell me."

She thought for a moment, picturing the nearly naked psychic making arcane gestures over the compass, the needle moving with his hands. "False fingernails with magnets beneath?"

"No, I know what you're thinking, but he doesn't gesture. At least, not so you'd notice. He does it by sheer 'mind power.' You're very close, though."

She shrugged. "So how?"

"Implants. The man's got more metal in him than the Terminator. I used the freeze frame on the video and augmented the images with the computer. Kristal has very small, very pale, almost invisible scars on his forearms, right above the flexor muscles. I also found one on the fascia lata, by the kneecap on his left leg. Unfortunately, I didn't have any footage showing the right." Stein took another sip of whisky, swallowed, and grinned. "I did, however, have several good shots of those washboard abs and found another pale scar right above the navel."

"Wait a minute," Laika said. "Are you saying he's had metal placed in his body surgically?"

"Yep. Both positive and negative charges, too. Like I said, he doesn't gesture, but he moves the way anyone would when they're concentrating—touches his forehead, rubs his temples, stretches his legs, shifts in his chair. He probably practiced for days to get the combination just right, but by performing these subtle, barely noticeable moves, he can make the compass do the tango if he wants it to.''

''You mean he had at least five incisions to do a lousy *trick?*''

''Ah, true artists must suffer for their art. No wonder he never flies—one time through a metal detector, and he's done.''

''What's he planning for his big climax?''

They paused for a moment while the waiter set their appetizers before them. Stein took an appreciative spoonful of his steaming cullen skink before he replied.''I don't know, but whatever it is, he's saying that he may do it one time and one time only. The psychic energy he has to expend could make him old before his time, you see.''

''So we have to discover what he's going to do before he does it so that we can expose it . . . whatever it is.''

''In a nutshell.''

''Have you thought about why yet?''

''No idea. Except that if Cloudy initiated it, it means bad news for somebody.''

''Cloudy?''

Stein looked mildly discomfited. ''Cloudy Skye.''

She laughed. ''I've never heard that one before.''

''Pretty common, I'm afraid. I suppose I should show more respect, but I always see storm clouds on the horizon when Richard Skye draws near.''

The taste of the smoked haddock soup was almost obliterated by the bitter taste that crept into Joseph Stein's mouth at the thought of Richard Skye. Skye was a field operations man all the way, and Joseph Stein had long ago had his fill of field ops. He had never wanted to travel under an assumed name again, never wanted to stay in a safe house or give code words to other agents, never wanted to see anybody die, or to have to kill.

He liked being Joseph Stein, the one the smart boys came to when they couldn't figure things out, the one who could take the round puzzle piece and figure out how to fit it into the square corner. Deskbound Joseph Stein, who had his own tiny office in Langley, even if it didn't have a window. Joseph Stein, who, under his own name, had actually had a letter published in *The Skeptical Inquirer*, and who wrote a quarterly column for *Fantasy Corners*, a slickly produced semi-prozine dealing with fantasy and science fiction in film and literature.

Joseph Stein, whose weapons and pleasures were thoughts and words. That was the Joseph Stein he liked being, not Joseph Stein/Donald Anderson/Thomas Feldman/whatever the hell the Company decided he should be called in the field that month.

He had had five hard years in the field, five years of blood and thunder, when the Cold War was still fought with warriors and he had no choice but to be one if he wanted to survive. But then the ones who counted started to discover his other talents, saw that he was more valuable behind a desk than in the field.

The field: he had always thought that was a perfect name for it. A battlefield. A field that was sown with blood and grew death. And now here he was, back in the field again, because Richard Skye had wanted him there and because his boss in Analytic Support didn't have the balls to tell Skye no.

This assignment was probably because of the mole that Joseph had ferreted out several months before. Joseph knew that his mind was fluid, that it could flow in directions other people wouldn't even consider. When they brought him all the information that they had on the mole, he began, quite simply, to think like the mole. After all, he had all the mole's thoughts as defined by his actions. It was a process that Joseph felt could not be taught, that was incomprehensible to anyone who couldn't do it. But Joseph could, and it came so naturally to him that it was impossible to explain.

It went beyond profiling, which was fast becoming a science these days. In retrospect, he supposed what he did was a combination of logic, deduction, acting, and self-deception, but while the first three could be taught, the ability to bury one's own consciousness and become another person transcended all three—even acting, which came the closest.

When he tried to verbalize it, it sounded as much like gobbledygook as did the beliefs, New Age and old alike, that he scoffed at. Still, it was real. His successes were the evidence of that.

When he had come up with the mole's identity, it had been so unexpected that he had been questioned for several days at Langley by those who suspected that only someone in partnership with the mole could have known so much. Fortunately, Joseph was able to prove his innocence, and his genius. Unfortunately, his success brought the attention of Skye. And if Skye had had this mission of exposing a phony psychic in mind, he would have seen instantly that Joseph Stein was his man.

Hell, Joseph thought, maybe it wouldn't be all that bad. After all, he didn't have to *kill* this goddamned phony. All he had to do was expose him. It might, after all, be fun. A little old-fashioned cloak-and-dagger stuff, and no one would end up dead. Just a psychic with a lot of egg on his artificially earnest face.

Joseph eyed the woman across from him, her attention temporarily on her langostino cocktail. Fine looking woman, he thought. Fine enough for him to consider his own appearance.

He had been starting to grow soft, but had hardened up over the past year. When he had first seen signs of his midsection drifting toward a middle-aged paunch, he'd begun to spend at least an hour a day in the gym at Langley after his work was over for the day. It kept him from the things that he would rather have been doing, like watching movies and reading books, but it was necessary. He had seen too many of his colleagues get old and fat before their time, and he swore it would not happen to him.

As chance would have it, it had worked out well. It was his first field op in a dozen years, but he felt physically ready for it. He wondered how he looked to Laika Harris, but only out of curiosity. He had been in the Company long enough to realize that you didn't get involved with another agent.

That was bad news for everybody, even if she'd be interested in an old, balding desk jockey.

"So when do we meet our third?" Joseph asked, patting his lips with his napkin.

"Tomorrow evening at Drumnadrochit." Laika Harris looked puzzled. "There wasn't anything in the dossier about the town. Why on earth would Kristal pick a remote Scottish village to put on his show?"

"Well, though it's remote, it's far from unknown. It's considered the official Loch Ness Monster center—where all the tourists start their monster hunts. Never been there, but I understand it's very tacky."

"I assume you don't believe in the Loch Ness Monster?"

"As a wise man once said, I don't believe in nuthin' I can't see. The whole Loch Ness legend began over a thousand years ago as a religious fable, so that makes it dubious right off the bat. And that famous photograph taken back in the thirties was proved to be a hoax, but that doesn't stop people from believing." Joseph shook his head, feeling a mixture of pity and superiority. "The human capacity for self-deception," he added, "may be our strongest trait."

The waiter returned with their entrees, and their conversation shifted to the excellence of Scottish cuisine as opposed to English. But after a while, Laika asked, "You don't believe in anything paranormal, then? That someone could actually be psychic?"

"No," Joseph answered flatly. "There's never been any evidence of it—of ESP or ghosts or anything of the sort."

"But haven't scientists been convinced of—"

He interrupted her with a laugh. "Scientists are the easiest people in the world to fool. But as soon as a magician shows up on the premises, the psychics suddenly lose their powers for fear of being exposed—'Oh, my, I feel negative vibrations in the ether. Antagonism and doubt are weakening my powers. . . .' Yeah, damn right they are."

"How about aliens?"

Joseph shrugged. "That's always a possibility. No one can say there's *nothing* in the universe but us—that would be the most amazing thing of all. But as far as having any evidence of it . . . well, I've seen the real files on Roswell, and there *were* no dead aliens.''

''What was it all about, then?''

Joseph chuckled. ''I'm a trained agent—you can't get it out of me that easily. All I'll say is that it was absolutely terrestrial in nature . . . though equally astonishing. But it's classified.'' He gave her a respectful nod. ''Even to my team leader. So what do *you* believe in? Your tone is slightly disapproving toward my heresy, as one who occasionally reads her horoscope.''

The stern answering look on Laika Harris's face told Joseph to be careful. His intensity at work was so great that he tended to get too relaxed during social engagements, which was why he planned so few of them. He had to remember that Harris was not his friend or his date, but his leader, according to the mission dossier.

''I read my horoscope when I come across it, but I don't believe it. I guess I have fewer . . . doubts about things than you do. Maybe it comes from my religious background.'' She smiled thinly. ''I was taught to believe in the supernatural from an early age. My father was a minister. So I tend to be more what I suppose you'd call *gullible*. Though I'm kind of lapsed now.''

Joseph nodded. ''The Company can do that to you. I started off lapsed. Both my parents were devout secular humanists, of that faith so loathed by the religious right.''

''So you never had the option of belief,'' Laika said without a smile.

The comment took him aback for a moment. He had never looked at it in that way. ''No,'' he said slowly, ''I suppose not.''

Their conversation flagged then, as a party of four sat at the next table. They finished their meal in relative silence and headed back to the safe house.

Lying alone in bed, Joseph thought about Laika's comment again and wondered if it were true. He had not come to a conclusion by the time he drifted off to sleep.

Chapter 6

*T*he following morning, Laika and Joseph headed toward the highlands. Joseph, who had lived for a time in England, offered to drive the Peugeot, and Laika accepted.

She was doubly glad as they drove up the narrow roads on the western bank of Loch Lomond, hugging rock walls on one side and coming within inches of trucks and occasional tour buses on the other. Still, they made good time and had lunch in the tourist town of Fort William, which, like the rest of the highlands, was sparsely populated during the chill of mid-April.

The further north they drove, the more beautiful the scenery became, and soon the long expanse of Loch Ness was on their right, appearing between the patches of trees that lined the roadside. A soft drizzle sprinkled the windscreen. "See any monsters?" Joseph asked.

Laika smiled and shook her head. "I wasn't really looking."

"Sure you were. You can't drive by Loch Ness, even if you're as big a skeptic as me, and not look at those deep waters with just a touch of expectation." He glanced out the right-side window and looked back at the road again. "But you're always disappointed." He gave a dry laugh. "So Loch Ness is a perfect place for Kristal and his humbug."

Three miles south of Drumnadrochit, they drove past a jacked-up minivan with frosted windows that was parked on one of the few dirt pull-offs along the shoulderless road. A heavily muscled man of medium height was leaning over the right front wheel well, using a tire iron on the lugs of a punctured tire. He glanced up for a second as they drove by.

"Let's turn around," said Laika. "We'd better help him."

"Why?" Joseph asked. "We're due to meet our third in twenty minutes in town."

"That *was* our third," Laika said. The face that had looked up at them had matched perfectly the photograph of Anthony Luciano in her dossier. "Turn around."

Joseph made a U-turn, drove back to the van, crossed the lane, and parked several yards from the minivan. The man straightened up, and his right hand went into his windbreaker pocket purposefully. His craggy face was an expressionless mask as he slowly turned away from them, showing them the smaller target of his side.

Laika got out of the Peugeot, making sure her empty hands were visible. Then she said, "And what in heaven's name brought you to Drumnadrochit?"

The man's deep-set eyes widened in surprise. Then he gave a snort of laughter and answered, "My health. I came to Drumnadrochit for the waters." He shook his head. "Jesus, I can't believe the passwords we're getting. Cloudy's got a goddamn Casablanca jones."

"Why am I the only one who never heard this 'Cloudy' nickname?" Laika said, as she walked toward the man, her hand outstretched. "I'm Laika Harris." He took her hand and shook it firmly. "And this is Joseph Stein." She gestured to Joseph, who was walking up behind her.

"Tony Luciano," the man said, shaking Joseph's hand. "And while we're on the subject of nicknames, I don't answer to 'Lucky,' okay, Laika? Joe?"

"Fine with me," Joseph said. "And I don't answer to Joe. Any relation to the gangster?" he asked, somewhat tactlessly, Laika thought.

"Very distant, Joseph," Tony said in a clipped tone. "You any relation to Franken, Stein?"

He rolled his head as he talked. Cocky, Laika thought. He was on the short side, compared to most CIA operatives, who were usually six feet tall or more, and she suspected he had a Napoleon complex. His personality profile in her dossier had stated, "Can be short-tempered," and she wondered if Stein knew that. If not, he might find out fast. There was a heavy dose of wiseguy to Tony Luciano, and despite his reluctance to be called after a gangland forebear, she suspected he cultivated the image. Otherwise, why bring it up in the first place?

Then Tony surprised her by breaking the ice with a laugh. "Just kidding. Glad you guys stopped. I hate changing tires alone. Tell you what, Joseph, maybe you could pull that dead one off while I get the spare, huh? Man, it is really gorgeous up here, isn't it? You believe these mountains, these lakes? Italy's nice, I've been to Italy a few times, but you don't have this heather and all. . . ."

He rattled on as he dug around in the back, uncovering the tire well, while Joseph groaned as he loosened the nearly rusted shut lugs. When Tony finally rolled up the spare, the tire was off. "Hey, good job," Tony said cheerily. "You wanta yank that off and put this baby back on now, while I tidy things up in the van—got all our equipment in there, everything we oughta need and more."

In a few more minutes, Joseph, his clothes now rumpled and soiled with grease, had the spare on and the lugs tightened. As he dropped the tire iron with a clatter, Tony reappeared from the back of the van. "Okay, everything's shipshape—hey, you got it on, that's great." He picked up the tire iron and gestured to the flat, lying on its side. "Okay, Joseph, just toss it in the back, there, and we'll be on our way. Laika, you want to ride with me? We can talk a little about how we're gonna handle this thing with Mister Mystic, huh?"

Laika looked at Joseph hauling the spare around to the back and thought that there should be something in Tony Luciano's file about his effortless powers of persuasion. "Sure," she said. "Let's go. Joseph, we'll meet at the hotel, all right?"

Joseph, a thin film of cooling sweat on his forehead, gave

a nod and headed back to the Peugeot. He stopped partway, turned back as though he were about to say something, then shook his head, gave a short, self-deprecating laugh, and walked to the car.

"I think," Laika said to Tony, "that he just realized how smoothly he was had. What were you doing in the van, anyway, reading?"

"Would you believe a weapons check?" Tony said in a deadpan voice so that she couldn't tell if he was joking.

"You think we're going to need weapons for Kristal?"

"I don't know *what* we're going to need for this guy," he said, climbing behind the wheel of the van. "What the hell is this all about?"

"You know as much as I do. Hopefully we'll find out more when we get there." Laika had to move several paperbacks from the passenger seat. "So, you read while you drive?"

"Only when the road's wide and straight. I tried it here, but no luck."

As they drove, Tony kept looking constantly toward the loch, and once drove slightly off the road. "Take it easy," Laika said. "What's so interesting over there?"

He glanced at her. "What, you never heard of the monster?"

"You're a believer?"

"Hell, yes. There's all sorts of evidence, you know—sonar, lots of people seeing it—there's *something* under there, all right."

"Well, why don't you keep your eyes on the road, and I'll do the watching. I'll be sure to tell you if I see anything."

Tony took one last quick glance out the window, sighed, and faced front the rest of the way to Drumnadrochit.

The little town was packed with visitors, even though it was the off-season, and Tony pulled through a throng of tourists bundled against the chilly winds blowing off the loch and into the parking lot of the Drumnadrochit Hotel. "Check it out," he said with a touch of awe, looking at the fiberglass version of the Loch Ness Monster that broke the surface of concrete between the hotel and the Original Loch Ness Monster Exhibition. "Is that where Kristal's doing his trick? At the exhibition building?"

"No," said Laika, recalling the dossier. "It's in the new one up the road—The Loch Ness Experience. Just past the *official* monster visitors' center. There's a large hall there, and that's where Kristal will perform."

There was a packet waiting for "Mrs. Sechrist" when they checked into their rooms—Laika and Joseph into a double as Mr. and Mrs. Ronald Sechrist, and Tony into a single as Thomas Capele. The rooms adjoined, and after they were checked in, Laika moved her things into Tony's room and he carried his soft-sided suitcases into the double room, which he would share with Joseph. Then Laika opened the packet and they sat down and made their plans.

"Kristal is coming in tonight," she said, scanning the information sheets in the packet. "He'll be with his assistant, whose name is supposedly Harmony. There will also be three roadies in a truck, but what it's carrying we don't know. They'll be going through a rehearsal of sorts tomorrow morning in the hall. It'll be closed to everyone but Kristal and Harmony. You're the one who'll spot the scam, Joseph. Any suggestions?"

"We have to see the rehearsal," Joseph said. "Odds are I could watch and figure out how it's done during the show, but we're not supposed to get involved. So the thing to do is figure it out beforehand and tip off somebody else."

"Like a reporter," Laika said.

"Exactly."

Tony cleared his throat. "Assuming he's a fake."

"Don't worry about that," Joseph answered. "This guy's as phony as a senator trying to pick up a stewardess."

"All right, then," said Laika. "Tony, you and I will have to get a video transmitter planted in the hall tonight. You do hardware, I'll do lookout."

"How's security?"

"Tight tomorrow, but normal tonight." She looked at Stein. "Joseph, you hit the bars and restaurants, schmooze the press boys, see if there's anybody out for blood. Tony and I will get some rest and hit the street at 0300."

Chapter 7

*N*obody looked at them twice. Hell, there wasn't even any-body to look in the first place.

Tony Luciano had walked out of his room at 0255 and met Laika behind the hotel, and together they dogtrotted through the back alleys of Drumnadrochit. Tony thought that he could find a bigger town than this under any rock, but he didn't mention it to Laika. No words would pass between them.

They were wearing the black that operatives usually donned during a night infiltration mission, and Tony felt nearly as dangerous as he really was. Despite his feeling that he should leave covert ops behind and really push for a desk job, he had to confess that this was what he liked doing best.

There was something about creeping through the night with a satchel full of toys and tricks, especially when you weren't expected to kill anybody or risk getting killed your-self. It reminded him of when he was a kid, and used to sneak out his window at night, dropping down off the porch roof onto the ground, and just rambling through the neigh-borhood like Batman or one of those other haunters of the night he'd read about in comic books. The killing part was what he'd never gotten used to and hoped he never would.

The Loch Ness Experience building was several hundred yards from the hotel. It was in the shape of a squat T. The cross of the T was a museum and display area facing the road, and the upright was the auditorium, where a multimedia presentation was shown. A small parking lot was behind the building, and a large van and a small enclosed truck were parked there, both rentals.

Tony and Laika walked along the edge of shadow until they reached the building. They looked around, but saw no one outside or watching from any of the windows that faced the lot. Moving from one pool of darkness to another, they approached the vehicles until they heard a low-pitched ding, like a small bell being struck once. A digitally produced voice followed:

"You are too close to the vehicle."

"Thanks for the tip," Tony whispered, and backed away, glancing at Laika. With what he had inside his satchel, he could shut that voice off in seconds, but Laika shook her head, and she was the boss. Besides, if this Kristal suspected that somebody was messing with his stuff, he'd probably say that the spirits weren't with him today and forget the whole thing, or postpone it for months.

They went up to the back of the auditorium. There were two doors, one large enough to drive a truck through, and the other far smaller, like a normal house door. Tony spotted the alarm system immediately. It was an old-fashioned wire-borne type, and he took his evasion box from his satchel. In another minute, he had intercepted the signal and deactivated it, while Laika scanned the area, watching for any sign of movement.

Then Tony looked at the lock on the door. No tubular here, just a plain old vanilla pin-tumbler. He selected a simple rake pick and put one end into a radio-sized electric device. Then he slipped the other end of the pick into the lock and flicked a small switch. There was a low hum and a soft clattering sound as the pins in the lock bounced. In a few seconds they were aligned and Tony felt the lock open.

"Bingo," he whispered, so softly even Laika would not hear. He turned the knob and pushed inward. He didn't look back as he went in. He knew Laika would remain at the door and alert him to any interlopers.

Inside, Tony found himself at the back of a small stage.

An enormous movie screen hid the rest of the auditorium, and the area backstage was dimly lit by a single forty-watt bulb. He listened for a moment, but heard nothing, and let the door close softly behind him.

In his crepe-soled shoes, he walked to the edge of the screen and peered around it. The auditorium was empty. Nothing was on the stage in front of the screen. That meant they would load in whatever they needed in the morning.

Tony walked down one of the side aisles to the auditorium double doors and gently pushed, but they were locked from the outside: no one would be coming in. Nevertheless, he listened at the crack of the door, but heard no radio, TV, snoring, or coughing—none of the telltale sounds of a night watchman.

Satisfied, he began to look for places to put his three cameras, each of them only an inch square. The walls of the auditorium were acoustical, rough-textured plaster, and he cut out three holes with a keyhole saw, one in the left wall, one in the right, and one against the back wall, all three well above eye level. He inserted the cameras, drilled small holes in each of the removed facings for the lenses, and then replaced the facings, sealing the edges with a fast-dry putty the same off-white color as the walls. He was finished in forty-five minutes.

When he looked, he could see no difference between the replaced patches and the rest of the wall, and the pinholes for the lenses were undetectable. The Office of Technical Service strikes again, he thought with a grin, and rejoined Laika outside, leaving the building like a ghost.

The following morning, Laika, Joseph, and Tony sat in front of a row of three small monitors showing the interior of the auditorium from different angles. The screen had been pulled aloft, and they watched as three men brought in a large box on a hand truck. It made a hollow sound when they removed the truck from beneath it and it hit the floor. "Plastic," Joseph said. "Molded plastic."

The surface of the box was smooth, its color a mottled

tan. The top of the box was six and a half feet from the stage floor, and from what they could see of it, the top was slightly indented, with a small hole in the center. "Air hole," Joseph murmured. "Of course . . . they'll seal the edges, keep all the light out. . . ."

The men opened the front panel of the box, revealing an empty interior. Then they went offstage and brought out a small table, a chair, a dressing screen, and an artist's easel, which they set ten feet to stage right of the box. From behind the cameras, a short but powerful-looking man with a long mane of silver-white hair came walking down the aisle from the back of the auditorium. He was wearing a blousy shirt and designer jeans. In his wake was a young woman with a peasant blouse falling over a pair of loose harem-style pants. A scarf billowed around her neck, merging with her long blond hair.

"Kristal and Harmony," Joseph murmured.

Laika smiled sourly. "Sounds like a Windham Hill duo."

The pair walked up onto the stage. Kristal carried only a pen and a pad of paper, and the woman had a sheaf of large sheets of white paper and some markers.

"Good morning, boys," said Kristal. Even through the half-inch mikes concealed behind the plaster, his Teutonic accent came through the monitors loud and clear. "Let's do a dry run, *ja?*" He stepped to the center of the stage. "All right, I'll take off the robe here. We'll get two men out of the audience, I'll go behind the screen, show them my balls." He chuckled. "Nothing up mȳ ass, shorts back on, come back out.

"Then I do the part about the guide, he will show me in my mind what the person draws, the people will examine the booth . . . 'Is there any camera, any holes?' They'll get inside, I'll shut the door, 'Do you see any light?' 'No, I don't,' they examine the air tube, not even any light can get in, blah blah blah, I tell them what I'm going to do when Harmony knocks once on the box. Fine, all right, then I let them look at the tablet, the pen, *ja*, I go inside now, all right?"

Kristal stepped into the box. "Go ahead, shut me up."

One of the three men shut the door of the cabinet and the two others took wide black electrical tape and sealed up all four edges of the door. "Kristal?" the woman called Harmony said, "can you see any light at all? Knock once for yes, twice for no."

Two knocks came from the cabinet.

"Ladies and gentlemen," Harmony said, "may I please have a volunteer from the audience, someone known to others here so that we may be sure there is no possibility of conspiring beforehand." She turned to one of the men. "Theo, stand in for now. Draw whatever you want, make it as complex as you like."

Theo sat down at the table, picked up a marker, thought for a moment, then began to draw on one of the large white sheets of paper. Harmony watched, relaxed, her hands in her pockets, until he had finished.

"Thank you, Theo. Now, if you will put the paper on the easel so that the audience may see."

The man secured it to the easel. "Well, well," Joseph said. "What an unoriginal mind."

The drawing Theo had done was apparently intended to be the Loch Ness Monster. A straight line intended to represent the surface of the lake ran along the bottom of the paper, and double half circles were the loops of the monster's snakelike body breaking the surface. Its neck and head protruded from the lake near the center of the picture, and the circle of its right eye was staring at a primitive boat in which a stick figure, its arms wide, looked at it in surprise.

Laika nodded in agreement. "Good old Nessie."

"I wasn't referring to the drawing," said Joseph. "I meant the trick. Blackburn and Smith did it a hundred years ago."

"Who were they?" Tony asked, but Joseph waved him into silence and they continued to watch the proceedings.

Harmony walked to the cabinet, knocked on it once, and returned to the table. They waited for perhaps two minutes, until there was a single answering knock from within the cabinet. Harmony then peeled away the tape from the edges of the door and opened it. Kristal stood there holding the tablet in his hands. On the top sheet, but reduced in scale, was a drawing identical to the one that Theo had made, complete with boat and startled observer.

"I stagger, I moan slightly with the effort, I *triumph!*" Kristal said, laughing. "So what you think, Theo?"

Theo could only shake his head admiringly and spoke some words in German which Laika, Joseph, and Tony all understood: "If I hadn't seen it, I wouldn't believe it."

"And the audience, and the scientists observing, will all be as believing and accepting as Theo," Joseph said, frowning. As they watched, Kristal, Harmony, and the three men left the auditorium.

"He didn't really do that, did he?" said Tony. "It was a trick, right?"

"Right as rain."

"So how'd he do it, then?"

"I know the principle," Joseph said, staring at the empty auditorium. "But not the exact process . . . yet." He turned to the others. "Leave me alone for a while, okay? Let me play back the tapes a few times, look at it from all three angles."

"Sure," Tony said. "You can only enhance it so much with the equipment I have here, you know."

Joseph nodded and started to rewind the three cassettes. Laika and Tony went into the next room, closing the door behind them, and Joseph started to watch. "See it," he whispered to himself. "It's there. *See* it."

An hour later, at 1100 hours, he opened the door, stepped into the next room, and smiled at Laika and Tony. "Got it," he said. "Want to see?"

Chapter 8

*B*y mid-afternoon, the three operatives had checked out of their rooms and were driving south, the loch on their left. Joseph and Laika led in the Peugeot, and Tony followed in the van.

Joseph had found the reporter from *Der Stern* with whom he had had a few beers the night before. After several pints, the reporter had told Joseph of his dislike for Kristal ever since the so-called psychic had humiliated him during an exhibition of his purported powers in Bonn, calling him a doubting Thomas (correctly) and telling him (also correctly) that the most prominent thing in his wallet was two condoms left from a pack of three, and that the missing one had been used with a young woman named Gerde. This was also accurate, and he might have found it amusing had his wife (now ex-wife) Sarah not been sitting beside him in the audience.

Hell, Joseph correctly assumed without psychic aid, hath no fury like a reporter paying alimony, so it was to this man that, the following day, he confided the secret of Kristal's upcoming demonstration of psychic powers, in exchange for which Joseph received a firm promise that the source would not be revealed. "Better," said the reporter gleefully, "to let this charlatan think that one of his own people, how do you say it, spilled his beans!"

Joseph regretted only slightly, as they drove away from Drumnadrochit, that those beans would be spilled without him. For him, the joy was in figuring out the scam, not necessarily in revealing it. Knowing that Kristal would be debunked was enough. He turned his attention to what was next. "Did the contact say anything else—anything at all—when you called?"

"No," Laika answered. "He gave me the location, and that was all. God only knows why he wants us to go to the Isle of Skye."

"Maybe to play ghostbusters at a haunted castle," Joseph said, and smiled when Laika laughed.

By eight o'clock, they had arrived in the small town of Kyle of Lochalsh, situated on the east side of the bridge that would take them to the large Isle of Skye off Scotland's west coast. They stopped for dinner at a pub that had a TV mounted prominently above the bar, so when the image on the screen became similar to that which he had seen on his three monitors, Tony signaled the others. "Check it out," he said. "Our pal Kristal."

The pub was noisy, but they were able to make out some of Kristal's comments about his "guide" channeling him information. "I am not a psychic," they heard him say, "but merely an instrument for—" The pub noise drowned him out again.

"Stop the presses," Joseph said dryly. "Kristal speaks the truth, for a change."

"Hey," Laika said, "look who's one of the volunteers." It was the reporter from *Der Stern*. Even on the small screen they could detect his anticipation.

"Screw this," said Tony. "Grab your drinks." He led the way to the bar. There were no stools available, so they stood there and watched the screen as Kristal stripped off his robe, revealing a compact, muscular body in a pair of Speedos. The reporter and another man went behind a screen and came out twenty seconds later. Kristal gave his pen and tablet to one of the volunteers, who examined them and handed them back.

Then Kristal asked the three men to examine the cabinet, including the corkscrew air hole at the top, the shape of which ensured that no light would come into the cabinet. One of the men was shut inside and when he came out was asked if he could see any light. He replied in the negative.

Then Kristal went into the cabinet, the door was closed and taped shut, and another volunteer was chosen from the audience, an older French woman who was on a bus trip with her friends. She sat at the table and drew a picture of a garden with a wall, two trees, and several flowers and birds.

Harmony set the drawing on the easel so the audience could see, then went over to the cabinet and rapped on it sharply. In just over a minute, Kristal rapped back. The volunteers stripped the tape off the door and opened it. Kristal stepped out, the tablet behind his back. He took a dramatic pause, looked at the picture on the easel, and then showed what he had drawn on the tablet to the audience. The two pictures were nearly identical.

"What a surprise," said Joseph, as the crowd burst into applause, and even the denizens of the pub murmured their admiration. On the screen the *Stern* reporter held out his hand with a look of amazement on his face and Kristal graciously gave him the tablet to examine the drawing.

But instead of looking at the drawing, the reporter flipped the pages of the tablet over, revealing its cardboard backing, and turned toward the audience. "This man is a fraud," he said. "And what you have seen is a simple conjuror's trick, and I can prove it!"

"Did you help him with his lines?" Laika asked.

Joseph shrugged. "I made a few suggestions."

"Turn out the lights—*all* the lights!" the reporter went on, "and you shall see!"

"This is preposterous," Kristal said. "This man is ridiculous; he wishes only to lie about me, he—"

"Turn off the lights!" the reporter insisted. "If your powers are real, what do you have to fear?"

The mob scented blood then, and some started shouting in agreement. One of the volunteers, who from his bearing might have been a "scientific" observer, nodded in agreement and signaled to the back of the house for the lights to be extinguished. Kristal protested vigorously, and Harmony looked around as though disoriented, but first the lights on the stage went off, then the house lights, leaving everything, including the cameras, in utter darkness.

Though they could not make it out on the screen, the three operatives knew from the cries of outrage that the audience was seeing the glow of the luminous powder that had been rubbed into the surface of the tablet's cardboard backing. "Turn them back on!" came the reporter's voice, and the lights returned, blinding the video lenses for a second, making the TV screen blaze with whiteness before recapturing the images on the stage.

"Now," said the reporter, "if the confederate will turn out her pockets—those spacious pockets in those spacious pants where she drew on a cigarette paper whatever she saw the volunteer drawing on her sheet. *Kommen sie*! Empty your pocket, *bitte*! The left one only!"

"The one," Joseph explained, "that was turned away from the audience. Not that it mattered much. Considering the size of those harem pants, she could've played pool in there and not attracted any notice."

The scientific gentleman pointed to Harmony and nodded. "If you please, madam."

The crowd roared again, and again Kristal protested. When Harmony reached into her pocket, he had had enough. "I will not be subjected to this inquisition!" he roared, and strode off the stage.

"He should have grabbed the girl," Joseph said.

The crowd was in an uproar now, shouting at Harmony to empty her pocket. Pale and shaking, she did, and from the folds of her voluminous pants brought forth a pen and a two-inch square of laminate to which was secured an equally small piece of either India or cigarette paper. The reporter snatched them away from her.

"You see?" he crowed triumphantly to the suddenly spellbound crowd. "She copied the drawing as the woman did it, then rolled the little paper into a tiny ball." He demonstrated as he spoke. "She palmed the ball, and when she knocked on the cabinet, she simply flipped it onto the top, where it rolled into and down the corkscrew airhole, right into Kristal's hands. He unfolded it and held it against the luminous tablet back; the paper was so thin he could see right through it and see the picture. Then he copied it, slightly larger, onto the tablet itself.''

"What did he do with the paper, then?" someone called out.

"Either put it in his shorts, or—'' The reporter rolled up the paper, popped the tiny ball into his mouth, and swallowed. "Either way, I wouldn't care to search for the evidence." The crowd laughed. "Especially after what I saw behind that screen!" The crowd laughed louder, and in it the three of them heard the end of Kristal's career.

"That," Joseph said, "was not one of *my* lines."

Chapter 9

After dinner, they crossed over the high, arching bridge to the Isle of Skye. Jagged hills rose darkly on either side of them.

"I just don't see," Joseph mused, "why the hell he would use such an old trick. Blackburn and Smith did the same thing over a hundred years ago. Only Smith did it under a blanket and blindfolded. Blackburn drew it on cigarette paper, but rolled up the paper and put it in a hollow pencil. Then Smith would pretend he'd lost his pencil, stick his hand out, and Blackburn would give it to him. Smith had a luminous slate in his waistcoat, and presto, there you were."

"Didn't it get a little obvious when Smith kept forgetting his pencil?" Laika asked.

"Apparently not. The scientists who observed this amazing phenomenon never even mentioned the pencil in their reports. The truth finally came out when Blackburn wrote about it years later. Guess he felt guilty."

"An emotion," Laika suggested, "totally foreign to Kristal, I suspect. You think he'll survive this?"

"Frankly, yes. He'll never be as big as he might have been without it, but people need so much to believe in this kind of junk that they'll assume Kristal's enemies conspired to frame him, or some such bullshit."

"You mean, maybe Harmony put the luminous stuff on the tablet, and carried the pen and paper in her pocket, but Kristal didn't really use it?"

"Right," Joseph said. "Maybe she was in cahoots with the reporter to discredit him. Remember, the only proof actually found on Kristal was the tablet, and if it was a frame-up, he might not have noticed even that."

"He would have if he was psychic."

Just before they reached the village of Ashaig, they saw the sign for the bed-and-breakfast to which they had been told to go. The Peugeot, the van behind it, pulled into the stone driveway that led them to a small car park behind the house. It was a long building with white plaster walls and a multitude of gables and pitched roofs. The path to the front door led through a colorless garden whose spring flowers had not yet begun to appear.

A woman in her forties answered their knock. Though she was slightly stout and had a face like a cherub, Laika could see a tiredness in her eyes that betrayed her field experience, and wondered what countersurveillance work she had done for the Company before being rewarded with the management of a safe house.

"I'm Laika Harris," Laika said, having been instructed by the dossier to give her real name.

"I know who you are," the woman said. "All of you. Mr. Skye is expecting you."

Laika was surprised. "He's here, then?"

"He was. We watched . . . some television together. Then he went out for a walk. If you came, I was to tell you to join him."

"Where is he?" Tony asked.

"Go out the lane, and turn the way you came. Three hundred yards down the road there's a dirt road to your right, toward the bay, that leads through some fields. You'll come over a rise and see the bay. There's a graveyard there. That's where Mr. Skye will be."

"Okay," Tony said, "let's take the car. I'll leave the van here."

"Mr. Skye wished you to walk," their hostess said.

"Walk? It's almost *dark.*"

"We're in the northern latitudes," said Laika, remembering that Tony had slept through the previous evening. "It'll stay this light for another two hours, anyway."

As they started back to the car, Tony asked Laika and Joseph, "Are you two carrying?" They both nodded, and Tony whispered, "Good," under his breath.

They didn't talk as they walked down the lane to the road. The only sounds were those of the stones shifting under their feet and the occasional car passing by them.

When they came over the rise, the graveyard was visible another hundred yards away across a pasture where cows lay sleeping or chewing their cud in the chill Scottish evening. The graveyard was surrounded by a low stone wall, undoubtedly hand laid hundreds of years before. As they grew closer, Laika could see a figure sitting on the far wall overlooking the bay, its back to them.

"Cloudy?" Tony said softly, but Laika could only shrug. It was light enough to see the figure, but too dark to make out any details.

The cemetery was larger than she had first thought, and as they passed by it, she saw very old stones side by side with more recent ones. Mossy Celtic crosses rubbed up against a group of a dozen Royal Navy casualties of World War II, while a bas-relief angel in profile held a garland of flowers for the dead.

The figure on the wall had not moved, and Laika could almost fancy that it, too, was a sculpture. They stopped ten yards away from it, and Laika spoke softly. "Mr. Skye."

The voice came before the figure moved. "Good evening, Ms. Harris. Mr. Luciano. Mr. Stein." Then the man slowly turned, and a familiar face smiled at her from under a brown oilcloth hat with a wide brim. "Very nicely done. My compliments."

Richard Skye got down from the wall with a swift economy of motion and faced the trio. Laika was startled once more to see how short the man was. "I doubt if Mr. Kristal will be plying his pseudo-psychic wares before many national audiences after this. If he's lucky, he might play a few clubs in Hamburg before he's forced to declare bankruptcy. I'm very pleased. All in all, this was an excellent, if non-critical, case for you three to get acquainted over, and, shall we say, cut your psychic teeth on before you move on to . . . greater matters. And you acquitted yourselves admirably.

"In fact, I'm *so* pleased that I'm sending you under the very deepest cover so that you can continue to do just this kind of work. As of today, you three no longer exist. You will be shadow operatives performing shadow operations." He smiled. "Ironic, isn't it? Shadows . . . bringing other shadows into the light."

Chapter 10

"Forgive me for being a little dense," Tony Luciano said, "but what do you mean, we no longer exist?"

Skye turned from them and looked out across the darkening waters of the bay, to where gray mountains rose on the other side. He removed his hat so that Laika could see his sandy-brown hair. "I mean that for all intents and purposes," he went on in his officious, almost prissy voice, "Anthony Luciano, Laika Harris, and Joseph Stein are gone. Everyone in the Company but a very high-ranking few will think you've been assigned to Eastern Europe and the Balkans. Even now, false trails are being laid. Nearly everyone at Langley will believe you to be working deep cover in Ankara, Bucharest, and Azerbaijan." The thin mouth beneath Skye's thinner moustache gave a half-smile as he looked at Tony. "Which is where we've put your shadow, Mr. Luciano. We expect to see a great deal of termination work there in the months to come."

Laika sensed Tony's tension, but he said nothing. "What about our personal lives?" Laika asked.

"For the time being, they will cease to be. I assure you that at some time in the future you will be able to reenter them, and you will be able to keep in touch with whatever loved ones you may have via letters only, which will be routed through the usual network. Communication by telephone or by Internet will not be possible."

"What's this all about?" said Joseph, sounding peeved,

Laika thought. She was peeved, too. She hated not being able to talk to her mother.

"It's about exposing lies and debunking the false," Skye answered. "What you did at Loch Ness was a trial run, which, as I said, you passed with flying colors. Having proved yourselves, you will be assigned to further projects for which there are no known natural explanations or solutions, cases that would suggest the paranormal to superstitious minds."

"What?" said Tony. "You mean, like professional ghost hunters, uh, UFO chasers? That kind of thing?"

"You put it a bit baldly, but yes, something like that, to mention just two of the more common delusions of the masses. You three will be called upon to produce the natural solutions for such absurdities."

"And what if we can't?" Tony said. "What if some of these things—" He shrugged. "Well, what if we can't?"

"Of the three of you," said Skye, "I expected that particular question to come from you, Mr. Luciano. It must be that good Catholic upbringing that makes you cling to outmoded beliefs."

"I didn't say I believed in *anything!*" Tony flared. "I just asked a question!"

"And I'll answer it," Skye said calmly. "If you find yourself unable as a team to disprove any so-called psychic phenomena, you simply report your findings to me. Some of us in the Company will do further research into a natural solution, and it will then be given to you, who will distribute it for public consumption."

"Wait a minute," said Laika. "I thought we were supposed to keep out of the public eye."

"You are. You will distribute your findings—or our conclusions—through channels."

"And what's our cover?" Joseph asked. "Do we just walk in and say to the authorities, Hi, we're your friendly freelance paranormal investigators, show us everything you've got?"

"You know better than that, Mr. Stein." Skye placed his hat firmly on his head. It added a good two inches to his spindly frame, but Joseph still towered over him. "You'll be working for a branch of the National Science Foundation with whom we have made some arrangements. It's a non-existent branch, but the cover will stand up to all but the deepest government scrutiny. Nothing short of a senate sub-committee will be able to disprove the provenance of the Division of Special Investigations."

"Special Investigations," repeated Laika. "Well, that sounds innocuous enough. I just have one concern, Mr. Skye." He nodded at her to continue. "If we're supposedly connected to the National Science Foundation, I would have to assume that we'd be working within the United States."

"That's correct. Possibly outside, but most of your operations will be domestic."

"There's the slight problem, then, of the CIA charter?"

"That," said Skye, "is precisely why I referred to you as shadow operatives."

"Why wouldn't the FBI handle something like this?" Joseph asked.

"Mr. Stein, I really don't think I have to explain government policy to you, do I? I was unaware that the DCI and even those far above him were answerable to you. Do you perhaps have your own senate committee of which I've not been made aware?"

Stein said nothing. Laika didn't expect him to, and, seemingly, neither did Skye.

"You will work wherever you are needed," Skye went on. "You have been assigned this operation, and if you do not choose to accept it . . . well, you know what your rights are. Do any of you wish to refuse this assignment?"

They looked at each other, but none of them spoke.

"Very well, then. Though I need not answer this question, I suspect you are wondering about it: why on earth would the government want to become involved in what seems to be an area that the private sector has been involved with?"

"You took the words out of my mouth," said Joseph. "Aren't we getting into CSICOP's territory here?"

"We're getting into matters of national security here, Mr.

Stein. The order for a group such as yourselves has come from high up—*very* high up. It expresses a deeply felt concern with our national character. The thought that pervades the reasoning behind the formation of this shadow group is that a superstitious citizenry is a weak and easily led—and *misled*—one.

"Tabloid trash has become daily bread to the majority of Americans. UFOs, ghosts, channelers, angels . . ." Skye gave a sardonic laugh. "Appearances of Jesus on plywood doors and in spaghetti sauce. Even cinnamon rolls that look like Mother Teresa. No side is spared. The left gets caught up in New Age garbage and magical thinking, while the right are suckers for religious appearances, angels, and Satanic cults hiding in every closet. And *everybody* from Maoists to militias is jumping on the UFO bandwagon."

"Not to mention reading their horoscopes," said Joseph, with a sidelong glance at Laika.

"Precisely. The more strange events that can be given rational explanations, the more reasoned our society will be. At least, that's the rationale behind what you'll be doing. I think it is not unimportant work."

"I tend to agree," Joseph said. "If there's anything that I don't mind pulling me away from my desk, it would be this."

"I'm so glad you approve," said Skye with a blend of sincerity and venom.

"How's the team structured?" Tony asked.

"All the details will be in the packets you will receive on the plane back to the States. But you already know that Ms. Harris is the team leader. She makes the final decisions, and you two gentlemen will be her support. Mr. Stein, you will concentrate on communication and research; Mr. Luciano, you will be responsible for covert operations. Your duties will overlap, but these are your primary functions. Any other questions?"

"What's our first assignment?" Tony asked.

"You will learn that later as well. Now," Skye said, looking up at the dark clouds overhead, "might I suggest we walk back to the house while we can still see our feet in front of us? There were some rather large piles of manure along the way that I should like to avoid.''

It wasn't hard for Laika to bite back the comment she would have made, were Skye not there.

Chapter 11

The three did not spend the night in the house with Skye. Instead, after the landlady rather grudgingly served them tea and scones, Skye gave them directions to a small private airport that was used mostly for medical emergencies. He gave them a brief and businesslike good-bye, and they went to their cars.

"He loves to hear himself talk, doesn't he?" said Joseph, when they had left their chief behind.

"I think it gives him an erection," Laika said without smiling. "Then he plays it back in his head at night."

"Did you check this car for bugs?" Joseph asked.

"I've said worse things he's probably overheard. I don't think he likes you very much—probably because you're a head taller than he is."

Laika heard more in Joseph's silence than mere agreement. After that they didn't say much of anything until they got on the plane. It was an eight-passenger Learjet that sat on the rough surfaced runway cutting between the craggy hills like a trench through rock. They were the only passengers, and the pilots asked nothing about customs. They told Tony to bring his personal luggage only, so he took a suitcase and the satchel with his picks from the van. Laika was sure he was used to leaving Company goods behind. They would be picked up, transported elsewhere, and used again. And when he needed such items in the future, they would be delivered. But picks were personal.

The plane lifted off without coming within five hundred yards of the end of the runway. Their trail would end there, and any reports of the flight would indicate that it had headed southeast, toward Eastern Europe.

Instead, it started across the North Sea, bearing toward Newfoundland, where it would turn south. After a half hour in the air, the co-pilot left the cockpit long enough to come back into the small cabin and ask if the three passengers wanted anything. "Just to know where we're going," Laika said.

The co-pilot smiled warmly. "You'll find that out soon enough. Would you like anything to drink?"

When he returned to his cabin, the ops discussed their assignment. "What I wonder is how long this is gonna be," Tony said. "Open-ended like this—hell, they could shuffle us back and forth from one goofy case to another for years. There are a lot of fortune tellers around."

"We'll do it as long as it please them, I guess," Laika said flatly. Then she looked closely at the two men. "What I want to know is, other than discomfort at the openendedness of this mission, how do the two of you feel about it?"

Tony jerked his head to the side, as if trying to shift his thoughts into place. "It's kind of cool, actually. Interesting. I got a little buzz, you know?"

"How do you feel about the paranormal?" Laika asked him.

Tony thought for a moment. "One thing I learned with the Company is that where there's smoke, there's fire. If several agents suspect there's a mole loose, there probably is. If a few think they can turn a foreign agent, they probably can. If enough of us think a government's ready to topple with a little push, it probably is."

"So if enough people believe in ghosts," Joseph said, "or UFOs or angels and demons and gods and devils, there probably are?"

"I wouldn't rule it out," Tony said hotly.

"I would," said Joseph, "unless there's some empirical evidence to back it up. No matter how careful he is, a mole leaves a trail, some physical evidence, behind. If an agent's ready to turn, other signs will be there—a persuasive and political lover, a busted bank account, the threat of blackmail. And nothing shows more physical signs of decay than a regime ripe for a fall.'' Joseph shrugged. ''But ghosts and angels and devils don't leave anything behind, and all UFOs leave is flaky witnesses who can't stop talking about their anal probes.''

''So you think it's *all* bullshit, then?'' Tony said, bristling.

''Let me just put it like this. In over two decades of looking into the paranormal, I've never come across a piece of evidence—not one single piece—that you'd be able to take to a court of law to prove the existence of any of this stuff people claim is true.''

''There are *pictures* of UFOs . . . and ghosts. . . .''

''Not one of which was ever proven to have been authentic. Under test conditions the results are always the same—negative. It's bullshit, Tony, it's all as much bullshit as Zeus and Jesus and the fairies.''

''Ah, what do you know? *You're* bullshit!''

''Now, *there's* a reasoned riposte.''

His cheeks flushed, Tony started to get up, but his seatbelt held him down, and a hard look from Laika kept him there. ''All right,'' she said, ''we're not going to work too cooperatively if we start insulting each other.''

''Don't tell *me* about it,'' said Tony. ''I didn't say *his* god was bullshit.''

''I don't *have* a god, thank you,'' Joseph replied.

''Yeah, 'cause no god would have *you!*''

''All *right!*'' barked Laika. ''What the hell am I, a kindergarten teacher? Now, take it easy, both of you. I'm just trying to get an idea as to where you stand concerning the paranormal. Let's keep religion out of it.''

''All right, fine,'' Joseph said crisply. ''And if it helps, I apologize.''

''Okay, I'm sorry I got pissed,'' Tony said after a moment, though Laika thought he still sounded annoyed.

''The only point I want to make,'' Joseph added, ''is that

it's the easiest thing in the world to ascribe supernatural causes to things that are all too natural. We seem to have a real proclivity to see patterns where none exist. That's why conspiracy theories thrive, and why people call unexplained lights ghosts and aliens, rather than looking hard for a natural explanation.'' He took a leather portfolio from beneath his seat and unzipped it. ''Look, let me show you what I mean. Here's *Fortean Times* magazine. It's named after Charles Fort, who collected volumes of unexplained phenomena.''

''*The Book of the Damned*,'' Laika said. She had read parts of it in college.

''Right, and three others. Anyway, the people who put this together aren't necessarily believers in psychic phenomena, but what they do is report the paranormal, or just strange things that happen. But strange things happen all the time, and strange things don't mean that the supernatural or aliens are at work. Like this article on the *chupacabras.*''

''The who?'' Tony asked.

''In Puerto Rico, they've found dead goats that are drained of blood: one puncture wound, weird slime over the corpses, and sometimes the animals are killed in closed cages. So naturally it follows that it's a supernatural vampire beast, right? Or the same UFOs that are responsible for the cattle mutilation in the States. But there's another perpetrator that makes a whole lot more sense.''

''Man,'' Tony said.

Joseph nodded. ''Exactly. There's nothing here that couldn't have been done by a sadistically clever human being.''

''Then it gets into questions of psychology,'' Laika said. ''What would make somebody do something like that?''

''The same thing that makes people create crop circles or tell about being abducted by aliens,'' said Joseph. ''Notoriety, or, if they keep it secret, just the thrill of knowing what nobody else does.''

''And scaring the hell out of them in the process,'' Tony added.

''Exactly,'' said Laika. ''And God knows that's a kick for

a lot of people.'' James came into her mind then, and she
pushed him back out again, concentrating on what Joseph
was saying.

''Here's another one. Listen to this:

> Plattsburgh, New York—Authorities were amazed to
> find the charred remains of eleven bodies in a burned
> down hunting lodge twenty miles from this town in
> northern New York State. The corpses were all male,
> and it has not yet been determined whether the men
> died in the conflagration or before the fire began. The
> identities of the men are unknown, as the lodge was
> rented under a pseudonym.
>
> Attempts to identify the corpses by dental records
> have led to the remarkable discovery that some of the
> teeth exhibit dental techniques that have not been in
> use for hundreds of years. The remains of bone and
> ivory dentures have been found, as well as guttapercha
> and lead fillings. Dr. Norton Thomas stated that he had
> never seen such techniques used on teeth, regardless of
> a patient's age.
>
> Witnesses who saw several of the men before they left
> for the lodge stated that they seemed to be in their thir-
> ties or forties and spoke with Scottish accents. These
> facts have led to speculation that the meeting was noth-
> ing more or less than a secret gathering of immortals
> that somehow went awry. Or perhaps the Society for
> the Appreciation of Dental History and Haggis?

''That's one thing I like about *Fortean Times*,'' Joseph
said, after he finished reading. ''Their sense of humor. If you
don't take any of this stuff too seriously, you never look like
a moron when it's debunked.''

''All right,'' Laika said. ''I'll play devil's advocate. How
do you explain away the teeth?''

''Well, my last assumption would be that the dead guys
are immortal. Maybe they are, however, part of a sect that
does things the way their ancestors did them. That might very

well give them a reason to gather in private.''

"A secret society," Tony said.

Joseph nodded. "I believe in secret societies—because they exist. The Masons are a secret society, after all. So are Skull and Bones and the Trilateral Commission. There have always been secret societies, and there always will be. But I don't believe these societies have paranormal powers, despite their supposedly ancient rituals.''

While Joseph was talking, the co-pilot came into the cabin with a large sealed envelope that he handed to Laika. When he left, she tore it open and read as Joseph went on.

"As for these victims being immortals, that's nuts. How can you deduce that somebody's immortal on the basis of a few guttapercha fillings? Why would an immortal even *need* fillings? And how could one true immortal die in a fire, let alone eleven of them?" Joseph and Tony both laughed.

"Inquiring minds want to know!" Tony said.

"In that case," said Laika, with no humor in her voice, "Richard Skye is an inquiring mind."

"What?" both men said at once.

"I think we've just seen either a terrific coincidence, or proof of synchronicity," Laika said. "We're going to Plattsburgh, New York, gentlemen. Home of the eleven burned immortals. We're supposed to prove that they're not."

Chapter 12

*T*he next afternoon, Richard Skye was back in his office in Langley. He picked up his telephone, hit a few buttons before dialing to ensure that the call would not be monitored, and dialed a number in Washington, D.C.

"Dr. Roker, calling for Mr. Stanley," he said, using his code name. He held the phone for three minutes before he heard another voice. Then he spoke softly and deferentially. "I've turned the matter of the Protectors over to the new team . . . oh yes, they're very good indeed. The Kristal thing? That was them. . . . You didn't? I'll send you a tape. You'll enjoy it . . . of course . . . of course I'll keep you informed every step of the way. As I said, they're very good. The only problem with them will be to make sure they don't learn *too* much. . . . Yes . . . yes, I certainly will. . . . Goodbye, sir."

Skye hung up the phone and let out a deep breath. The buzzer on his desk startled him, and he slapped the button and half-shouted, "What?" at his secretary.

"Agent Daly here to see you, sir."

"Send him in."

In less than ten seconds, a man entered the room. He was tall and so muscular that his carefully tailored suit could not disguise the thick boluses beneath. Some of the other agents called him Popeye.

"Talk," Skye told him.

* * *

When Peder Holberg had finally shown up at his mid-town studio at six o'clock in the morning, fourteen hours after Adam Guaraldi had found him missing, he'd been barely coherent, and Guaraldi thought he must have been taking drugs, wherever he had been. But a few hours of sleep restored Holberg to his usual energetic self, and once again he swore that he remembered nothing about his disappearance.

A few days later he started going uptown to hang with the goths. Guaraldi had seen goths around town and at some of the clubs. Most of them were kids, teenagers, or in their early twenties. Their attitudes bored Guaraldi's ass off. Okay, maybe love and death were the only two great things in life, but Jesus Christ, you couldn't think about them *all* the time.

These goths were different, Peder had told him. There was an earnestness, a seriousness, a *danger* that he felt somehow drawn to. "There is something about them," Peder said. "It's as if . . . they *know* something I don't. But I should. Maybe from them I can find it out."

"Find *what* out?" Guaraldi asked. "Where you go? Is that where you've been going, then? To be with these kids?"

"They are not kids, Adam," Peder said, as if pleading with his lover to understand. "They have not the, what is it, the *attitude* the children who play at being the vampires have. And no, I do not go to them when I have these blackouts—I think not, anyway. You can come with me when I go to them, you know."

Guaraldi went only once. He wanted to see if these goths played with sex or drugs, if that was what Peder was finding so attractive. But he learned quickly that such was not the case. He also learned that he did not want to see any of them again.

As the weeks passed, Peder got more and more taciturn. He would visit the goths, always telling Guaraldi when he went, and he would also disappear. For some reason he couldn't name, Guaraldi began to disbelieve Peder when he told him he couldn't remember where he had been. Peder seemed daily to grow more inward. And though he had been able to function well on only a few hours of sleep a night, he looked constantly tired now, and terribly worried about something he did not share with Guaraldi.

Three weeks before his next showing was due to open, Peder split with the goths. Guaraldi remarked that it had been several days since Peder had gone uptown to see his "kohl-eyed friends," as Guaraldi put it.

Peder simply told him in a flat tone that he did not want to see them anymore: "If they ever call here, I am not in to them."

Guaraldi tried to get Peder to tell him what had happened with the goths, what he had learned, if anything, about his fugue states, and why he was so unhappy of late, but Peder would share nothing with him. He had become increasingly more secretive, locking himself up for hours at a time in a loft that they had used for storage, and to which he retained the only key.

Through all this, Peder somehow managed to continue working. He had always been of the peculiar belief that his works of art were best seen in the context of the space in which they had been created. Guaraldi and most of the critics had to admit he was right. The burned and battered wooden floors, the iron wall racks holding iron, the high, dark ceilings, the acetylene tanks—all paid testimony to the physicality of the work involved and made even the finished pieces seem parts of a work in progress that was Peder Holberg's life.

Eight new sculptures were finished the week before the five-day showing was due to open on March 15. Five days was all the time Peder Holberg felt he could tie up his studio. He was an artist, after all, and it was his duty, and had been his joy, to work. Showing and selling pieces were tasks for merchants, and though his idiosyncrasy of showing in his studio required his participation, he did not like mingling with the arty set any longer than necessary.

But this showing, unlike the previous ones, was hell getting ready for. Lionel Garraty, Peder's agent, was in charge of making all the arrangements for press releases, mailings, food and drink, valet parking (a real bit of organization, since the nearest garage was three blocks away from the studio), and everything else it took to make such an unorthodox manner of showing art seem uncompromising and daring rather than a pain in the ass. It was always a relative nightmare, but it was made doubly so by Peder's preoccupied air.

He seemed to have no opinions on any of the matters that Lionel or Guaraldi brought up, and might either disappear or lock himself in the loft storage room at any time of the day or night. Finally, the day before the showing, Lionel lost his temper. "Don't you *care?*" he bellowed. "Don't you care at all? Because if you don't, let's forget it right now, I'll make calls, I'll call the whole thing off, just let me know, Peder!"

The outburst was great enough to bring some life back into the sculptor. He assured Lionel that everything would be fine, that he wanted to have the show, and that he was sorry he was so preoccupied, but that he was thinking about his work, which was a bald-faced lie if Guaraldi had ever heard one.

The goths didn't help matters any that last week. Peder might have broken with them, but they, for one reason or another, had not broken with him. Several calls came in every day asking for Peder. Guaraldi knew from the sepulchral tones who it was. At first he made excuses, next he hung up on them, and finally he stopped answering the phone completely, letting the machine take the urgent and finally threatening messages.

The day before the showing, after coming back to the studio with Chinese food, Guaraldi saw two of the sallow-skinned ghouls standing outside the studio door. They seemed to know who he was and stood in front of him, blocking his way. "We want to see Peder," the more lively looking of the pair announced.

"I don't doubt it. Sorry. He's getting ready for his showing."

"No, you don't get it. We *have* to see him."

"No, *you* don't get it, Dracula. Peder can't see anybody

right now, and he especially doesn't want to see you guys. So take a hike.''

The talker stared at Guaraldi then as if he were trying to hypnotize him. Guaraldi wasn't scared of them, unless they had knives or guns or something he couldn't see. They were so skinny he thought he could snap their arms and legs in two if he had to. So he stared back at the man, bugging his eyes mockingly. "Sorry, sweetheart," he told him, "you're not my type. Now, back off.''

The man gave one more glower, then moved aside as Guaraldi walked past him and unlocked the door. As the locks disengaged, Guaraldi looked back over his shoulder. "Don't even *think* about it. Just go hit another midnight showing of *The Crow*, okay?'' He went in and slammed the door behind him, whispering, "Assholes," in the dark. He didn't mention the goths to Peder. There was already enough on the artist's mind.

Peder kept to himself the day of the showing, while caterers and cleaners and Lionel's assistants and hangers-on scurried about the studio, preparing for the eight o'clock opening. He spent much of his time in the apartment, and an hour or so alone in the windowless loft.

Still, when his fellow artists, patrons, and critics began to come in shortly after eight, he seemed to brighten, chatting with those he knew, being introduced by Lionel to those he did not, accepting compliments, and making small talk. But for all Peder's surface amiability, Guaraldi thought he seemed preoccupied, and he wasn't surprised to watch the sculptor moving away from the crowd and up the stairway to the sanctuary of the locked loft.

He *was* surprised, however, when, only a minute after Peder had gone in and locked the door behind him, an explosion rocked the studio.

The sound was enormous, a gigantic *crump* that felt like someone had slapped both of his ears with open palms. The building shuddered and seemed to take several seconds to settle, the sculptures teetering precariously. Some people fell to their knees, others grabbed whatever was handy. Men and women shouted and screamed, and several ran out the door and down the stairs.

Most, however, finding themselves unharmed except for the ringing in their ears, looked around the studio to try and determine the source of the explosion. When Guaraldi looked up toward the loft, it was all too obvious.

Thick, dark smoke was drifting out of the room. The door hung only by the top hinge, and the concrete block wall bulged outward slightly. For an instant, Guaraldi thought of the naked belly of a pregnant woman. Then he realized that Peder Holberg was still in that room.

He cried out Peder's name and ran toward the wooden steps and raced up them two at a time. The stairway had been damaged by the blast, and one of the steps buckled under his weight, but he grabbed the railing and hauled himself up. He heard other people behind him.

"Peder!" he cried again, yanking the broken door aside and looking into the room. It was large, twenty feet square, with a high ceiling. The lightbulbs inside had been shattered by the blast, and in the darkness and smoke Guaraldi could see nothing but a few stray tongues of flame that were going out even as he watched. He could not see Peder.

"Call 911!" he shouted down to the people on the floor. "Lionel! Bring me that cord light!" He pointed to a coiled mechanic's light hanging on a peg on the wall. Lionel grabbed it and cautiously brought it up the stairs.

Guaraldi plugged it into a socket on the outer wall, and it flashed into light. He took it inside, trailing the cord as he went. Several men followed.

The room was chaos. Pieces of sculptures that Pēder had rejected were stored here for salvage, and the iron was now twisted as though an unseen force had rent it. A huge work table that used to sit at the far end of the room had become nothing but shards and splinters. Those sculptures closest to the table had been wrenched apart by whatever had caused the blast, and rods and bars of iron lay scattered like a giant's toothpicks.

The tiles on the ceiling twenty feet above had been blown

from their grids and covered the floor, charred brown squares that no longer hid the naked plaster and the pipes that, having burst from the blast, sent water hissing onto the hot surfaces below.

"Peder?" Guaraldi said, but though he shone the light all around the room, kicked aside the shattered table, and clawed away the fallen tiles, he could see no trace of Peder Holberg.

There was not a drop of blood, not a scrap of flesh.

And most puzzling of all, there was no way that Peder Holberg could have gotten out of the loft.

"Where is he?" Adam Guaraldi whispered, and then everyone was asking the same question. But the ruined room gave no answer.

Chapter 13

"**W**hat have we got?" asked Laika.

She sat in a small room in Plattsburgh Memorial Hospital. Tony Luciano sat across from her on a smooth leather chair whose seat showed more duct tape than leather. He was dressed in medical whites, and his hands bore traces of the white powder he had worn under his latex gloves in the adjacent autopsy room. "We've got a mess," he said. "It doesn't help that these guys have been on ice for a few months. They're really burned, burned bad."

"That follows," Laika said. "The local police have already established that the lodge was torched. At least six gallons of gasoline, sparked by white phosphorous."

"Tallies with what we're seeing in there. They must've been soaked with the stuff."

"Were they dead when they were torched?"

"Yeah. The locals got that right. There was enough cyanide in their stomachs to kill three times as many men."

"What about the teeth?" A doctor walked into the room from the hall, but stopped dead at the sharp looks he received from Laika and Tony. He mumbled an apology and went back out.

"I think we scared him," Tony said.

"We should. I told the administrator that we were to be left alone. Hinted that if anybody interfered in our research, this hospital might not only lose some grants, but a few people might even be—" She shrugged.

"Audited?" Laika nodded. "Man, you're wicked. What's Laika mean anyway? 'Ass-kicker' in Swahili?"

"It's Russian. I'll explain later. Besides, I'm Flo, did you forget?"

"Dammit," Tony said, lowering his voice, "I always have trouble with cover names." Their National Science Foundation papers identified them as Dr. Florence Kelly, Dr. Kevin Tompkins, and Dr. Vincent Antonelli.

"Anyway, the teeth?"

"Oh, yeah. What's left of them looks like really old stuff. There are traces of this guttapercha, what they used to make golf balls out of? And a lot of lead. There was even the trace of a *wooden* denture, and those haven't been used for decades."

"Was there anything . . . how shall I put this . . . *alien* in nature about the physiology of the corpses?"

"You mean, like *Alien Autopsy, Part 2?* No, they're just normal human beings, except for their teeth. So far, anyway."

"What about prints?"

"That's what we're working on now. Most of the flesh is burned so badly that I doubt we'll get any. Still, you never know. I'd better get back to it."

Tony returned to the morgue, and Laika went back to the makeshift office she had been given and began to go over what data they had on the men who had gathered and died at the lodge. Several cars had been found near the lodge, and by interviewing car rental agencies and airplane and rail counter clerks, she had been able to determine where several of them had come from.

One had flown in from New York City, another had rented a car in Baltimore and driven it to the lodge, and a third had purchased a car in Albany. But the payments had all been made in cash, and the credit cards used for identification and as security on the rental car had all been fakes.

The surnames were of English or Scottish origin, and Laika now ran them through the data banks, but the character of the responses told her that they were most likely temporary aliases. Whoever these dead men were, they had been good at covering up their trail.

After another hour, there was a knock on her door and Joseph Stein opened it. There were black and rust stains on his hospital whites, and Laika didn't much like to think about what had made them. "We've got three," he said. "Three good fingerprints out of, what, a hundred and ten?" He gave a grim smile. "One of them must have clutched a table leg when he fell. His fingers were still around it during the fire, so the tips weren't totally burned."

"Fine. Let's run them then," Laika said.

With the codes Skye had given them, their new covers had connections to every major police department in the world, including the FBI, Scotland Yard, the *Sûreté*, Interpol, and, of course, Langley. And with the state-of-the-art laptops with which they were equipped, they had nearly instant access over any data transmission line.

"*Vincent's* sending them now," Joseph said—rather smugly, Laika thought. She heard footsteps in the hall, and Tony stood in the doorway behind Joseph. "Make that *sent*," Joseph said.

"How long before we hear back?" she asked.

"Hopefully hours, I'd think a day at most," Joseph said.

"Well," Tony said reluctantly, "it might take longer than that. I told the data hounds at Langley that I wanted them compared with every print on file worldwide." He paused.

"Yeah?" said Joseph. "So?"

"I told them I wanted a check back to the 1890s." Tony looked quickly down at the floor, his tongue probing inside his lower lip.

Laika felt her face flush and heard Joseph give a snort of disbelief. "For Christ's sake, *why?*" she said.

"Well, the rumor is that these guys were supposed to be immortal, right?"

"Uh, excuse me," Joseph said, "but their corpses prove they're not."

"Okay, so really, really old, then," Tony replied. "I figured we might as well go as far back as we can . . . just in case.''

"In case of *what?*'' Joseph said. "In case they were committing crimes a hundred years ago? You think that seems likely?''

"No, I don't mean in case they're really that old. This helps prove they're *not*, see? To prove that, we have to go back as far as we can.'' He sighed. "Look, these guys may have been up to something weird, and they apparently had some nasty enemies, so odds are more than even that one of them has had a run-in with the law. If this one guy has, we'll get a match.''

"Maybe,'' Joseph said. "But if we do, you know damned well the match will be no earlier than the sixties. The *nineteen*-sixties, that is.''

"Sure,'' said Tony. "But this way, nobody says we didn't find out who this guy was because we didn't go back far enough.''

"Prints that old won't be on the computer,'' Laika said. "Do you have any idea how long it's going to take to compare them to the prints in those old files?''

Joseph nodded. "I imagine they'll be pulling yellowed cards out of dusty files at Scotland Yard for several days, depending on how many people they have working on it.''

"I *did* request highest priority,'' Tony said, "and Skye set us up with a lot of juice.''

Laika looked at him with hard eyes. Right now she *felt* like a Swahili ass-kicker, sure enough. But maybe he was right. This way the *National Enquirer* or the *Star* or the other rags that might cover this story couldn't say that the government ghostbusters hadn't done their homework.

"All right,'' she finally said. "There are other things to do. We haven't seen the lodge yet.''

There wasn't much to see. The only thing left standing was the fireplace and its chimney. The rest of the lodge was a pile of ashes and blackened timbers, thrown helter-skelter when the authorities pulled out the bodies. Small green plants were already beginning to push up from the ashes, and birds were singing their spring songs in the trees that surrounded the lodge site.

"They have no idea who was responsible for the murders," Laika told the others. "The local police chief suspects a mass suicide, but when I asked him how the victims were able to immolate themselves, he said he figured that the last man did it, set the fire, then took the poison."

"After dousing himself liberally with gasoline," said Joseph.

"He did confess that it was a little farfetched, but it's possible. What do you think?" she asked Tony, who was kicking at the ashes, lost in thought.

He shrugged. "Somebody killed them, then torched the place, to cover up his tracks, maybe."

Joseph looked up, as if he'd just thought of something. "What if somebody killed them and somebody *else* torched the place?"

"What makes you think that?" Laika asked.

"The chemical levels in some of the tissues of the bodies. If they'd been burned immediately after death, I'd expect them to have been higher. But if they were burned four or five hours after—or even later—why did the murderer wait that long?"

"Maybe," Tony said slowly, "waiting for number twelve?"

"That makes sense," said Laika. "Eleven is a strange number to meet, but twelve . . . especially if there was some secret aspect to their meeting—"

"Hold it," said Joseph. "I'm talking about science, and you two are reading some cabalistic society into this. Next you'll be telling me that Judas killed the rest of the apostles, or something."

"Nooo . . ." Tony said, still looking down at the ashes as though he could read an answer in them. "But maybe Judas got here late."

"What?"

"I'm talking logic, Joseph. Eleven is a number that

doesn't work for anything except craps. But twelve is logical. That number reoccurs throughout Christianity.''

"And *other* mythologies, too,'' Joseph added.

Tony didn't rise to the bait. "Suppose there were supposed to be twelve, but the last one didn't make it? There were blizzards all over the northern United States that night. So what if number twelve shows up late, after the killer's all done and gone. He sees everybody's dead. We don't know who any of these guys are, right?'' He looked at Laika.

"Not so far,'' she agreed.

"So they're secretive as hell,'' Tony went on, "and number twelve wants to keep things that way. He takes everybody's ID, real or phony—remember, there were no burned wallets found anywhere—and sets fire to the whole thing as a cover-up. The secret's safe.'' Tony shrugged and spread his arms wide as if to ask, *Why not?*

Joseph slowly nodded. "Maybe. Or maybe not. It's someplace to start, anyway.''

"When we get back to town,'' Laika said, "let's start checking out any other strange occurrences that may have happened that day or the night before. People . . . desperate to get to this area. We can use Langley's resources. Airports, bus and train stations, car rental agencies—anything out of the ordinary that happened.''

"What, through the whole country?'' Tony asked.

"Just the area that was affected by the belt of blizzards,'' Laika said. "God knows that's a big enough territory, but maybe something will stick out.'' She looked around at the barren space in which they stood. "Anything else here?''

Both men shook their heads, and they seemed as relieved as Laika to be leaving.

On the way back to town, Tony asked, "I wonder why they kept the bodies for so long? You'd think they'd have buried or cremated them by now.''

Laika looked out the window at the few patches of nearly melted snow. Spring had come late this year. "I already checked. They received orders from the governor.''

"And I wonder," Joseph said, "who he got *his* orders from."

None of them had an answer, but Laika thought she knew.

After two days of waiting and routine investigation, everything suddenly seemed to happen at once.

"Bing-frigging-o," said Joseph, looking at the screen of his laptop, while the other two looked up from theirs. "This sounds mighty promising, friends. Seems there was a man named Kyle McAndrews who, on the evening of December twenty-eighth, tried to charter a plane to take him from a tiny airport in Minnesota to guess where?"

"Plattsburgh," Laika said.

"Precisely. The pilot won't go, so Mr. McAndrews, who, by the way, had a Scottish brogue, offers to buy the plane. The pilot won't sell, so McAndrews overpowers him and steals it. Little Cherokee, of all things, which disappears somewhere over Wisconsin. Last month they found it in the woods two miles outside of Eau Claire, but there was no trace of a body and no parachute in the wreckage. Could very well be our boy."

"Have them run a check on car rentals or purchases on that date in Eau Claire," Laika said. "Limit it to cash transactions." After a moment, she added, "Tony, you feel like some legwork?"

"Absolutely." She was sure he did. They were all getting office fever.

"Do the same for Plattsburgh. See if you can find anybody who sold a vehicle for cash that day and several days afterward. He couldn't have driven all the way here. He'd probably take a train if the weather was bad. Joseph, what's the nearest major city to Eau Claire that's served by Amtrak?"

Joseph twiddled with his computer for forty-five seconds, then said, "St. Paul, but he'd pay cash on a train ride. They don't ask for IDs."

"Maybe he'd take a train or bus to Plattsburgh, then, but he'd need some way out to the lodge. In that weather, rentals would be unlikely, but this McAndrews might just buy another four-wheel. The Minnesota police have a description on this guy?''

Joseph nodded. ''From the pilot. Five-ten, one-eighty. Light reddish-brown hair, brown eyes, pale complexion. No identifying marks or scars on his face, which is all the pilot saw. He was wearing a camel-colored topcoat, wool fedora, and gloves, which, I'd suspect, are in some land fill by now, along with OJ's knife.'' He glanced at Laika and frowned. ''Sorry.''

''Don't be. I think the sonovabitch is guilty, too. Just because I'm black doesn't mean I'm blind and stupid. Minnesota police make any progress?''

''No, the guy seems to have vanished.''

''Then let's materialize him.'' She turned to Tony. ''See what you can find.''

Several hours later they received word of a transaction in which an Eau Claire resident sold his Suzuki Samurai to a man in the early hours of December twenty-ninth. The man had received a call about the ad he had placed in a local advertising paper and told the caller the vehicle was still available. The man arrived shortly in a taxi, paid twenty-one hundred dollars for the five-year-old Samurai in a combination of fifty- and twenty-dollar bills, and drove away in it. He answered the description of the man called Kyle McAndrews.

''So Mr. McAndrews drove off into the sunrise,'' said Joseph. ''And there the legend ends.''

''Until something else comes in,'' said Laika.

It came at six o'clock in the evening, when Tony returned. ''Found it. Our boy bought a twelve-year-old Jeep from a guy who owns a local Mobil station. It was sitting in front with a 'for sale' sign on it, McAndrews spotted it, paid in cash, no questions asked. Description matches.''

''Wonder where the Jeep is now?'' Joseph said.

''Probably at the bottom of a lake,'' Laika replied, ''or in some impoundment garage after our man dumped it at an airport parking lot. But let's get out a description of the Jeep just in case.''

They took a break for dinner, then came back to their office in the hospital and planted themselves in front of their computers. Laika heard the chirp that indicated that Tony had received e-mail.

There was silence for a moment as he started to read it, and then she heard him whisper, "Jesus . . . ," then, again, "Jesus. . . ."

"What is it?" Laika asked, turning toward him. Joseph had already slid his chair a few feet closer.

"We got a match from the *Sûreté*," Tony said softly. "On the prints. The name is Robert Gunn, arrested at Rennes-le-Château in France on suspicion of burglary." He looked up at the others, and his face was pale.

"On October eighth, 1907."

Chapter 14

"*I*t's a mistake," Joseph said bluntly. "They screwed up."

"No," Tony said. "There's a message here from the head of their records division. He apologizes for the delay but says that their fingerprint files before 1930 were not placed on computer. He sounds more than a little pissed at the manpower it took. He's sent the complete file zipped."

"Unzip it," Laika said.

Tony did so, and they all gathered around his small screen to read it. It told them little, only that a man who carried no identity papers had been apprehended by a local *gendarme* in the village of Rennes-le-Château in the act of trying to break into the Villa Bethania, a house owned by a local dignitary. He was taken to the police station, where he was fingerprinted, photographed, and locked inside their only cell. The next morning the cell door was open and the man had disappeared. Though an alarm was put out, he was not seen again, and the case remained open until 1957.

"And was probably forgotten in 1908," Joseph said.

"There's a .jpg of the photo," Tony said, opening it up. It had been scanned from a yellowed photograph, cracked along the edges. The man was wearing a coat and necktie, and faced the camera. His hair was light colored and wavy, his face long and gaunt, with a prominent cleft in his chin.

"Got a Kirk Douglas doughnut," Tony said.

"Forward this to Langley for enhancement," Laika said. "I want it to look modern, like it was just taken yesterday.

You show this picture to people and ask if they've seen this guy around, they'll say no, but ask my grandpa.''

Laika filed a full report that evening before she went to bed and sent it, encrypted, to Richard Skye. The next morning they received the enhanced photo from Langley and printed several copies, which Tony took into town, while Laika interviewed the owner of the burned lodge.

His name was Garrett, and he owned a real estate business. He had been contacted the previous summer and asked if he had a property far from town where a small meeting could be held. He never saw the face of the man who'd rented the lodge, since all proceedings were done over the phone and through the mail, including the delivery of the key to a post office box in Los Angeles.

"I've heard the rumors—about the teeth and all?" said Garrett, a rotund man with a gray moustache, dressed in a suit tailored as well as possible for his dumpy body. "But I know what it was really about. I know why you're here."

"And why is that, Mr. Garrett?" Laika asked.

"It's an organized crime thing, isn't it?" The man looked scared. "You know, I was afraid of that—I mean, a place twenty miles from town, they want their privacy, everything's done on a cash basis, leave no paper trail, you know? But I thought, hey, I don't know, these guys could be insurance salesmen, for all I know, and you can't rent lodges that far out the week after Christmas, so my greed got the better of my common sense, I guess, and then one family bumps the other family off and . . . hey," he said, looking even more worried. "I'm not gonna be charged, am I? You know, for aiding and abetting or anything like that?"

Laika fixed the man with a cold stare. "I may be back," she said, not smiling until she was outside. "That'll learn ya," she whispered softly to herself.

Laika met up with Tony at noon, and she was glad to learn that his visits had been more productive than hers. "Got a positive ID from a clerk at the Holiday Inn," Tony said. "Guy called himself Daniel Simpson, from New York City. Stayed there for two nights, paid cash in advance, no credit card. Checked out around the time of the lodge deaths.''

"Anyone with him?" Joseph asked.

"No. A single."

"What was the address he gave?" Laika said.

"Three-forty-six Madison Avenue."

Laika had to smile. "That address is Brooks Brothers."

"Was he well dressed, did she say?" said Joseph.

Laika didn't wait for Tony to figure out Joseph was kidding. "You run McAndrews's description by her?"

"Yeah, but she didn't see anybody looked like him. There were a few other singles in around that time, though. I got a list—and some paid in cash."

He handed it to Laika, who scanned it. She recognized two of the New York City addresses as fabrications. "These two, Barnes and Robinson?"

"She described them for me as well as she could remember. Mid-thirties, medium height and weight. Said there wasn't much memorable about them, except that they seemed very polite, to use her word." Tony's face soured. "Said they kind of reminded her of the way her grandfather used to be."

"Courtly," said Joseph, and deepened his voice to try what Laika thought was a Rod Serling impression. "As though from another time."

"Funny," Tony said without a smile. "We'll see how long you keep laughing."

"Come on," Joseph said. "You don't buy this, do you? The *Sûreté* had to make a mistake. That's the French for you. We have no actual evidence that—"

"Except for fingerprints," said Laika. She was tired of hearing denial when the evidence showed otherwise. "Fingerprints don't lie. And the clerk identified that photograph—a photo ninety years old. To me, that's proof that Robert Gunn and McAndrews are the same person."

"Me, too," said Tony. "Unless we got a time machine, this is as much proof as I need."

"But ninety years—" Joseph looked at the photograph again. "He looks thirty here—hell, he'd have to be a hundred and twenty, and nobody *that* old is going to look *this* good! It's not *possible.*''

''Well,'' Laika said softly, ''we are, after all, the Division of Special Investigations, and this is sure as hell special as it gets. But I'm damned if I can think of how to explain all this bullshit away.''

''I say we just keep digging,'' Tony said. ''There's got to be an answer here somewhere—even if it isn't one Skye's going to want.''

Joseph nodded. ''That's for sure. We're supposed to be debunking, not proving that this weird shit is actually real. And we've been going more in that direction.''

''That's Skye's problem,'' Laika said. ''We'll report what we find, and he can do whatever the hell he likes with it.''

They found out later that day what Skye wanted done.

''Gather round, folks,'' Laika said, as the message began to come in. ''God is in the house.''

They read the words as they scrolled across the screen:

You will immediately cease your current investigation. Proceed in the morning to New York City. Lodging will be at 39 West 72nd Street. Two cases there bear more serious interest to us than the current investigation, which, you should be happy to learn, may be considered closed.

Other agency sources, unconnected to the Platts-burgh investigation in any way, have coincidentally uncovered several documents that reveal the identities of the eleven victims found outside Plattsburgh. We have overwhelming evidence that these men constituted the total membership of an extreme right-wing religious group. Feeling that there was no place for them in this sinful world, they decided to commit mass suicide by swallowing cyanide.

According to a letter one of these men had sent to a relative shortly before his death, one was chosen to survive the others and douse the building with gaso-

line, then poison himself and immediately set fire to the
building. Their primitive dental practices were a result
of their retreat from the world, as was the absence of
any identification.

You will receive directives on the New York City
investigations when you arrive there.

The message was unsigned.

"Some 'coincidence,' " said Joseph. "And where did
they find that convenient letter?"

"In Skye's word processor," Tony answered, with a trace
of bitterness.

Joseph sat on his edge of his desk and crossed his arms.
"Not that I hold any sympathy toward the religious right . . .
or the religious in general . . . but it won't do the current
administration any harm to have another example of Bible-
beating extremism in the headlines. Skye is a clever man."

"All right, gentlemen," Laika said as sternly as she could.
"We are Mr. Skye's operatives, and we've been told what
to do. Let's just do it without any paranoia."

"There's something *here*, though!" Tony said.

"You just read what's here."

"But the fingerprints—"

"Forget the fingerprints, Dr. Antonelli. We never saw any
fingerprints, and if the subject ever comes up, which it won't,
it was a case of misidentification."

"I suppose we conveniently forget the chemical levels in
the tissues, too," Joseph said calmly. "What do we do with
the files?"

"You know what to do with them," Laika said. "Delete
them. And see that any hard copies are shredded or burned,
including the photographs of Robert Gunn, original and enhanced. That man died a long time ago." She folded up her
laptop and walked out of the office, her teeth clenched so
hard her head hurt.

What the hell was Skye playing at? These dead men
weren't magic. Maybe the solution was something just as
pedestrian as the one Skye had provided. But it wasn't the

truth, and Laika had felt that they were approaching it.

Still, she had always walked the walk, even if she hadn't talked as much talk as she just had to Stein and Luciano. If you were Company, you did what the Company told you, no questions asked. You didn't say "But," and you tried not to think it.

This time, however, she couldn't help herself. There was something terribly strange about those eleven dead men, and something strangely terrible, as well. They were close to it but wouldn't be allowed to continue. She felt frustrated and furious, like a dog trained for killing that had been given the scent and was trailing its quarry when it heard its master's whistle.

She made the official farewells, and by the time she got back to the office, Tony and Joseph had finished what they'd had to do. Joseph looked glum, but Tony looked like a kid who had been told there was no Santa Claus.

"Got another e-mail," he said. "From the *Sûreté*. They say that the print identification was a clerical error, that the person who made the match had been up for twenty hours straight."

"There were similarities," Joseph said, "but when they rechecked, they said it wasn't a match after all."

Tony shook his head sadly. "Goddamnit, we had people ID the photo, though."

"It's not impossible," Joseph allowed, almost grudgingly, "that one guy could look like another." Then he smiled. "Coincidence," he said. "The single thing that gets people believing weird shit more than anything else. Like I said before, seeing patterns and links where there aren't any. I almost did it myself this time."

"Whaddya mean, almost?" Tony said.

They drove back to the motel and went to their individual rooms. Laika stayed awake for a long time before she was finally able to sleep.

Chapter 15

*T*he next morning they left without checking out. Their bill would be sent to a government address. Joseph was already behind the wheel of the car as Laika and Tony came out. When they opened their doors, they didn't hear the sounds of a sharp click and a whirring that instantly followed.

The camera was in a room three doors away, the photographer's name was Taylor Griswold, and he took pride in the fact that he was descended from the Rufus Griswold who had blackened the name of Edgar Allan Poe after Poe's death. He tried to get another shot, but it was too late. Everyone was now in the car, and between the window he was shooting through and the car windows, he knew he'd be lucky if the image he got was as good as the 1936 Raynham Hall ghost shot.

Griswold had only gotten the tip the day before and had raced up to Plattsburgh from the offices of *The Inner Eye*. His source, as usual, was confidential to the rest of the world. He had been aware of the occurrence at Plattsburgh, and a stringer had done a story on it, offering the theory of a secret cabal of immortals. The editors of the tabloid had added their usual soupçon of sensationalism. Though Griswold thought he knew what it *really* was all about, it was not his assignment, and he could only wait until he was called upon.

Finally the tip had come in, and his editors were all too happy to wish him *bon voyage* in his investigation of a secret

government agency investigating the deaths. He had been
given the name of this motel; now, here they were, the first
he had seen them, and already they had their suitcases as
though they were leaving.

He jammed the camera into its bag, grabbed his coat and
suitcase, and opened his door a crack. The car was pulling
out of the lot. Time to follow.

Griswold ran out to his rental car, unlocked it, threw in
his gear, and climbed in. But when he turned the key in the
ignition, nothing happened. He tried it again, futilely pump-
ing the gas pedal. Hissing through his teeth, he reached desperately under the dashboard, found the hood release, jerked
on it, and got out and opened the hood.

Everything looked normal. He didn't realize what had happened until a service mechanic told him two hours later that
his spark plug wires had all been taken out and replaced in
the wrong order.

The man who had done that was Sir Andrew Mackay, and
while Taylor Griswold fretted and fumed, waiting for his
service call, Mackay was driving down Route 87, keeping
the car with the three government investigators in sight at all
times. Now that he'd found them, he didn't want to lose
them. He knew where they were from, but he wanted to
know more. And when he finally learned all he could, he
would kill them.

It was the least he could do for his brothers.

While Taylor Griswold and Sir Andrew Mackay saw the
three ops leave Plattsburgh, other eyes saw them come into
New York City.

When they got out of their car after Joseph had pulled it
into the unloading space in front of their West 72nd Street
address, a young African-American man was walking by on
the other side of the street. He glanced appreciatively at the
long-legged woman who got out of the car with the two
white men. All were carrying suitcases.

But just as he was about to look away, something familiar

about the woman caught his eye, and he looked more closely, staring at her until she and her companions went into the building. Then he went into a phone booth at the end of the block and dialed a number.

"Yo, James? 's Pipe . . . sorry I woke ya. Listen, man, guess who I just saw? . . . Naw naw, *listen*, man! A *sister*. Friend of yours, James—*ex*-friend, you dig? . . . You on it, man. Right up here on West Seventy-second. Number thirty-nine. Went in the door with two white boys, look like an Eye-talian guy and some *old* dude . . . yeah, what if she is, what you gonna do about it? . . . Oh yeah, I bet. Then what?" Pipe listened for a while, then chuckled appreciatively. "All *right*. You still not all white after all . . . and right back *at chu,* niggah. And thassa compliment."

Pipe hung up and smiled long and slow. That damn James and his hot-shit job. Might make a lot of green working with the white man, but that didn't mean shit if he couldn't hang on to his woman. Pipe had seen him when he came up to the old neighborhood to visit his mama. Boy had had a red face and a big old scab on his cheek. "What 'samatter?" Pipe had said. "Your woman bitch-slap you?"

He had been kidding, but from the look on James's face, he knew he had hit on the truth. Wasn't that a laugh, old downtown James getting stomped on by his old lady? James had gone on and on how he was going to make her pay, and Pipe had said, sure, yeah, just like he was going to tell those mothers at his firm to stuff it up their white asses.

So when Pipe saw James's woman with two white boys, he just couldn't resist sharing the news with Uncle Tom/ Uncle Ben/Uncle James. As much as Pipe hated sisters who messed with white boys, he hated black men who forgot where they came from. Maybe he'd be lucky and they'd mess each other over bad.

Pipe rattled the vials in his pocket and headed east toward the park. He still had a lot of sales to make before he could head back uptown and get some for himself.

*   *   *

James put down the phone and lay back in bed. He'd had a long night before, doing a lot of drinking and trying to forget about Laika.

It had been weeks, and he still missed her, goddamnit. All those Saturdays he had woken up next to her, early and happy—maybe to make love and make breakfast, go out and see an art show, or a matinee at the Met, or just walk with her through Chelsea.

And now, here he was at 1:30 in the afternoon, hung over from the night before, his dick sore from having humped that dumb punk white bitch against the outside wall of the club he'd gone to, feeling like a dumbass because he'd been too drunk to use a condom, and she'd been too stoned to care. Probably an AIDS-carrying junkie bitch.

And it was all Laika's fault.

Maybe he'd loved her once, maybe he still loved her. But he also hated her for what she'd done to him. Sure, he had hit her, but she had deserved it. His old man had hit his mother for a lot less. Laika had been a goddam prize, beautiful, smart, a sweet lovemaker, and independent. And maybe that last one was the problem: she didn't know that a woman had to be subservient to her man. She wasn't supposed to give him shit, and if she had the guts to do that, then she'd better have the guts to take a whipping for it.

He had gone back to her apartment several times, but nobody'd answered the door, and when her phone rang, he heard only her tape say, "If you'd care to leave a message, please do so at the tone." He hadn't. Several nights he had gone to her building and looked up at her window that fronted the street, but there were never any lights on. He assumed she had probably gone out of town for the export business she worked for.

But now here she was, back in the city, heading into a building with two white men. Now, what the hell was *that* all about?

Well, he'd find out. You bet your ass he would.

Trying to hold his head steady, he got up, showered, and dressed.

Chapter 16

The apartment was adequate, Laika thought. It was laid out in a haphazard manner, as so many of these renovated buildings were. There was a living room and a large dining room that they would turn into a work area with the desktop computers that already sat on the floor, waiting for them. The new cables snaking out from the phone jacks at the baseboard told her that fiberoptic connections had already been made.

A narrow hall led to two fair-sized bedrooms, the larger of which Tony and Joseph would share. There was a toilet off Laika's room, and a bath with a shower and tub off the hall. The kitchen was small but well appointed, and the shelves and refrigerator were stocked with food.

Windows were always a matter of concern, but she noted that no windows were in the dining room, and those in the living room and kitchen looked out onto an airshaft. The bedroom windows faced blank brick walls.

By the time they'd finished unpacking and getting the place in order, it was nearly 5 o'clock. "I'm hungry," said Tony. "Anybody for an early dinner?"

"We could see what's in the fridge," Laika said.

"Nah, I don't wanta cook. I'll make you guys spaghetti tomorrow, okay? But let's go out somewhere tonight."

"You like Cuban food?" Laika asked. "There's a good Cuban-Chinese place over on Broadway."

"Cuban-Chinese? Never had it, but I'll give it a try. Joseph?"

"I'd rather set up the network. You two go without me, and I'll just make a sandwich."

Tony and Laika walked over to the restaurant, where Tony learned that he did indeed like the food, though he joked quietly, "Don't know if two spooks should eat at a Cuban-Chinese joint."

By the time they were back on the street, it had grown dark. "Any bookstores around here?" Tony asked. "I need something to read."

"There's a Barnes and Noble four blocks that way," Laika said, pointing. "I think I'm going to head back. Hopefully the new assignments have been delivered by now."

"You be okay going back—" She knew he was about to say "alone," but he stopped, slightly embarrassed. "That was dumb, wasn't it? I think I went into automatic date mode . . . *sure* you'll be okay. Catch you later."

He turned and walked up Broadway, and she watched him go, thinking that the concern, even if misplaced, was nice. There was nobody anymore, beside her mother, who showed concern for her.

She sighed and started walking back east toward the apartment, planning to head south at the park along Central Park West. She stopped now and then to look into store windows, and went into a used CD store on Amsterdam, where she found a two-disc live recording of *Das Liebesverbot* on the Melodram label. It was one of the few Wagner operas she didn't have, so she happily paid the fifteen dollars and tucked the CDs into her purse. She would let them play her to sleep later.

At the apartment building, she unlocked the outside door and stepped into the lobby, letting the door swing slowly shut behind her. But as she crossed the marble floor in the dim light, she became aware that she could still hear the sound of the street, and glanced back to see a dark figure moving swiftly toward her. There was no time to reach into her purse for her pistol, so she swung around into a defensive stance and moved forward, anticipating the attack.

But the attacker stopped dead, his arms up as well, and just looked at her, a half-smile, half-snarl on his handsome, brooding face.

"James—" she said, and he nodded.

"Happy to see me?" He slowly lowered his arms, and she did the same. "Not gonna blindside me and pour hot soup in my face?"

"You were holding a knife on me."

"You were gettin' mouthy." He shrugged. "Look, I'm sorry, okay? I'm sorry I held a knife on you, I'm sorry I hit you. You come on back, now, and it won't happen again."

"Just go."

"Hey, I mean it, I promise. I miss you, you know? You come on back, try to be a little less sassy, I'll try not to get pissed off so easy, we'll get along again, right?"

"James," she said quietly, but with an edge intended to cut flesh, "you get out of here now, while you still can."

His face puckered up like he was going to spit. "Whatsa matter, you got a *white* boyfriend now? Don't you forget who you are, girl! What is this shit, movin' in here with two white men?"

Laika felt a chill in the pit of her stomach. How much did James know? "You heard me, James. Forget you ever saw me. I'm not joking. You know I don't joke." She smiled savagely. "I can still see a scar."

He started to move toward her then, and she got ready to do what she had to, when the sound of a key turning in the lobby door grabbed her attention. James whipped around, dropping his hands like a little boy caught stealing from the teacher's desk, as Tony Luciano walked through the door. She saw that he sensed the tension.

"Problem here?" he said, his face and voice calm.

When James saw a short Italian guy holding a Barnes and Noble bag instead of a security guard or a cop, his attitude grew cocky again, and his voice echoed the streets. "Nah, we don't got a problem. What, *you* got a problem?"

Tony looked away from James at Laika, still calm, asking

her with his eyes how she wanted him to play it. She didn't know what to do. This was personal, and personal business mixed with company business was bad. Getting no answer, Tony looked back at James. "You live here?"

"None of your damn business where I live, man. I'm talkin' to the lady here, so why don't you just piss off?"

"I happen to know the lady," Tony said.

James cocked his head. "No shit . . . goddamnit, you the Eye-talian guy?"

Tony's temper finally flared, and he took a few steps toward James. "Yeah—you the Af-frickin' guy?"

James involuntarily backed away from Tony, who advanced like a force of nature. Still, he blustered as he moved. "Back off, man, don't push me . . . I'll . . . I'll call a goddam cop, you, you—!"

Tony dropped his bag of books, yanked his pistol from behind his back, pushed James up against the wall, and stuck the muzzle right under his nose. Then he snarled through clenched teeth. "I *am* a goddam cop. Now, listen to me— you get your dumb ass *out* of here. Don't come back to this building, or this street, or anywhere within ten *blocks* of this street. Don't ever bother this woman again, don't ever bother *me* again, or you're gonna *eat* this gun while I pull the trigger several times, and there won't even be enough left of your tiny brain to make one stupid thought, not even 'Ow, that hurt.' "

Tony took the gun away, grabbed James's shoulder, and flung him toward the door. "Get outta here."

With a frightened but sullen look at Laika, James tore the door open and ran out into the street.

"That was a little extreme," Laika said.

"I was afraid he was gonna call me a goombah. Or a guinea," Tony said, shoving his pistol back under his jacket and picking up his books. "Then I would've had to get mad." His face quiet again, he looked at Laika with a combination of curiosity and concern. "You knew him." She nodded. "Was this a personal thing?"

"Old boyfriend." She pushed the elevator button, and the

doors opened. Tony followed her into the car. "He got abusive on me, I didn't like it."

Tony shrugged. "Who would?"

"I beat him up. A little." She pushed the button for 7, and the car started to move.

"Didn't seem to do him much good. He's still stupid." He blew out a long breath through his nose. "How'd he find out about you? And me—the 'Eye-talian' guy?"

"I don't know."

"I had to scare him off, you know that."

"I know."

"You know what might happen, he shows up again."

"Christ, I know a lot of people in New York."

"Around here?"

"No. Way downtown—the Village, Chelsea."

"So I guess that's why we're up here."

"I guess."

"Maybe you'd better stay off the street."

She turned and glared at him. "I'm head of this team. *I'll* decide when I stay off the street. And I'll tell you not to mention this incident to Stein."

"He ought to know."

"Do I need to repeat that order?"

He gnawed on his lower lip for a few seconds, looking at her. "No."

Joseph hailed them as they came into the apartment. "We're all hooked up," he said joyously. "On line and ready to go. And guess who sent Ms. Harris an encrypted file?"

"Skye," Laika said.

"Your perspicacity is second only to mine," said Joseph.

Laika sat at the center machine and ordered the decoding process to begin. It took nearly five minutes before the sentences appeared on the screen. She noticed that Joseph and Tony were politely holding back, making an effort not to look at her monitor. Still, they were tense and expectant.

"Anything *we* should know about?" Joseph asked with a grin.

Laika wasn't ready to smile yet. It would take awhile to push James from her thoughts. "Just the usual," she answered. "A haunted house and a man who vanished from an exploding room."

Chapter 17

*T*hough the next day was Sunday, they'd been told to meet with Clarence Melton at 4 in the afternoon at the row of townhouses he owned. The three operatives spent the early part of the day looking over the files that had been sent about the building, as well as others they downloaded concerning Melton himself.

Melton had made his considerable fortune in New York City real estate. He would buy up decaying blocks near reasonably upscale neighborhoods, gut the buildings while keeping what was architecturally viable, rebuild them, and regentrify the neighborhoods. He made large contributions on both sides of the political fence. Both Dole and Clinton had benefited from his largesse in the most recent presidential election, and so had most New York State congressmen and city officials. As a result, he had smooth sailing for all his projects.

The smoothness stopped, however, with the Park Project, located on East 77th Street and Fifth Avenue, overlooking the park. It was a slight change for Melton, since the row of eight townhouses he'd purchased were already in a good area. However, an absentee and uncaring landlord had let the property depreciate, until the forty apartments within were barely habitable.

When the landlord, now eighty years old with no heirs, ignored the city's demand to bring the buildings up to code, the city declared them unfit for habitation and ordered the premises vacated. It was time for Clarence Melton to move in.

He lost no time in looking over the property with an architect and a structural engineer, and made the decrepit owner an offer that would keep him in nursing care and Depends for the rest of his life. Melton and his crew of architects presented the city with their plans, which were quickly approved. But when Melton brought in his first work crew, weird things started to happen, and it was the responsibility of the Division of Special Investigations to find out what had happened and why.

The buildings had sat vacant now for nearly three months, while the tabloid press had a field day with Clarence Melton. *The Inner Eye* ran a cover story: "Melton's Madness— America's Borley Rectory!" And even the *Post* ran a page three story, "Ghosts in the Attic, or Bats in the Belfry?" Clarence Melton didn't like being laughed at, and he particularly didn't like having a multimillion-dollar investment sitting empty and untouched.

Joseph pushed his chair back from his computer, stood up, and walked away from the screen full of words to the window that looked out on the airshaft. "So what do you think? Melton called in some of his markers?"

"Sure," Tony said, looking up from a paperback titled *The Two-Bear Mambo*. He had already gone through all the files on the computer. "He calls some senator, or maybe Clinton himself, Clinton calls Carey, Carey gives it to operations, and it naturally ends up with Skye."

"Why 'naturally'?" Joseph asked.

"Because it's weird, and Skye's in charge of weird shit. And we're his weird-shit crew."

At 3:30 they walked through the lobby, but Laika stopped at the door. "Tony, get us a cab," she said.

"A cab?" Joseph said. "We've got plenty of time to walk, it's just across the park."

"We'll take cabs or the car. I don't want us seen on the street if we don't have to be." She glanced at Tony, and he nodded and went out to the sidewalk. Joseph shrugged, but waited with Laika.

Their cab arrived ten minutes before their scheduled meeting with Melton, so they crossed Fifth Avenue. There, in the shadow of Central Park's trees, they stood and observed the buildings.

The eight brownstones were all connected, with overhanging walkways between the second and third, fourth and fifth, and sixth and seventh. They were all four stories, and were laden with an anachronistic combination of Victorian and gothic ornamentation. The stone was heavily soiled with soot that Laika thought might have survived since the turn of the century, and the windows were so heavily coated with a layer of grime that it was nearly impossible to see through them.

"*Looks* pretty spooky," said Tony.

Joseph patted him on the shoulder. "Don't worry, I'll hold your hand."

Tony had just opened his mouth to make a comeback when a limousine pulled into a reserved space in front of the buildings. Two men got out of the back. One carried a briefcase and had the subservient air of a longtime assistant. The other moved with a fluidity of motion and a physical sureness that told Laika he had spent long hours working out on a variety of machines. She had only seen blurry newspaper photographs of Clarence Melton and had not expected him to be so young.

It was only when they crossed the street and she introduced herself and the others to him that she realized he was older than he appeared. From his face, she could see that he was in his mid-fifties, but grooming, exercise, and hair dye made him look little older than forty to the untrained eye. His topcoat fitted perfectly, and the tie and shirt visible beneath were immaculate.

"Dr. Kelly, Dr. Antonelli, Dr. Tompkins," he said, repeating their cover names as though it were an exercise in a memory course, "it's very good to meet you. This is Dennis Tweed, my assistant. Come, let's go inside."

They followed Melton and Tweed up the steps of the fourth brownstone and waited while Tweed opened several locks and pushed the door open. The sour smell of mildew and dried urine struck them as they walked in.

Melton made a face. "I'm sorry about the odor. It'll disappear completely when we're able to get started in here, which I hope will be soon, with your help." He pointed down a short hall that led past an open staircase to the back of the house. "It's less nasty back there. Shall we?"

What had once been a sitting room was furnished with some plastic stacking lawn chairs. The silent Tweed pulled a large white handkerchief from an inner pocket and wiped the surfaces of them. Melton waited until the ops were seated, then sat himself. Tweed remained standing, clutching his briefcase, looking at them without expression from behind a pair of thick bifocals.

"How much do you know about the houses?" Melton asked.

"As much as we read in our reports . . . and the newspaper stories," Laika said.

Melton nodded sadly. "Yes, they were pretty sensationalistic. Dredging up the sordid history of the place. It's true, several decades after they were built, they were prostitution row for the Upper East Side dandies. They were built in 1882, as townhouses for those just under the Four Hundred in wealth, or for rich widows—that range of income. But in twenty years, who knows what happened? Rumor has it that one railroad magnate purchased one of them for his mistress. Then another tycoon, not to be outdone, did the same for his paramour.

"Well, after all, who wanted to live beside what were essentially kept women? So the gentry moved out, and more monied riffraff moved in. The rich men tired of their playthings and gave them the houses to pay them off." Melton gave an eloquent shrug. "These ladies knew only one business, and they began to recruit others to fill the empty rooms. Since the neighborhood was still good, they were appealing to wealthy men, whose . . . How shall I put this? . . . whose normal desires were easily satisfied, so they looked for more *exotic* thrills.''

''Kinky stuff,'' Tony said.

''Exactly. Things could get fairly rough. Girls, even young girls and boys, might be the victims. We know some were tortured. We think some probably died, but the customers' money ensured that the bodies would be found floating in the East River . . . or never be found at all.''

''But there was never any proof of murders committed here?'' Joseph asked. ''No bodies, no skeletons found?''

''No,'' Melton said. ''But admittedly, some of these walls could contain bones, and the cellars go down two stories. The subcellars have concrete floors, but that wasn't poured until the thirties, so who knows what might have been buried under dirt floors before?''

''We've read all kinds of horror stories in the papers about what's gone on here recently,'' Laika said, ''but really, to your knowledge, what kind of things have happened?''

''Unfortunately, the same sort of incidents you read about in the papers. Strange things started happening as soon as the workmen went in. It seemed the minute they began to do any demolition—tearing out walls, pulling up floors—there would be noises, from pounding on the floors and ceilings to screams right in the ears of the men. They would spin around, and nobody'd be there.''

''No one ever saw anything?'' Laika asked.

''No. Several of the men said they thought they'd catch something . . . some movement . . . out of the corners of their eyes, but when they whirled around, nothing was there.''

''Was there any history of haunting before the workmen came in?'' Joseph asked. ''From the last tenants? Or *any* tenants, for that matter?''

''Apparently. A number of them have talked to the press and have said they've heard voices, seen figures. Some mentioned poltergeist activity.''

Joseph raised his eyebrows. ''Did any of the workmen experience that?''

''Oh, yes. Several of them left things unattended—toolboxes, machines, even their lunchboxes. They leave the room for a minute, they come back, and the machines are on and the toolboxes and lunchboxes are open and everything's thrown all around. And there's no other way in or out of the room except the way they went, and nobody went in or out.''

"Have you had dogs in?" Tony asked.

"Yes. They hate the place. Can't get a scent of anything in this stench. I assume they're overwhelmed by it all.''

"Someone had mentioned cold spots," said Laika.

"Oh, yes, we have those, too—I've seen them, in fact. Well, not *seen*, but, you know, felt them. And there are the lights.''

"Lights?" Laika said.

"We've been able to keep that to ourselves, thank God. Otherwise, people would show up around midnight across the street every night." Melton sighed. "These lights appear in a couple of the windows every night. We've had people inside the very room at the time, but they don't see a thing inside.''

"And is there any rumor about that particular room?" asked Joseph. "I mean, did someone die horribly there, or commit suicide or floss too hard?''

Melton smiled. "I think you're a skeptic, Doctor.''

"You're right, Mr. Melton. You know, this very well might be America's Borley Rectory, like *The Inner Eye* said. Because what people tend to forget is that Borley—the most haunted house in England—was a total hoax. Even the Society for Psychical Research said that there wasn't a thing that happened at Borley that couldn't have a rational, nonsupernatural explanation. And all the things that couldn't be explained were probably done by Harry Price. He was the ghost hunter who built his reputation on Borley.''

"So you think all these things have a rational explanation? The lights . . . the poltergeist activity . . . the screaming?''

"If there's a light, someone has to shine it. A scream, some throat has to make it. And if tools are thrown around, somebody's hand had to do it. Yes. They all have a rational explanation. And it can be found.''

"You sound like Frank Hardy," Melton said with a grin.

Joseph frowned. "I'm sorry?"

"Frank Hardy in the Hardy Boys books. I read them all when I was a kid. When there was a ghost somewhere, Joe always believed in it, but Frank never did. And Frank was always right."

"Smugglers," said Tony. "I read them, too. And it was usually smugglers."

"Or counterfeiters," Laika added. Then she chuckled. "They were a *lot* more exciting than Nancy Drew."

"Well, I wish it *were* smugglers," Melton said, "and I'm a pretty practical man. But I don't know . . . there's enough to this that I've hired a psychic to come in and look the place over."

Joseph groaned.

"I take it you disapprove."

"There hasn't been a so-called psychic yet who has the ability to do anything but deceive their clients and the media."

"What about all those psychics who help the police catch murderers? Leading them to bodies, giving them descriptions?"

"It doesn't happen," Joseph said. "There's no police force in the world that asks psychics for help—it's the other way around. Psychics beg to be allowed to investigate, especially in high-profile cases. If they get lucky, they've written their ticket. If not, they don't mention it to a soul. Tell me, your psychic, did you contact him? Or vice versa?"

"*She* contacted *me*. Elissa Meyer."

"Oh, Jesus—" Joseph muttered.

"You know her?"

"Of her. And she's promised she can put a stop to your 'manifestations.' "

"Yes, she has."

"All right, Mr. Melton, I'll tell you what: we'll look around today and this evening, then we'll come back. And when we do, that's when you should invite the psychic Ms. Meyer here—"

"Dr. Tompkins," Laika said to Joseph, trying to caution him.

"—And then you can see which approach best suits your particular needs—scientific inquiry—"

"Dr. *Tompkins*—"

"—Or mumbo-jumbo charlatanry!"

"I'm *sorry*, Mr. Melton," Laika said, turning a basilisk eye on Joseph. "Sometimes Dr. Tompkins gets a bit over-zealous in his crusade to debunk what he considers fraudulent claims. Perhaps you and Mr. Tweed would care to show us around the place now?"

Melton glanced at Tweed, who forced a small smile. Laika quickly got the feeling that the man would rather not be anywhere near this place. "Of course," Melton said. "Let's start with the cellars first, and we'll work our way up. Mr. Tweed?"

Chapter 18

*T*weed opened his briefcase and from it took five small but bright Maglites, one for each of them. "The electricity is off," Melton said. "I bought a place four years ago, and while I was gathering the crew for it, some old wiring caused a fire and the place was totaled. Ever since then, I always cut off the power when there's no work being done. But with five of these," he said, holding up his light, "we'll probably have more light than we'd get from an incandescent bulb."

The cellars and subcellars were as dank and dingy as anything Laika had ever seen, and the smell seemed to be worse. Joseph ran a hand along the damp wall and sniffed his fingers. "No smell, but it almost seems as though the sewer lines are getting into the groundwater."

"No," said Melton, shaking his head. "The pipes have all been inspected. But I know what you mean. The smell seems to come from the very walls."

"Has the water been turned off?" Laika asked.

"Yes. No water at all."

All of the upstairs rooms were in a state of decay. Yellowed wallpaper hung in strips, and what carpet remained on the floors was tattered, worn, and mildewed. The woodwork was still handsome beneath its patina of dust, and the hardwood floors could, Laika thought, be sanded and refinished. But it would take a lot of work, she thought, to get the stench to disappear.

It was 7 o'clock by the time they finished going through

115

four of the houses, and there were as many again to see. Darkness had fallen outside, and the Maglites were necessary everywhere, since the street lights pressed only fitfully against the built-up detritus on the windowpanes.

They were going down the second-floor hall of the fifth building, and had just finished picking their way around a pile of uprooted ceramic tiles that lay near the window, when Tony stopped. "Hey," he said softly. "Wait a minute."

They all stopped then, and Laika felt a chill stir the hairs at the back of her neck. It was cold here, probably ten degrees colder than anywhere else they had been on this floor, but she wasn't going to be the first to say it; Joseph did. "It's colder here."

"I didn't want to say anything," Melton said. "I wanted you to be the ones to notice it."

"Well, you can't help it." Joseph shone his light over the walls and ceiling. "There must be someplace here that a draft is getting in."

"I don't think so," said Melton. "Mr. Tweed?" Tweed took from his pocket a slim, gold cigarette lighter and lit it. The yellow flame wavered as Tweed's hand shook from nervousness. "Here," said Melton, and plucked the lighter from his subordinate's fingers. Melton held it steady, and the flame did not flicker, not even when he slowly moved it all around the area in which they stood.

"No draft, then," Joseph said. "I wonder—"

But he didn't finish his thought. Suddenly, from what seemed like all around them, a voice pierced the foul air of the hall. It started as a low moan, then, in only a couple of seconds, surged higher, like a siren increasing in frequency, until a shriek like the sound of a hundred nails scraping a blackboard made Laika grit her teeth and shut her eyes. It continued to remain at that impossible summit of pitch, a sound full of pain and hate and madness.

Just as Laika forced open her eyes to confront whatever had made that terrible scream, it stopped. It didn't fade off, but stopped dead, as if the head that had made it had been severed. There was not even an echo remaining.

She whipped her light down the hall, then up in the other direction. Joseph and Tony were doing the same. But their flashlights' beams caught nothing except each other, Clarence Melton's stern-jawed, pale face, and Mr. Tweed, whose eyes were still pressed shut, and whose grimace told Laika that he was still hearing the scream.

"What the hell was that?" asked Tony, and she was glad that she had not been the first to speak. She wouldn't have trusted her voice not to quaver.

"I heard it once before," said Melton. "Several weeks ago. Can you see now why the workmen don't want to come in here?"

"Not really," said Joseph. Laika was amazed to see that he was smiling calmly. "It's a voice, that's all. And voices have to have people to make them work."

"Do you *see* anybody except us?" Tony asked, then added, "*Doctor* Tompkins?"

"I didn't *have* to see it. I *heard* it."

"Then you think it was a live person? And not a ghost?" Melton asked. Tweed was just starting to open his eyes.

"Since I don't believe in ghosts, that's the only possible conclusion. It's a horrible scream, yes—but it was no sound that couldn't necessarily come from a human throat."

"If we discuss this further," said Laika, "I suggest we leave this particular spot. Mr. Tweed, do you agree?"

Tweed nodded, and a small "Yes" escaped his mouth. As they left the hallway, Laika thought that they were all walking a bit faster than when they'd entered. Even if whatever had screamed was human, she had no desire to hear the sound again.

At last they arrived on the stoop of the fifth building, where they paused. Melton took a deep breath. "I think maybe we'll conclude the tour tonight. I do have another appointment later on, and the other buildings are very similar to those you've seen. Let me make one suggestion, though. Please—"

He led the way down the steps and across the street. "The fifth building, the one we were just in? That's where the light appears—that second window there on the third floor. Like I said, it always happens around midnight."

"We'll come back, then," Laika said. "We'll need some time to study this further and to prepare a thorough investigation, Mr. Melton, but we'll be back in touch in a day or two."

"And we'll fix up this problem for you," Joseph promised. "I hope you'll invite Miss Meyer to investigate at the same time. I think it would be useful to compare her technique to that of our team."

"I'll do that," Melton said. "I'm sure she'll look on it as a challenge."

"*I'm* sure she'll be scared . . . stiff," Joseph countered. "You might expect an excuse."

Melton said good-bye, and, after offering to drop the ops off, he and Tweed drove away in the limo, whose driver had been waiting patiently for hours. Tweed was still trembling as he opened the limo door.

"Doesn't talk much," Tony said, as they watched the limo drive down the street.

"Fear," Joseph said. "It makes people either run at the mouth or shut up entirely. I'd bet a hundred bucks that man has moist shorts right now. So—" He turned to Laika. "What's next?"

"Tell me—you're the expert. You think it's a hoax?"

"Now, I'd bet a *thousand dollars* on *that*. Sure, it is. Somebody, or *somebodies*, are in those buildings. We just have to come back and find out who, and where they're hiding."

"Okay, I admit the scream might have been human," Tony said, "but what about the cold spot?"

Joseph shrugged. "It seems weird, but fluctuations in temperatures are common in old buildings. No big deal."

"What about the poltergeist activity?" Laika asked.

"The *presumed* poltergeist activity," Joseph said. "Sure, somebody threw that stuff around, but it wasn't a ghost."

"And the lights?"

"We'll see about the lights. How about some dinner first? We've got a few hours till midnight."

At 11:45, they stood across the street from the townhouses and waited. Twice they were accosted by panhandlers, but a few threatening words from Tony drove them away.

Two minutes before midnight, they saw the light in the window on the left. Laika, in spite of herself, felt a chill. It was a white light, dim at first, then brightening slightly before it moved to the other window, where it remained for several seconds and then vanished without fading, just winking out like an extinguished candle.

"Well?" asked Laika. "You think somebody's in there?"

Joseph shook his head. "Not that room. No, I believe Melton when he said they investigated the light. They just didn't do it the right way." He smiled. "Borley Rectory. More so than they think?"

"Huh?"

"Never mind, Tony." Joseph lowered his voice. "All will be revealed . . . in time. Nyah-hah-hah."

Tony frowned. "You make this job a lot of fun, Joseph."

"I strive constantly to amuse. But I *am* getting tired— shall we return to the bat-cave? I long to go to sleep with the memory of that screaming ringing in my ears."

Though he was joking, an hour later Laika found that was precisely what she was hearing. She put her new opera on her discman, trying to get the sound out of her mind, along with thoughts of James Winston.

How had he found her? She hoped he had taken Tony's warning seriously, because if he showed again, things would be worse for him—a lot worse. She didn't want him to die. There were too many good memories along with the bad for her to be comfortable about that.

Finally she sat up in bed, took off her earphones, and decided to get herself a drink. The Company always stocked their safe houses with liquor.

She was surprised, when she went into the living room, to find Tony Luciano reading a paperback, his feet propped on the coffee table. On the television screen was a home shopping show, the sound turned all the way down. Tony was holding a rocks glass containing an amber liquid and melting ice.

"Don't get the wrong idea," he said. "I'm not an alcoholic, or anything. I just thought a drink might help me get to sleep."

"I had the same idea." Laika went to the sideboard and poured some scotch, then got some ice cubes from the kitchen. She sat in an easy chair in the living room and glanced at the TV. "Why do you have the sound off?"

Tony took a sip of his drink. "I don't care about it. It's just company while I read." He held up his book so that Laika could see the title, *Down in the Zero*. Cheery stuff, she thought. "What'd you think about tonight??" he asked, looking at her. "The spook house?"

"I don't know. It was unsettling . . . that scream."

"Yeah, I still hear it. Old Joseph, he's really got brass balls, hasn't he?" He shook his head in grudging admiration.

"Yes, he does. Nothing seems to rattle him. The only thing about being so confident is, what happens if you find out you're not always right?"

"You don't think he's right? About the house?"

She shook her head sharply and took a long drink. "No, he's right, I'm sure. I just don't know if he's . . . right about everything. After all, 'There are more things in heaven and earth, Horatio—' "

" 'Than are dreamt of in our philosophy.' " Tony grinned. Laika thought he was feeling the drink. "And you thought I was dumb."

"No, I didn't."

"Sure you did. Dumb dago, all muscle and no brains."

"You forget I saw your record, Tony. Graduated cum laude from Columbia. Your score on the Company's qualifying test would blow every other agent I ever knew out of the water, including me. No, I never thought you were dumb."

"Well . . . I feel dumb tonight. Joseph is so dammed savvy

about all this shit, and me . . . I'm like one of those pop-eyed black guys in the Charlie Chan movies . . . 'Oh Lawd, Missah Chan, I done seed a ghos'!'" He suddenly became embarrassed, as though he had just remembered Laika was black. "Sorry . . ." he muttered.

" 'Ey, datsa arright," she said in a cheesy Italian accent. "Issa no problem, paisano." They laughed together, and the racial tension fled.

"Ah, you know what I mean, though. I don't really believe this stuff, but hell, it's gotta give anybody the creeps, and Joseph just acts like . . . like—"

"I know how Joseph acts. Like a superior smartass."

"You nailed *that* right on."

Laika thought for a moment. "But Skye knew what he was doing. We need a total skeptic, and I don't think it's unfair to any of us to say that Joseph is the brains of this outfit. He's got the interest, the experience, and the attitude. If there's a rational answer, he'll find it. With our help."

"Well." Tony raised his nearly empty glass. "Here's to us and our help." He emptied it and set it down on the coffee table next to another book that he picked up. "Now, this one's Joseph's. You believe this? This guy is a total skeptic, and look what he reads. *The Alabaster Hand*, a collection of old ghost stories. Like a dentist who spends his vacation looking in people's mouths."

"He doesn't believe in it, so maybe it *is* escapist for him." Or maybe he just wants to believe, she thought, but didn't say.

She finished her drink and stood up. "Better try to sleep, Tony. Big day tomorrow."

"The Case of the Vanishing Sculptor, huh? With Frank and Joe Hardy, and, uh. . . ." He pointed at her. "Their girlfriend—what was it, Ilona?"

"Iola."

"Yeah, Iola. Goodnight, Iola."

"Goodnight, Joe." She started walking out.

"Iola?" he called. She turned and looked at him, and he winked. *"Smugglers."*

"Smugglers." She went to get some sleep.

Chapter 19

*T*he next morning, Quentin McIntyre was looking over the newspapers in his office at FBI headquarters in Washington, D.C. It took him from half an hour to an hour to do so, but since he always arrived an hour early, he never felt guilty about it cutting into the time during which he should be performing his duties. Besides, who was going to criticize an assistant director?

Another rationale was that he considered this daily scanning of the papers part of his duties. He was exploring the country, seeing what strange things popped up in front of his face. His assistant had suggested he do the same thing on the Internet, but it was not possible. On the Internet, you depended on key words and branching searches, and he never knew what it was that he was searching *for* until he found it. As for the Bureau's official readers, their heads held nowhere near the storage capacity that Quentin McIntyre, twenty-five years in the Bureau, possessed.

So, three cups of black coffee already under his belt, he attacked the pile: fifteen morning newspapers from across the country, as well as weekly tabloids such as the *Star*, the *National Enquirer*, and even *The Inner Eye*.

It was there that he had seen a photo of a confidence trickster, who had vanished fifteen years before, selling "psychic tangrams" out of a post office box in Trenton. The man had lost a hundred pounds and several inches of hair and had grown a beard, but McIntyre had recognized him instantly.

Federal agents staked out the post office and arrested him when he came to empty his box. Ever since then, McIntyre went over the tabloids with as much zeal as he did the New York *Times*.

This morning, it was not the headline on the fifth page of *The Inner Eye* that attracted McIntyre as much as it was the smaller of two photographs that accompanied the article. The first was of a desolate piece of earth surrounded by pine trees. A blackened chimney was all that remained upright of a burned building whose ashes darkened the ground.

The second was of a man and a woman getting into a car. The woman's back was toward the camera, but the man's face was visible. He wore sunglasses and a baseball cap with no insignia, but McIntyre still thought he recognized him. It was a square, craggy face, but still somehow gaunt, with high cheekbones and a pouting mouth. The neck was thick and the shoulders wide, and if the car was the model that McIntyre thought it was, the man would be about Tony Luciano's height as well.

McIntyre finally read the headline: "Secret Gov't Psi-Team Investigates Immolated Immortals!" He chuckled and read the rest of the story, by one Taylor Griswold, "Special to *The Inner Eye*." It stated that a top secret government team of psychics had been sent to Plattsburgh, New York, to try and establish psychic contact with the spirits of eleven charred corpses found in a burned-down lodge near the town. *The Inner Eye*'s on-staff psychic and seer, Imelda Santana, gave reporter Griswold the tip.

"These men are immortal and cannot die," she was quoted as saying. "Their souls remain in their ruined bodies, and the government has sent psychics to contact these miserable souls in the hopes of finding the secrets of immortality so that the President, his family, the Joint Chiefs of Staff, and other important officials can survive in the event of nuclear or ecological destruction."

McIntyre snorted and hoped the chain of immortal command would extend down to his level. He pushed a button on his desk and was answered by Phillips's voice. Good, he was there early. It seemed McIntyre's influence was rubbing off. "Al," he said into the speaker, "got something for you here."

In a matter of seconds, Alan Phillips was standing on the other side of McIntyre's broad desk. "Sit down, Al. See that fella in the picture there? I think that's a guy named Anthony Luciano, a CIA operative. Got to know about him when he performed a number of low-level political sanctions a few years back. We had some interest in one or two. Read that and you'll know as much as I do about it. See if you can find out anything."

Phillips had been reading the article while listening to McIntyre. "New York State," he said. "That's a little out of CIA territory, isn't it?"

McIntyre smiled. They both knew damn well that certain subdivisions merrily broke the CIA charter right and left. Sometimes McIntyre thought that as many clandestine operations were going on within the country as there were outside it. It was a rare month when his agents didn't trip over a spook or two operating within the U.S. They could go crying to a congressional subcommittee about it, but after all, they were all on the same side. Most of the time.

"Just see what you can learn," McIntyre told Phillips. "Try and find out if it's Luciano, if it's CIA, what it's all about, and who in the Company is responsible for it." He thought for a moment, then added, "You might see if Richard Skye has his long fingers in it."

Phillips nodded and left the room with *The Inner Eye*.

Yes, this was something Richard Skye could be involved with, all right. The CIA charter had never bothered Skye in the past, and Skye was unlikely to have changed his outlook on such things in the six years since McIntyre had last crossed swords with him. Skye had stepped on the agency's toes back then, and McIntyre had figuratively kicked Skye in the shins, an act from which Skye was probably still smarting.

The psychic tie-in was what had made him think of Skye. Several years before their semi-official run-in, Skye had been involved in a project that had entailed kidnaping Russian psychics working with the KGB and smuggling them into the States. It was when they arrived stateside that McIntyre had entered the picture. Skye, unwilling to compromise his hold over the purported psychics, would not turn over responsibility for the human cargo to the stateside bureau, and by the time the orders to do so came down from on high, the Russians had disappeared. Though the bureau was never able to determine what had happened to them, McIntyre was sure that Skye had "disappeared" them.

Or maybe he was wrong. Maybe even now the psychics were being held prisoner in some secret Company cell, using their powers to the CIA's—and Skye's—advantage.

McIntyre laughed at the thought, as he did each time he had it. Psychics, he was convinced, were bullshit.

Chapter 20

*L*aika was unimpressed with the building in which Peder Holberg's apartment and studio were housed. It seemed utilitarian to the point of absurdity. There were hardly any windows looking out onto the busy midtown street, the wall was a flat gray sheet of concrete, and the door was a slab of dull steel with a handle. "Hardly what I expected," she said, and Tony and Joseph murmured agreement.

She pressed a recessed button beside the door, but no voice came through the speaker grill. Instead there was a sharp click, and when she pulled on the door handle, it opened. They stepped inside.

A long stairway rose in front of them, and against the light at the top, they saw a thick-set man in an ill-fitting suit. "You the people from the science institute?" he called down.

"National Science Foundation, yes," Laika called back, starting to climb the stairs.

"Come on up, then," the man said gruffly, and disappeared.

"How hospitable," said Joseph softly.

At the top of the stairs was a short hall. On the left side was a carved wooden door, and on the right was another steel door similar to the one downstairs. It was open, and they went in.

At last Laika was impressed. Peder Holberg's studio was huge, with mammoth constructions of iron everywhere. The

anarchical sculptures were so disordered that it took her a
moment to notice the scene of the explosion. An entire wall
at the top of a wooden staircase had been taken out, leaving
only a jagged hole behind.

"Blew this place a new asshole, didn't it?"

Laika turned to the chunky man. His hair was fashionably
cut, but the rest of him was as rumpled as the two chins that
hammocked beneath his twisted mouth. "I'm Detective Ser-
geant Havisham."

"*Great Expectations*," Joseph said quietly.

Havisham's mouth pulled up on one side in what Laika
figured was a smile. She was sure it wasn't the first time
someone had alluded to the literary significance of his name.
"Hope I don't disappoint you. And you guys are from . . .
what is it again?"

"National Science Foundation, Division of Special Investigations," Laika said.

"You mind showing me your IDs?" When they presented
their cards, Havisham nodded. "And this ranks in your book
as something *special*, huh?"

"Apparently, somebody thinks so," said Laika.

"Yeah, well, God forbid that the cops should try and figure anything out when there are always feds to do the job.
No offense."

"Some taken," said Tony. "Don't you like us, Ser-
geant?"

"I think you're just peachy, fella."

"Really? Well, you know, I don't even give a shit."

Christ, thought Laika, if it wasn't Joseph smartassing Melton, it was Tony with this cop. "Okay," she said. "Would
you just show us the scene?"

Havisham's face was starting to redden, but Tony was so
cocksure that the cop said nothing more to him. "Sure,"
Havisham said tightly. "I was told to give you the *utmost*
cooperation—that was the exact phrase—so sure. Come on."

He led them up the stairs to the opening in the wall.
"There it is. Holberg went in and never came out. Boom.
No Holberg."

"And there were no traces of body parts? No blood or tissue?" Laika asked.

"None at all. You got the reports?" She nodded. "Then you know that the lab found quantities of plastic explosive. And what probably was part of a timing device."

"Any idea," Joseph asked, "whether Holberg had made the bomb, or it was planted by someone else?"

"Well, I wouldn't know," said Havisham. "You see, we got orders from the feds to cease our investigation before we could ask the boyfriend much of anything about Holberg. For all I know, *he* could have made it."

"You mean . . . the boyfriend?" Joseph asked. "This, uh—" He referred to a clipboard. "Adam Guaraldi?"

"That's the guy. He's living in the apartment across the hall."

"Anything else you can think of that might be helpful?" Laika asked.

Havisham half-closed his eyes and shrugged. "You've got the witness list and all the reports. The boyfriend's expecting you. Here's my card." With nicotine-stained fingers the man withdrew a gleaming sterling silver card case from his coat pocket, opened it, and proffered a perfect white pasteboard to her. Surprised, she took it, thanked him, and put it into her shoulder bag, as Havisham walked down the stairway and out the door without another word.

"Cheery sonofabitch," Tony said.

"He resents us." Joseph was looking around the room, brightly lit by police floodlights. Every detail of the destruction was starkly visible.

"Look," said Laika, joining the search. "This was a table. The bomb must have gone off—" She looked around at the way the wood had shattered and splintered. "Yes, on top of it. The impact pressed these boards down."

"I don't get this," Tony said. "Look at these statues here . . . if that's what they are."

"See what you mean." Joseph touched the bent and twisted iron. "You'd think the blast would have ripped these apart . . . at these welds. But instead, they're just twisted."

"Corkscrewed," Laika suggested, and Joseph nodded. "Like it got caught in a tornado, but wasn't picked up or knocked down," she added. "Weird."

"Weird's a good word for it," said a strange voice.

Laika spun around to see a man standing on the other side of the blown-out doorway. He appeared to be around thirty, and his arms and shoulders were bared by the sleeveless T-shirt he wore. He was of medium height and muscular, but they were the muscles that grew from hard work, not the kind that were sculpted in a health club. Laika noticed a number of red scars on his forearms, as though he had been burned. "I'm Adam Guaraldi," he said in a high-pitched but husky voice. "I was Peder Holberg's companion."

Laika introduced herself and the others. "You're still living here, is that right?"

He nodded. There was nothing at all effeminate about him, Laika thought. "I own the place now. I didn't know, but Peder had named me his sole heir. His parents in Norway are dead, and he had no brothers or sisters. So. . . ."

"Have the police talked to you?" Laika asked.

"Just after the explosion, that's it."

"Was this room kept open?"

"No, it was always locked. Peder had the only key." He smiled uncomfortably. "There are other people who will swear to that. And I say that because I think I know what you're thinking. That if Peder died, I stood to come into a lot of money. And that's true. But I had nothing to do with the bomb, if that's what it was." He looked around the brightly lit room, squinting against the glare of the lights. "Where did he go?" he asked in a pleading voice. "Where the hell did he go?"

"That's what we'd like to find out, too," Laika said. "Is there someplace a little more comfortable where we could talk for a while?"

"Sure. Let's go over to the apartment."

The main room there was huge and stark, but it felt enriched by the few pieces of warm furniture and the sensuous canvases that spanned the walls. There seemed to be none of Holberg's work there. Guaraldi poured them freshly made coffee. Then they sat and he told them about Holberg's seeming fugue states and his disappearances. "He seemed very strange, withdrawn, as though his mind was constantly on something else. A few weeks before . . . the explosion, he asked me some questions about explosives."

"Like what?" Laika asked.

"Like where you get dynamite. 'Adam, if you wanted to get dynamite, how would you do it?' Hypothetical questions, but so damned obvious. I asked him what the hell he wanted to get dynamite for, but he'd say he was just curious. Yeah, sure. And hell, *I* didn't know where to get dynamite, how would I? But after I asked why he wanted to know, he never mentioned it again. That was the only hint I had that he might be . . . cooking something up." He gave a deep sigh. "I guess he was."

"Well, these fugue states and mentions of dynamite are odd enough," Laika said, "but was there any other strange behavior on Mr. Holberg's part in the past few months?"

"Yeah. His infatuation with the vampire kids." Guaraldi gave his head a bitter little shake. "That's what I called them. They were goths. You know the lifestyle? Pale skin, dressing in black, lots of makeup on the women *and* men, most of it black or very dark red—the blood thing, you know."

"Mooning about *liebestod*," Joseph said. "Maybe drawing a little blood during sex."

Guaraldi nodded. "You keep up with things down in D.C. Anyway, he hung with these creeps for a while—and I mean *creeps*. I got the feeling that there was more to them than just an infatuation with vampires and full moons. Peder implied that he thought maybe he could find out where he went and what he did in his fugue states from these kids somehow. It didn't make any sense to me, still doesn't, but I think that's what he believed. The problem was that when he decided he'd had enough of them, they didn't want to let him go. Guess he was their first celebrity, or something."

"So what'd they do?" Tony asked.

"Called, showed up here. I finally chased them off, but they were persistent."

Laika set down her empty cup. "Where did he meet them?"

"A club down in SoHo. One of those dank cellar places—pretty big, though. I went there once with him. That was enough." Guaraldi got up and rummaged through a drawer in a pecan end table until he took out a card. "Here it is," he said, handing it to Laika.

"Thanks. Did Mr. Holberg have an office, someplace he kept his private papers?"

"Yes." Guaraldi walked to a door at the far end of the room, and the others followed. He opened the door, and Laika was surprised to see a small room as cluttered as the living room was open and bare. "I hardly ever went in here. Everything's just the way he left it. Feel free to look around all you want . . . files, desk drawers . . . the computer's running Windows 95."

"Thanks, I've heard of it," Joseph said with a smile, flicking on the power switch.

Guaraldi chuckled, then lost his smile. "Let me know what I can do. I'll help you any way I can."

"Thanks," Laika said. "Just one more thing before we start digging in here—that room that exploded, did it have any other ways in or out? Anything at all that you could think of?"

Guaraldi shook his head. "One door. I saw Peder go in. If he had come back out, I would have seen that, too. But I didn't, and *he* didn't. Please find him. Or at least find out what happened to him. Peder was my friend—he still is, I hope, and I love him. I was told that if anyone could come up with an answer to all this, you people could."

"We'll try."

Guaraldi seemed to realize that there was nothing more to be said. He nodded and left them to their work.

Chapter 21

Joseph opened up the computer files while Tony explored the desk drawers, then the bookshelves. Laika busied herself with the four-drawer filing cabinet.

After ten minutes, Joseph said, "Nothing much here at all. I think he used this more as a toy than a business tool. *Doom*, *Quake*, aha, *Civilization II*. An intellectual."

"Keep looking," Laika told him. "Open everything up, just in case."

A few minutes later, Tony stepped down from a short stool that provided access to the higher bookshelves. "Here's something," he said, riffling a small sheaf of papers. "These were stuck behind some books. They're bills and canceled checks. I found some others in the desk—usual stuff, rent on this address, Amex, utilities, art supplies. But these are for rent on a place in the Bronx. The landlord's address is out on Long Island, but the property is listed as 'Brennan Warehouse.' Looks like it's just off the Third Avenue Bridge." Tony flipped through the checks. "The checks in the desk were made out by a different hand than Holberg's— maybe Guaraldi. But *these* checks are all in Holberg's script. And it's even a different *account*."

Laika took the checks and went into the other room where Guaraldi was sitting, and asked him if he knew anything about the warehouse.

"No," he said, looking puzzled. "I wrote all the checks for Peder to review and sign, but I never wrote these. That's his handwriting, all right.'' He looked up at her, an idea dawning on his face. ''Do you think that's where—''

''Where he went during his fugue states?'' Laika finished. ''Maybe. We'll go up there and see what we find.''

''May I come along?''

She hesitated. ''Not yet. I think we should go up first. Maybe later.''

''He could be there,'' Guaraldi said hopefully.

''Maybe. Did Mr. Holberg have a key ring?''

Guaraldi nodded. ''It was still in the door when it blew open. It held together, though. I'll get it.''

He stepped into another room and came back with a simple metal ring with seven keys on it. The metal of both ring and keys was scratched and dusty. ''These three are to the downstairs door, the studio, and the apartment. This is the car key, which he hardly ever used, this one's the key to the loft in the studio. I don't know what these two are. Maybe this warehouse?''

''Can we hang on to these?''

''Sure. Come in and check out the studio whenever you like. Or the office. Just ring beforehand so I know you're coming up.''

The three ops spent another hour in the office. On the same shelf where he had found the other hidden papers, Tony found some bills for iron pipe and other metal pieces, as well as acetylene torches, to be delivered to the Bronx warehouse. The checks paying for the supplies were also made out and signed by Holberg. When, on the way out, they showed the invoices to Guaraldi, he claimed to know nothing about them. ''But Christ,'' he said, looking through the papers, ''that's one helluva lot of pipe.'' He shook his head incredulously. ''I don't think Peder would use that much in the studio in a *year*.''

''These bills for materials and rent stretch over a period of four months,'' Laika observed. ''About as long as you say he had these fugue states.''

''You think he was . . . *working* all that time?'' Guaraldi asked.

"Depends on what we find out when we visit the warehouse," Laika said.

They spent several hours looking through the rubble of the studio, but found nothing to explain how Peder Holberg might have escaped the explosion that tore the loft to pieces. "You don't think," Joseph said, half seriously, "that he could have disintegrated, do you?"

"You mean, been blown to bits?" Tony said. "There was a lot of plastic here, but there wasn't *that* much. No, they'd have found something red and sticky. Might blow him apart, but the flash wouldn't burn blood, muscle, and bone. Hey, you know better than that."

"Just making conversation."

"You know how long it takes just to *cremate* a guy?"

"I *know*, I *know*, forget I brought it up. . . ."

Tony shook his head and continued to pick through the rubble. " 'Disintegrate' . . . jeez. . . ."

When they decided there was nothing more to look through, they said good-bye to Adam Guaraldi and promised to tell him the following day what they found at the warehouse. They went back to the apartment, where Laika boiled spaghetti while Tony whipped up a quick but tasty sauce, and made plans for the evening. Laika and Joseph would drive out to the Bronx warehouse, while Tony would take a cab to the Blud Flat in SoHo, the club where Holberg had met his goths, and try to find out what Holberg's relationship was with them.

"You going to pack?" Joseph asked, as they were washing and drying the dishes.

"I always pack," said Tony.

"Well, you'd better pack this, too." Joseph put a dishtowel around Tony's neck, then raised his right hand, fingers down like a spider, and said in a poor imitation of Bela Lugosi, *"They biiiite. . . ."*

"You asshole," Tony said, and tossed the dishtowel back. But he smiled, and so did Laika.

"Da cheeldren of da night," Joseph proclaimed. *"Vat music* dey *make!"*

Tony patted the .38 special in the hollow of his back. "Yeah," he said. "Rock and roll. . . ."

Chapter 22

Children of the night, Tony thought. That Joseph was one piece of work. Smartass know-it-all, a cross between the class clown and a computer nerd. Still, Tony had to admit he liked the guy. He nearly made him laugh, and Tony didn't laugh a whole lot. He had left too many people dead behind him.

He hadn't gone to mass for several weeks and hadn't made a confession for longer than he cared to remember. Though he didn't know whether he still believed the way he had when he was younger, confession always made him feel better, though he suspected it didn't do the same for the priests.

He could tell them only so much, and if he said that he had been sanctioned by the government to do what he did, that would have been blowing his cover, and Tony didn't even trust a priest to keep that secret. So he let them think he was a mob guy, though he never actually came out and said that, since lying was a sin in itself. It probably gave the priest a thrill, and he was sure that in some parishes where he had made confession he wasn't the only hitman, sanctioned or otherwise, who'd ever come to be shriven.

Sitting back in the cab, watching the lights of the city blur past, Tony wished he had sins of a more carnal nature to confess. He hadn't been with a woman for months and was feeling the absence. Laika was very attractive, but she was a colleague, and that was one rule he had never broken. Maybe he'd pick up a vampire babe tonight. He thought about it for a moment, then shook his head. Fat chance. The average age of these goths would probably be around fifteen.

"Lemme out at the corner here," he told the cab driver. According to the card, the Blud Flat was in the middle of the block. As he paid the driver, he watched an assortment of kids, nearly all of them dressed in black, moving back and forth along the block. They were young, all right. And the few older ones he spotted looked worn-out, like they really *had* had their blood drained over the years. Tony wondered if they actually tried to look like junkies, or if it just came with the territory.

He paid the driver and walked toward the club. He had chosen an all-black ensemble himself—black T-shirt, black jacket, black slacks—but he felt ridiculous as he looked at his reflection in the store windows. Usually when he went undercover, it was as a businessman or a construction worker or a hotel employee, all roles in which he felt comfortable. But being a thirty-year-old goth didn't sit well with him, and he just felt silly. The occasional snickers he heard from some of the drunker and younger kids didn't help his self-image any. At least he didn't have a spare ounce of fat, even if he wasn't the walking skeleton that so many of these goths seemed to find the height of desire.

A dozen gawky, black-clad kids were hanging around a stairway that led down. A blood-red neon sign read, "The Blud Flat," and more red neon formed an arrow pointing straight down. Without excusing himself, Tony pushed through the kids and walked down the steps. He figured that courtesy would be suspect.

If the attitude of the doorman was any indication, he was right. "Ten-buck cover," he said, holding out a hand. His eyes were ringed with kohl, and his lips were defined by a dark shade of lipstick outlined with black eyeliner. Tony put a ten in his black-nailed hand and pushed open the door.

A haze of smoke, thick with the smell of cloves, engulfed him. He took one more quick breath of the far fresher New York City air and let the door drift closed behind him. The club was illuminated with red and blue lights, giving a sickly cast to every exposed bit of flesh. A few blond and white heads shone like floating islands in the murk, but nearly everyone's hair was black, so that the large room seemed filled with white masks.

A band played on a stage at the far end of the cavern, but the ceiling was so low that their heads nearly touched it. There would be no leaping and pogoing from this crowd, Tony thought. A bar was along the left wall, and most of the stools were taken. Tables were in the center and on the right, and those farthest back were lost in the smoke and the dark. A few people seemed to be dancing on a small area in front of the stage, but Tony couldn't be sure. Maybe they were only swaying.

He walked to the bar and sat at the empty stool at the end. The bartender ignored him until Tony raised a hand and asked for a draft lite. He could drink a number of them without feeling it. Drink in hand, he moved through the thick crowd, looking for people who appeared to take everything a little more seriously than the usual pierced-nose-and-surliness throng.

At the far end of the room, Tony found a door he assumed led to whatever passed for backstage. But on the right wall, there was another opening covered by a black curtain. He started to look behind it when someone said, "Hey. . . ."

Tony turned to his right and saw a Brandon Lee lookalike, his chair leaned back against the wall, his feet propped on the table. "Can't go back there."

"Looking for the john," Tony said.

"Either side the stage—boys left, girls right."

He had been wrong about them being stage doors. "Nothing's marked," he said.

"Nothing has to be. Everybody knows." Tony definitely felt a sense of exclusion.

He thought he heard some voices behind the black curtain, singing, or possibly chanting. "What's goin' on in there?"

"The Order's meeting."

"What order?"

"You *are* a newbie, aren't you?" The man pursed his lips. "Maybe you'd like a friend to explain it?"

Tony got it and smiled. "Sorry. Don't travel that way."

"The road of blood has many paths," the man said enticingly.

"Yeah, well, I'll take the high road tonight. Thanks for the offer." Tony saluted with his beer glass and walked back toward the front of the club. There he finished his beer and watched the band, keeping an eye on the black-curtained doorway.

Just after midnight, what Tony assumed was "the Order" began to come though it. There were eight of them, five men and three women. Though their faces and attitudes bore the despair and hedonism of the other goths, their eyes were more alive. An extreme intensity seemed to roll off them in waves like a thick scent.

They crossed the room, ignoring the band and the greetings of those bold enough to address them, walking to a large table that suddenly emptied as they approached. A barmaid, dressed in black, of course, brought over a tray of drinks as though by a prearranged signal. In the strange light, the liquid in the long-stemmed glasses looked black, or at least dark green.

These, Tony surmised, were the people he needed to talk to. They seemed to be the dark princes and princesses of this dingy realm. But they didn't look like the type you'd just walk over and start chatting to. In fact, none of them was saying a word. They must have done all their talking in the back room. Now they were just sitting there, looking dead ahead like zombies, every now and then bringing whatever concoction they were drinking to their lips.

After ten minutes or so, one of the girls, who had blond hair cut in a pageboy, said a few words that Tony couldn't hear over the music, got up, and walked back to the women's restroom. Tony, making sure the remaining seven weren't watching him, followed.

The girl came back out a short time later. She was tilting her head and sniffing. She appeared to be older than most of the teenyboppers in the club. Without the Vampira makeup and the dozen or so knobs and hoops that pierced her nose, lip, and eyebrows, she'd be pretty cute, he thought. Time to see if the old guinea charm still worked. He had a way with the women, but whether it extended to those who'd rather suck blood than other things, he didn't know. Maybe it would take blood to break the ice.

As the girl walked by him, he held up a hand to stop her, and then pointed to her lip, which was pierced, along with other pins, by a hooded skull less than an inch in diameter. " 'Blood,' " Tony said solemnly, " 'was its avatar.' "

The girl smiled loopily. " 'And its seal.' Yeah, you got it."

Tony smiled back. "*Masque of the Red Death*. One of my favorites. You wearing any other Poe on you?" he asked, looking appreciatively at her ornaments.

"No. A lot of other symbols, though."

"Yeah, I see—the ankh, an inverted cross—very nice, pentagram, magic circle. . . ." Then he looked at her rings, an assortment of gold skulls and serpents. "Those are wonderful," he said, taking her hand with the excuse to see them better. She didn't pull away, but only smiled all the more at his compliments.

Then he noticed a dark spot on the inside of her wrist and turned her hand over to reveal a small but highly detailed tattoo. "My God," he said. "Now, that is really exquisite."

He wasn't lying. The tattoo was of what appeared to be an octopoid creature mounted atop the globe of the earth. The shapes of the continents were discernible when he looked closely. The thing's tentacles were wrapped about the planet, and all around it, stars shone dark on the pale background of the woman's skin.

"Amazing," Tony said. "That took a real artist."

"We all have them," the woman said dreamily. "It's Cthulhu, you know—the sign of the order."

Tony remembered the books he had read in high school. "Lovecraft. The, what was it, Esoteric Order. . . ."

"Of Dagon," she finished.

"Right. But I thought that was fiction."

She shook her head. "No. Truth disguised, that was all. The Holy One spoke to Lovecraft, and Lovecraft wrote what the Holy One told him, but he changed things so that the people who *knew* would recognize things, but those who didn't would just think they were stories."

Jesus, keep me from hard drugs, Tony thought. "Somebody I knew was telling me about your group," he said.

"Yeah?" He saw interest in her clouded eyes, and maybe a bit of lust, too, if he wasn't overestimating his attraction.

"Yeah, an artist. Sculptor named Peder Holberg?"

As the name penetrated her thoughts, she frowned. "Him . . . the Holy One could talk to him. He can't talk to any of us, but he could to Holberg. Only Holberg didn't want to *listen.* He turned his back on him, on the Holy One, can you believe that? To have such a gift and just shit it away! No *wonder* he got blown the hell up!"

She had gotten louder now and had drawn the attention of her companions. One of the men, who reminded Tony of a tall, lanky scarecrow dressed up for Halloween, stood and started toward them, followed by two of his fellows. "Elaine!" he said, loudly enough to be heard over the band. The crowd parted for him, so that in another moment he was by the woman's side. "Who's this?"

"My name's Bill," Tony said. He didn't put out a hand. These weren't the type who went in for shakes and howdys.

"So?" said the tall man with a total absence of warmth.

"He knew Peder," Elaine said.

"You did?" the man said, his nostrils flaring as if he'd caught a scent.

"Maybe I still do. We don't know that he's dead."

"He was in a room when it blew up. Even if they found no body, how could he be alive?"

"If they didn't find a body," Tony said, "how can he *not* be alive?" He attempted a thin smile. "I know he was hanging with you. I just wondered if you might have any idea of where he may have disappeared to. You know, if he said anything about taking off, leaving the city—"

"He left *us*," the tall man said. "We taught him so much, and then, when he finally saw what benefit he could be to us—and to the Holy One—he went chickenshit, turned his back on us. And you're his *friend*?"

The other two men were flanking him now, and Tony felt as though this could escalate very quickly. He didn't want that to happen here. Injuries, police, questions . . . his papers would see him through, but the less light shone on him, the better. "I knew him, like I said."

The tall man fixed him with a steely glare. "You think he's alive?"

"Maybe."

"I think you know more than you're telling us. If Peder Holberg's alive, we want to talk to him. Now, what do you know?"

The tone was commanding, even if the guy did look like Ichabod Lugosi. The two on either side of Tony towered over him as well. The thought that he could probably kill all three of them in as many seconds without pulling his pistol was reassuring, but he preferred a more peaceful solution. "Not much," he said. "But maybe we oughta take this outside."

"No," Ichabod said. "We want privacy; we'll go in the back." He turned to the table where the remaining members of the Order sat and beckoned them with a sharp little jerk of his head. This guy was good, Tony thought. He had his minions nicely trained. They stood and moved to the black curtain as Tony felt the two men press his shoulders, telling him to start walking.

The tall man led the way, and Tony followed him through the curtain and down a short hall. There was a heavy door at the end, and someone ahead of them rattled what sounded like a large key in the lock. The door opened on squeaking hinges, but showed only blackness. Then he heard the sound of footsteps on metal stairs, and in another moment he too was walking down the long black stairway.

That was good, he thought. The further away they were from the club, the less likely the goths upstairs were to hear gunshots if Tony had to use his weapon. Or at least, so he thought before he walked into the vault.

There were torches glowing through an arched doorway, and Tony was inwardly congratulating his captors on getting the ambience right when he felt the unmistakable hardness of a gun barrel being pressed to his head. "You carrying, asshole?" a harsh voice said, and then hands began to move up and down his body, searching.

There was no point in waiting to see what happened next. Tony had seen too many people do that and die. Besides, people felt too confident when they were holding a gun to your head. They expected you to be scared and not to move, and when you did, they didn't know what the hell was happening. His greatest fear was meeting someone someday who did, and would put a bullet in his head at his very first twitch.

But these goths weren't anywhere near as professional as they thought they were. Tony slapped the gun away easily with his left arm, using a knife hand that broke the wielder's wrist, so that a shot went wild as the pistol flew away from him. At the same time, he shot his right heel backward, knee-capping the man behind him, so that he screamed and staggered backward, falling.

A millisecond later, he struck to the right, hitting the man there in the throat, pulling the blow just enough so that it would not crush the windpipe. By that time, his left hand had come about in a circle from the first blow into a dangerous uppercut that caught the front man under the chin, snapping his teeth together with a sharp crack and dropping him unconscious to the floor.

Those who weren't out cold or nursing their wounds didn't seem to know what to do, and when Tony's .38 special jumped out from under his jacket, they grew even more confused. Of the men, only Ichabod was left, and he stood in a stupor, looking down at his fallen and screaming warriors.

Elaine, however, was a woman of action. With a shriek that echoed through the damp-walled vault, she flew at Tony, fingers outstretched to claw his face. He sidestepped and came down with an overhand left that collided with her temple and dropped her to the stone floor.

"You sonofa*bitch!*" one of the other women screamed. "How could you hit a woman?"

Tony didn't pause to inform her that he had already killed more than one woman in his life. Instead, he stepped over the writhing bodies behind him and went out the door. He paused just long enough to close it and turn the key in the lock. Then he yanked it out and tossed it into the darkness.

" '*In pace requiescat*, Fortunato,' " he whispered, then quickly walked toward the dim light that shone at the bottom of the long stairs. As he went he hoped that Laika and Joseph had had a helluva lot more productive night than he had.

Chapter 23

*L*aika Harris and Joseph Stein's night did indeed turn out to be more productive than Tony Luciano's, and nearly as dangerous. The address of the warehouse was not merely *off* the Third Avenue bridge, but *under* it as well. They drove their car uptown and across the bridge to the Bronx, waiting until after midnight in the hopes that fewer people would be about at that hour.

They were right. There were fewer people, but those left on the streets were predators and foolish prey, cut loose from the herds that fled to their dens when daylight and, later, the comforting neons of evening faded and the darkness came. Luckily for Laika and Joseph, the Company had trained them to feed on carnivores.

Except for the carcasses of two stripped and rusted cars, the small parking lot of the warehouse was empty. When Joseph turned off the engine, all they could hear was the sound of traffic on the bridge overhead and the thin whisper of music from a waterfront bar two blocks away. All of the street lights in the area had either burned out or been shot out. In any event, they had not been replaced, and the glow from the city across the river provided the only light.

"How the hell could Holberg have gotten out here without a car?" Joseph asked.

"Cab," Laika said simply. "And there's an IRT stop three blocks away. Tomorrow, let's check to see if any cabbies have a record of taking a party over here—if they'd be willing to make the trip. Don't think there'd be many people coming right here.''

''Amen to that.''

They sat in the car for a moment, observing the warehouse. It towered four stories high and was perhaps sixty yards long by forty wide. Lichen crawled twenty feet up its concrete sides, making it look as though it had been there forever. The huge painted words ''Brennan Lading'' were pale ghosts, nearly exorcised by years of sun and the scouring acids in the rain and the air.

Spray-painted graffiti ringed the building's perimeter, letters and codes and symbols that were foreign to Laika. Whatever windows the warehouse had once had were now boarded up. There was a large metal delivery door in the side of the wall. Around the corner on the shorter wall was another, smaller door that looked more promising.

''Well,'' Joseph said, ''it's not going to get any prettier.''

They got out of the car and went up to the small door. The keys Adam Guaraldi had given them unlocked both the heavy padlock and the inset lock, and the door creaked open. Just as they were about to go inside, a voice from behind them said, ''Burglars.''

Laika whirled around and went into a crouch, her right hand slipping inside her jacket for her weapon. Beside her, Joseph did the same, but more slowly. Then she froze.

Half a dozen African-American kids, none of them older than sixteen, were standing thirty yards away. Their hands were in the pockets of their jackets or the pouches of their hooded sweats, and they seemed very much at ease. They should, Laika thought. This was their territory. One of the boys switched on a boom box, and the harsh words and sounds of gangsta rap filled the night.

''They burglars, all right,'' said another one over the music. ''Breakin' and enterin', that what they doin'.''

''Man, that ain't good. Goddam Jew owns that shithole, he catch you, he be mad. Fac', we catch you, maybe he give us a reward.''

''Got *that* right.''

"We're not breaking in," said Laika, straightening up.
"We have keys, see?" She hoped they'd just go away but
didn't think it was likely.

"Keys? Now ain't that somethin'? What else you got
there, sister, a white boy? What you keepin' him for? Or he
keepin' you? He a rich Jewboy, like the black meat? You
ought be ashamed of yourself, sister."

Joseph looked at Laika and breathed a deep sigh, both
apologetic and weary. Why the hell did it have to be like
this, she wondered. "You boys go away now—we're busy
here."

"Yeah, you gonna get busier." The boy in the lead started
walking toward them. "You gonna be busy gettin' your asses
kicked, and we gonna do the kickin'. Maybe we do more
with your sweet ass, sister. Bust you down, bitch."

God *damn* it, but Laika hated that word. The boys were
ten yards away by now. Hell with it, she thought. Even if
they *were* packing, she and Joseph could take them all.

She took out the automatic and was glad she'd thought to
attach a silencer. Still, the sound of the shot was like a giant
spitting. The bullet smashed into the boom box, shattering it
and stopping the music. The boy holding it dropped what
was left and glared at her in mixed fury and fear.

Two of the others reached deeper into their pockets, but
Laika targeted the one on the left and Joseph the one on the
right. "Do it and you're dead," Laika said, and they stopped
moving. "Take them out slow."

One of the shooters had a cheap Saturday night special,
its butt wrapped with electrical tape, but the other had a
sweet little Glock. "Now empty the cylinder and the clip
and throw the bullets over there into the dark. Go on."

They did it, though she was amazed at their barely disguised hatred. Here they were with two guns held on them,
and they still looked only a thought away from jumping at
her anyway.

"Now," she went on, "you want to be able to buy another
box? You want to make a little money, more than you'd get
if you tried to mug us? Then listen up. We're gonna be

coming in here from time to time. You don't give us any shit, and you leave our car alone, and we'll drop a hundred dollars at the door there each time we leave.''

"*Two* hundred," said the lead boy, as though he actually had a bargaining chip instead of a gun pointed at him.

Before Laika could respond, Joseph chimed in, "How about two-fifty?" She swung around and glared at him as if he were crazy, but he only smiled at her. "It's out of Skye's account," he whispered.

She thought a moment, then turned back. "We'll make it two-fifty," she said. "Only we'll want a receipt. Suit you?"

"A *what?*" the boy said.

"A receipt. You write on a piece of paper that we paid you two hundred and fifty dollars for . . . security."

"We do that now, you pay us the money?"

"You got it?" Laika asked Joseph.

"Barely," he said, taking out a money clip with bills.

"All right," Laika said. "A hundred now, the rest when we leave—*if* the car's still here." Peeling off some bills, Joseph walked up to the boy and handed them to him, still holding his gun.

"Hey," said the boy who had had the boom box. "What about my box?"

Laika shook her head. "Don't press your luck, kid. Take it out of the two-fifty." She put her gun back in its holster. "Write it off as a business expense."

She opened the door, which had drifted shut, and held it for Joseph to enter. She went in after him, closing and locking the door behind her.

They found themselves in total darkness, so they both took out flashlights and turned them on. They were in a dingy eight-by-eight-foot anteroom. One wall showed a spot free of dirt where a time clock had once been installed. Against the other, an ancient Coke machine sat, the kind in which you opened a door and yanked out one of the bottles. No caps were visible beneath the grimy glass.

There was a closed door opposite the one they had come in. Laika walked across the wooden floor, pushed it open, stepped through, and shined her flashlight into a spiderweb of iron.

Chapter 24

"**M**y God," she whispered, as Joseph turned on the lights, and she saw that it was more than a web; it was a jungle.

"Now we know what he was doing up here," Joseph said, and she heard the unmistakable tone of awe in his voice. "And what that stack of invoices for iron was all about."

The room was filled with a gigantic ruined sculpture. Laika thought it must have been made up of thousands of pieces of iron. The bright fluorescent lights overhead cast the shadows of the bars upon the floor and on the iron below, so that from their vantage point it was impossible to tell what was true and what was shadow.

In some places the iron towered thirty feet high. In others the foot-wide boards had been removed so that the iron could descend beneath the level of the floor.

Red-brown puddles dotted the floor, and the smell of rust and corrosion hung in the air. There was another unpleasant note to the odor that Laika could not define until Joseph said, "Smells like when I was a kid . . . and mice would die in the walls of my grandmother's house."

That was it, all right, the smell of death. Despite her experience with severed lives, the rank odor and the sight of the twisted labyrinth of iron made Laika feel ill in both her stomach and her soul. She had never experienced such a sense of total awe and complete revulsion. It was like coming face to face with God and learning that he was a monster who wished only death and torment for his children. Even half ruined, the work was appalling and, in an aesthetic sense, nearly obscene.

Laika closed her eyes, took a deep breath, and tried to push the sickness away. There was work to do. When she looked at the sculpture again, she felt better, though the sensation of examining a decayed and skeletal corpse would not fully leave her. She steeled herself and studied the work.

Many of the bars had been disconnected from the main work and lay on the floor like huge pick-up sticks. Others reminded Laika of the tortured sculptures back in Peder Holberg's other, more public studio. They were wrenched and bent, as though by that hypothetical tornado that had twisted the smaller pieces in the destroyed loft. But whether they were merely bent or actually separated from the mass, whatever Peder Holberg had meant to represent was no longer clear, if it had ever been.

Near the wall, tanks of acetylene lay on their sides, and at several places in the work, portable steel stairways that had no doubt allowed Holberg access to the higher levels of the sculpture were knocked over as well.

"He was coming up here to build a sculpture," Laika said. "Why on earth—"

"*How* on earth," said Joseph. "Imagine all the time he must have spent here, coming and going at all hours of the day and night. Will you please tell me how Holberg, gay and foreign, managed to avoid being made into cube steak by those gangbangers out there?"

"Maybe . . . they're not as bad as they seem?"

Joseph said nothing, but only turned on her a look of withering scorn that she realized she deserved. "Or maybe God was watching over him," Joseph finally said, with sarcasm even deeper than his look.

"I don't know," Laika said, held by a dark fascination to the bizarre ironwork. It seemed God was very far away from this place.

She walked slowly around the sculpture, looking into its complex maze, seeing far finer filaments in the bright light.

Spiders had begun connecting the spaces between the bars, building their own traps of death, and she heard, from time to time, the scuttling of what could only be rats.

Nearly halfway around the work, she stopped and examined an area closely. "Joseph?" she said, and he came to where she was standing. "Look at that. It looks as though it . . . came outward."

Where she was pointing, iron had been twisted and wrenched away from the mass. It seemed to leave a definite path back toward the middle of the sculpture, and there they could clearly see where the sculpture had burst outward from the center, from a force that had left no sign of its passing but the bent iron. There was not the slightest scent of flame or powder or ash or any of the other olfactory evidence that a true explosion would leave behind.

"What the hell happened here?" Joseph asked.

"An explosion? Some force—"

Joseph looked at the tangle of iron for a moment. "You know," he said slowly, "maybe Holberg *intended* it to look like this. We know that he was asking Guaraldi about explosions . . . maybe because he was working on this—sort of an intentional *artistic* destruction."

"But remember," Laika said, "Holberg wasn't even supposed to *know* that he was working on this."

"I don't buy that. You can't do something this complex— rent a warehouse, order supplies, create this thing—and not know it. And he knew enough to hide the records."

"Maybe he was hiding them from himself," Laika said, then sighed. "Or maybe you're right . . . maybe it was all planned and Holberg just faked the fugue states to surprise Guaraldi with the piece later. There's just one problem with that."

"What?"

"Look at the size of it, and look at the door. He'd never have gotten it out of here."

Joseph looked at the door and nodded. "But what if he just intended to show it here?"

"In this neighborhood?" Laika was glad to see him nod again in agreement.

They continued walking around the vast sculpture and at the far end of the room found a rickety wooden table. On it were a number of badly soiled and stained sheets of paper, each of them eighteen by twenty-four inches. They all contained enigmatically complex pencil drawings and series of numbers running down the sides.

The drawings were mostly of angles and lines, and what looked like measurements were written next to every line and angle. The pile of papers was nearly six inches thick, and she and Joseph were careful not to get them out of order as they leafed through.

"Plans?" she asked.

"I think so. You know who has to see this?"

"Yes. Guaraldi. He worked closely with Holberg, so he might be able to make something out of it all."

They examined the rest of the sculpture, but found only more iron joinings interrupted by seeming chaos. The longer Laika looked at it, the more her sickness waned, as if the work were slowly seducing her, until, in its own bizarre way, it seemed dangerously beautiful, like a monument to bone and sinew. The rust that crawled up the pipes somehow added to its gritty glory, and the puddles on the floor reflected the discordant structure above like pools of blood.

"We need to take photos," Joseph said, breaking in on her reverie. "I'll get the camera in the trunk."

"No." Laika shook her head. "Let me go. I need a breath of fresh air." She did not realize how badly she needed to get out of the warehouse until she spoke. The air was cloying and thick, with a trace of salt. It was like breathing through a bloody nose.

"Let me go with you. Those kids—"

She waved a hand dismissively. "They'll be no problem now. Besides, even if they were. . . ."

"I know. You could take 'em." Joseph smiled. "I'll just poke around here. Don't be long, though. This place even gives *me* the creeps."

Laika took out her flashlight as she opened the front door and stepped into the parking lot. She thought about holding her pistol, but decided not to. After all, she could draw it in two-tenths of a second, should the need arise.

As she shut the door behind her, she hesitated for a moment, checking the terrain, listening, watching, and even smelling the air. Once, in Haiti, the scent of an enemy agent's body odor had alerted her to his presence as she'd entered her hotel room. His plan had been to kill her, but he had died instead. Ever since, Laika had used all of her senses to fight her battles.

It was a good thing she had. There were probably many men who used a little-known German scent called Knize Two, but she knew only one who did, and had told him several times that he splashed it on too liberally, until he got angry and told her to mind her own business.

James.

For a moment she could not believe that he could have been so unbelievably stupid as to follow her and Joseph out here to no-man's land. He probably figured since he was a brother, he had nothing to fear. He would learn otherwise soon enough, if she had rightly sized up the gangbangers she and Joseph had confronted.

Laika looked around slowly and saw, parked far down the street, a car that hadn't been there before. James's Jaguar. There were the long, lean lines he was so proud of, even though he kept the car garaged most of the time. As she watched, shadows came out of the night around the car, and in the flurry of movement she could imagine busy hands stripping what they could from James's vehicle.

She wondered why he had come, what he wanted. The only thing certain was that his stupidity knew no bounds. Shaking her head slowly, she walked out onto the cracked and uneven parking lot, shining her flashlight on the ruined asphalt in front of her. She would easily enough hear his feet on the loose stones if he came running up to her.

She had just unlocked the trunk and was lifting up the lid when something beneath the car grabbed her right ankle and pulled hard. She was off balance, so let herself fall backward, twisting to cushion the fall with her forearms and hip. A single kick and she was free, spinning into a crouch, ready to draw her gun.

Her flashlight had fallen so that it shone under the car, and James's angry, surprised face looked out at her. He scrambled out from under the car, more slowly than he would have liked, she was sure, for by the time he was out, Laika was on her feet, standing with her arms at her side, her flashlight in her hand.

"What the hell was that all about?" she said.

He was panting with the exertion of getting out from beneath the car, and it took him a moment to get his wind back. "I need to talk to you," he said breathlessly.

"Well, you think a good way to do it is by hiding under my car and grabbing me? Talk, hell—you wanted to hurt me, James."

He shook his head as though he wasn't sure, and then said, "Yeah, maybe—shit, you hurt *me*, and that sonofabitch guinea did, too." Laika felt her temper build like a cold fire, as James gestured to the empty parking lot. "Other boyfriend's in there—nobody here to protect you now, baby. So I want *you* back, or *pay*back."

"You'd better take payback, asshole. If you can."

Chapter 25

James Winston's nostrils flared in fury, and he started for her. His wild charge was pitifully easy to evade, and her leg sweep took him to the ground without a follow-up strike.

Then she knelt over him and hit him four times hard in the face. The second blow broke his nose, and the fourth his jaw. She stopped when she heard it crack.

James lay there, gasping in pain, his eyes open wide in shock. Laika grabbed his shirt and hauled him up toward her until his bleeding face was only inches from hers. "You don't know what you're into here. Get the hell out while you can, James. The 'guinea' you're talking about would have killed you like *that*. And next time I see you, *I'll* do it."

As she spoke, the panic in James's eyes was slowly replaced by understanding and then rage. "I'm gonna kill *you*—" he grated out, trying to sniff back the blood that ran copiously over his mouth and chin. "You bitch. . . ."

She shook her head, amazed at his spirit and his stupidity. "I still don't think you get it." Then she struck him hard once more, just at the bottom of his rib cage so that ribs cracked and the air went out of him in a tremendous burst, making him start to vomit. Somehow, he rolled onto his side so that what came up didn't choke him.

"Get up," she said. "Get out of here." She kicked him lightly in the side, and he pushed himself to his hands and knees, still vomiting. She waited until he stopped, then kicked him again, harder. He fell over onto his side, holding up his hands in a gesture of surrender. "You're going to keep hurting, James, unless you go now," she said. Another kick in the side, and now he rolled over again and stood up slowly.

Her next move was purely out of anger. She slapped his face with her open hand, hard, across his cheek. *"Run."* It was as much a growl as a word.

James whimpered and staggered away from her, toward the dark street where the boys were stripping his car, destroying still another dream. She tried to watch him go without a trace of sympathy.

She knew that she should have killed him, driven the bridge of his nose up into his brain with the heel of her hand. She and Joseph could have weighted his body down and dropped it in the river, or just let it float, for that matter. He was lucky, very lucky, to get away with his life. She wasn't concerned with how the gangbangers would treat him when he returned to his car, if they were still there. Let them kill him, she told herself. She should have. She knew she should have.

Laika picked up her flashlight and lifted the trunk lid. She took out the camera bag and closed the trunk, concentrating on the task ahead, trying to cleanse her mind of what had just happened. But when she turned back toward the warehouse, she saw Joseph standing in the doorway.

"You knew him," he said, as she walked up to him.

"Yes."

"Is he connected?"

"No. He's got nothing to do with our business."

"Personal, then. What did he want?"

She thought for a moment. "Revenge, I think."

"Then he'll be back. You know what you should have done."

"Of course I know. But don't make it sound so damned easy—you don't know a damned thing about it."

"You're right, Laika, and I don't *want* to know a damned thing about it. But even more, I don't want *him*, whoever that was, to know a thing about *us*."

She looked at him long and hard. "You're a desk jockey, Joseph. Have you ever killed anybody?" He didn't answer. "Have you ever looked in a person's eyes and seen life there, and you knew, you knew absolutely, that you were going to take that light out forever?" She jerked her hand in the direction in which James Winston had disappeared. "I gave him what he deserved. I made him hurt. But he didn't deserve to die. Not yet."

"What if he comes back?" Joseph said softly.

"Then I'll kill him," she said, just as softly. "I promise that I *will* kill him."

They went back inside then and took several rolls of film of the sculpture, recording it from many angles. Then they rolled up the papers they had found, turned out the lights, and, with a nearly palpable relief, locked the warehouse behind them. Joseph, with a lopsided smile at Laika, took a hundred and fifty dollars in bills from his money clip and put it half under a piece of concrete block.

When they got into their car, Laika noticed something she hadn't when she'd gone outside earlier. There was a circle on the front windshield in white chalk. Several squiggly lines were drawn through it. "It's a gang mark," Joseph said, as he brushed it off. "Probably to tell everybody else to leave the car alone."

As they drove away, Laika noticed that James's car was still there, what was left of it. James himself was nowhere to be seen.

Tony was sleeping on the couch in the living room when Laika and Joseph came through the door of the apartment. He awoke immediately and insisted on hearing what they had found at the warehouse. After they told him, he filled them in on his adventures with the Esoteric Order of Dagon, and Joseph nodded.

" 'The Shadow Over Innsmouth,' " Joseph said. "That's the Lovecraft story the Order appears in. So they think Lovecraft had a divine visitation from Cthulhu before he wrote his story, huh? Next thing you know, he'll be the new Joseph Smith.''

''There wasn't anything vaguely Mormon-like about this bunch,'' Tony said. ''But I think they know even less than we do about what happened to Holberg.''

''Did they say anything about this sculpture?'' Laika asked. ''Whether or not Holberg had told them about it?''

Tony shook his head. ''Not a thing, but we didn't have much of a conversation. So when do *I* get to see it?''

''We'll go over tomorrow,'' Laika said. ''Take Guaraldi with us, see what he makes of it, and if he can interpret the papers we found.''

Tony snapped his fingers. ''Jeez, speaking of tomorrow, Melton called. That medium, Elissa Meyer? She's going off on a book tour in two days, so the only time she can visit the house in the next month is tomorrow night.''

''What?'' Laika said. ''That doesn't give us *any* time. Joseph?''

He merely smiled. ''We don't need any. We can take Guaraldi over to the warehouse tomorrow and still show up Elissa Meyer tomorrow night. I'll just have to pick up a few things.''

''Crucifixes and holy water?'' Tony said with a smirk.

Joseph ignored him. ''We'll call Melton in the morning, tell him we'll be there. Now I'm ready to get some sleep.''

Sometime just before dawn, long after the gang had retrieved their money that Joseph had left for them and returned to wherever to sleep off a rough night's work, two figures slipped furtively from the shadows surrounding the warehouse. They were dressed in black from head to foot, and seemed not so much to pass through the night as to wear it. One of them carried a small black bag.

They glided to the door of the warehouse through which Laika and Joseph had left several hours before, and after a few minutes of small, economical movements, the locks yielded to their efforts. Not until they were inside with the door shut firmly behind them did they turn on their powerful flashlights.

For several minutes they stood looking at the structure of iron towering above them, and at the burst and broken pieces scattered here and there. They walked around the whole work, shining their lights everywhere, though they did not turn on the overhead bulbs.

Then they started to examine the wooden sheathing that covered the wall separating the anteroom from the warehouse area. When the man with the bag found the proper spot, he handed the bag to the other person, who opened it and began to take out several small tools which were passed to the technician.

Within fifteen minutes they had finished what they had come to do. They left the building, locking it behind them, placing the padlock precisely the way it had been, and blended once more into the darkness. There was no trace of their presence, save for what was now hidden between the wooden panels of the wall.

Chapter 26

When Quentin McIntyre went into his office the following morning, he was happy to see that, along with the daily quota of newspapers, Alan Phillips had also put a CIA report on his desk. Phillips was going to be a winner, McIntyre was certain. One of those agents whose life is their work and vice versa.

He read the report first. It was a précis of an internal CIA memo that concerned Anthony Luciano's latest assignment. It stated that Luciano had been assigned to Azerbaijan and had supposedly been there for the past six weeks. McIntyre smiled and shook his head. Skye, he wondered, just what are you up to?

He pressed a buzzer on his desk, and Phillips came in. "Alan," McIntyre said, "I want you to start a three-priority search for Anthony Luciano. I don't believe a word of this memo. I know that was him in Plattsburgh, so let's begin with New York State and branch out from there if we strike out."

"You think it's a Company operation here in the States?"

McIntyre nodded. "There's no other reason Luciano would have for being in Plattsburgh. He was investigating those deaths at that hunting lodge, I don't know why. But I'm sure someone in the Company does, probably Richard Skye. Let's try and check all his internal correspondence, see if there's any mention of Luciano in connection with other

161

agents. He had two other people with him in Plattsburgh. Let's see what we can get to mesh.''

After Phillips left, McIntyre took out the clipping from *The Inner Eye* and looked at it again. "I know you," he whispered. "Azerbaijan, my ass. . . .''

At 10:30 that morning, the people Adam Guaraldi knew as Drs. Florence Kelly, Kevin Tompkins, and Vincent Antonelli of the National Science Foundation were driving Guaraldi to the warehouse in the Bronx. As they crossed over the Third Avenue bridge, Guaraldi was still flipping through the pile of papers they had shown him when they'd picked him up a half hour earlier.

Laika was sitting with him in the backseat, looking at the papers and watching his face for any reaction. "Does it make any sense to you?" she said.

He nodded. "It's Peder's work all right, but much different from his usual manner. I mean, he prided . . . *prides* himself on controlled chaos. But this is *un*controlled. I don't know what he's saying here. And the draftsmanship . . . it's Peder's, but almost in a different hand—more rushed, hurried. He was usually real meticulous in his plans. This isn't like him." Guaraldi turned a few more pages. "But I can see how this might fit together."

"Do you think the pages were in order?" she asked.

"No. I don't believe so. Like here. . . .'' He took a page from near the top of the stack. "See, this piece would seem to go with . . .'' Then he pulled a piece from the center. "'. . . this one. You see?" Laika didn't, but she nodded anyway. "It's like a huge jigsaw puzzle," Guaraldi said, riffling through the sheets.

Wait until you see the sculpture, she thought.

As they drove down the street to the warehouse, Laika noticed that James's car was no longer parked there. If he'd gotten past the gang, he probably had had what was left of it hauled away. She figured that was what had happened, since if it had been up to the police, the vehicle would have sat on that street until it had rusted out.

Joseph parked the car near the door, and they got out. Guaraldi looked around in amazement. "Here? Peder came here? My God, how?"

"We're not sure," she said, "but we checked this morning, and there was no record of any cabs taking riders to this location. So either he used unlicensed cabs, took the subway, and walked a few blocks, or he drove himself."

"That's impossible," Guaraldi said. "He didn't know how to drive."

Laika unlocked the door, walked through the anteroom, and turned on the lights. Guaraldi followed, and let out an unbelieving gasp when he saw what occupied the huge room.

"My God," he said. "Peder did all this? It's . . . it's *impossible*."

"Why?" Joseph said.

"Well, it's . . . too *much*! I mean, in size and scope, this is more than a year's worth of work—and that would be with me helping him. He couldn't have done this by himself in just a few months."

"Do you know anyone else," Laika asked, "who could have helped him with this?"

Guaraldi shook his head. "No, I don't *think* so. The only people he was seeing were those goths, but. . . ."

"Forget them," Tony said. "I talked to them last night, and they didn't know anything about this place."

Guaraldi's eyes took in the massive structure, the metal staircases, the pipes tossed helter-skelter by whatever force had torn them from the mass. "I just don't see how . . ." he began, then sank into silence. After a long moment, he spoke again. "I can hardly believe that this is Peder's work. I don't mean just the size of it, but the . . . the *aesthetic*. I knew him better than anyone else, and I can't conceive that he was capable of something so. . . ." He searched for the word.

"Monstrous?" Laika offered.

Guaraldi nodded thoughtfully. "Monstrous, yes . . . but fascinating as well. It draws you in even as it repels you. Like a dark maze you're afraid to lose yourself in, but that you can't keep from entering. I can't help but feel that somewhere in this . . . gigantic chaos may be the answer to what happened to Peder.''

''I was thinking the same thing,'' said Laika. ''This seems to be our only clue. But we can't really know what it means until we see it as it was intended to be. Do you think it would be possible to reconstruct it? From the plans?''

''That might not be necessary,'' Joseph said. ''We could do it virtually, on a computer. Did Holberg ever do any plans on his computer?''

''No. He tried, but it just didn't work. He called it soulless and just played games on it.''

''If you could interpret these plans for me,'' Joseph told Guaraldi, ''I could possibly reconstruct the statue in a CAD program. Just take it step by step.''

Guaraldi shook his head. ''I don't think I could do that. This isn't as methodical as it appears. I don't want to sound too precious, but the plans alone aren't enough—this would take the eye of an artist. It's not a matter of mechanics as much as it is organic. Besides, you can't really know what one sheet of plans signifies until you've done the necessary construction on the previous one. I could never make all of this . . . coalesce with just lines on a screen.''

Laika didn't understand everything Guaraldi had just said, but she knew it meant no. She took a deep breath. ''Do you think you could reassemble it physically, then? With the plans, could you reconnect the pieces that were . . .'' She was about to say ''blown off,'' but didn't. ''. . . That were detached? With our help?''

Guaraldi walked closer to the structure and ran his hand along the rusting iron. ''I think so . . . it would take some time, some trial-and-error, but I think so.'' He looked at his fingertips where the red rust clung, then at the iron he had exposed. ''The rust has eaten into the metal,'' he said. ''It's even red underneath.'' Then he whirled about and looked at them, his face stirred and angry. ''I can do it. It looks as though only a third or less of the whole is compromised. If Peder did the whole thing alone in a few months, I can do the same with some help.''

"I thought you said it was impossible," Tony said.

"I know I did. But I don't think I reckoned with, what would you call it, the *drive*. Peder was driven to do this—by what, I don't know. But I do know what drives me to repair it, and that's finding out what happened to him. And if maybe the way to do that is to finish this work, then I can work that way, too." Guaraldi looked at the highest spot on the structure. "Like a man possessed."

The first thing Guaraldi needed to do was to get the plans in a rough approximation of the proper order. Laika suggested that he might more comfortably do that back in his apartment, but Guaraldi said that it would be easier if he could see the structure itself and how the pieces fit together.

So he set up shop on the large table at the far end of the warehouse, while Laika, Joseph, and Tony planned their next step.

"We need to relocate here," Joseph said. "This is going to take months."

"Agreed," said Laika. "We'll have to get some more computers out here, have fiberoptic lines put in, order desks."

"I'll take care of all that," said Tony. "Maybe a minifridge and microwave." There were bathrooms off the anteroom, along with running water, as well as showers.

"You know, though," Joseph said, "although it seemed fairly cavalier last night, I really don't want to pay those kids two-fifty a day for a few months just to park the car."

Laika grinned. "I'll talk to them, maybe work out a long-term lease. Someone should be here with Guaraldi at all times, though. I don't want to leave him alone out here."

"But if the place is locked up," Joseph said, shrugging.

Laika looked at where the unseen force had torn the structure apart. "I'm not as much concerned with what's outside as with what may be *inside.*"

"Invisible force, huh?" Joseph said with a curl of his lip.

"Can you explain it? And can you convince me that nothing like it will happen again in here?"

The sneer disappeared. "No."

"Then we protect him. Okay, let's get started making this place livable."

They spent the rest of the day organizing. Laika figured that the ideal cover would be to have most residents think the mob was setting up a drug factory, a scenario that assured they wouldn't be bothered, and the others agreed.

Tony called in their requirements from his cell phone, and by late afternoon most of the equipment they needed had been delivered by Company vans, all of which bore the names of Italian businesses on their sides. Although a few kids walked by, nobody bothered to watch or to ask what was going on. You didn't do that in this neighborhood if you wanted to stay healthy.

In the afternoon, Joseph took the car to get some of the things he would need that evening at Melton's townhouses, while the other two continued to assemble their new office and Guaraldi kept trying to make sense of Peder Holberg's manic blueprints. Laika watched the man from the corner of her eye as he feverishly flipped through the large papers, then leapt up with several sheets in his hand, walked around to a certain vantage point, intently stared at a junction of pipes, then at the papers, and ran back to the table to resume his work of getting the plans in order.

They ate take-out at both lunch and dinner, but Guaraldi was concentrating so on the work at hand that he let his sandwich sit and go dry at lunch, and at dinnertime merely waved a hand when asked what he wanted. At Laika's insistence he ate a few bites of the soup and egg roll she had gotten for him, but he was immediately back at the papers again.

Elissa Meyer had set the time for the evening's ghostly meeting at 11 o'clock, so at 10, Laika and Joseph got into the car and headed back to the city. Tony remained at the warehouse with Adam Guaraldi, who showed just enough signs of tiring that Tony was able to talk him into taking a break.

They sat on a worn sofa in the anteroom. Guaraldi sipped a Coke while Tony had another cup of coffee. "This is how I get my caffeine fix now," Guaraldi said with a smile. "Peder hated coffee, couldn't even stand the smell of it. 'Burnt leather,' he always said." Guaraldi chuckled as Tony took a sniff of the steaming mug he held.

"In this case, he wouldn't be far off the mark," Tony said. "Chinese places aren't known for their coffee." He smiled at Guaraldi, then looked back down at the black surface of the coffee. Tony was uncomfortable with gay men. It was all right when there were other people around, but when he was alone, he never knew what to do or say.

"You okay?" Guaraldi asked. Despite the chill of the warehouse, his chest and arms were glistening with sweat.

"Yeah, sure," Tony said, looking up as though surprised at the question.

"You seem kind of 'out there.' Of course, I don't know many scientists. Maybe they all act kind of 'out there.'"

"Sorry."

"No problem. Or maybe you're just straight."

"*What?*" Oh shit, was the guy coming on to him?

"Ah, I can tell straight guys, they're always edgy when they're alone with people like me. Don't wanta be too friendly because they don't want me to think they're making a move on me, and they don't want to be too *un*friendly, because they don't—"

"They don't wanta be a jerk." Tony nodded. "You got me. Ever do any profiling?"

Guaraldi gave a little smile and shook his head. Then he raised an eyebrow. "Straight."

"As an arrow."

"Well, relax, you're not my type," Guaraldi said seriously.

"I'm Italian, too."

Tony didn't mind flirting when he knew it was safe, but Guaraldi didn't crack a grin. He just shook his head and said, "I'm a one-man man." He got off the sofa, walked to the door, and looked toward the sculpture. "But I can't find him."

"We will."

"You mean that, Doctor?" Guaraldi looked back hopefully.

"Yeah, I mean that. And forget the Doctor stuff. Call me . . ." He had to think for a minute. ". . . Vince."

"Okay, Vince. Well, I've got a few more hours in me, I think."

There was a knock on the door, and Tony was up in an instant and looking through the peephole he had installed earlier that day. "It's just the car," he said. "I had another one brought out in case you want to leave before the others come back from the city."

When he opened the door, a young, nervous agent handed him the car keys without a word, then got into the passenger side of a second car and was driven away. Tony saw several young men across the parking lot start to move toward the warehouse.

"I'll be right back, Adam," he said.

"Where you going?"

"Dr. Kelly asked me to take care of the, uh, parking attendants. Try and negotiate a long-term deal." He stepped through the doorway, locking it behind him, and waited for the boys who were growing nearer, their shoulders hunched, menace in their strides.

Tony smiled. He could handle these negotiations. Easily.

Chapter 27

"So what did you buy?" Laika asked, as she and Joseph drove south toward Manhattan.

"Simple things. Tape measure, stud finder, crowbar, hammer, mirror, thermometer, couple of Coleman lanterns, the usual ghost-hunting equipment."

"No holy water?"

"Never drink it."

They arrived at the townhouses at 10:45 to find Clarence Melton's limousine parked in front of the third house. Melton and Dennis Tweed were there waiting for them. "Miss Meyer hasn't arrived yet," said Melton, "but we can go in if you like."

"That would be fine," Joseph said. Laika had decided that he would be in charge of tonight's little adventure. "If you wouldn't mind, could Dr. Kelly and I go in alone to do some preliminary groundwork?"

Melton agreed, and Joseph and Laika went into the fifth house, the one where they had previously heard the scream. "Whatever you hear, 'Doctor,' " Joseph said, maintaining the illusion, "don't let it worry you. And if you see anything, it's going to be totally natural in origin. Remember, I'm not Dr. Montague, and you're not Eleanor Vance."

"Sorry, I didn't get that."

"*The Haunting of Hill House*—the ghost hunter and the sensitive. Maybe you saw the movie—*The Haunting*?"

"Yeah, I did, but frankly, that's the last thing I'd like to think about right now. It scared the shit out of me when I saw it on TV when I was a kid.''

''Common experience,'' said Joseph. ''But I'm old enough for it to have scared the shit out of me in a theater. Let's get these lanterns on.''

Laika hadn't seen similar lanterns since she'd gone camping with her parents, so she was newly amazed at the amount of light they gave off. ''Makes it homey,'' she said, ''though home always smelled a lot better than this.''

''Mmm. That was part of what tipped me off. Where there's piss, there's people.''

''What about cats and dogs?'' she said, following Joseph up the stairs.

''Seen any around here? Cats and dogs, in a situation like this, would leave their scat anywhere. But we haven't seen a single pile of it. Still, we're smelling it.'' She understood what he was saying and began to feel the edginess she always felt when there was a live enemy around. Even so, the narrow stairway felt almost cozy in contrast to the vast nightmare of Peder Holberg's warehouse and its looming and broken sculpture. And she preferred even the smell of human waste to the smell of death.

''Okay,'' Joseph said at the top of the stairs. ''This is where we heard the scream, right?'' She nodded. ''Here, grab the end of this tape—hold it right there, and let me go into the next room.''

They measured several rooms and hallways, and although Joseph wrote nothing down, she saw that he was carrying the figures in his head. He opened several closets throughout the house and peered into them, lifting his lantern high, examining every surface.

''Secret passageways, Mr. Hardy?'' she asked.

''You bet your magnifying glass.''

Finally, Joseph took out an instrument that Laika didn't recognize, and examined it at several places in the hall. ''Come on,'' he said, slipping it back into his pocket, ''let's see if the psychic Ms. Meyer has materialized on this plane.''

Outside, a small red Lamborghini was parked behind Clar-

ence Melton's limo, and a tall woman with flame-red hair
was standing next to Melton. She appeared to be in her mid-
forties and was wearing a short jacket of silver fur over a
pair of black slacks that Laika thought was at least two sizes
too tight.

"Nice fur," Joseph said quietly to Laika, as they walked
down the steps to the street. "But it's a wonder she isn't
tortured by the psychic screaming of the foxes. 'Do you still
hear them, Clarice?' "

"Knock it off, Dr. Lecter," Laika replied, "or it's back
in the hockey mask."

Melton introduced Elissa Meyer to Laika and Joseph, and
though she shook their hands, her attention seemed to be
elsewhere. Her head jerked here and there, as though she
heard sounds no one else did.

"Picking up some psychic transmissions, Ms. Meyer?"
Joseph asked, in a surprisingly sincere tone.

She nodded and answered in a low, thick voice. "This
entire street is teeming with them. I can't begin to describe
the intensity I feel here. I . . . I'm almost afraid to go inside."

"Don't be," Joseph said. "We've just been there, and it
seems pretty quiet tonight." He opened the trunk of the car
and took out the crowbar he had bought earlier, then gestured
with his hand like a *maître d'*. "Shall we?"

They went up the stairs of the fifth house, Joseph leading
the way with his lantern, Elissa Meyer behind him, then
Laika with her lantern, and Melton and Tweed bringing up
the rear. Meyer stopped dead in the foyer. "Oh, God," she
whispered. "Oh, dear God. . . ."

"The smell *is* pretty bad," Joseph said, "but you'll get
used to it."

The woman seemed oblivious to Joseph's sarcasm. "No
. . . there is great pain here . . . and madness . . . and death."

"Where, specifically?" Joseph asked. His words made
Laika angry, though she could not express why. This woman
was probably a charlatan—no more psychic than Laika or
anybody else, for that matter. But there was something about
this place, a sadness, a sense of tragedy, that went beyond

its appearance and the odor that pressed on them like a cloud. It made Joseph's easy mockery almost sacrilegious.

"It's everywhere here," Elissa Meyer said, her eyes shut tightly. "All around us."

"That's not too specific."

She forced her eyes open and looked at Joseph. "You doubt," she said, "and you mock. But I tell you, I am not wrong. There is real horror here."

"Spirits of the dead?" Joseph asked.

She did not move her head, but only said, "The dead themselves."

Joseph smiled. "Then let's go say hello to them. The cold spot—and where we heard a pretty severe scream—is upstairs."

He led the others up the stairs and down the hallway. "Mind the tiles, there," Joseph said, stepping around the hundreds of ceramic tiles that the workmen had apparently pulled up before they'd been chased out. "Feel a change in temperature, Ms. Meyer?"

"Oh, yes. . . ." she said. "Yes . . . it's here. Right near here. The locus of all the pain, the horror."

"So, this cold spot," Melton said, "is, in your opinion, a paranormal occurrence?"

"It undoubtedly is. Something dreadful happened here . . . or close by."

"Oh, I don't know if I'd call solar energy dreadful," Joseph said.

They all looked at him oddly. "Solar energy?" Melton said.

Joseph nodded. "Mr. Melton, have you ever noticed this cold spot on cloudy days?"

Melton thought for a moment. "I can't really say. I've only been in here a few times, and most of those were at night, so I don't know."

"Well, it was sunny today, wasn't it?" Joseph said. "And these windows," he continued, "are among the few in these houses that have been cleaned, I assume by the workmen who were working here to let a little light in. Now, Mr.

Melton, may I suggest that you feel one of those tiles?''

Melton frowned, but then walked back to the end of the
hall, with Laika lighting the way. He knelt next to the tiles
and picked one up, running his hand over its dusty surface,
both the smooth front and the rough back. He gave a small
sound of surprise. ''The back's warm,'' he said.

''Ceramic tile really soaks up the sunshine,'' Joseph said.
''I think you'll find that the tile at the other end of the hall
is only a few degrees cooler. That gets the morning sun,
while the tile you're holding gets the setting sun. All that tile
increases the temperature at the back end of the hall by four
degrees, at the front end by two. Our bodies sense the difference, but because we're more sensitive in a tense situation,
the difference in temperature seems far greater than it is. So
we wind up with a cold spot that's really no colder than the
rest of the building, but *is* colder than the ends of the halls
through which we've come, and into which we pass.''

''You may be right,'' Elissa Meyer said, before Laika even
had a chance to be impressed. ''But there is still something
here . . . or near here.'' She was qualifying, Laika thought—
covering her tracks.

''You're absolutely right,'' Joseph said. ''There *is* something here.'' And he took the crowbar and swung hard at the
wall.

The hooked end had no sooner gashed away the wallpaper
and plaster than a terrible sound filled Laika's head. It was
the scream of a few nights before, sawing through her brain
like an ax through a head of lettuce. She winced but kept
her eyes open, watching as Joseph smashed the crowbar at
the wall again and again. Plaster and laths showered to the
floor, and the sound stopped, cut off as it had been before.

''There are passages between the walls . . .'' Joseph said
between blows. ''Narrow enough for one person at a time
. . . to go through sideways . . . put in for voyeurs . . . to see
what was going on in the bedrooms. . . . The entrances were
covered up years ago . . . when it was converted to apartments. . . .''

As the hole Joseph made widened, the vile smell that hung

in the air grew stronger, so that all of them were wrinkling their noses in disgust. It was a combination of feces, piss, and death, as well as other things Laika couldn't and didn't want to name.

At last it was big enough for Joseph to slip through, and he did so, dropping the crowbar and taking a Maglite from his pocket. "Dr. Kelly?" he said to Laika. "Perhaps you'd like to accompany me to find our hidden friends?"

Laika nodded and stepped to the gaping entrance. "The rest of you, stay here," she said. "We'll be right back . . . I hope," she added under her breath, as she squeezed into the passageway.

Chapter 28

*I*t was like something out of a nightmare, like crawling through the guts of a creature of wood and nails. The stench was awful, and she saw all too clearly why. Piles of feces dotted the filthy floor, dark mounds in the dust that their passage stirred up. The dust swirled into her nose like a physical manifestation of the foul odor, and she tried hard not to gag.

Their lights jerked about constantly, so that there was never a chance to actually focus her vision on anything. Sight was a montage of splintered laths and cracked plaster, lit for split seconds by brilliant flashes of white.

They sidled, like crabs, sideways through the passageway, for there was no room to turn and walk. "Get your gun out," Laika said, extricating her own weapon.

"All right," Joseph replied, and paused just long enough to take out his pistol.

"Where the hell are we going?"

His voice came back in a series of grunts. He seemed to be having more trouble navigating the narrow space than the slimmer Laika. "About twenty more yards. It turns left up here. According to our measurements, there's about an eight-by-ten area unaccounted for. . . ."

The turn was ahead, as Joseph had promised. Laika flashed her light down the opposite passage and was chilled to see that it stretched away into darkness. It was like shining her flashlight into the night sky. She looked away from it and followed Joseph.

"Douse your light," she heard him whisper. She held her fingers over the lens, separating them just enough to let a needle of light shine through, and Joseph did the same. Ahead, she saw another light, dim and yellow, in which the dust particles performed their *danse macabre*.

Joseph shuffled ahead a few more steps and then turned another corner and vanished into the dim light. Laika side-stepped as quickly as she could, fumbling along, feeling as though she were moving through the thick broth of dream.

When her head cleared the corner, she saw the room and who and what were in it. The sight froze her for a moment, and then one of the creatures moved and the scream that had assaulted them before filled the room with its pain and fury.

She fumbled to bring up her gun, but before she could there was a sudden flash and a roar of gunfire that was deaf-ening in the small room. The woman, if that was what the thing truly was, fell back, and something dull and gray-white dropped from her arms.

It was a baby. It landed on the filthy floor with a terrible liquid sound, and the woman who had held it struck the far wall and slid down it into a sitting position. Her eyes and mouth hung open, and Laika heard a bubbling sound in her throat. She coughed a mass of blood and phlegm that clung like a huge leech to her chin, dripping down upon the bloody wound in her chest, and did not move again.

The baby lay where it had fallen. Joseph's bullet had passed through its soft body into the chest of the woman holding it and had nearly ripped its left arm from its shoul-der. But its sickly gray flesh told Laika that it had been dead a long time. It was so thin that it scarcely looked like a baby, reminding Laika heartlessly of nothing so much as a large, hairless rat. It was naked, and Laika saw that it had been a little girl.

She turned her eyes away from it, toward the only living stranger in the room. He was crouching in the corner, his eyes darting back and forth between Joseph and her, never looking at the dead woman or her child. His hair was a rat's nest of dirty brown curls, his face was gaunt, his frame spindly. Laika could tell that his mind was not right. He did not speak, but only looked at them, back and forth, back and forth, as though he were watching a tennis match.

Holding her gun, Laika crossed the floor, kicking aside the hatchet with which the woman had attacked Joseph, and knelt by the woman's side. There was no pulse. She looked up at Joseph. "Did you bring any cuffs?" she said.

He did not respond. Ignoring her questions and the wild-eyed glare of the man in the corner, Joseph was looking with horror at the dead baby on the floor.

"*Dr. Tompkins!*" Laika barked. "Look at me! Did you bring any cuffs?"

He nodded, reached into the pocket of his coat, and took out a pair of handcuffs. Laika stepped between Joseph and the sight of the dead and took the cuffs. "The baby was dead, Doctor. It was dead long before tonight."

She stepped over to the man in the corner and beckoned him to get up. He didn't move, and she could see both his hands, so she jerked him to his feet, spun him around, and slapped the cuffs on him. He made no protest.

They went out the way they had come in, the bound man between them, stepping sideways through the filth and the dust. Laika led the way. When they reached the opening, Laika pushed the man's head down and pulled him through. Joseph followed, still pale. The man looked at Clarence Melton, at Elissa Meyer, and at Tweed in the same uncomprehending way in which he had previously looked at Laika and Joseph.

"There are two more at the end of that passageway in a secret room," Laika said. "A woman and a baby, both dead."

"Dead!" Melton said.

"The woman attacked us with a hatchet—Dr. Tompkins had no choice. The baby's been dead for a while. You'll have to contact the police." Tweed quickly made a cell phone appear. He dialed it and spoke into it softly. "Tell them to come without lights or sirens," Laika cautioned the man. "There's no need."

"Was it the woman who . . . ?" Melton left the question unfinished.

"It was the woman who was screaming, yes," Laika said. "Probably from behind the wall. It must have made a pretty good sounding board, and she was loud to begin with." She looked at their captive. He seemed to have lost interest in them and was now staring down the hall, into the darkness at its end.

"They probably stole food from the workmen when they could," Laika went on, putting the pieces together. "And the so-called poltergeist activity was due to them. The areas between the walls are wide enough to walk through." She looked at Joseph. "Isn't that right, Dr. Tompkins?"

Joseph nodded, then spoke haltingly. "Yes . . . the place is honeycombed. The ceilings of many of the closets are false. That's probably how they got in and out of rooms without being seen." He seemed as though he was about to say something else, but simply waved a hand in the air.

"And that's all there were?" Melton asked. "Two of them?"

Joseph gave a slight shrug, and Laika answered for him. "There might be more. But if there are, they're behind the walls. Get a force of armed security people in here and track them down. You may find more, you may find nothing."

"But what about the lights?" Melton asked. "The lights in that room?"

Joseph sounded tired, but did his best to explain. "They're reflections, that's all. I checked the flight schedules at Kennedy, and there's an international flight that leaves at 11:53 and circles east of the city. Its takeoff light reflects in one of the new taller buildings across the park."

"The Bradoff building?" Melton asked.

Joseph nodded. "Its windows are angled slightly downward, so the light bounces across the park and hits the windows on the upper floor for just a few seconds as the plane banks. You can't tell from inside, because it's not bright enough to notice it shining through the window. But it's enough to be noticeable from across the street." He shook his head sadly. "There are no ghosts here, Mr. Melton." Then he looked at Elissa Meyer and gave a weak smile. "There are no ghosts here, Ms. Meyer."

She smiled back at him. It was sad, and Laika thought it seemed sincere. "You are wrong, Dr. Tompkins. These poor people might have caused the recent disruptions, but there is still something here." Then her smile faded, and her look was less kindly. "And it is *stronger* now. It has the strength of those who have just died."

The look on Joseph's face was unmistakably guilt—*undeserved* guilt, Laika thought. But she had never fired a bullet through a baby, even a dead one. What Joseph must have initially felt when he thought he had killed a child must have been unbearable. It would take some time for that shock to wear off.

"Well, I hope you're successful in exorcising it for Mr. Melton," Laika said, with venom in her voice. "We've done everything *humanly* possible to show what was wrong with this place. Now it's your turn to sweep out the invisible. Doctor?"

She took Joseph's arm and pushed him gently toward the stairs. Then she grasped the cuffed man and led him in the same direction.

By the time they reached the sidewalk, a police car was there. Laika and Joseph turned their prisoner over, gave the officers in charge the necessary information, and showed the credentials that would ensure they would never be questioned on the matter again.

They waited while the officers called in their IDs. When they were cleared, they got back into their car without saying good-bye to Melton and drove toward the West Side, Laika at the wheel.

"You didn't kill the kid," Laika said into the silence. "And you had to kill the woman. You didn't have any choice."

"I know."

"Joseph?" she said after another minute. When she glanced at him, his face was lit only fleetingly by the street lights they passed. In the quick seconds of illumination it looked pale and sickly.

"Yes?"

"I hope I'm not out of line here, but have you ever terminated anyone before?"

He didn't answer right away, and she was ready to rephrase the question when he said, "Yes," softly.

She didn't know whether to believe him or not. She could log in and check his files. His kills would be in there.

But then she thought, why bother? It wouldn't change anything. And maybe if he hadn't before, it was for the best now. She had killed, and she knew Tony had more terminations on his conscience than any other five people she knew in the Company. So wasn't it time that Joseph Stein, far older than either of them, joined the club?

The thought made her angry at herself. Killing wasn't the measure of a person; she knew that well enough. Maybe she just wanted Joseph to be a killer so that the terminations she had carried out wouldn't seem so special. There were nights when some of them weighed more heavily on her than others. She had never killed except in self-preservation, but she had known a few of the dead, and even known the people some of them had loved. Thinking about them was what was hard.

She didn't say anything about those thoughts to Joseph. If he had killed, he already knew. If not, nothing she could say would make him feel any better about it. You had to deal with dealing death yourself. If you did it, you lay down with it in the nighttime, and you were alone with it. That was how it worked.

When you died, you died alone, no matter how many died with you. And when you killed, you killed alone, no matter who else was by your side. And if you didn't know that, you learned soon enough.

And once you learned, you could forget. She buried the dead woman and the dead baby deep down in her mind, with all the other dead, and began to think about Peder Holberg and his mad, final work of art.

Chapter 29

*T*he following day, Richard Skye was speaking on the telephone to Mr. Stanley. The connection was encrypted and unbreakable.

"Melton's houses were a negative," Skye was saying. "Everything had a perfectly rational explanation. The operative Stein was forced to kill a woman who attacked him, but we've already glossed it. They're clean as a whistle. . . . Yes, most of the tabloids had something on it. Melton's happy, and we should be happy, since there's no mention of the team in the papers. . . . The Meyer woman? No, she won't say anything. I've had someone . . . talk to her."

Skye sat back and listened, then spoke again. "It was disappointing in that regard, of course. But this Holberg situation still looks promising. . . . Yes, the other man, Holberg's queer lover, is working on it now. Feverishly, it seems . . . I don't know, but I would expect within a few weeks. . . . Yes, I most certainly will. . . . Good-bye, sir."

Skye hung up the phone and sat back in his chair. He looked at the closed door of his office suspiciously, but then smiled. No one was listening. There were no bugs in this room. Jenkins and Bailey went over it twice a week, and Skye secured his own phone lines himself. He knew the wires and the guts of this place. He should, after twenty years in it.

He tried to continue smiling at the thought, but his smile twisted into a sneer. In another year, if he played it all right, and found the captive and turned him over to Mr. Stanley, his life would finally begin.

Aldrich Ames and Harold Nicholson were pikers next to what Skye was capable of attaining. And best of all, he was selling information not to his country's enemies, but to Mr. Stanley, who was considered one of America's greatest patriots. That made a difference to Richard Skye. He was not a traitor, he was an entrepreneur.

And a good entrepreneur had to know when to make sacrifices. His pawns were moving on the board, and when they had the king in position, he would bring in his knights, regardless of what happened to the three operatives.

Pawns were, after all, expendable.

Although Laika Harris, Joseph Stein, and Anthony Luciano didn't know that they were considered pawns by Richard Skye, during the next few days they certainly felt like it. Sweatshirts and jeans seemed to be their uniform as they helped Adam Guaraldi reconstruct Peder Holberg's massive and clandestine work.

They had set up shop in the Bronx warehouse, complete with computers and cots for occasional naps. Guaraldi worked nearly around the clock, pausing only for quick catnaps of less than an hour. Laika estimated the man slept only four hours per day.

The three operatives worked two eight-hour, staggered shifts a day. Laika and Joseph might start, then Laika would go back to the city and sleep, while Joseph and Tony took the next shift. Then Laika would return, letting Joseph go sleep, and he would return to let Tony get his break.

Every week or so the pace would catch up with Guaraldi and he would return to the apartment he had shared with Holberg and sleep for twelve hours straight. At these times he seemed almost bitter about the inability of his body to keep up with the tireless pace he set himself.

The operatives helped him in any way they could and told him to consider them always at his service. Although he worked alone much of the time, particularly when dealing with the enigmatic plans, at other times he required their help, fitting large pipes and welding them into place, carrying tanks and hoses up and down ladders, moving piles of toppled iron to its new launching site.

The great structure had begun to be resurrected slowly, but with each passing day it seemed to Laika to grow exponentially, faster and faster, looking one day like some madman's idea of a rollercoaster, and the next like the skeleton of a building found only in nightmare. On another, it appeared to Laika as a helter-skelter mess of entrails, and on another as a pile of thin hands with long, branching fingers. Sometimes it seemed terrible, at other times, laughable. But it never stopped changing, shifting, growing.

She uneasily noticed several times how the lights on the ceiling above cast strange shadows of the sculpture's evolving contours onto the floor. At times it seemed to her that she could almost make out symbols or runes on the dusty boards. Sometimes she could almost see faces, and then she would quickly look away.

The warehouse, despite Laika's efforts to keep the atmosphere light, continued to be oppressive, becoming more so as the once fallen iron pipes took up more and more of the space as Holberg's work continued to rise. Guaraldi seldom joined in the conversation, but on one of his infrequent breaks, Laika got him talking about Holberg's work in general.

"Peder believed in beauty," Guaraldi said, and Laika grimly noted that now he used the past tense. "But he saw reality. He saw life as it was, often ugly and raw. So he tried to see beauty in those things, too, tried to show that to others in his work. It may be too simplistic, and I doubt if he would have put it quite like that, but I think that's what his art was about." Guaraldi's gaze went to the insistent presence of the sculpture. "But I look, and I look, and I look again, and the beauty . . . I can't find it here, not in this."

Then he went back to his work, sadly, but with purpose.

As the weeks passed and the sculpture grew, Laika started to see a pattern in it, but one that she could not define, like sentences in some unknown language, seen clearly, but impossible to decipher. The more it grew, the stronger grew the idea within her that somehow she *knew* this thing, that it spoke to her and showed her something with which she was greatly familiar—indeed, almost intimate. It was like trying to remember the name of a person you once knew very well, and whose face you can clearly see, but whose name is always just out of memory's reach. It was teasing and frustrating and challenging at once.

She was not the only one of the three to whom this sensation came. Late one night, when she was working the shift with Tony, he stopped dead, stared at the thing, and said to her, "Goddamn it, I *know* this thing. There's just something about it. . . ."

"You think you've seen it before?" Laika asked.

He shook his head slowly and thoughtfully. "I don't know, but I've seen what it *means*." Then he snorted. "That doesn't make much sense, does it?"

It did, more than he knew. She hadn't heard a similar conviction from Joseph, probably because she hadn't heard much of *anything* from Joseph in the past few weeks. The day after the incident in the townhouse, she had congratulated him on his acumen, but he had not accepted it gracefully. "It was simple," he said vacantly. "The comparisons to Borley made me think of the train. That's how I figured out the lights."

"What train?" she asked.

"There were lights in Borley Rectory, too," he said, "and no one knew where they came from, either. It turned out they were the reflections of the headlight of a train that wasn't readily visible from inside the room, and not at all from down on the ground. That's why they appeared at about the same time every night."

One evening they were alone together in the warehouse, while Guaraldi was taking a catnap on a cot in the small anteroom. She took the opportunity to ask Joseph if he was troubled by what had happened in the house.

"By the shooting?" he replied, and she was glad to see

he didn't pretend not to know what she meant. "A little, at first, but not anymore."

"Did you think you hit the child?" she asked.

"I *knew* I hit the child. What I thought was that I killed it. Two at one blow. That wasn't the case, and I was glad. But still, I killed the woman."

"You didn't have a choice."

Joseph kept his eyes fixed on his monitor screen. "I shouldn't have had to do that. We're trained to deal with situations like that without gunfire."

"No, Joseph. It was the only way—the closeness of the room, she was already on top of you . . . you did the right thing." He didn't respond, and she added, "Don't worry about it."

But he did. Joseph Stein, in his many years in the Central Intelligence Agency, several of which were spent in field operations, had never been forced to kill an enemy before. He had incapacitated several, and had even shot an agent in Bucharest in the right lung, but the man had survived.

This madwoman in the house had not survived. Joseph's bullet, after passing through the body of her dead child, had entered her heart and killed her almost immediately. As he had told Laika, for a long and terrible moment he'd thought he had killed the baby as well. There had come upon him a clutching and writhing sickness that would have left him vulnerable to anything that the man in the corner might have wanted to do. It had not been until Laika had spoken sharply to him that he'd regained his senses and realized that he had not killed the child, just the mother.

Just the mother. Just a poor insane woman doing what any animal would have done, trying to defend what she thought of as her home and her child, even though the baby was dead. And he had been so cavalier about it all, tracking the mysterious squatters down through the hidden passageways, just like the goddamned Hardy Boys, with a plucky grin on his face, right up until the second that the ugly truth stared him in the face out of its empty, hollow eyes.

And came at him with an ax, Laika might have added. But Joseph thought that Laika, for all her belief in things he had long ago discarded, was more of a pragmatist when it came to humanity.

Humanity was all Joseph had left to believe in, and though he knew it was a foolish, liberal, outmoded concept, he sought the potential for good in most people, not the evil, and he was more ready to forgive that evil. Since there was no afterlife, this life was only that much more precious, for friend and enemy alike. It was all any of us had. And it was all that Katherine Lambden had had, and he had taken it away.

In his spare time in the warehouse, Joseph had found out much about Katherine Lambden. His passwords gave him access to police and medical records, the New York City Department of Welfare, and a multitude of other agencies through which Katherine Lambden's brief and tragic life had wound. The more he learned about her, the more he wanted to know, and slowly her life spread itself before him in every appalling detail.

She was twenty-eight when she died. As a girl, she had lived in Brooklyn, and she had been impregnated by her father when she was fourteen. An abortion followed. She dropped out of high school shortly thereafter and became a prostitute to support a crack habit. She lived in that manner for several years, until she began to display signs of mental illness during her frequent arrests.

She then spent two years in a public mental institution and released herself at the end of that time, turning again to prostitution, and was arrested several times in Central Park, where she apparently turned tricks under the shelter of bushes. Her last arrest had been for vagrancy, a year and a half before. The court transcripts stated that she showed signs of mental illness, but she had served her six weeks in prison. After her release, she disappeared not to be seen again by the officialdom of New York City until she was discovered with a man, still unidentified, in Clarence Melton's townhouse.

Joseph thought that he could fill in the blanks. She linked up with this loser, probably as crazy as she was, but still streetwise enough to ensconce the two of them in a deserted and crumbling block of houses and hide like rats there, stealing food out of garbage cans and crapping in the walls, both of them growing crazy as bedbugs if they weren't already.

But even crazy people had sex, and then the baby came along. The man probably helped her deliver it, but it couldn't have lived long. The medical report that Joseph downloaded estimated the baby's age at death as approximately two weeks old. Joseph was surprised it had lasted even that long.

He had had plenty of time to think about Katherine Lambden and what her last few weeks must have been like, having enough mother love to drag around a dying and then dead baby, but not enough mental faculties left to keep it alive, or enough caloric intake to ensure a supply of breast milk for her new child. The medical report had established that pitiful detail as well.

Then, when an interloper had come into their inner sanctum, invaded what passed for their hearth and home with crowbars and loud voices, she had reacted as any mother would, and he had killed her for it. He felt guilty over that, and that guilt would be a long time leaving him, if it ever did.

Now, at last, there was a dead end. He could learn no more about Katherine Lambden, and he sat back from the computer, looking at the message, "No further files," and sighed.

"What is it?" Laika asked, looking over his shoulder at the screen.

"Nothing," Joseph said, then turned and smiled at her. "Just trying to track down an old . . . friend."

"Girlfriend?" Laika asked.

"Not really. It never quite went that far." He clicked on the mouse, and the words on the screen vanished.

Laika walked away from Joseph and his computer and turned her attention back to the sculpture. Adam Guaraldi was high on one of the portable stairways, soldering several small pieces of iron into place with the acetylene torch. He had been working nonstop for the past eighteen hours, and prior to that had had only a half-hour nap.

It had been five weeks since the reconstruction had begun, and there was hardly any iron remaining on the floor. It would not be long now, she thought, if Guaraldi was able to hold out.

Laika walked slowly down the length of the room, her eyes, as they nearly always were, on the mighty shape rising before her. She heard Guaraldi coughing and looked up at him high above, grasping the rail of the stairs as coughs shook his body. With all the dust and the rust particles in the air, Laika thought it was a wonder they all weren't in some lung ward by now. The spasms passed, and Guaraldi resumed his work.

Laika stopped at the end, where the sheets of paper that had been Peder Holberg's plans were piled. She noticed that only one sheet was on the right-hand pile. The others were all facedown next to it. Could Guaraldi be that close to completion?

She almost barked a cold laugh. And then what? she thought. Figure out what the hell this hunk of cold, rusted metal was all about—come up with an explanation of how it was involved in Peder Holberg's disappearance, a logical, rational explanation that would make Skye happy.

She let her fancy wander to ridiculous extremes. Maybe the thing was a spaceship, and all it needed was some pixie dust to make it fly. Maybe Skye could provide that. Or maybe Peder Holberg had been reading too many Calvin and Hobbes books and had made a transmogrifier. Maybe they could lure Skye into the middle and he might become a human being. Or it could be a Star Trek transporter, a little bit bigger than Scotty was used to, and it just transported Holberg to another planet.

She could almost hear Skye demand loudly, "What planet?"

"Uranus," she whispered aloud, holding the A a beat.

Then she chuckled to herself. This was one hell of a way for an agent of the Central Intelligence Agency to be acting. She was working too long, that was it. Too many damned hours in this warehouse, surrounded by this nightmare of a sculpture. It was enough to make anybody nuts.

She turned around and looked at the goddamned thing, towering above her and nearly surrounding her where she stood. At that moment, it looked like some monstrous city of iron, and she imagined futuristic monorails whining along under the horizontal iron rods. She followed the route of one such imaginary train, balancing on top of its round iron rail as it whirled across and spiraled down, down to nearly touch the dusty wooden floor before turning upward again and shooting off in a different direction.

But Laika's gaze did not follow her imaginary train upward. Instead, she kept looking at the floor near the end of the warehouse. There was something beneath the dust that she had not previously noticed. It was just at the edge of the sculpture, a pattern on the boards.

She put out a foot to wipe the dust away, but then thought better of it and went back to the anteroom for a broom. Though Guaraldi did not look down at her from his perch, Joseph looked up from the monitor. He frowned as he saw the seriousness of her mien. "What is it?" he asked, getting up.

"I don't know," she said. "Something on the floor."

They walked back to the far end of the sculpture, and Laika took a few swipes at the wood with the broom, sweeping away the dust and debris from a square-foot area. What was revealed was a letter nearly a foot long, scratched into the floor.

"N," Laika said.

"Or Z," Joseph suggested. "Depending on from where you look. Or it could be something completely different. A symbol, perhaps."

Laika looked at the letter again, then at the structure that lay before them. A quick movement caught her eye, and when she looked at where Guaraldi was working, she saw him slipping down the first few steps at the top of the metal staircase.

Guaraldi tried desperately to grasp the handrail, but failed, and then he was rolling underneath the rail and out into space, falling from a height of thirty feet.

His tiny cry was swallowed up in the immensity of the room.

Chapter 30

Adam Guaraldi did not land directly on the floor. If he had, he might have lived. Instead, his body struck a thick iron bar six feet off the floor, and Laika heard the sharp, sickening sound of his back breaking.

Guaraldi hung there for a moment across the bar, as if uncertain which side to fall over. Then his body slid head downward as limply as a fried egg sliding off the edge of a plate, and he landed roughly on the wooden floor.

Laika and Joseph had started to move the instant they saw Guaraldi begin to fall, but could do nothing to arrest his flight. When they reached his side, Laika was amazed to see that he was actually laughing, despite his pain, in small bursts as sharp as the shards of bone that must have been prodding his flesh. Blood trickled from his mouth and nose, dabbling his chin and upper lip.

"Slipped . . . damnit . . . just goddam *slipped* . . . but I finished. . . ." Guaraldi said weakly. "Jesus . . . Jesus . . . got the last piece in . . . the *last* goddamn . . ."

His voice trailed away as his final breath hissed softly from his throat. His eyes remained open, looking upward at the iron monstrosity that he had re-created and that, according to his eyes, had killed him.

As she checked for a pulse and found none, Laika wondered if his open eyes saw any answers there. She wondered if he saw Peder Holberg.

"Joseph," she said, a thickness in her throat, "check the

ladder . . . see if you can tell what happened."

Joseph walked almost dazedly to the metal stairway while Laika grabbed a cell phone from one of the desks and dialed the number that would bring removal experts from the Company. A party on the other end answered, and Laika spoke only a few words and snapped the phone shut. She looked up at where Joseph stood, high above, his hands clinging with white knuckles to the railings.

"There's a wet spot," he said dully, and so softly that she could barely hear him. She saw his fingers touch one of the steps, saw it move to his mouth. "Salt," he said. "He slipped on his own sweat . . . just slipped." He shook his head and came slowly and carefully down the ladder.

"They'll be here in a few minutes," she said, as Joseph knelt next to Guaraldi's body, looking at the man as though he couldn't believe he was dead.

"Who?"

"The clean-up crew. They'll take him away, make it look like the accident happened somewhere else."

Joseph looked up at her. "Cover it up."

"We're in the business of cover-ups. We can't have any attention directed at this place. Not now, not ever."

Joseph slowly nodded and stood up, his eyes still on Adam Guaraldi's twisted corpse.

Laika then called Tony in the city. He must have been sleeping, for his "Hello" sounded slurred. "Tony, it's Laika. Good news and bad news. The good news is that the sculpture is finished. But Guaraldi . . . he had an accident. He's dead."

"What . . . *what?* Jesus! What happened?"

She told him, and he said that he'd drive right over. He sounded far more upset than Laika had thought he would. She had assumed that Tony was used to death, but he had sounded genuinely shocked at the news about Guaraldi.

The crew arrived less than ten minutes after Laika had called them. It always surprised her how quickly the Company got the necessary people where they needed to be. In a way, it was nice to think that she and her colleagues were being watched over so carefully, yet in another way it disquieted her.

She talked to the person in charge, told him what had happened, and was assured that everything would be taken care of. Then she and Joseph watched the unmarked van drive away with Adam Guaraldi's body, leaving them alone in the night with the completed statue.

Just as they were about to walk back inside, a car drove into the lot and Tony Luciano hopped out. His face was grim, and his first words were, "Was that the crew just left?" Laika nodded. "Okay. Let's see the thing."

He didn't ask about Guaraldi and didn't act as though he wanted to be told anything, either.

They went inside and walked around the sculpture, and Laika showed Tony the letter scratched into the floor. "N," he said. "North?"

Laika had been thinking the same thing. "It's a map?"

Joseph didn't respond at first, but then grabbed the broom and started to sweep away thin layers of dust and rust to reveal the hardwood underneath. "If it is, maybe there are other markings." He moved around the sculpture in a counterclockwise direction, to the west, if the N did indeed indicate the north.

There was only one broom, so they took turns sweeping, stepping over the rods and moving in toward the center of the piece, then out again, trying to expose every square inch of the wooden floor before they had to sweep the dust back over it again. They found a number of marks, but on closer investigation they saw that they were probably random markings made in the floor over the period of years in which the place had functioned as a warehouse.

But several yards from where they had started, at the north-northeast area of the sculpture, Laika swept away the dust to expose not one, but several letters. There was a freshly carved X, and four other letters near it: BHLM.

"X marks the spot," said Joseph.

Tony knelt and ran a finger along the grooves of the dugout letter. "You think X is where we'll find Holberg?"

"Maybe."

"Or," said Laika, "X as in, 'You are here.' " She looked up from the letters at the towering mass of iron and frowned for a moment. Then her face grew totally blank as the truth came to her all at once. "Oh, my God," she whispered. "It *is* a map. It's New York. . . ."

She ran along the side then, looking at it. "Look at the shape, the length of it. And here. . . ." She ran back to the X. "See the piece going across there?" She pointed ten feet above at an arching rod of iron. "It's the Third Avenue bridge. And the X is *here*. We're *on* the X! The Bronx is here, near the top—northeast. This rod over here must be the Willis Avenue Bridge, and look—the X is right beneath the Third Avenue pipe. That's got to be the warehouse we're in. This thing is a map of New York City!"

Tony and Joseph looked at the work with such awe and recognition on their faces that Laika knew they agreed with her theory. "But then," Joseph said slowly, "what's BHLM? The name of a demon or something? Like the letters YHWH represent the Hebrew god Yahweh?"

Tony looked down at the letters and frowned as if concentrating. Then he gave a weak laugh. "You know the old maps?" he said. "The ones where they hadn't sailed any further and didn't know what the hell was ahead? Remember what they wrote on the edges? I think Holberg is trying to tell us something."

Laika nodded. "BHLM—'Beyond here lie monsters,' " she quoted.

"Right," Tony said. "Beyond here . . ." He gestured expansively to the huge warehouse in which they stood. ". . . Lie monsters."

Chapter 31

"All right," Joseph said, always the skeptic. "It *looks* similar, but that could be coincidental."

"Coincidental, my ass," Tony countered. "Look at it— Jesus, I *knew* there was something familiar about it. For *weeks* I've been thinking that, and now . . . New York," he finished quietly.

"Yeah, it's a hell of a town," Joseph said. " 'The Bronx is up and the Battery's down,' but maybe you're right. Actually, I think you are, but I want more than just a few matchups and gut reactions to make sure."

"What's your suggestion?" Laika asked, knowing that his reluctance to accept the theory immediately was prudent.

Joseph started to walk around the sculpture as if stalking it. "Let's make a computerized schematic of this thing. Three dimensions, as detailed as possible. It should take a couple of days. Then we'll lay it down over a computerized map of the city, see how well it really matches."

"That puts us off Holberg's track even longer," Tony said.

Joseph turned a jaundiced eye on him. "Think about it. If it *is* a map of the city, it probably *leads* somewhere. But how can you read *that?*" he said, pointing to the iron chaos that surrounded them, "and if you *could*, how the hell can we follow it or stick it in your pocket without doing what I just suggested?"

"Joseph's right, Tony. We have to have an overlay." She

turned to Joseph. "How do you want to start?"

"Now we can use the plans—we couldn't before, but Guaraldi filled them in well as he went—and if we're uncertain about anything, we always have the sculpture to refer to."

"We have the software we need?" Laika asked.

"There's imaging software on all the machines," Tony said.

"And I can download the New York maps once we have our schematic done," Joseph said.

"Anybody want to go out and get a decent dinner first?" Laika said, even though she knew what their answer would be. "It's the first chance we've had in weeks."

Tony and Joseph looked at each other, and then at her. Their faces told the story. "I'm not hungry," Tony said. "Let's get working."

It took four days to create the computerized schematic of the sculpture. When it was completed, they could manipulate it in any way and view it from any angle. It looked, Laika thought, like an early wire-frame computer game, but infinitely more complex.

Joseph downloaded an extremely detailed map of New York City from Langley and spent another hour juggling the mouse, fiddling with coordinates, and tweaking the program's capabilities until he pronounced it ready to view. "It may slip off the grid every now and then," he said, "so we might have to readjust it, but it's a near-perfect match. You were right, Laika."

It was uncanny, she thought. The smallest they could get the scale was to have one crosstown block equal an inch on the screen. "It goes beneath the street in some places, doesn't it?" she asked.

"Yeah. But all I could get on the map is current subway tunnels. Those that aren't used anymore, or basements, or any other tunnels, aren't shown. It only does that in a few places, though."

They examined it for several hours, jotting down notes of

possible locations where the tubes and pipes joined. Some were street crossings, while others seemed more random, but could have been small alleys or walkways not shown even on so detailed a map.

The longer they worked with the schematic, the more convinced Laika became that Holberg had indicated no ultimate destination, no actual X-marks-the-spot to which they could immediately proceed. Tony agreed.

"It's not much of a help to tell us where to go specifically," he said, "if that was what it was supposed to do. It's pretty clear that it tells us where *not* to go—wherever there are no pipes, I guess."

"Has the thought occurred to either of you," Joseph said dryly, "because I confess it has to me, that this thing isn't telling us to go anywhere at all? That maybe it's just a map of New York that Holberg made the way somebody else would spend months making a ship in a bottle?"

"People don't generally go into fugue states when they make ships in bottles," Laika said. "And there are a few other reasons against that argument. Holberg was obsessed with this place, and that obsession had something to do with violence, because otherwise, why had he made a bomb? When there are *two* secrets in your life—this sculpture and a bomb in the workroom—I think there's bound to be some connection, don't you?"

Tony nodded. "Damn right."

"She wasn't asking you," Joseph said.

"Besides," Laika went on, "this thing is a simulacrum of the city that's perfectly to scale. The pipes match up with streets, where it's high, there are buildings—"

"There are buildings everywhere in the city," Joseph said. "That's why it's a city."

"All I'm saying is that this thing is too perfect to be . . ." She knew what she was about to say and bit it back, but Joseph finished it for her.

"Natural? Too perfect to be natural? Which implies that there is something *unnatural* about this sculpture . . . dare I say, even paranormal? What we can't immediately explain *naturally* has to be the result of some strange powers, right? I mean, we couldn't assume that Peder Holberg—who was, after all, an artist—might have those talents of perspective and depth and measurement and spatial relationships that would allow him, given several months, to create something like this. It's much easier to assume that he was affected by a strange curse or an alien or dead Elvis, right?''

"Wrong," Laika said coldly. "All I'm saying is that this thing has a purpose. It wasn't a . . . a folly of some sort to kill time. You don't risk your life coming up to this neighborhood for something like that . . . and that's something else I have to wonder about."

"What?" Joseph said, with more than a trace of scorn.

"How *did* he get up here and stay up here unharmed? Why wasn't he hassled, beaten up, even killed?"

"It's like he was protected," said Tony.

"Angels now?" Joseph asked.

"I don't know, Joseph, and there's something else I don't know. Have we found any other map of New York City in Peder Holberg's possession?" Tony didn't wait for an answer. "No, we haven't. So even if he was this super-duper genius that you suggest, how did he achieve this kind of accuracy without any guide at all?"

"So he had a *spirit* guide?" said Joseph. "Look, I'm just trying to be logic's advocate, since I don't believe in the devil, either. I don't go along with *any* supernatural theory, but I can almost agree with you that Holberg might have been trying to tell us—or somebody—something with this monstrosity. The question is *what.*"

"And *who,*" Laika said. "We can be sure he didn't build it to show three CIA operatives where to find his vanished body."

"Yeah," said Tony, "who the hell *was* it for? Only people he hung around with were Adam and the goths. Could it have been for them?"

"Maybe," said Joseph. "Remember, he stopped disappearing once he broke with them. Could be that this was his gift to them."

"Or," said Laika, "his offering to whoever it was they worshiped."

"The Holy One," said Tony. "Or maybe Cthulhu."

Joseph snorted. "Oh, yeah, right, the fictional octopus god. How *could* I have forgotten? Well, whatever the reason for it, this *is* a map. And the only way we're going to find out if it leads anywhere is to follow it somehow."

"Where do we start?" Tony asked.

"Why not start where Holberg possibly intended us to?" said Laika. "We're at X, and everything else is beyond here." She smiled. "Including the monsters. Let's just follow the pipe across the Third Avenue bridge and see where it takes us. Can we chart a path of sorts on the computer?"

Joseph nodded and turned back to the screen. "Problem is, there's no telling which way to go at the junction of the pipes, which are the junctions of streets, for the most part."

"Well," said Laika, "maybe we could examine the anomalies, the places where the rods meet but there are no corresponding streets on the map. Those could be certain buildings or locations where Holberg thinks there's something important."

"Or where he just measured wrong," Joseph said.

"Possibly. But we won't know until we go there." Laika gestured to a place on the structure where an iron rod passed into the shattered floor and then up again. "And we'll see what's beneath the city, too."

"Wonder what we'll find," Tony said, looking at the darkness into which the iron sank. "Maybe Holberg?"

"Or his body," Laika said.

"Or a hole in the ground, or nothing," Joseph added. "I'd just like to find out how the hell he got out of that room."

"Me too," said Laika. "And so would Skye."

"Skye, you sonofabitch," Quentin McIntyre muttered as he went over the latest report intercepted from the CIA. It had originally been sent by Richard Skye to his superiors and had been filed weeks before the previous report McIntyre had read on Anthony Luciano's assignment to Azerbaijan.

This current but older interception explained the reason for Luciano's activities in Scotland.

There were two other agents involved as well, Joseph Stein and Laika Harris. McIntyre had copies of their dossiers in front of him, too, another welcome example of Alan Phillips's anticipation of McIntyre's needs. McIntyre had heard of Stein, but not of Harris.

After he read their dossiers, he concluded that a team of the three would be most formidable. Skye's memo stated that the three had performed the Scottish exposure of Helmut Kristal as an experimental preface to a mission designed to investigate government-controlled psychics in Eastern Europe. All three were part of the same team but had been assigned to different locales in the region.

McIntyre didn't believe a word of it. This was a cover if McIntyre had ever seen one. It said nothing about Luciano's presence in New York State, and McIntyre would have been willing to bet that the unidentifiable woman in the *Inner Eye* photo was Laika Harris.

McIntyre had wasted no time in sending a team of his own to Plattsburgh, but by the time they got there, the three "doctors" from the "Division of Special Investigations," whatever the hell that was supposed to be, were long gone. McIntyre's people had gotten descriptions of the three from the doctors who had worked with them, and he saw this morning that they matched perfectly the physicals on Harris, Luciano, and Stein's dossiers.

The evidence was overwhelming that these three were in the country on a black-ops mission orchestrated by Skye. Maybe it had something to do with paranormal occurrences, and maybe it didn't. Maybe that whole psychic crap was just a cover for something else.

Unfortunately, the search in New York hadn't landed a thing. No one reported spotting Tony Luciano, or, after Phillips sent out the descriptions, his two companions. But that didn't mean they weren't out there somewhere. New York was a big city.

Still, it wasn't worth putting a whole shitload of agents on this thing. There were already enough crimes to keep every goddamned FBI agent in the country working round the clock, so it didn't make much sense to bust anybody's balls tracking down a trio of rogue spooks, especially since the only thing they had done so far was investigate what might have been a mass murder or a Jim Jones–style mass suicide. After all, it wasn't like Luciano, Harris, and Stein were the killers, if murder was indeed involved.

Still, with Richard Skye at the helm, you never knew what might happen next. McIntyre's agents wouldn't dedicate their lives to the search, but they sure as hell would keep their eyes open.

And McIntyre would keep reading the newspapers.

Chapter 32

It took another long day to chart what the operatives considered to be anomalies on Peder Holberg's bizarre map of
New York City, but when they left that evening, they had a
list of places they'd investigate. Some seemed obvious, since
certain of the buildings were marked on the map, but there
were other locations at which they had no idea of what they
might find.

By the time they got back to Manhattan, it was 9 o'clock,
and they had steaks and beer at a small tavern, where they
relaxed and talked about their private interests. Joseph
brought up fantasy and horror movies, and mentioned *Carnival of Souls*, which Tony had seen, but which Laika had
never heard of.

"I've watched it several times," said Joseph. "Very
weird. Like a nightmare."

"Could we get a copy and watch it?" Laika asked, looking eagerly from one to the other and back again. The apartment was equipped with a VCR.

After dinner, they stopped at a Tower video store where
Laika found the movie for $14.99. Back at the apartment,
they made microwave popcorn, opened three more beers, and
sat on the couch and watched *Carnival of Souls*.

Joseph and Tony had been right: the film *was* scary, despite its obvious low budget and less-than-stellar acting. It
had the ambience of a bad dream, and at the end, when Laika

found out the reason why, she felt slightly sick, but attributed it to the beer and popcorn.

"You guys were on the money," she said. "That was weird, all right."

"The weirdest," said Tony. "There's something that's almost too real about it. Brrr. . . ." He pretended to shake it off. "I'm gonna have to watch something else to get my mind off it. Anybody want to see who's on Letterman?"

But Joseph begged off, saying he was tired. Laika wondered if it wasn't something more than that, if, despite the anticipation of tomorrow's hunt, he was still bearing the guilt of the woman's death in the townhouse. He had seemed all right at the tavern, but when they'd started watching the movie, a change had come over him. He hadn't eaten any popcorn, nor had he drunk more than a sip of his beer. Now he went directly to the bedroom he shared with Tony and closed the door.

Laika said good night to Tony and went down the hall to her room, where she undressed, slipped into a robe, and went to take the first long, relaxing bath she'd had in weeks. After she'd slipped into the bubbles that came to nearly the top of the tub, she put on her portable headset and started to listen to the second disc of Sir Thomas Beecham's recording of Puccini's *La Bohème*, her favorite performance, the one with Bjoerling and Merrill and de los Angeles. She could never listen to the fourth act's "*Ah, Mimi, tu piu non torni*" without chuckling at Beecham's answer as to why he wanted to record Bjoerling and Merrill's duet again when the first take was perfect: "Because I simply *love* to hear those boys sing it!" So did Laika, and she hit the repeat button and listened again.

Joseph lay alone in the darkness. He had taken off most of his clothes, but by the time he got down to his underwear and T-shirt, a heavy lassitude had come over him so that he lay down on top of the single bed's blankets and let his head drop down onto the pillow. He was afraid he would dream. He wished he had not viewed the movie they'd just seen.

He had forgotten how haunting it was, how the dead man's blackened eyes looked like the deep-set eyes of the woman he'd killed. He had dreamed about her before and several times had awakened sweating on the cot in the warehouse anteroom.

Now he was afraid she'd fill his dreams again, running at him with that hatchet raised over her head, holding something else that he could not identify until it was too late, until his pistol had fired, splitting the poor little creature she held, then killing her, the lead dragging the child's death into the mother's body.

Oh, Christ, he wished he could just stop thinking about it. For a while tonight, he had. The camaraderie of his colleagues, the thought of getting out of that damned filthy, dusty warehouse and onto the streets tomorrow, the good food and drink had made him feel almost human again. And then they had watched that movie.

He rolled over, feeling half sick, and buried his face in the pillow. A few minutes later, he thought he was asleep.

He thought he was asleep because he thought he was dreaming. When he became conscious of an existence beyond the waking world, Joseph felt terrified, but when he found that he was not shuffling sideways through the walls of Clarence Melton's townhouse, the terror faded, replaced by awe.

Joseph found himself high in the air. There was a blue-black sky above and to either side of him. Below there was nothing—an inky, palpable blackness into which, if he fell, he knew he would vanish completely, and cease to exist. A black hole, a dark star, death, nothingness.

He was standing on a dark red bridge, the color of rust or dried blood. It was rounded, and there was nothing to keep him from falling off to either side except his balance. As he shuffled forward like a tightrope walker, afraid to lift a foot for fear that it would unbalance him, the surface beneath his bare feet felt gritty and dirty, and then he knew that the bridge was the color of rust because it was actually coated with it.

Joseph was walking on a bridge of iron.

It arched up so that he had to lean slightly forward as he walked, and he held his arms out and up for balance, as though he were being held at gunpoint. When he paused and looked ahead of him, he could see nothing but a light brighter than the blue-black that surrounded him, and the nonreflective rust on which he walked. And then he heard a voice. It was a man's voice, but the sweetest, the purest, the most melodic voice he had ever heard.

Find me, it said.

Only that, only two words, but they moved him to his very soul. He shivered at the sound of them, and an instant later was struggling to maintain his tenuous balance upon the iron rod on which he stood. When he felt secure once more, he breathed a sigh of longing. Then he said, "Yes, yes, I'm coming. . . ."

Suddenly, the most important thing in the world, or wherever he was, was answering that summons that had spoken inside his head, inside his dream. He shuffled forward faster, thrilling to the voice as it spoke again: *Come. Seek me. Find me.*

"*Yes,*" Joseph said louder. "Yes, I'm coming. I *will* find you."

Chapter 33

*A*fter Mimi had coughed herself to death one last time and Rodolpho had cried her name, Laika rubbed a tear from her eye and took off her headset. As she did, she heard another sound over the gurgle of the water whirling down the tub drain.

It was Joseph's voice. She couldn't make out the words, but she recognized the tone. It was impassioned, almost desperate, and she wondered what had been going on while she was engaged in the musical tragedies of the Paris Bohemians.

She quickly got out of the tub and slipped on a terrycloth robe without drying herself first. Then she opened the door and edged into the hall. Tony was already standing outside the bedroom door, listening.

He held a finger to his lips and beckoned her. She walked to him, silently sliding her feet along the worn carpet. Joseph's voice spoke again.

"I'm coming. . . ." he said. "I'm looking for you . . . are you here? Tell me where to find you. . . ."

Tony turned the knob and pushed the door inward a few inches, enough for the two of them to see Joseph. He was not in bed. He was standing next to it, facing the far corner of the room. His arms were out, feeling his way toward something, and his body was moving slowly, tentatively, walking ahead as though he were on a stair-stepper, his heels raising, but his feet never leaving the ground.

But the two things that sent a chill over the back of Laika's neck were that Joseph's eyes were wide open, staring ahead of him blankly, and his body was leaning forward so far that she thought he would topple over at any moment. Yet amazingly enough, he did not.

She glanced at Tony, and he gave her a look that unmistakably said, "What the hell's going on?" She couldn't answer.

Now Joseph was walking into darkness, or something that seemed like darkness. The blue-black sky faded, lost in a flat darkness from which no light reflected.

Then the leaden walls closed in around him and the bridge of rust beneath his feet was gone, replaced by the same heavy, lusterless substance of the walls. He was no longer in danger of falling, but he felt instead the danger of suffocation. The dark walls seemed to leach the oxygen from the air, and Joseph's breath came harder. Soon he found himself panting, trying to get enough air into his lungs to keep from blacking out and falling down, becoming one with the heavy blackness that surrounded him.

Then he saw the man's face and he could breathe again.

The sweetest and purest air he had ever tasted flowed into his lungs, and his gaze rested on the man. He was standing against the center of the wall, and Joseph could see manacles around his wrists and ankles, connected to chains that held him to the wall, chains that seemed to enter the blackness rather than be fastened to hardware upon it.

The man was dressed in a single white garment that was nearly as luminescent as his face, which was framed by long, shining brown hair. A brown beard and moustache, neatly trimmed, adorned his jaw and upper lip, and his nose and mouth were in perfect proportion. He appeared to be in his early thirties.

But what Joseph focused on most were the man's eyes. They were softer and gentler than any eyes he could remember, and the man's expression was one of infinite kindness and love.

The man looked at him with pleading in those soft eyes,

and although his lips did not move, Joseph heard the words inside his head: *Find me. Help me. Save me. And then I may save you.*

Joseph wanted to do what the man said. He wanted to so badly that he began to cry, and at that moment he knew that he would do anything, go anywhere, to help this man, to free him and save him.

Because Joseph wanted, more than anything, to have this man save *him*.

"I'm going to wake him up," Laika said to Tony.

"He's not *sleeping*—look, his eyes are open. Is he in a fugue state, or what?"

"I don't know *what* the hell he's in." But Laika did know that her colleague was in pain. Joseph was looking into that dark corner of the room, holding out his hands like he was drowning, and sobbing in a totally desperate way that Laika had heard from men only a few times before. They had been men facing certain and unrelenting death.

She started to move into the room, but Tony put a hand on her shoulder. "You're not supposed to wake sleepwalkers, are you? What about something like this?"

Laika looked at the hand meaningfully, and Tony took it away. "He's not sleepwalking, and I'm not going to leave him like this." It was her decision. She was the leader, and she would be responsible for the consequences.

She pushed the door open all the way and walked into the room, going up to Joseph. She didn't know if she stepped into his field of vision whether or not he would see her, and decided not to. Instead, she reached out and touched his trembling left hand, then tightened her hold on it until she held it firmly. "Joseph," she said. "Joseph, it's Laika."

He continued to sob and pant for a few seconds, but then his breath came more easily, and he took deeper, longer breaths. He swallowed several times, and his eyes seemed to refocus from directly in front of him. He blinked the tears away from his eyes, opened them wider, looked down the wall at the floor, and then, slowly, over at Laika.

"Where were *you?*" she said gently.

He didn't answer right away, but turned his hand over so that his fingers could grip her hand. He clung to it tightly, looking around the room, taking some more deep breaths through his nose as if to clear his head. Finally he gave a ragged, breathy laugh. "Whoa...." he said. "*That* was weird."

"What?" Laika asked as Tony walked into the room.

"A dream, but—" Joseph looked around again. "Was I standing here?"

"Right here on the floor," Tony said. "With your eyes open."

"What did you see?" asked Laika, unable to look away from Joseph's awestruck face.

"I saw...." He laughed again. "I think I saw *Jesus!*" Then he laughed harder, until tears came to his face. Neither Laika nor Tony joined in.

"Where?" Laika asked, when Joseph's laughter had subsided and he was sitting on the bed, shaking his head as if at his own absurdity.

Then he told them about his dream, if it *was* a dream. He described the rusting bridge of iron, the dark sky, the darker room in which he had found himself, and the face of the man who had spoken to him. "Oh, it was Jesus, all right," Joseph said, grinning. "You know all those pictures you see in churches of Jesus knocking on the door and praying in the garden, and that one of just his head, looking real, real waspish and not at all like a Semite?"

Laika nodded. They had had them all in her father's church.

"Well, that was this guy to a T."

"So it *was* Jesus," Tony said. The somber tone of his voice made him a perfect target for Joseph.

"No, it wasn't *Jesus*, Tony—it was the American Christian *concept* of Jesus. The perfect savior, beautiful in every way."

"You must have thought so," Laika said quietly. "You were deeply affected by something."

"It was a *dream*," Joseph said defensively. "In case you didn't realize, sometimes you act differently in a dream than you do in real life?"

"Bullshit," Tony said. "You weren't dreaming, Joseph. You had your eyes wide open, man, and you were walking and talking up a storm. Hell, we *heard* you."

"What? What did you hear me say?"

"You said you were coming and you were going to find somebody," Tony said. "I heard it crystal clear. How about you, Laika?"

"I heard it, but I couldn't make out the words. But you were talking loudly, Joseph. And when we opened the door your eyes were wide open. You were looking at something that you apparently saw right there," and she pointed into the corner. "If it was a dream, you were up and around during it, and seeing something, too."

"I saw the shit in my *dreams*, that was all!"

"Dreams *mean* something," Tony said, "not all the time, but sometimes. That bridge you were on—that's the sculpture, the map, see? And it was leading you someplace—"

Joseph threw up his hands in frustration. "Sure! To *Jesus!* This dream brought to you by Jews for Jesus Incorporated! Tony! It was a goddamn *dream!* Now, if you want to psychoanalyze me, go right ahead, but don't make it a spiritual visitation, okay?"

"Did you ever have anything like this happen before?" asked Laika, still calm.

"A dream? Sure, lots of times, nearly every night!"

"You know what I mean. Standing up, pretending to walk, eyes open, not mumbling, but talking out loud."

"I don't know, Laika, I never *watch* myself when I'm sleeping, okay?"

"Joseph, you were not dreaming. Whatever that was, it wasn't a dream. Hallucination, maybe . . . maybe something else. But not a dream."

"Sleepwalking, then," Joseph said stubbornly. "Just because I never did anything like that before doesn't mean it's something paranormal! You think it was a visitation from Jesus, for Chrissake?''

Tony shook his head. ''I don't know how you can blaspheme after what you just—''

''Jesus Holy Christ driving with Mary in the sidecar!'' Joseph shouted. ''It all came out of my head! Will you two please face the facts and kindly not impose your childish superstitions on me? It came out of my *head,* and that's all!''

''Maybe it did,'' Tony said. ''But what put it there, Joseph? What put it there?''

Joseph opened his mouth to answer, but seemed to despair of the battle. Finally he just shook his head. ''Arguing religion with Christians is like talking to a brick wall. Now I'm tired, and I would like to go back to sleep. Notice I said *back* to sleep, as in, that's where I was before I was so rudely interrupted. I'm sorry that I bothered you with my little *dream.* So good night, sweet pains.''

He threw himself back down on the bed and turned his face away from them. Laika beckoned to Tony with her head and walked out of the room. Tony closed the door behind them.

They didn't talk until they were in the kitchen, the room farthest from the bedroom. ''What do you think?'' Tony said.

''I don't know. I really don't know why I should think anything other than that it was a dream, even if his eyes were open. He's probably right. I mean, I've been dreaming about the damn sculpture, too, and after that movie tonight, hell, it'd be enough to give anybody nightmares.''

''I think there's more to it,'' Tony said, looking at the floor. ''I didn't want to say, not in front of him, but I was closer than you. I could hear him talking, and I could hear. . . .'' He gave a little snort and shook his head. ''Damn it, Laika, it sounded like another voice. Like somebody else was in there with him. I couldn't hear the words, but I could hear the tone of voice, and believe me, it wasn't Joseph.''

It was Laika's turn to shake her head. ''That's not possible, Tony. Maybe you heard somebody out in the hall, or next door.''

"Uh-uh. The voice—the *voices*—came from in there with Joseph. I'm sure of it."

"Then maybe it *was* Joseph. Maybe he was talking in different voices. Why couldn't he do that in a dream state?"

"Because Joseph's voice couldn't have *sounded* like that. Laika, even though I couldn't make out a single word, it was the most beautiful speaking voice I ever heard in my life. I mean, Charlton Heston, James Earl Jones—it had that kind of depth to it, but it was . . . just *beautiful*. Like the voice of God."

Laika raised an eyebrow. "Or like the voice of Jesus?"

Tony nodded. "Yeah. Maybe. Whoever it was, when Joseph talked about the chains, and about this person asking to be freed? Well, I think that somehow somebody's telling us that the map will lead us to somebody we have to free. . . . a prisoner."

"Would you think this if you weren't a Catholic?"

"That's got nothing to do with it." He smiled. "I'm just a sucker when it comes to *any* heavenly visitation."

"Maybe Skye ought to reassign your ass to Lourdes," Laika said, and they both laughed softly before they started to think and talk again about what had just happened.

In the bedroom, Joseph's eyes were open, seeing only the dimly lit room in which he lay. But in his mind's eye, he saw the flat black room and the man in it, remembered with the vividness of life, not dream.

He had argued with Laika and Tony, and he had lied to them. He knew that what he had had was not a dream, but something he had not experienced before. He felt as though he had traveled, that the spirit in which he did not believe had left his body and found the man who had spoken to him, asking for freedom.

No, he told himself over and over, it *must* have been a dream. *It must have.* . . .

Then why did it seem so real? And why could he not put

the beauty of that man's face, the ecstatic song of his voice, out of his mind? Why was helping that man the only thing that he could think about, saving him, and being saved, in turn, from his life of unbelief?

Chapter 34

*T*he next morning, Laika showed them on a map of the city where their first stop would be. "Down here, in lower Manhattan," she said, pointing to a spot in the middle of a block, "near the Brooklyn Bridge. There's a large area here that isn't intersected by major streets, so the fact that a number of the pipes pass through it would seem to indicate there's something there."

"Or not," Joseph said.

"Or not," she repeated, agreeing. This was going to be, as was so much investigative procedure, guesswork. Show up and hope you find something. Ninety-nine times out of a hundred you didn't, but you always hoped for that hundredth.

Tony got the car, and they drove downtown to the Lower East Side. "Let's park a few blocks away," Laika said. "If we're being followed at all, we can lose them on foot."

They found a place to park on the edge of Chinatown, and walked several blocks without observing anyone tailing them. Then they cut over to the spot on the map where the pipes conjoined. It was a small block, completely surrounded by a black wrought-iron fence. When Tony saw what was on the property, he grinned at Joseph. "Oh, ye of little faith," he said, and turned his gaze back to the church.

The sign, rusted and badly in need of paint, read "St. Stephen's Parish Church, Est. 1848," and included the hours of mass. Ivy twined up around it, covering the words painted on the bottom.

The ivy was only the beginning. The entire block was shrouded by a mass of vegetation. Thick oaks and elms loomed up from the ground, which was nearly devoid of grass. Bushes and shrubs grew wild, trailing runners for yards in every direction. Through the foliage, at the far end of the lot, Laika saw dozens of tombstones and three tombs that still looked impressive in spite of their cracked columns. A stray beam of sunlight that managed to make its way down through the leaves shone on a metal lock on one of the doors. Some things, she thought, were still sacred.

The trees arched over three buildings that shared the lot with the graveyard. The church itself was the largest, an edifice of dark red stone that years of city soot had darkened even further. It reminded Laika of rust—but then, she thought, nearly everything red or brown did these days. She'd had enough rust for one lifetime. The church had stained-glass windows, but no lights were shining inside, so Laika could make out no images in their dark panes.

Behind the church was a small outbuilding that looked like a gardener's shed. Laika wondered what was stored in it. It didn't look as though anyone had done any gardening around St. Stephen's for years. It had large double doors with a padlock less shiny than the one on the vault in the graveyard.

The third building was the rectory, its two stories almost hidden by greenery. It was made of red brick, and Laika guessed that it had been built at the same time as the church. A wide porch coated with chipping gray paint surrounded it, and the steep roof showed a pale surface beneath where slates had fallen out, like patches of missing hair displaying a scrofulous skull. All in all, it was the most unwelcoming place of worship Laika had ever seen.

"Okay, it's a church," said Joseph. "Now what?"

"Now we play Hardy Boys," Laika said. "The door to God's house is never locked."

"How long *you* lived in New York?" said Tony, and Laika smiled.

As they approached the church door, she watched Joseph from the corner of her eye. In spite of his religiously symbolic dream, he wasn't holding back. In fact, he seemed anxious to enter the gloomy building, probably to prove to her and Tony that he hadn't been fazed by his vision.

The double doors were of a dark wood so oily that they appeared almost greasy. A large iron ring was mounted on each, and Laika pulled the one on the right. When it yielded, she was mildly surprised, since she had thought to find it locked in spite of her comment to the contrary. She had also expected it to open with a squeal of rusted hinges, but instead it drifted toward her soundlessly, and the three entered the church.

The interior was lit only by candles and censers, and a single, dim overhead bulb that hung near the top of the nave. Laika was surprised to find that the church seemed much larger inside than it appeared. There was one wide center aisle, and aisles on either side that went past the stained-glass windows. Laika went down the left aisle, directing Tony to the center and Joseph to the right.

Now, with the dim light from outside, she could see the windows as they were meant to be seen. They depicted biblical scenes such as Adam and Eve being cast from the garden, heading through the gates into a broken world; Noah, alone at the front of the ark, looking out toward a landless horizon; and Moses, throwing down the tablets of God. All, Laika noticed, depicted the biblical characters from the back.

On the other side of the aisle were glass scenes from the life of Christ. She saw that Joseph was not even bothering to look at the works of art as he walked down the aisle. His eyes were on the darkness near the front of the church, or the interior of each pew as he walked by it.

Laika was looking everywhere, surprised they'd found that the church doors opened. Why had the place not been vandalized long ago, she wondered. Anything not nailed down should have been stolen, since nothing was sacred to junkies. But a gold chalice still sat on the altar, and the candlesticks stood untouched. There was not a mark of graffiti on the walls, and missals and hymnals were tucked in every pew rack. Maybe God watched over the place.

As she walked slowly down the aisle, looking for whatever she might find, she noticed that the last window on the right side, the one nearest the altar, did not conform to the other windows. The style was different, and the glass was somewhat brighter in color. It was an image of a man in a white robe. His head was bowed, but tilted just enough so that you could see his eyebrows, nose, and chin. It was the only face depicted in any of the church windows.

As she looked at it, she saw Joseph stop next to it and look across at her. Her gaze must have been intense, for he turned and followed it up toward the window. His back was to her, but from his stance she could see that the image on the stained glass had immobilized him, and she wondered if it was similar to what he had seen in his mind the night before.

Then he turned back to her. Much of the blood had drained from his face, but he still forced a smile and shrugged and gave a "move ahead" signal, then walked toward the altar, where the three of them met.

"Okay, now what?" Tony said. Even though he spoke softly, the words still echoed weakly off the arched ceiling.

"Let's find the priest," Laika said. She glanced meaningfully at the stained-glass window of the man in the white robe, staring down at the chains that bound him, then looked at Joseph, but he did not respond.

At the rectory door, they waited two minutes and were about to leave before they finally heard footsteps inside, and saw, through the sheer curtains that covered the glass panel of the door, a black form approaching. A wizened face looked out at them from around the pulled-back curtain, and Laika showed her false credentials. There was a sharp click as a lock withdrew and the door swung in.

The priest must have been tall once, but was now so severely stooped that Laika suspected he suffered from a degenerative disease. He peered at them from over the top of a pair of wire-rimmed bifocals, an attitude that was more vulturine than quaint. Laika introduced herself and the others to the priest, who identified himself as Father Thomas Grady, and asked them what they wanted. The inquiry was curt, and Laika felt there would be no cheery conversation on the priest's part.

"Sir, the character of our investigation is classified," she said, trying to be as charming as possible to thaw his wintry countenance, "but certain things we've discovered have led us to your church. Has anything recently happened here out of the ordinary? Strangers hanging around, or anything missing? I notice you keep the church unlocked."

"And why shouldn't we?" he answered in a brittle voice. "It's a church. People should be free to come in and worship."

"You don't have a problem with theft?" Tony asked.

"No. People here respect the church." Laika heard in his tone a broad implication that the current visitors didn't.

"But there must be others, a criminal element," Joseph said.

"Criminals don't bother us here. They know better."

That sounded to Laika like a veiled threat, but she smiled nonetheless. "You haven't seen a gentleman around lately with a Scandinavian accent, have you?"

"No. I haven't seen anyone but parishioners."

"Is there anyone else who lives here who might be able to help us?" she asked. "A housekeeper, or—"

"No one else lives here. A woman comes in to clean twice a week. I don't need anyone else. I can't help you."

"Well, sorry to disturb you, Father, we'll just—"

"Father?" Joseph said, interrupting. "Just one question of an historical nature. That one stained-glass window? The one with the man in chains? When was it done? It wasn't installed when the rest were, was it?"

"No," the priest said, showing a shadow of interest. "The others were installed in the 1880s, but the one you mention— the St. Stephen window—was done later."

"1910, I'd guess," Joseph said with an air of superiority.

"You'd guess wrong," said the priest. "1919. Now, is there anything else?"

Laika glanced at Tony and Joseph, but they both shook

their heads no. "Thank you for your time, Father. Sorry to disturb you."

"Well, you government people are used to disturbing folks, I'm sure," Father Thomas said, and closed the door.

"Did anyone detect," said Joseph, as they walked away from the house, "a distinct note of hostility from Father Flotsky?"

"Yeah," said Tony. "He wasn't your usual priest—should've seen more Barry Fitzgerald movies."

"I had the feeling he blamed us for abortion," Joseph said.

Laika nodded. "And the national debt and the decline in his church attendance. It doesn't seem like a thriving parish." On the street, she turned to Joseph. "Why did you ask about the window?"

"All right, I'll tell you. But no reading any cosmic significance into it, okay?"

"The guy in the window looked just like the guy in your . . . dream," Tony said.

"Yeah. That's right, he did. Same robe, same hair, and he was chained up the same way."

"And you don't see anything weird about that?" Tony asked.

"It's weird, but not inexplicable. It's improbable, but totally possible that I was taken to that church when I was a little kid, saw that window, and retained it in my subconscious. Years later, it came back to me in a dream."

"And it's just coincidence that we happened to come here the very next day after you had your so-called dream." Tony waved an arm in the air. "I don't buy it, Joseph. This is some very, very weird shit. That vision—because it wasn't a dream, damnit—had something to do with this church and something to do with that sculpture, and you can deny it all you want. But when all these things mesh, calling it a coincidence is the *real* anomaly."

"All right," said Laika. "Let's not get into another argument. Let's just work from the facts. The main thing is that the map brought us here. Now, we didn't find anything in the church except for the window. The priest is definitely hostile, which may mean that he has something to hide, and what he's hiding may very well be what we're looking for.''

"Whatever and wherever the hell it is," Joseph said scornfully.

"I already know *where* it is," said Tony.

Joseph grinned lopsidedly. "Now you're psychic?"

"No. Just logical. You remember what was special about the iron pipes that indicated this area?"

"Two of them dipped under the floor at one place," Laika answered. "You think it's under the church?"

"Has to be under something," Tony said. "And there's no subway line runs under here."

"Then let's check the church basement," Joseph said, turning back toward the building.

"That's not where I was thinking," said Tony, just loudly enough for Laika to hear, but he followed Joseph toward the church doors. "That priest is gonna be watching us," he added.

"We're the government," Laika said. "For all he knows, we can go anywhere we damn well please. He'll probably appreciate our feeding his paranoia."

Back inside the church, they quickly found a heavy door that could lead nowhere but downward. "Locked," Joseph observed.

"Gee, isn't that a shame?" said Tony, taking out a small packet of manual picks. In five seconds he was pushing the door open. Then he flipped on the light switch, illuminating a broad stairway leading down. "One of us ought to stay here."

"You're elected," Laika said, and started down the stairs. Joseph followed.

The cellar was exactly what she had expected. It was large and open, filled with ancient cardboard boxes containing old issues of Catholic magazines and church records. A few broken pews were piled against one wall, and an old oil furnace with a dozen octopoid metal arms sat silently in a corner.

The only sound was the tiny patter of mice feet over the old newspapers that covered the floor. Laika raised one of them with her foot and saw dirt beneath.

They made a circuit of the cellar, lit dimly by three bare bulbs, but found nothing of interest, no secret doors hidden in the brick walls, no areas of rebricking. "Well, they didn't bury any pregnant nuns alive down here that I can see," said Joseph, slapping the dusty bricks. "You satisfied?"

Laika took one last look around and nodded. They climbed the stairs and turned off the light, and Tony locked and closed the door. "Anything?" he said.

Laika shook her head. "Where were *you* thinking?" she asked Tony.

"You're gonna laugh," he said, and looked at Joseph. "I know *you* will, but I don't care. I think there's something in that crypt."

Joseph didn't laugh, but he gave a disgusted noise deep in his throat. "What crypt?"

"There are three of them out there in the graveyard," Tony said. "Now, with everything else around here being in lousy shape, why would that one crypt have what looks like a brand new shiny lock on it?"

"Because vandals busted into it?"

"My ass. This place isn't well kept, but there's not one sign of vandalism here, not one. No graffiti, no beer cans, no *nuthin'*. I know you don't get into churches much, Joseph, but that alone makes this church just a little unique in New York City. Now, some of these crypts go down into the ground, right?"

"Right," Joseph said.

"Well, that's below the surface, and I bet that's where Holberg was pointing."

"Jesus Christ," muttered Joseph, "why couldn't he just have written a note?" He looked at Laika. "You agree with this nutty theory?"

"I don't think there's much else we can try, short of exploring the priest's basement," said Laika, "and I doubt if he'd let us down there without a warrant. The lock is new, it's true. There has to be a reason.''

''Great,'' said Joseph. ''Maybe we should have watched *Children Shouldn't Play With Dead Things* last night instead.''

*A*t 2 o'clock the following morning, the three operatives went back to St. Stephen's Church. They were dressed in dark colors to blend into the night, and Tony had brought along a more potent set of B&E tools.

The lights in the rectory were all off, and no candlelight came through the stained-glass windows of the church. Although Laika tensed for some recognition of their intrusion onto the church property, none came. How did this place stay undisturbed, she wondered. The gates were wide open, yet no druggies were pushing crack under the trees, no whores were doing their johns in the bushes.

Ghosts? She had to admit, the place was eerie. But that wouldn't have stopped the lowlifes that dirtied up the rest of the city. What, then?

The night was cloudy with no moon, but the glow of the city all around them provided them with enough light to find their way through the overgrown grounds to the large granite tomb with the name Peters carved on the lintel above the door. As it turned out, there were two locks. The newer padlock secured an ironwork gate that covered the heavy door of the tomb itself, a massive slab faced with marble that had an inset lock like a house door.

"You going to pop it?" Joseph asked in a whisper.

Tony shook his head. "Don't want anybody to know we were here and gone." It took him three minutes with a feeler pick, a ball rake, and a tension wrench to get the padlock open, and another eight minutes for the door. When he turned the lock, he whispered, "This hasn't been opened in a long time. Some of the tumblers were rusty. Maybe I was wrong."

"We're here now," Joseph said. "I wouldn't miss this for the world. Open 'er up."

The heavy door opened hard, and with a high-pitched squeal, and Laika thought that the top hinge had partially given way and was dragging the bottom of the door over the marble floor. Tony wrapped his fingers around the edge of the door and lifted it upward, and it opened more easily.

Laika expected the smell inside to be rank, filled with decay, but there was only the dry odor of dust. They stepped inside, not wanting to use a light until the door was closed again. Tony and Joseph pushed it shut, and then they turned on their flashlights.

The vault was empty. There were no caskets, no markers on the walls, no niches or urns or decoration of any kind. But there was a four-by-six-foot slab in the middle of the marble floor, and a heavy iron ring set into it.

"What are we waiting for?" said Joseph, more loudly now that the door was closed. "A flashing neon sign that says, 'Pull tab to open?' "

The ring was large enough so that each of them could get their fingers around it. They pulled upward and the slab moved slowly. "You read Lovecraft, right, Tony?" Joseph said, panting. Tony nodded. "What would Lovecraft have put under this slab?"

"Whatever it is," Tony said, "I hope it tears *your* face off first."

They shifted the slab to the side, and a strong smell of human waste and body odor that made Laika wince drifted up from the opening. A wooden staircase led downward, and when Tony shone his light down, they heard a feeble gasp from below.

"Jesus," said Joseph, "there's somebody *down* there!"

They all three drove the strong beams of their lights into the hole, and Laika saw what looked like two fat, white spiders crawling about in a whiter nest. Then she realized that she was looking at a white-haired man dressed in black, who was attempting to cover his head with his hands. A cry of anguish surged up at them, and the thin, twisted fingers stretched, futilely trying to shelter the head beneath like an umbrella. If this was Peder Holberg, his hair had gone white.

"Move your lights away," Laika said, turning her beam up, out of the hole. The others followed suit. "We're coming down," she said to the man below. "Close your eyes and cover them with the palms of your hands." Without waiting to see if he obeyed, she started down the narrow stairs, shining her light in front of her. The man scurried into the corner of what looked like a room eight feet square.

At the bottom of the stairway, Laika stepped onto the floor of the room. It was black, and the beam from her light merely sat upon it without casting any reflection. The walls and ceiling were similar. On the wall opposite was an opening six inches high and a foot wide. There was one wooden chair in the room, and a thin mattress lay on the black floor, a dirty woolen blanket over it. A metal basin, partially filled with urine and feces, was in the far corner.

"Who are you?" she asked the man, whose face she could not see. "Let us see your face." He didn't move, and she prodded him with her foot, ready to move should he attack. "I mean it. We won't shine the lights directly on you, but we want to see your *face!*"

Laika shone her light into the opposite corner, and the others turned their lights out at her direction. The man, now only dimly lit, slowly turned, lowered his hands, and raised his head. He was not Peder Holberg.

Beneath the mop of white hair, the face was lined and wrinkled, punctuated with a few pustules that glistened redly. The man was cadaverously thin, his neck a bag of wattles, the pouches beneath his closed eyes like hanging half-moons filled with liquid. His partly opened mouth revealed no teeth, and his thin lips were as cracked as old parchment. The skin of his face, lined deeply with the map of his years, was a sickly gray-white.

"Tony," Laika said, "pat him down." Tony moved to the

old man reluctantly, but did his job quickly and efficiently. The old man grunted and whined as Tony's hands explored him, and his fingers fluttered like fire-crazed moths. He never once opened his eyes.

"All right, I'm going to turn the light out now. Then we'll talk, understand?" There was no answer. "Do you understand me?" she said more firmly.

"Yeh... yes...." the man said. Though Laika assumed he must have been down here for some time, his voice, though weak, did not sound rusty from disuse.

If there was one thing she did not want, it was to be in this vile tomb with this man in the dark. But even her single light seemed to stab his eyes like nails, and she knew she would get no answers until he was comfortable once more. She put the fabric of her jacket over the lens, reducing it to a dull crimson glow so that the tomb seemed bathed in thick blood. Then she reached into her jacket pocket, took out a microcassette recorder, and pushed *play*.

The old man's whining subsided, and she heard him breathe out, "Thank you ... *thank* you ... I have no light ... never, never anymore. The pain was so great ... so *great* ... that I wasn't ... quite *myself*." He stressed the words too dramatically, and Laika realized immediately that the man was not sane.

"And who are you?" she said, glad that her voice sounded firm.

"I am Samuel," the voice intoned. "*Father* Samuel, oh yes, *Father* Samuel, a servant of our Lord, trying to live my life for *Him* now, for *Him*...."

"You're a priest?" She recalled all the old legends of the ghosts of nuns who had been walled up and left to die by their superiors for pregnancy or other sins, and the thought flashed through her mind, "Now they're walling up *priests* instead." A nervous laugh came to her lips, but she bit it back. There was already enough insanity here.

"I am ... I *was*. Oh yes, I was ... a *good* priest, yes, a very good priest, I cared, you see, I did, for *everyone*, not just my parishioners, oh no, but all who came here, all who needed, needed. . . ."

"Needed what?"

"Oh, needed *Christ*, yes, so many, always so many. . . ."

"Why are you down here?" Laika asked.

"Should be . . . *should* be . . . for my *sins*."

"Penance?" she heard Tony's voice say, and was glad to have aural proof that her team was still there.

"Oh yes . . . yes, penance. . . ."

"Are you being held here against your will?" Laika asked.

There was a long silence, and then the priest's quavery voice slithered through the near-darkness. "Noooo . . . noooo . . . *I* chose. *I* chose this, none other. For what I *did*, I *did*. . . ." Then Laika heard a scuttling, and although his form had not moved, she had the uncomfortable feeling the old priest had crept closer to her in his eagerness to explain. The smell of his body was strong and cloying.

"I *like* it now, I *like* it down here, you see, you see? I have the time now, time to meditate on the Holy Mystery, on what I have done. I pray always, *always*, I pray and say my rosary, and He is *with* me, yes, even down here, and *someday* He will forgive me, and grant me absolution, yes, even *I*. . . ."

"What was it that you did?" Laika asked gently.

There was a long sigh and another silence, and when the priest spoke again, his voice was pinched, as though he was struggling to hold back tears. "I set him free . . . I set him free . . . I couldn't help myself . . . you see, I thought *he* needed Christ, too, I was so foolish, yes, that's *how* great a fool *I* was . . . to think that *he* needed Christ. . . ."

"Who was he, this one you set free?"

"Oh, who he was, who was he, I thought . . . so many things I thought, he told me, he spoke to me in *here*, in here, the son of the father, I said, yes, that I said, the *son* of the father . . . but no, not that, *not* that . . . the holy ghost, *unholy* ghost. . . ."

"Where did they hold him?" Laika asked, trying to steer

the conversation back into a more rational channel. If they lost him now, they might never get him back.

"Oh here, oh here, yes, here, who'd look here? Who'd think . . . who'd think here?" he ended weakly.

Laika heard Joseph's voice in the darkness behind her. "Father, the prisoner," he said softly. "Was he the one in the window? The man in chains?"

"Yes . . . yes . . . he. . . ." The voice was getting more breathy now, and Laika could sense that the man's mind was becoming even more muddied. He had probably not carried on a conversation like this in decades.

She shuddered at the thought, then tried to prompt the priest. "Yes, the prisoner—what about him?"

". . . Hail Mary . . . Lord is with thee . . . fruit of thy womb. . . ." The words stopped with a sharp intake of breath, and for a moment Laika was afraid the old man had died. But then they started coming again. ". . . Fruit . . . thy womb . . . thy line . . . lineage of David, *house* and lineage of . . . David . . . descend . . . into   Hell . . . descending . . . descendant . . . line, lineage, Hail Mary, full of grace . . . Hail Mary. . . ." His words, which had been growing ever more incomprehensible, trailed off into mere mumbling.

"Father Samuel," she said, but he gave no response except for low babbling. "Father, would you like us to help you? Would you like to leave here?" She asked again, but there was no change in the priest's demeanor. "All right," she said at last. "Let's go."

She turned off her recorder and slipped it back into her pocket. Then she climbed up the narrow staircase in the dim red glow and heard Tony and Joseph coming behind her. At the top, she set the flashlight against the wall so that it would create as little light as possible. The vault was lit by a soft glow no brighter than a night light. She gestured to the marble slab, and together the three of them dragged it back over the hole and fit it into place. The babbling from below ceased immediately. Laika wondered if even a scream would be heard through the heavy slab.

Then they turned out their lights, opened the vault door,

and went outside into the New York City night. The sickly air smelled sweet in comparison to the pit from which they had climbed. Tony locked the door behind them and fit the padlock back onto the wrought-iron gate. There would be no evidence that they had ever been there.

"Let's get out of here," Laika said, leading the way through the rank vegetation toward the far cleaner street.

Chapter 36

*T*wenty minutes later, they were sitting in the back booth of a well-lit all-night coffee shop in midtown. They were all drinking coffee, and Tony was eating a piece of apple pie. Laika had no appetite, and Joseph didn't look any too hungry, either.

"Thoughts?" Laika said, after the bored waitress moved away.

"How long has that man lived down there?" Joseph said softly, staring down at the light brown surface of his coffee.

"If that window was installed in 1919," Laika said, "and that's when this prisoner was held, it would seem he's been down there for close to eighty years."

Joseph shook his head and looked up at Laika. "How could he be that old? If he was a priest, he had to be at least in his mid-twenties. Add eighty years to that, and the guy's over a hundred. You're telling me somebody could live in those conditions for eighty years and be a centenarian? I don't think so."

"What does he *eat*?" Tony said.

"The priest we met today must feed him through that small door in the wall," said Laika. "There's probably a tunnel between the rectory basement and the tomb. His toilet basin probably goes through there, too. But, my God, how could they *let* a man live like that? I can't believe he chose it himself."

"Probably didn't," said Tony. "I know a little about

Catholic guilt. Times have changed a lot—I mean, the Pope now says evolution's okay—but if this priest committed some mortal sin, and it's worse if a priest does it, then this . . . imprisonment might have been suggested by the bishop as penance, maybe for an appointed time. But when it was over, Father Samuel might have decided on his own that it wasn't long enough, that he still needed to do penance, and stayed down there himself. Or maybe he was just crazy by that time."

"Or maybe," Joseph offered, "the church wanted to keep him quiet."

"Quiet about what?" Laika asked.

"Churches aren't supposed to hold prisoners, okay? Maybe it was kosher when popes had their own armies in the field, but not in this century. So here's the church, and they've got this guy the priest was talking about. He's locked in this crypt, and Father Samuel lets him go."

"Or *tries* to," Tony said. "We don't know if this guy got away or not."

"Okay, *tries* to let him go, so what's the church going to do? Are they going to go through normal channels to discipline Father Samuel? Hell, no. That means exposing what they're doing, which is imprisoning someone against his will. So they feed old Sam this crap about needing to repent, and stick him into the ground. Nobody ever sees him again."

"We need to learn his identity," Laika said. "There should be records of what priests served St. Stephen's in the 1910s. Let's find out and see what *officially* happened to Father Samuel. And then maybe we can also find out precisely what he did, and the identity of this prisoner he freed."

"Whatever it's all about," Tony said, "I think the church took it seriously. You notice the name on the tomb that Father Samuel's living under?"

"Peters," said Laika. "You see a link to Peter the apostle?"

" 'On this rock I will build my church' Peter?" Joseph asked. When they looked at him in surprise, he shrugged. "I had comparative religion courses in college, okay? I mean, myth and fantasy have always fascinated me,'' he added dryly.

''Yeah, that Peter,'' Tony said to Laika, looking away disgustedly from Joseph. ''Only that's also the Peter who denied Christ three times, remember?''

Of course she did. ''So you think that's why they carved 'Peters' on the tomb?''

''Look,'' said Tony, ''that tomb was never built to hold any bodies, but it *was* built to hold something else, and something—or somebody—that was really important. It was built to house a prisoner. Now, either that 'Peters' was carved there later to ironically indicate that the church fathers thought Father Samuel was a blasphemer or something of the sort, or it was carved there when the thing was built, and it was built as a prison, so the 'Peters' refers to the prisoner.''

''Maybe the prisoner's *name* was Peters,'' Joseph said.

''Sure,'' said Tony. ''And they're going to hide this guy and then put his name right on the front of his prison? Please.'' Laika glared at him, and Tony continued in a more moderate tone. ''Another reason this thing is big is the window. Why would the church have put that window in if it somehow wasn't meaningful?''

''It was,'' said Joseph. ''You heard the priest—it's the St. Stephen window. And it's St. Stephen's Church, right?''

''You didn't learn enough in comparative religion,'' Tony replied. ''St. Stephen was brought before the Sanhedrin, and after he spoke to them, they dragged him out and stoned him. But Stephen was never imprisoned, Joseph. He never wore chains.''

Joseph said nothing. He just looked down into his coffee again. ''The flat black walls, Joseph,'' Tony went on. ''You mentioned them in your dream . . . your own vision of St. Joseph. They were flat black walls in Father Samuel's cell, weren't they? And the window showed the same man you saw in your vision, too, didn't it? But that's just a coincidence, huh?''

''Lead,'' Laika said, realizing what the surface was.

"That's also why the slab was so heavy, isn't it? The cell was lined with lead."

"Joseph, I asked you a question," Tony said.

Finally Joseph nodded. "Yes," he said softly. "The man in the window, the room in the crypt. They were just like my dream." He looked up at them, pleading, almost desperate. "I didn't make it up. I told you last night, before we ever came here."

"I know," said Laika. "I can't explain it either."

Tony finished his coffee and gave Joseph a small smile. "I think we're all pretty tired. What do you say we head back and dig out the information on Father Samuel in the morning . . . the *late* morning?"

Laika paid the check and followed Tony and Joseph out the door into the street. Just as she let the door swing closed behind her, there was a sudden flash. Although she heard no gunshot, she crouched immediately, only to see Tony take off running across the street after someone in retreat. Joseph and Laika followed.

It wasn't much of a race. Tony caught the runner in an open plaza in the middle of the block, grabbed him by the shoulder, and yanked him around. A camera with a flash attachment swung around with him, and Tony grabbed it with his other hand, jerking it from around the man's neck. Then he pushed the man away from him.

"Hey!" the man yelled. "Give me my camera!"

There were only a few people on the street. A couple of winos sat on a bench under a spindly tree that the building owners probably hoped would lend a bit of sylvan charm to their vista of concrete, and a young couple walked by on the sidewalk, very careful to ignore completely the shouting photographer. There were no policemen in sight, and none of the cars cruising by had bubble tops.

Laika didn't think Tony would have cared if there were cops around or not. He popped open the back of the camera and yanked out the film, then threw the camera back at the man, who just missed it. It clattered on the concrete, and he retrieved it with a moan of fury, while Tony pulled the length of film out of the cartridge, exposing it to the bright New York night.

Then, before the photographer could decide what to do next, Tony grabbed him and patted him down, removing several rolls of film from his jacket pocket. Tony jammed them into his own pocket, then continued to search the man. He tried to break away, but Tony grabbed his wrist and tugged the man's arm up behind his back. "Screw around with me and it breaks," he said, then finished his search as Joseph positioned himself on the other side of the photographer.

Satisfied, Tony swung the man around again and grabbed his lapels, the way he had done to James in the apartment lobby. "Who are you?" Tony said.

The man, who stood a head taller than Tony, but seemed powerless in his grip, only shook his head, his mouth opening and closing. Tony's hand disappeared behind the man and reappeared with a wallet. He flipped it to Joseph, who caught it deftly and opened it, examining the cards.

"Taylor M. Griswold," said Joseph. "You don't mind if I take a business card, do you, Mr. Griswold? Now I'll know who to call the next time aliens give me a rectal probe." Joseph reached into his pocket and brought out a pair of sunglasses that he slipped on. Then he went up to Griswold, whom Tony now released, and stuck his face only six inches away from the man's.

"Mr. Griswold works for *The Inner Eye*, my friends, that paragon of journalism. I'll also memorize your home address, Mr. Griswold, just in case you should ever annoy us again and we have to pay you a visit. You see, we *are* the people in the black hats, the ones who show up to ask questions of folks who die the next day? The ones who visited the Kennedy witnesses? Who dropped in to Marilyn's house that last night? Who caution people not to mention the black helicopters that fly over their farms?

"We don't want to see you again, Mr. Griswold. And we don't want to see anything about us in your newspaper, or anywhere else. Do you understand, Mr. Taylor M. Griswold of 204 West 96th Street, Apartment 37M?"

Griswold nodded nervously.

"Comply with our request," Joseph said, "and neither myself nor Comrade X-9 nor the feminine demiurge of the solar system shall trouble your earthly frame again. And Heil Zantarp, master of all the universe." Joseph crossed his hands over his chest in an X, and looked at Griswold expectantly. "I said 'Heil Zantarp,' mortal."

"Heil Zantharp," Griswold responded incorrectly.

Joseph looked skyward and sighed, then back at Griswold. He stuffed the wallet into Griswold's pocket and tapped him on the chest. "Move your ass."

Griswold moved it, walking quickly away from them, heading uptown. They waited until he was out of sight, then turned back toward their car, which was parked a few blocks away.

"Think you scared him?" Laika said to the men.

"Reporters are pussies," said Tony. "We won't see him again. He not only thinks we're mean, thanks to Joseph he thinks we're crazy, too, and mean and crazy is a magical combination that most people won't screw around with."

"Let's check this magazine he works for," said Laika.

"It's a tabloid," Joseph informed her.

"Whatever. See if there's anything about the Scottish affair or the Plattsburgh case, or worse, the Melton thing. There's got to be some reason this guy has made us."

"We're not made," Tony said. "If he thinks we're anybody, he thinks we're from the National Science Foundation, and there's no way he'll learn any different."

"Do people from the National Science Foundation usually threaten reporters and steal their film?" she asked, climbing into the car.

That shut Tony up for a minute. "Well, some scientists can be pretty strange," he finally said as he started the car.

A half hour later, Taylor Griswold sat in his car and spoke quickly into his cell phone. "Yes, I'm sure it's them," he said. "They were the same ones I saw in Plattsburgh. . . . I did, but they took my film. . . . of *course* they know who I am, they looked in my wallet! . . . Yeah, they know who I work for, and where I live, for that matter. . . . Sure, I'll move out tomorrow afternoon. Set it up.

"Anyway, I followed them back uptown, but I lost them at a light on Sixty-fifth . . . there was *traffic,* okay? I can't drive through a bus! They kept going uptown, so wherever they are, they're above Sixty-eighth. I lost their lights after that. . . .

"No, it was just a freak. I had a tip on a psychic party, but it turned out to be a bust, and I'm just walking past this coffee shop, look in, and there's the Italian guy sitting in the back. So I waited until they came out. . . . How? The flash was on. I thought I had it off, but I must've bumped it. If it hadn't gone off, they never would've spotted me. . . .

"Okay, fine, I gotta get some sleep. Gonna call *The Inner Eye* first—they have to get their pound of flesh, too. . . .''

Chapter 37

*L*aika woke up at 8:30 in the morning, after four and a half hours of sleep, slipped on her robe, and walked down the hall. The door of Tony and Joseph's room was closed, so she assumed they were still sleeping, and she went into the kitchen to make a pot of coffee.

When she heard a key jiggle in the front door lock, she grabbed a pistol from the silverware drawer and took a combat stance in the living room. The door opened, and Tony Luciano stepped in with several bags.

"Jeez," he said, "you wouldn't shoot a guy with bagels, would you?"

"Depends," she said, lowering the gun. "Any onion?"

He frowned. "Not a one. All plain, poppy, and sesame. H&H, best in the land."

"Good. I hate onion bagels. Come on in, I've got coffee going." She took the bagels from him and noticed that he was holding a bookstore bag as well. "Run out of reading material again?"

"No, this is something else. I didn't sleep very well."

"Don't tell me you've started having dreams, too," Laika said, carefully cutting two of the bagels in half. The bloodiest wound she had ever gotten had occurred when a knife had slipped while she was cutting a bagel, and she had gashed the web between her thumb and forefinger. Blood had sprayed out. She still had the scar.

"No. No dreams. But I kept thinking about what the old

237

man said, especially at the end, you know, when he was babbling?" Tony went back into the living room and got the microcassette recorder. "Listen to this. . . ."

He pushed the button and Laika heard the words of the old man, thin and tinny from the tiny speaker. ". . . Fruit . . . thy womb . . . thy line . . . lineage of David, house and lineage of David . . . descend. . . . into Hell . . . descending . . . descendant . . . line, lineage . . ."

Tony turned off the machine. "All that about a descendant, and lineage? He harps on that, doesn't he? And I was thinking, lying in bed, about the idea of a descendant of Christ, and then I remembered this book I read in high school, must have been fifteen years ago."

"Isn't it a little bit early for a literary discussion group?" Joseph had come down the hall so silently they hadn't heard him until he thrust his head and shoulders through the kitchen door. "Ah, coffee. And bagels, too. H&H?" Tony nodded. "Excellent."

"Go on, Tony," Laika said, as Joseph helped himself.

"Anyway, this book—maybe you know about it, Joseph— came up with a theory that Christ didn't die on the cross. He was alive when they took him down, and survived the crucifixion."

Joseph took a sip of coffee so hot he couldn't speak for a moment, but nodded his head vigorously. "*Passover Plot*, right?" he said finally.

"No," said Tony. "*Holy Blood, Holy Grail*."

"Oh yeah, that one—the Merovingian bloodline thing."

"Whoa," said Laika, "you lost me."

"Baigent, Leigh, and . . . and. . . ." Joseph said, trying to recall.

"Lincoln," said Tony.

"*Right!* Baigent, Leigh, and Lincoln came up with this wild theory that Jesus survived, ran off to India—or maybe that was some other book—got married, and had children. Started a whole bloodline which, so they claim, came down to the present day through the old Merovingian kings."

"And who were the Merovingian kings?" Laika asked.

"Jesus, I can't be expected to know everything," said Joseph. "I never read the book myself, just about it, enough to know it was bullshit." He looked from Laika to Tony. "What brought this subject up, anyway?"

"The old priest talking about descendants, and I started thinking about descendants of Christ, and. . . ." He shrugged, and pulled a paperback from the Barnes and Noble bag: *Holy Blood, Holy Grail.*

"Oh boy," said Joseph, "here we go again. You're gonna read that and figure that all of this somehow ties into it, aren't you?"

"No," said Tony. "I've read it. But *you* haven't. I got this one, too." He pulled out another paperback from the bag. "It's the sequel."

Joseph shook his head. "Forget it. I will not piss away my time on those books."

"Yes, you will," said Laika, trying hard to keep from smiling. "Think of it as research on how this case might *not* tie into the book's thesis. Or if it does, maybe you'll realize how it was *made* to tie in."

"Would you like me to do all our horoscopes when I'm done? Or maybe read your palms?"

"Maybe he's not a reader," Tony said casually to Laika.

"Sonny, I was reading the Harvard Classics before you were a sinister gleam in your daddy's eye." Joseph snatched the books from Tony's hand. "And you're not manipulating me—I'm just following orders." He tossed a toasted bagel onto a plate and filled his cup with coffee. "I'll be reading in my boudoir, if anyone wants me."

"Not in your boudoir," Tony said, and even Joseph laughed.

After breakfast, while Joseph was reading the books, Tony connected to Langley and requested a search for a Father Samuel UNSUB who served St. Stephen's Church in the 1910s. The answer came back by early afternoon, and Tony called Laika and Joseph around his computer.

"There *was* a Father Samuel at St. Stephen's," Tony said. "Father Samuel Doherty. He was swimming in the East

River in the summer of 1919, when he vanished from sight. He was assumed drowned, and his body was never recovered.''

''Why doesn't that come as a surprise?'' asked Joseph.

''Well, maybe this will,'' Tony said. ''St. Stephen's was Father Samuel's third church. He served it beginning in 1909, and before that he had had two other parishes—St. Aloysius' in Brooklyn from 1902 to 1909, and St. Vincent's in Harlem. He started there as a young priest in 1887.''

''What?'' Laika said, and Joseph made a throaty sound of disbelief.

''Father Samuel Doherty,'' Tony said quietly, ''was born on August twentieth, 1863.''

''It can't be the same man,'' said Joseph. ''Maybe it's . . . it's a crime so great they have a new scapegoat every generation or so.''

''It's ridiculous,'' Laika said, ''to think the Catholic church would have an innocent man suffer for the sins of somebody else.''

''Ridiculous?'' Joseph said. ''Forgive me, but I've always thought that was the whole *premise* of the Catholic church.''

''You know what I mean. That's a farfetched idea, Joseph.''

''And a hundred-and-thirty-five-year-old man living in a tomb isn't?''

''Sure it is,'' Tony said. ''But this isn't the first time we've hit the longevity thing. What about that Scotsman, Robert Gunn?''

''That case has no connection to this one.'' said Laika.

''Oh yeah?'' Tony said. ''Maybe the priest and that Gunn guy were taking the same tonic.''

''Look,'' said Joseph, ''no offense, Tony, but the Catholic church has a long and dishonorable record of scapegoats. What was that Inquisition thing all about?''

''That happened hundreds of years ago,'' Tony said.

''Sure, but even in the early part of this century, the church was still playing fast and loose with morality. Hell, they made Ralph Reed look like a kid soaping windows. All I'm saying is that it's possible whatever Father Samuel—the *original* Father Samuel—did in freeing this prisoner, maybe it was a sin so terrible that someone has to keep paying for it. Neither of those two at the church were spring chickens, and this whole thing could have been set in place long ago.''

''It's possible,'' said Laika.

''Of *course* it's possible, more possible than a hundred-and-thirty-five-year-old man living in a damp hole for most of this century.''

''Speaking of possibilities,'' said Tony, ''you finish the books yet?''

Joseph nodded.

''And?'' Laika asked.

''And I think it's all pretty preposterous. Oh, it's very clever, there are all sorts of connections that look impressive, but it really hinges on flimsy evidence. Here's the deal.

''In the late 1800s, this poor French parish priest finds a couple of old manuscripts hidden inside a column in his church. In the next few years, the priest gets a lot of money—enough to fix up the church and build several structures, including a tower and a new villa. So where did the money come from?

''One possibility is that the priest discovered something that let him blackmail the church. There were some ciphers in the documents he found, and by interpreting these in a certain way, the conclusion is that this priest discovered that Jesus didn't die on the cross, but married Mary Magdalene, with whom he had children. Another theory is that he *did* die at the crucifixion but had impregnated Mary Magdalene first.

''Whatever happened to him, Mary Magdalene's children got married to Visigoths, the ancient Germans from whom the Merovingians were descended. Now, history says they were all wiped out, but the theory is that the line survives in some of the European royal families, and this secret society called the *Prieure du Sion*, or the Priory of Zion, wants to put these descendants of Jesus back on the European thrones.''

"What European thrones?'' Laika asked dryly.

"Yeah, that does pose a problem,'' Joseph said.

"Before I even ask you what you think of this,'' Laika said, "I'd suspect that if this theory had firm evidence, it would've gotten a lot more publicity by now.''

"Right. The evidence is very shaky. A lot of it apparently comes from a French nobleman who claims to be a descendant, and so stands to benefit if the throne is restored—fat chance. And much of it comes from these secret dossiers that no other historians have even seen. One of the rumors, not surprisingly, is that some of these documents were taken by British agents at the request of the CIA.''

"Hell,'' said Tony, "it wouldn't be a good conspiracy if it didn't have us spooks in it.''

"You've never heard any of this at Langley?'' Laika asked.

Joseph shook his head. "Just as jokes—the CIA–P2–Knights of Malta connections, tabloid stuff that our people have laughed about for years. Some people think the Company's in bed with every secret society in the world.''

"So all in all?'' said Laika.

"I think it's preposterous,'' Joseph said. "It's this gigantic grab bag of clues tied into everything you can think of—not just the Company, but the Knights Templar, the Holy Grail, the Masons, you name it. It's very *clever*—a lot of time was spent concocting this theory—but it's basically. . . .'' He searched for the word. "*Baseless.* 'Wackier than shit' would be a good description, too. So thanks, Tony, for letting me spend a very entertaining morning. Thank God I can speed read and didn't have to spend *more* time with these books.''

"Look,'' Tony said. "I've just got one question. From everything you've read, you're saying that this whole thing is very improbable, right?'' Joseph nodded. "I just want to know—is it *possible?*''

Joseph crossed his arms and shook his head. "All right,

all right, Tony. This theory, like everything else, is *possible*. UFO abductions complete with lost time, implants, and the ever-popular anal probes are *possible*. Bending spoons by telepathy *may* be *possible*." He smiled grimly. "People having prophetic dreams may be *possible*. Happy now?"

"Yeah."

"But," Joseph went on, "I see absolutely no connection between what's in these books and the ramblings of a crazy old man. Now maybe, if nobody wants me to look into reading the entrails of birds, we could get back to following Peder Holberg's map."

"I haven't been totally idle while you two were working," Laika said. "I've been looking into another confluence of iron pipes. This one here seems to indicate this spot." She pointed to a map on her computer screen. "The only thing is, it's another one of those locations where the pipes went under the floorboards. So odds are good it'll be underground. Now there's a subway entrance right here, so I overlaid our schematic of the sculpture on the Transit Authority's subway map, found the location, and placed *that* on the outdated maps that we requested—they were downloaded to us this morning. It so happens that there's an abandoned subway station right at that site."

"What's the nearest station?" asked Tony, looking over her shoulder at the computer monitor. "Cortlandt?"

"Actually, Rector," Laika said. "Closer by about fifty yards."

"We have to walk down the tracks?" said Joseph, and Laika heard the concern in his words.

"Actually, I think running would be a better idea." Then she smiled. "Don't worry, I've got the schedules. Three or four in the morning, those stations are pretty dead down there. We'll just drop off the platform, walk down to the closed-off entrance, there'll be plenty of time. Tony, bring your picks."

"Always," he said.

"So what are we going to find," Joseph said, "in an abandoned subway station at three in the morning?''

"Jimmy Hoffa?" Laika suggested.

"Nah. He's at Giants Stadium," Tony said offhandedly. "Under Gate B."

Chapter 38

*A*t 3:30 the following morning, the three agents stepped off an empty 1/9 train and entered the Cortlandt Street subway station. They had come equipped with plenty of firepower and wore long coats to cover it all. Joseph had said that it seemed like overkill, but Laika had only smiled and stashed a second weapon in the voluminous folds of her coat.

The station, as Laika had predicted, was nearly empty. A couple stood, their arms around each other, at the uptown platform's edge, but didn't even glance at them. Drunk or stoned, Laika thought. Maybe the gods would see them safely home.

As they waited for the couple's train to arrive, Laika could almost feel the weight of the World Trade Center directly overhead, pressing down on them. She thought about the skells and "mole people" who lived on the subways, sometimes even squatting in the many abandoned stations that dotted the system like ghost towns. Or ghost *tombs,* she thought, far underground.

She hoped they wouldn't run into any of the subterranean dwellers. Their firepower gave them clear superiority, but many of the squatters were clinically insane and might disregard the threat of guns. Laika didn't want to shoot any crazy people.

At last a nearly empty train stopped and the couple got on, but no one got off. The train pulled away, and they waited until its lights had disappeared around a bend in the tunnel. Then they took a look around, and, unobserved, hopped down onto the track and dogtrotted into the darkness. "Don't step on the third rail," Laika said for Joseph's benefit.

"Thanks for the tip," he replied, hugging the opposite side of the tunnel as if even proximity to the electrical rail would fry him.

When the light from the station faded behind them, other bulbs shone dimly along the tunnel wall, but it was hardly enough for safe walking, so they turned on their flashlights. Occasionally Laika heard things skittering ahead of them in the dark, but her light was never quick enough to find any of the creatures. "Rats," Tony said, after something scuttled near them, making her stop and shine the light around. "They won't bother us," he went on. "More scared of us than we are of them."

She didn't argue that she *wasn't* scared of rats, since Tony had used the plural. If he was willing to admit the rodents creeped him out, so was she, at least tacitly. At least they hadn't come across any of the sad human creatures who called these tunnels home.

A few minutes later, the beam of her light found a small door that, according to the Transit Authority plans, led to the abandoned station. Tony eyed the large padlock, turned it over in his hands, and smiled. Within two minutes it snapped open, and he took it from the hasp and opened the door.

Six steps led down, and they descended into a wide hallway. Dark puddles spotted the floor, and the ceiling was slightly higher than that of the tunnel through which they had come.

They walked down the hallway, shining their lights into the openings on either side. Some were simply small rooms, while others were halls that vanished into darkness.

"So is right here the area on the map?" Tony asked in a whisper which was probably unnecessary, but which the damp and shadowy chamber seemed to demand.

"I think a little further ahead," Laika answered in the same soft tone.

A moment later, Joseph, who was in the lead, stopped dead and turned his light off, signaling to the others to extinguish theirs as well. When they did, they saw a yellow glow reflect softly off the damp surfaces of the hallway. There was an opening ahead where the light was coming from, and they advanced slowly, trying to avoid splashing through any of the frequent puddles.

The opening was the size of a double door, and the three operatives approached it hugging the shadows of the walls. A landing lay before them, with stairs to either side leading down into a very large room, with the arched mouths of tunnels visible both to the left and right.

But in the middle of the room, twenty people were gathered. Laika had expected to see the skeletal and ragged inhabitants of the tunnels, but instead, the occupants were all dressed in black and red, and none was older than his mid-thirties. Some sat in ratty chairs, while others were seated around tables. Still others stood talking to each other. None was at rest. They were in constant motion—moving their hands as they talked, or crossing and uncrossing their arms. Even those seated jiggled their legs, or jerked their heads to and fro, as if looking for something. Laika hoped it wasn't them.

"These folks seem wired," Joseph whispered to her.

But before she could respond, if only to signal him to keep quiet, Tony spoke softly. "I know them." She turned to him questioningly, and he explained in whispers, "They're the cult that was hassling Holberg. The Esoteric Order of Dagon. They look harmless, but they pack heat." He pointed to a long, lanky man with stringy blond hair who seemed to be berating several of the others. "That's the leader, I think."

"Will they pull on us if we try to talk to them?" Laika said.

"Don't know. They're pretty damn crazy, but they really wanted to know whatever *I* knew about Holberg. There's *some* reason the map showed this place. I think we oughta try it. They try anything funny. . . ." He shrugged. "Nobody'd ever know, not down here."

"There are twenty of them, Tony."

He shrugged again, and Laika nearly shuddered at the cheapness of human life that his shrug implied. She hoped it was just macho bullshit, but wasn't sure. "I think we show our guns first," Tony said, "they might not be so anxious for a fight."

"Perhaps a little display of firepower?" Joseph suggested. "Just to get their attention?"

Tony shook his head. "I've seen these people. They're spooky. We fire over their heads, they'll return fire quicker'n hell. Let's just *look* bad." He reached under his coat, detached two sling holders, and brought out a SIG SG 550-1 assault rifle.

"Hunting sewer moose later?" Joseph said, taking out a standard Uzi.

"They just look at this and they shit ice cubes," Tony said.

Laika said nothing as she pulled out a Finnish Jati-Matic, folded down the front grip, and clicked in a twenty-round clip. Joseph nodded admiringly. "Fearless Leader looks like she's ready," he said.

"Tony, you've dealt with them before. You want to do the talking?"

"Sure, but what the hell am I asking for?"

"Let's feel them out," she said. "Ask what they're doing here, what they wanted with Holberg. Maybe they've gotten a little closer to their goal, which, for all we know, might be the same as ours."

Tony nodded. With his rifle in front of him, he moved slowly into the light. Several of those below saw him before he spoke, and pointed toward him, uttering shrill barks of surprise. Laika and Joseph flanked him, their weapons exposed, their faces grim with unmistakable threats.

"We see a gun," said Tony loudly, "and people die." The words were few and sharp and did the trick. Everyone stopped moving, except for a few hands that went up slowly into the air. "If you're packing," Tony went on, "take the weapon out slow, pop the clip or eject the shells from the cylinder, and place it on the ground, don't throw it.''

Laika knew that was a bluff. There was no way to tell who had guns, short of patting them down, but four of the men reached gingerly into deep pockets and into the small of their backs and took out pistols, which they carefully set down. The gaunt man Tony had pointed out looked at them as though they were stupid. He was right, thought Laika.

"Hey, Ichabod," Tony said, gesturing with the barrel of his gun at the gaunt man. "I know *you've* got something. Let's see it." The man cast an even sharper glare at Tony, but reached under his leather vest and came out with a .44 Magnum hand cannon. "Ooh. I'm impressed. Empty it and drop it." Ichabod did as ordered.

"Now," said Tony, "suppose you tell my friends and me what exactly it is you're doing here."

"We're waiting for a train," said Ichabod, and the others laughed bitter, nasty laughs. "Why the hell should we tell you?"

"Because we've got the guns. And because I think we may be after the same thing."

"We all look for the Lord," said Ichabod, and though his intensity remained, he seemed sincere, as though he were proselytizing. "The junkie, the whore, the priest, the killer. We all need Him."

"So where is the Lord?" Tony asked.

"In all of us. The Holy One's in you, friend. Oh yes, I see Him in you. He was there that night you escaped us. You nearly killed Dante, you know. He just about choked to death. And the way you hit Elaine when she went after you . . . oh yes, my dark friend, He was in you, all right."

"But you're still looking for him?" Tony asked.

"So are *you,*" Ichabod said. "What are you, man? Who are *you* with?"

"I'll answer your questions when *you* have the guns."

Then Ichabod tilted his head, and his expression grew cagy. "We were waiting for you, you know, or somebody like you. We knew somebody would come sooner or later. The Holy One wouldn't let us just sit and wait forever, just because none of us had the power to hear His voice. We thought the Iron Warden was going to show us."

"Iron Warden? You mean Peder Holberg?"

"Yeah. But he was chickenshit. He got scared."

"Scared of what?" Tony asked.

"Of His strength, His power. You know, man. It's the same thing *you're* looking for. But why the hell did you come to us? How did our Lord send you?"

"He works in mysterious ways," Joseph said, "His blunders to perform."

"Oh, He sure does," Ichabod said. "He can even deliver you out of the hands of your enemies, did you know that? And deliver them into your hands. He can make the plain places rough, and the straight crooked. He can do some really, really cool shit. Why, He brought you here, to show us where He is. There's no other way you could've found us, except through Him. And if He led you to us, He can lead you to Him. And we'll be following you, all the way."

"I don't think so," Tony said.

"But I do." Then Ichabod started to laugh, a very unpleasant sound that echoed all around the large room. "You think you've got the drop on us? Shit, man, we've had the drop on you all the time. I was just *playing* with you."

He lifted his hands and made a small, beckoning gesture, and out of the shadowed alcoves stepped eight men dressed in black. Pale faces stared like moons at Laika, Tony, and Joseph, and the small black eyes of gun muzzles looked equally threatening.

Ichabod seemed delighted by the Mexican standoff. "I could've had you shot down any time. All I hadda do was scratch my ear, man! But I didn't, and you know why? Because you're gonna take us to *Him!*"

Laika spoke for the first time. "I'm afraid not." She made sure her gun was pointing directly at Ichabod.

"You *have* to," he said.

"We can't. We don't know where . . . your 'Lord' is any more than you do."

A wave of fury swept over Ichabod's long face. "Then there's no reason to keep you alive."

"There's one," Laika said. "I have you right in my sights. You're the first one dead."

"Careful," Joseph said softly. "Religious maniacs love martyrdom."

Joseph, in this case at least, was all too right. Ichabod's eyes got crazy, and he threw himself on the ground, scrambling for the .44 and the dropped bullets. It would have been a suicidal move, had Laika not been trained. It would take at least five seconds for the man to grab the revolver, open the cylinder, grab one cartridge, load it, snap the cylinder closed, and aim. In that time, every one of the eight gunmen already armed could shoot an entire clip.

Laika ignored Ichabod and went for the gunmen.

Since she was standing on the right, she took the ones on that side. Tony went for those in the center, and Joseph fired on the left. One of her targets went down, and she ducked and fired a burst across those who were going for the weapons they'd thrown down.

But answering fire drove them back into the dark mouth of the hallway from which they had come, a place they could not hope to defend. It was so narrow that all the cultists had to do was to sweep it with fire and the ops would stand a good chance of being hit. The side alcoves and passages could easily be dead ends, and the fact was that they were outnumbered. Their best chance, Laika thought, was to retreat down the hall and continue to lay down return fire to keep the cultists away from the mouth of the hallway.

"Joseph," Laika barked, "light the way; Tony and I will return fire." Joseph's flashlight went on as they ran. Eight paces, turn and fire, another eight paces, fire again. Bullets whirred past them as they ran, and once Laika felt a bullet tear through the hem of her coat.

The sound of gunfire was loud in the low-ceilinged hall, but suddenly, just as she had turned to run again, it seemed to explode almost beside her. She crouched and whirled, and saw a shadowy form leaning out from one of the alcoves, firing back in the direction they had just come. Then another was there, on the other side of the hall. Against the pale light from the large room, Laika saw one of the pursuing cultists throw up his arms and fall.

Someone was covering their retreat.

Laika didn't pause to look a gift horse in the mouth. Whether it was backup somehow sent by Skye (which was impossible, she realized after a second's thought) or Transit Authority police or armed aliens (both equally unlikely), she took advantage of the covering fire and ran, almost outdistancing the beam of Joseph's light.

At last they reached the six steps and were up them in two bounds. They went through the door, and Tony slammed it shut, fit the padlock through the hasp, and snapped it so that it locked.

"Somebody was covering us," Joseph said, breathing hard. "What about them?"

"What *about* them?" Tony said, turning from the door and walking down the tunnel toward the station.

"You gonna leave them in there?" Joseph said. "Christ, they saved our asses!"

Tony stopped and turned to Laika. "You're the team leader. You want me to unlock that, let them through?"

Laika shook her head. "We didn't ask for cover. We don't know who they were. They could've been more of those crazies—guards, maybe, who just got confused over who was shooting at whom."

"They *could* be from the *Company!*" Joseph said.

"No. We would've been notified if Skye was sending backup. And even if they were, they take their chances, just like we do."

"But they were friendly fire, you can't just let them—"

"*Look!*" Tony shouted. The tunnel echoed with it, and he spoke more quietly, but no less intently. "Don't you give us any shit about life and death when you're not even backing up your partners!"

Laika eyed Tony narrowly. "What do you—"

"He wasn't shooting to kill, he was firing over their goddamn *heads!*'' Tony said. "These assholes are trying to cap us, and Joseph here's trying to *scare* 'em!"

"That's not true. I was going for center mass, just the way that I—"

"Oh, *spare* me! I've seen more firefights than walks in the park—I know when somebody's doggin' it! Don't you care about living?"

Laika hadn't noticed at the time, but now that she thought back, she couldn't recall anyone being hit on the left until Tony had turned his attention there. "The door stays locked," she said. "Now, let's clear. We'll discuss this later."

As they trotted down the subway track, Laika hoped a train wouldn't come. She looked at her watch and saw they'd be damned close, but didn't tell the others.

She didn't know what to say to them now. If Joseph had indeed been basically firing blanks, that would have to be dealt with. She thought it must have something to do with the incident in the townhouse. Joseph had been hit hard over having had to shoot the madwoman. If that had made him stop short of killing, it was understandable, but not forgivable.

Then she thought about the people who had defended them during their retreat. She felt confident that whoever they were, they hadn't been trapped by the locked door. The cultists certainly hadn't gotten in through the door, since it was locked from the outside. There were probably dozens of ways in and out of the place. They might have been able to get out without losses. But who *were* they?

Then she heard a low rumbling sound, and her attention was immediately centered on the fact that a train was fast approaching. There was no way they would beat it to the platform, or even take a chance on hurdling the two low third rails between them and the empty uptown tracks. So she hugged the wall, and told the others to do the same.

Laika closed her eyes as the train sped by, and she felt as though the force of it could have pulled her against it had she not clung, spiderlike, to the wall. Dust and grit stung her exposed skin, and she pressed her head further down into her collar.

As quickly as it had come, the train was gone, the sound of it fading down the dark tunnel. She looked at the others. Joseph looked shaken, but Tony seemed unfazed, and she turned and ran toward the station once more, the others behind her.

Chapter 39

*I*n the apartment, they sat in opposite corners of the room. Only one lamp was burning. Outside the first rays of dawn added a touch of warmth to the city's ever-present ambient light.

"Before we discuss anything," Laika said, "I want to know if what Tony said was true, Joseph. Did you shoot over their heads?"

"Hell, yeah, he shot over their heads," Tony said.

"I'm asking Joseph," Laika said sharply.

"Yes," he said, looking down at the floor.

"Why?"

He looked up at her. "I thought . . . I thought maybe I wouldn't have to kill them."

"All right," Laika said. "I'm going to say this, and then the matter's going to drop. Joseph, I don't know why you did that. But by doing it, you endangered my life, and Tony's, and your own. You endangered the mission. We were being fired upon, and your only duty was to fire back with intent to terminate those targets.

"Now, I don't know what got into your head. I *do* think I know you and your record well enough to feel fairly certain that you're not in alliance with those cultists. Maybe you're still feeling bad over putting a bullet into that woman and her baby. If you are, get over it. That baby was dead, and the woman was as good as dead. So get over it. Now.

"Because if you ever—and I mean ever—do anything like

that again, I'll consider it an act of betrayal, and I will execute you then and there. And Tony can feel authorized to do the same. If you are ever in a firefight with us again, you either shoot to kill, or you expect to die. Do you understand?''

He started to say something, but then seemed to change his mind and simply nodded.

''I'd like a verbal response,'' said Laika, trying her best to sound like the biggest hard-as-nails bitch either man had ever run across. She had no choice; their lives were her responsibility.

''Yes,'' Joseph said. ''I understand. It won't happen again.''

''Then we won't have to talk about it again,'' she said, and took a deep breath. ''We'll take a break, and then maybe we can start to try and figure out what the hell else went on tonight.''

Laika made a big pot of coffee, while Tony ran out for fresh pastries at the all-night deli. Joseph sat down at his computer, but Laika didn't look to see what he was doing. When Tony got back, the coffee was ready, and they ate and drank while they talked.

''All right,'' Laika said to begin. ''Lots of questions. Why did Holberg's map lead us to that station? For that matter, why St. Stephen's Church? What was Holberg doing at those places, and what did he want . . . whoever was reading the map to find?''

''Could the map have been created for those crazies?'' Tony asked.

''But then, why would it have led to their secret meeting place?'' Laika said. ''They know where they were.''

Tony shrugged. ''Maybe that was meant to be the original starting point on the map.''

''Joseph, any ideas?'' Laika didn't want him to withdraw. It was obvious he wasn't a team player at the best of times, and she didn't want her reprimand to put him at still a further remove from her and Tony.

''Holberg made the map,'' he said slowly, thinking it out.

"And he had to have made it for the purpose of showing someone where someone or something else was. And it sure wasn't us, that's obvious. So maybe it was for them, the cultists, to show them where . . ." He paused and gave a thin smile. ". . . Where the *Lord* or the Holy One was, whoever he may be." Only when Joseph had taken a bite of Danish and chewed and swallowed did he continue.

"But *why* would he have done it for them?" Joseph asked of himself. "He broke off with them, didn't start the map until then. No, it doesn't make sense."

"Not if Holberg was doing it on his own," said Laika, trying to make the pieces fit, no matter how ridiculous it might seem at first. "But what about those fugue states? What if he was doing it—"

"While he was in a trance?" Tony said. "Maybe this 'Lord,' or whoever they were talking about, made him do it?"

"When in doubt, go for the paranormal, huh?" said Joseph. The sneer in his voice told Laika that he was getting back to his old self again. That was good. They needed him to keep them grounded in reality, even the twisted reality of what they had already experienced.

"Okay," said Tony, "then you tell me why Holberg made it. Why he took months to *consciously* create this goofy map when he could have just written all these instructions down on paper, or called somebody and *told* them where these places were. Joseph, this is the only solution that makes any *sense*. Holberg was a sculptor, he lived for his art. If another consciousness was at work inside him—"

"Oh, *Jesus*," said Joseph.

"If it *was*," said Tony, "what better way than to get its message across than by inspiring Holberg's *art?*"

"By possessing him and making him build one gigantic mother of all ironmongery," said Joseph in disbelief. "Don't you think this . . . possessing entity, for lack of a saner term, could have made a little *smaller* sculpture? A desktop model, rather than an IBM Univac that took up a warehouse?"

"I don't know." Laika could hear the frustration in

Tony's voice. "Maybe this thing just thinks big."

"As gods are wont to do, no doubt," Joseph replied. "All right, all right, supposing we *do* opt for possession as the raison d'être for Holberg's little project. Where does that lead us?"

"Possibly to the conclusion," Laika said, "that Holberg didn't know what he was doing when he did it."

Joseph ran a hand through his hair and shook his head as if to clear it. "So he drew all those plans, rented that warehouse, ordered all those supplies, and built that entire iron Tinkertoy without ever knowing what he was doing?"

"Maybe he knew what he was doing," Laika answered, "but he didn't know why."

"Because the 'Lord' told him to," Joseph said. "And who is this oh-so-powerful entity, anyway? God? Satan?"

"Christ?" Tony said. "Or maybe his descendant?"

Joseph laughed. "Are you back on that kick again?"

"So where's the map leading, then?" said Tony, his cheeks flushed. "Why did it take us to that church? To the place where those cultists met? And how will where it takes us next tie into churches and guys imprisoned in tombs?"

"I don't know, Tony, I'm not psychic. But I want to check the sculpture again before we go running off to any more conjunctions of iron rods."

"Why?" Laika asked.

"Because I think there's a mistake in the schematic. I was checking it when you made coffee and Tony went out, and I think I may have entered some of the original data wrong. Or what's more likely, I entered it right, but Adam Guaraldi put it together wrong."

"What makes you think Guaraldi screwed up?" Laika asked.

"Because our next stop seems to be right in the middle of the outdoor plaza at Lincoln Center. And somehow I don't think we're going to find any bricked-up nuns there."

They slept for a few hours and got up at noon, then walked the few blocks down to Lincoln Center. There was nothing there, Laika thought, that hadn't been there before, and the fountain seemed the same as usual.

" 'Look in fountain,' " Joseph said. " 'Take coin.' " When she looked at him curiously, he smiled. "Old computer game, text based."

"Are you sure it's not *below* the plaza?" she said. "A subway station, or cellars, or something?"

"No, that's another thing that made me think this site is a mistake. It's supposed to be up in the air, fairly *high* up, which would probably indicate a high story on a tall building."

"What if," Tony said, "it was indicating a building that had *been* here, but was torn down?"

"That's a thought," said Laika. "Can we find out what used to be here before it was demolished to build Lincoln Center?"

"Sure we can," Joseph said. "But frankly, I think it's a lot more likely that Guaraldi made a mistake than that Holberg's guiding mental bugaboo had him make an old map. So can I suggest that we head out to the warehouse and try and figure out what that mistake was?"

Laika nodded. "You're probably right, but let's ask for the old data anyway."

"All right," Joseph said with a sigh. "I'll submit the request before we leave. Maybe we'll have it by the time we get to the Bronx."

Back at the apartment, Joseph requested the data while Tony brought the car around, and they headed north to the warehouse. It was 2 o'clock in the afternoon when they arrived. As usual, there were no cars in the parking lot, but there was a visitor outside the door. A tiger-patterned cat, its fur surprisingly clean for a stray, lay in the sunshine, washing itself. It looked up as they walked toward the door and blinked lazily.

"Nice kitty," Tony said, leaning down to scratch behind its ears. "How you doin', huh? Who do *you* belong to?"

"Nobody, probably. It's a stray," Joseph said, slipping the first of the keys into a lock.

"Stray would've run away," Joseph said. "This is a pet."

"Or *was*," Laika said. "Somebody probably dumped it."

"Is that true?" Tony said, picking it up and cradling it like a baby in his arms. "Somebody didn't want you? Sure, you're a pet, see how nice you are. . . ."

Joseph unlocked the final lock. "Come on, put the cat down and let's go in."

Tony set down the animal, which rubbed against his legs. He patted it one more time and joined the others inside, where Joseph immediately started going over Peder Holberg's plans, while Laika checked to see what information had come in concerning the buildings that had been razed for Lincoln Center.

"Nothing very interesting," she called out, as she read the file. "Office and apartment buildings, that's all. Nothing to indicate anything suspicious."

"Well, I'm suspicious about *this,*" said Joseph, holding up one of the large sheets of paper. "Where most of the damage was done? That area that seemed to have blown outward? I think Guaraldi was looking at this goddamned plan wrong way up."

"You're kidding," said Laika. "It's no wonder—he was working with next to no sleep."

"Yeah. These pipes shouldn't be in this area at all, but nearer to that end. Look . . . shit, if he hadn't been in such a damn hurry—"

"He might still be alive," said Tony coldly. "But that's such a small thing, isn't it, compared to our work?"

"Look, I'm sorry, I didn't mean—"

"Save it, Joseph. Let's get this crap straightened out."

The three of them pored over the plans, and Laika quickly saw what Joseph meant. The bundle of pipes to which Guaraldi had joined several of the detached pieces was a mirror image of a similar juncture several yards away that had seemed complete on its own. But when they crawled inside the webwork of the sculpture, they could see the uneven ends where the pieces had been ripped away.

"You're right," Laika said. "He welded them into the wrong place."

"And sent us to Lincoln Center instead of where we're supposed to go," said Joseph.

"Which is?"

"We won't know until we get those pieces off from where they're not supposed to be, and reattached."

"We helped Guaraldi enough to know how this is done," said Tony. "The tanks and torches are still here, and we can see the seams where Guaraldi put them in wrong. All we have to do is saw them off and put them in the new position, according to the plans. And unlike Guaraldi, we'll be awake while we do it."

Chapter 40

*T*hey started by cutting off the mistakenly placed rods with hacksaws and carrying them to the correct area of the sculpture. By the time they were finished, it was nearly 6, and they were all hungry. Tony called a pizza place a few blocks away where they had been regular take-out customers when Guaraldi had been reconstructing the structure, and ordered a large pepperoni for "Vinnie Antonelli," a variant on his cover name.

"Hey, Vinnie," said the girl who manned the phone, "been a while, where you been?"

"Hey, around, Patty. Twenty minutes?"

When he went out the door, the cat was still there, and he rubbed its ears until it purred. Then he hopped in the car, thought for a second, and went back to the cat, picked it up, and brought it into the car with him for company. It purred nearly as loudly as the engine and curled up on his lap.

The pizza place was hopping when Tony went in for the pie. The two waitresses were scurrying from table to table, and he had to wait a few minutes before Patty could grab the box with his order. "Looks like you scarcely got time to breathe," Tony told her, as he handed her a twenty.

"Ah, the short order guy got sick and took off. Barely been here two weeks. He wasn't so damn good, Sal woulda kicked his ass outta here for good." She handed him the change. "Thanks, Vinnie."

Tony said good-bye and went out the door. *Vinnie.* He

262

liked the sound of that. It made him feel like he was in the old neighborhood again. He grinned and rubbed the cat's ears with his free hand. It purred, but got up and hopped in the back with the pizza. "Don't open that lid, now," he said with a chuckle, but when he heard the sound of cardboard crackling, he realized that was exactly what the cat had done.

"Aw, shit," he muttered, then pulled the car over and looked into the backseat. The cat had somehow gotten a paw under the box lid and pulled it up enough to get his muzzle inside. Tony grabbed the cat by the scruff of its neck, pulled it away from the pizza, and lifted it into the front seat again. Then he examined the pie.

It was okay, except for a few missing pieces of pepperoni that the cat had stolen. "Can't take you anywhere," Tony said. He put the lid down firmly and held the cat for the remainder of the trip.

"You wanta come in, you little crook?" he asked the cat, when they pulled into the parking lot. The cat only licked its chops in reply. "Okay then, come on, you can have the rest of my pepperoni."

The cat followed him to the warehouse and stepped inside when he held the door for it. He called out that he was back, and saw Laika and Joseph entwined in the bowels of the ironwork. From what he could see of them, Laika was holding a rod in place, while Joseph was welding it with the torch.

"We're almost done," Joseph called back. "By the time you get the drinks from the fridge, we'll have this one on."

Tony waved in agreement, but before he went back into the anteroom, he set his jacket over the pizza box. "Stay out of there, pal," he told the cat, who was sitting on the floor, looking up at the box on the table.

When Tony came back less than a minute later with three cans of soda, he thought the cat was napping again. It was lying on the floor, its legs out. But then he saw its eyes were open, and there was a touch of red at its mouth and nose. Damnit, had it gotten into the pizza again? But no, his coat was still on the box.

Then Tony noticed that the red was not tomato sauce, but froth, and as he watched, the cat's mouth slowly opened as if in a yawn. More blood trickled from between its jaws, and it spasmed once, then was perfectly still. He didn't have to touch it to know that it was dead. And he was sure he knew what had killed it.

Laika and Joseph were walking toward him, pushing their safety glasses back up onto their foreheads. "What's that cat doing in here?" Joseph asked testily.

"Nothing," Tony answered. "It's dead." He pointed to the box with his coat still on it. "Don't eat the pizza."

"What?" Laika felt suddenly chilled.

"The cat ate a couple pieces of pepperoni maybe eight, nine minutes ago. It was fine, then this happened, just in the last minute or so."

Joseph took Tony's coat off the box and threw it to him. Then Joseph opened the lid and examined the greasy, uneven surface of the pizza. "There are very small crystals on the surface," he said. "I'm not going to taste it, but there's a chem kit at the apartment. We'll take a sample back."

In the meantime, Laika had examined the cat. "Apparently it doesn't have any effect until it hits the central nervous system. And then it's all over." She looked up at Tony. "Where did you get this?"

"All-Nite Diner, like always. Nobody could have gotten to it after I picked it up." His frown deepened. "So it had to be done there. Patty said they had a new short order cook who got sick and left. I thought she meant earlier, but maybe it was after he poisoned the pizza."

"Let's go," Laika said.

They locked up the warehouse and ran to the car. Through the dying light of day, Tony drove the few blocks to the diner quickly but not recklessly. They didn't want anyone to know they were coming.

"You think this was a random thing?" Joseph asked. "Or were we targeted?"

"We were targeted, all right," said Laika. "This assassin

got our location somehow, learned that we got a lot of take-out from the All-Nite, and then got a job there with the express purpose of waiting until we called in an order. When we came back today, he had his chance. You gave them your cover name, didn't you, Tony?'' Tony nodded. ''He saw it on the order slip, and went to work, then fled. Question is, how far?''

They pulled up in front of the All-Nite Diner, and Laika and Joseph waited while Tony went inside. He came back two minutes later, looking grim.

''Got his address,'' he said, climbing back in and starting the engine.

''What, you just asked for it?'' Joseph said.

''Yeah, after I told Patty I found a hunk of phlegm on my pizza. Told her I wanted to pound the guy who put it there. And I was right—the guy left right after he closed my pizza box and put it on the rack. Patty said Sal—he's the owner—would fire the guy's ass. She said Sal never liked him anyway, he's not Italian.''

''So what is he?'' Laika asked.

Tony smoothly guided the car around a sharp corner, and headed north. ''They all called him 'Scotty.' That give you an idea?''

Chapter 41

"They never saw his social security card, guy worked off the books," Tony went on. "Gave his name as Brian Chambers."

"You get a description?" Joseph asked.

"Nah, Patty just told me this while she was finding his address. He's at the Emerson Hotel, a transient place ten blocks north. Pretty rough, she said."

The Emerson did look rough. The bricks were stained with decades of soot, and all that was left of the paint on the wood around the windows were curled chips. Joseph watched the side of the building while Laika went around the back. Tony walked inside.

The clerk was in his early twenties, but as dissipated as a man in his forties. His long, greasy hair was tied behind his head with a thick brown rubber band, and his cheeks were cratered with acne scars. He looked at Tony but said nothing.

"You got a tenant named Chambers?" Tony said. "Brian Chambers, maybe goes by Scotty?" The clerk didn't answer. He just kept looking at Tony in that same cold, reptilian way. "Got a Scottish accent?" There was still no response. Tony pulled out a fake NYPD ID and showed it to the man. "Let me see your register."

"You gotta warrant?" The voice was slurred and nasty.

"I don't need a warrant. Now you wanta do this easy, or you wanta do it rough?"

"What you gonna do, arrest me? I know my rights."

"No, I'm not gonna arrest you. What I'm gonna do, if I don't see that register in the next ten seconds, is call some guys I know and they'll come over and torch this shithole. With you in it."

"You wouldn't do that, you're a cop."

Tony couldn't decide if the guy was stubborn or just stupid, but he didn't have any more time to debate. He reached across the narrow counter and grabbed the guy by the front of his T-shirt. When the guy reached under the counter and brought up the .38 with the taped butt, Tony was ready for him and snatched it out of his hand before he could even stick his finger in the trigger guard. Then he whipped the man across the face with it.

The front sight split a gutter of blood across the man's cheek, and Tony knew it would add another scar to his arsenal. Tony stuck the muzzle of the gun under the clerk's jaw. "Are you starting to see that I'm serious about this?"

An old man who had been reading a racing form in what passed for the lobby started to get up slowly. "Sit down, pop," Tony said, and the man obliged.

The clerk reached beneath the counter again and passed a large faux leatherbound book to Tony. Tony kept the cheap gun fixed on the clerk and opened the register. There was no listing for a Brian Chambers, nor were there any other remotely Scottish names in the book.

"The guy's not here," said Tony, looking at the clerk with mild surprise. "Why didn't you just *tell* me that? Show me in the first place?"

The man shrugged, holding the collar of his T-shirt to his bleeding face. It was true, he probably didn't know why. He'd just been trained since birth to hassle anybody in authority or, hell, anybody at all.

Tony shook his head and walked out, the gun still in his hand. Outside, he kicked it down a storm sewer and honked twice on the horn, a signal for Laika and Joseph to rejoin him. They showed up within seconds, and Tony gave them the bad news.

"Not going to be that easy," he said. "Apparently this

guy gave Sal a phony address, which makes sense. Hell, you're gonna pop somebody, you don't want people knowing where you live.''

"Let's go back to the diner and get a description," Laika said. "Maybe we can...."

But she trailed off as the old man who had been sitting in the lobby came tottering down the cracked concrete steps of the Emerson Hotel. Tony tensed, knowing that there had been more than one case in New York of a senior citizen blowing away neighborhood bad guys.

"Hey, son," he said, as he walked up to them, "you lookin' for the Scotchman?" The old man's cracked voice held the musical phrasing of Italy. He reminded Tony of his grandfather.

"Guy with a Scottish accent?" Tony said. "Yeah, why?"

The man pointed at him with a crooked finger, as if tapping on an invisible door, and chuckled. "You ain't no cop. I know who you are, I know the style...."

"Oh yeah? So who am I?"

"You're a made guy, ain't ya? I know, I can tell ... now, don't get mad, see, I been in the rackets myself."

"You have?" Tony asked, thinking the old man was bullshitting him, but not sure.

"Aw yeah, Gambino family. I never done nothin', you know, like killed nobody, but I knew a few that did, you know—enforcers, muscle guys. I was more an errand guy, you know—run errands and stuff, go-between kind of thing. But I seen you, I seen how you handle that punk, I say, there goes a made guy. And I say, I wanta help that guy out if I can."

"You'd be in my debt," Tony said, more formally.

The old man waved a hand as if to dismiss the idea. "Nah, nah, for old time's sake. I seen this Scotchman. I walk around the neighborhood a lot, you know, got nothin' much to do, the people, they leave me alone, the word's out, I don't gotta tell *you* that. You do good, you play right, and you get taken care of. But I know this Scotchman 'cause I seen him cookin' down at the All-Nite, you know the place?" Tony nodded. "And I hear him talkin' to Sal down there, and I'm thinkin' this guy sounds *funny*, you know? Because he's talkin' Scotch. And I said to Sal when the guy's not there, Sal, how come you hire this Scotchman, how come you don't hire a nice Italian guy, and Sal, he just says the guy's a great short order guy, so I don't think nothin' of it.

"But then I see this sonofabitch about eight blocks north of here, and that's as far as I walk, 'cause the moolanyans know me around here, but up past there they don't, and who wants to get mugged, you know? Fact I know who I know don't cut nothin' with *them* moolanyans, no offense, lady. So's I see this Scotchman go up to the old Drummond Building, place been closed up for years, most of it boarded so the bums can't get in, and I'll be damned if this Scotch sonofabitch don't unlock the front door and go right in, closes it up behind him. He don't see me, I'm inside this coffee shop, you know.

"So I wait, I have another cuppa coffee and a doughnut, which I can't eat many of 'cause it binds me up too bad, and I'm there an hour and this guy don't come out."

"What's the Drummond Building?" Laika asked.

The old man looked at Laika as though he was sore at being interrupted, but told her. "Old office building. Big one, eight stories, used to be a goddamn busy place, but hell, things changed, moolanyans took over—again, no offense— and it closed up, everybody moved away."

"Things change," Tony said.

"You can say that again." He looked at Laika and grinned, showing several missing teeth. "Now the families are using moolanyan dames. But lookers, yeah, some of them are lookers."

"Thanks," said Laika, not sounding at all grateful.

"And Jews," said the old man, examining Joseph. "You're a Jew? Hell, we had some good Jews back then, too—Meyer Lansky, he was a Jew, I never knew him, but we worked a lot with Jews."

"I endeavor to give satisfaction," said Joseph.

"Hah?"

"So where's this Drummond Building?" Tony asked.

"You go up here eight blocks, take a right, another two blocks over, it's on the corner, still got the name on it, can't miss it."

"I deeply appreciate your help," said Tony, "Mr. . . ."

"Cicero, Vito Cicero, like the Godfather, you know, he was Vito, too. And you're . . . ?"

"Vincenzo."

"Hey, that's a good name—my father, he was named 'Vincenzo.' You take care of yourself now, you hear?" He waved his hand from Laika to Joseph and back again, over and over. "Take good care of your people, too, they can't help what they are, we gotta be tolerant, times change."

"Oh, they're not *my* people," said Tony, unable to resist. "*She's* the boss, my capo."

Vito looked as though he didn't understand, but then his puzzlement was replaced by amazement. "*She's* the capo?"

Laika finally smiled. "If ever I can do you a service, feel free to call upon me. Honeychile Brown." She put out her hand, and Vito tentatively shook it.

"My God," he whispered, "times *do* change. . . ."

Chapter 42

"All I want to know is," Laika said as they headed north, "what the hell is a moolanyan?"

"It's a derogatory term for blacks," said Tony. "*Melanzana* means eggplant in Italian, and 'moolanyan' is Sicilian dialect for *melanzana*—just slurs the original word."

"Eggplant?" Laika said. "Why an eggplant?"

Tony shrugged. "They're black, I guess."

"Great. Now we're vegetables."

"Don't take it so hard. When I was a kid, we called ourselves dagos all the time."

"We called ourselves Jews," Joseph said quietly.

They parked two blocks away from the Drummond Building and walked the rest of the way. The building was, as Vito Cicero had described it, eight stories high, but the windows on the first two stories were boarded over. Laika guessed, from the decorative stonework that covered the top of the building, that it had been constructed in the early part of the century. Several of the third- and fourth-floor windows had been broken, but apparently no one had a throwing arm powerful enough for rocks or bottles to reach any higher.

The front door was formidable and appeared to be an addition rather than part of the original building. It was steel, and strong enough to keep out any marauders or squatters who didn't pack TNT for their B&Es. Inset in the steel door was a high-security tubular lock. Tony regarded it with what

Laika thought was respect. "This might take a while," he said, reaching into his jacket pocket.

He came out with a white-handled device that looked like a power screwdriver. "Tubular lock, tubular pick," he said, inserting it into the lock and moving it delicately.

Laika and Joseph stood in front of him to hide him from view, but Laika wasn't too worried. Hardly anyone was around, and though they were visible from a coffee shop across the street, no one seemed to be looking out the window. Also, night wasn't as brightly lit here as it was further downtown. Most of the stores were closed by now, and many of the street lights were either burned out or broken.

After ten minutes, they heard a pronounced click, followed by Tony's sigh. "Got it," he said as he pushed the door open.

The Drummond Building smelled stuffy, as though no fresh air had blown through it in a long time, but it was clean enough. Their flashlights shone on a thin layer of dust that coated the floor, but Laika saw that the layer had been disturbed by the passage of feet.

"Let's follow the footprints," she said. "Go single file." If they had noticed the footprints down the center of the hall, it followed that Brian Chambers would notice two pair of footprints on either side of the channel through the dust that he had previously made.

The footprints led to a stairway, and they went up it quietly. They shone their lights everywhere, looking for sensors or traps, but found none. On the eighth floor, they followed the tracks in the dust down the hall to the end, where a glass-paned door was locked against them.

Laika listened for a moment, but heard nothing inside. Tony swept the door and frame, then shook his head. It took only a few seconds for him to pick the lock, and then they went into the room.

It had apparently once been a waiting room, but was now denuded of furniture. An inner door led to a small office. There, on the swept floor, was a clean, thin mattress without any sheets or pillow. A small Bible lay on the floor beside it. On a clothes tree in the corner hung a winter topcoat, a dark suit, two other pairs of trousers, and two clean and pressed shirts, a white one and a powder blue one. All were hung neatly on hangers. Next to the clothes tree a large, closed suitcase sat on the floor.

"It's like a monk's cell," Laika said.

"Does have a touch of the ascetic to it, doesn't it?" agreed Joseph, who stepped over to the suitcase and knelt down to open it.

"*Hey,*" Tony breathed, freezing them. Laika looked at him, and he gestured to the door, then doused his light. Laika and Joseph did the same. The lights coming in the window gave just enough illumination for them to see each other as shadowy forms. She heard the footsteps coming down the corridor and hoped that whoever was approaching had not seen their lights or heard them.

Taking out their weapons, the three moved next to the door, Laika and Joseph on the right, Tony on the left, the side on which the door would open. A light went on in the waiting room, shining through the frosted glass pane of the inner office door. On the floor, the shadow of a man grew larger as he approached their hiding place. Then the door opened and someone stepped inside.

"Don't move," Tony breathed, as he thrust the butt of his pistol against the back of the man's head and placed his free hand firmly on his shoulder. Laika and Joseph came around the door, pointing their pistols at the man.

The man obeyed, holding perfectly still.

"Turn on the light," Tony said to the others, as he patted the man down, but they could find no switch inside the room.

Finally the man spoke. "I use the light from the waiting room. Anything brighter might be seen from the street." His voice had the flat vowels and the slightly trilled Rs of a Scot.

"He's clean," Tony said, stepping back, but keeping his gun trained on the man's chest. Laika opened the office door all the way, and the secondary light was enough for her to get a good look at the man. He was tall and seemed to be in his mid-thirties. The face was angular and not unhandsome. He was dressed in dark slacks, a collarless dark blue shirt, and a plain dark green baseball cap with no logo.

"You tried to kill us," said Laika. "Poison us."

"Aye, I did. The fact you're here shows there's no use in denying that."

"Why?"

"Why? You know all too well. I only tried to do to you what was done to my brothers. Or do you kill so many that you've forgotten already?"

"Your brothers?" Then Laika realized. "You're Kyle McAndrews."

The man almost smiled. "So *that's* how you know me, is it?"

"Up in Plattsburgh," Laika said. "You were with them."

"I *should* have been with them. I was late. I think God made me late on purpose, so that there would be someone left to avenge us on you."

"We didn't kill your friends."

"My *brothers*," he said. "You, your organization, what difference does it make? You work for him, there's blood on your hands." He nodded toward the thin mattress on the floor. "May I sit down? I had a long walk up here from your warehouse." Laika nodded, and he sat carefully, his long legs bent in front of him so that his chin nearly touched his knees.

He took off his baseball cap and set it on the edge of the mattress, then ran a hand through his dark hair. "Went all the way down there to make sure you were dead, but then your car was gone. I don't mind telling you I was very disappointed. So I came back here to try and decide what to do next."

"Do you mean how to kill us again?" she said.

"Yes. Really, you'd be better off dead. You have no idea who it is you're looking for, no idea at all."

"*Who?*" said Laika. "Then it *is* a *person* we'll eventually find?"

Now the man did smile, a thin smile that somehow showed both anger and pity. "Who," he repeated, "or *what*." He shifted his weight until he was crouching and picked up his cap, turned it in his hands, and set it back down so that it was resting on top of his hand. "If you had any sense at all, you'd forget all about this—"

And then he moved. He leapt out of the crouch, directly at Tony, flinging his cap into Joseph's face and bringing up the long knife he had hidden under the mattress, and then under his cap. Tony fired, the silenced pistol coughing once. Laika saw the man stagger, but the initial force of his charge kept him moving. Then Laika fired and simultaneously heard three quick bursts from Joseph's pistol.

The Scotsman flew to the side as Tony fired again, but Joseph's bullets made the second shot unnecessary. The man they knew as Kyle McAndrews crashed into the far wall with five bullets in his chest and side. Three were Joseph's, one was Laika's, and one Tony's. The tip of the long knife had missed Tony's face by inches, and that knife remained clutched in McAndrews's dying hand as he slid down the wall, leaving a smear of red behind.

Laika was the first at his side and took the knife from his hand. His eyes were looking into the middle distance, where he must have seen death coming. His mouth was panting as he tried to draw air into bullet-riddled lungs, but he seemed to be trying to say something.

"An . . . andra . . . andra. . . ." The syllables rode up from his throat on bubbles of blood.

Laika ripped open his shirt to try and give him CPR and keep him alive long enough for him to say what he had to say. But when she saw Tony's bullet hole directly over his heart, she knew death was only seconds away.

There was something else on his chest, and she examined it as his speech faded, and the rise and fall of his chest ceased. It seemed to be a tattoo, but done with red ink, and it was not until she wiped some of the blood away that Laika realized it might have been branded on rather than tattooed.

The image, though worn, was identifiable as two people riding on the back of an animal, probably a horse, although the beast's head was directly where the bullet had pierced the flesh. Laika's attention was drawn from it momentarily as McAndrews's last breath hissed away through his teeth. Then she looked at the others.

"It's a symbol of the Knights Templar," said Tony. "I've read about them. They boasted about the poverty of their order by making their seal two knights riding the same horse."

Laika picked up the knife and looked at it. On the hilt was the same symbol, much clearer than the brand on McAndrews's chest. "That's an old knife," said Joseph, looking over her shoulder. "See the way it's joined together?" He ran a finger delicately along the blade. "Probably Toledo steel."

Joseph's voice shook, and Laika looked up at him. "Are you all right?" He nodded. "That was fast shooting," she said. "You probably saved Tony's life."

"Yeah," Tony said quietly. "I hit him, but he kept coming. Thanks, Joseph."

Joseph pressed his lips together and nodded.

"Tony," said Laika, "go through his pockets, lining of his coat, anyplace anything might be hidden. Joseph, you lift his prints. I'll check the suitcase."

When she opened it, she found underwear, socks, a zippered bag with some toilet articles, three large rolls of fifty- and twenty-dollar bills, and something bulky rolled up in a sweater. She folded back the layers of wool and found a carved wooden box nine inches square.

The surface of the box was covered with intricate designs of swords, knights, garlands, and crosses. A small metal clasp kept it closed. Laika opened the clasp and slowly lifted the lid of the box. Inside, lying in a bed of velvet, was a wooden cup.

Laika lifted it out and knelt there, holding it. Its dark wood gleamed, and she thought she could see not only her reflection and that of the room around her, but something else moving in that almost fluid blackness, faces and forms drifting nearly into focus, but passing away before she could be confident of their reality.

After an indeterminate time, she became aware that Joseph and Tony were near her, looking into the dark, shining depths of the cup with the same intensity she had brought to bear on it. "What is it?" Tony said in a whisper.

"A cup of some sort," Laika said. The shape was simple, almost homely. There was no base, no fluted stem. It was a wooden cup, shaped like the kind of plain jelly jars that her mother would wash for the family to use as drinking glasses. It was about eight inches high, and slightly wider at the top than at the bottom. The wood of which it was made was a half inch thick, and it seemed thicker at the bottom so that the extra weight would help prevent it from tipping. It was solid and practical and sturdy.

"The Knights Templar," Laika said, trying to remember things of which she had read, and with little interest, a long time before. "Weren't they the guardians of. . . ."

"Of the Holy Grail," Tony said. "Yeah. They were."

"Okay," said Joseph, and she could hear his voice trying to break the spell that the wooden cup seemed to hold over all of them. "Okay, let's not get carried away here. We've got a guy with a Knights Templar brand on his chest, and we've got an old cup, and that's all we've got for now."

For some reason, Joseph didn't sound as dubious as Laika had supposed he would. Though the words were those of a skeptic, she had the feeling that he was saying them because that's what they would expect him to do. And even though he seemed insincere, she realized that the words, at least, were correct: they would run the risk of making an absurd mistake if they jumped to conclusions at this point.

"You're right," she said. "But I think we should have this cup and the box examined and dated, if that's possible." Then she thought about what the man called Kyle Mc-Andrews had said: "Your organization . . . you work for him, there's blood on your hands."

"And I think," she went on, "that we should have it done by someone not directly connected to the Company."

Chapter 43

*T*here was a sudden hush in the room, as though, like Kyle McAndrews, they all had stopped breathing.

"Are you taking what he said seriously?" Tony said. "About . . . the Company being behind the assassinations?"

"I don't know," Laika said. "I don't know why he'd have said that if he hadn't believed it. Why would he have tried to kill us otherwise?"

"Maybe," said Tony, "because we were on the trail of something he didn't want us to find. Something the Templars didn't want revealed."

"I feel a conspiracy theory coming on," Joseph said, but Laika still didn't feel his heart was in it. "Tell you what," he went on, "I've got a friend at the Metropolitan Museum of Art I met some years back, doesn't have a thing to do with the Company. I'll take him the cup and the box—the knife, too, for that matter, see what he makes of it. In the meantime. . . ." He looked at the body on the floor. "What do we do with Mr. McAndrews?"

Laika nodded. "We do need to get rid of the body. No one should know what happened here, and no one should know about that brand. The twelfth man of that group should vanish completely."

Tony sighed. "Leave it to me. Let's get his clothes off, and everything here packed into that suitcase."

They did what Tony had suggested, and Laika examined the Bible on the floor. It was a King James version that had been printed in the 1980s, and there was nothing at all distinctive about it, but she put it into the wooden box, along with the knife and the cup, and placed it back in the suitcase.

"He's got no ID at all," Tony said. "Just the single key to the building, and a lot of cash sewn into his clothing. Traveled very light."

When everything was in the suitcase, Joseph carried it out of the room and down the stairs, while the others followed. As far as they could determine, no one saw them step out into the street.

"Go to the car and go back to the warehouse," Tony said. "I'll meet you there when I'm finished." Then he turned and headed toward an all-night drugstore whose lights were shining feebly a block away.

"What's he going to do?" Joseph asked, as they watched him go.

"He'll buy plastic garbage bags, a meat saw, and maybe some acid. There were sinks in the building, maybe even showers or tubs. The water might still be turned on, if he's lucky. Even if he's not, all that's left will be blood." She looked up at the building. "We need to find out who the owner of this building is. It might help us learn more about McAndrews, if that's really his name."

"You don't think it is?" Joseph said as they headed for the car.

"Apparently he's used a series of aliases. There's no reason why Kyle McAndrews wouldn't be just another one."

At the warehouse, they continued working on reassembling the sculpture in its proper configuration. As she worked, Laika was unable to stop thinking about McAndrews's accusation, and about Richard Skye.

It would not be unlike Skye to order an assassination, but was he capable of the slaughter of eleven men? She was afraid he was. And if he'd been responsible, that meant there was much about the Plattsburgh case he was not telling his operatives.

It logically followed, then, that he didn't trust the three of them. And if that were the case . . .

Laika looked around the warehouse, at the high ceiling, the concrete block walls that rose everywhere except for the wooden paneling that separated the warehouse from the anteroom. She looked at the smooth surface of the wood intently. Then she dropped the iron bar she was holding and walked away from the sculpture, toward the wooden wall.

"Christ, Laika," said Joseph, turning off his torch and raising his goggles.

She tossed her goggles aside and stopped a foot away from the wall. She scanned its surface like a laser, leaving nothing unseen. Then she noticed it and felt furious that she had not seen it before.

Eight feet up there was a small hole that had been drilled in the unfinished paneling, no bigger than a quarter inch across. She also saw the ghosts of lines where the piece of paneling had been removed with a keyhole saw, then replaced and smoothed over with a combination of sawdust and putty. It was crude work, but good enough that none of them had noticed.

"There's a bug behind the paneling," she said to Joseph. "Sonofa*bitch*."

"Christ, who?"

"Let's dig it out and see."

They wheeled one of the metal stairways over. Laika climbed it, loosened the sawed-out piece easily with a few raps of a hammer, and pulled it out with the claw. She reached inside, wiggled the mechanism back and forth, and freed it. Then she took a long look at the tiny microphone. "This is not pretty," she said, disabling it and handing it to Joseph.

"What do you mean?" he said, examining it carefully. "This looks like standard Company issue."

"That," said Laika, "is what's not pretty about it. Somebody's keeping tabs on us, and either they stole that bug from the Company, some rogue supply person sold it to them, *or*—it's the Company itself."

"Skye?"

"Mr. Control Freak himself. I suggest we search the rest

of this place, then the car, and finally the apartment. If it's Skye, he could have bugs everywhere.''

But though they looked, they could find nothing else in the warehouse—no cameras, and no other mikes.

Tony walked in two and a half hours after they had separated. He looked exhausted, and Laika noticed some dried blood around his fingernails.

"Nobody will ever find Kyle McAndrews," Tony said. "And if they do, no one will ever know who he was. Now, if you two wouldn't mind, I'm really tired. I could use a night of flat-out sleep.'' Then he seemed to notice that they were on the ladders, but nowhere near the sculpture. "So what are you two doing, shall I say, climbing the walls, for lack of a better term?''

Laika climbed down and told Tony what she had found and what she expected. "I think that's all too possible,'' Tony said. "Skye's a user. I never mentioned this, because I couldn't confirm it, but a field agent told me once that a friend of his had been on a mission that Skye had backed, and then backed *out* of. He scrubbed it because of political pressure, and left this guy and another agent in a damn war zone, when he could've gotten them both out safely. But if he had, he'd have lost face in the Company. So he wrote them off. They were expendable, not just to the mission, because we always know we're that, but to his career. Like I say, I never got it confirmed, but that's what I heard.''

"Skye's a weasel,'' said Joseph. "He'd sell out his own mother if it meant even a slightly vertical move.''

"All right,'' Laika said. "I tend to agree with you. But we don't know for sure it was him—''

Tony pointed at the bug in Laika's hand. "I know that bug well enough.''

"Matériel has gotten outside the Company before,'' she said. "But just in case, I think, even more than before, that we ought to . . . be discreet in what we report to Mr. Skye. Now, let's get some rest. But we won't say a thing about any of this on the way home, and not at the apartment, either, until we give it a clean sweep—agreed?''

They were all too tired to talk anyway. Tony played the radio on the way back to Manhattan, an oldies station that was playing all-night doo-wop. By the time they got to 72nd Street, Laika was singing along softly.

"I thought you were an opera gal," Tony said, as he pulled the car into the garage under the building.

"There's more to black culture than Leontyne Price and Kathleen Battle," she said.

Even so, she put on her headset and listened to Price's *Tosca* as she drifted off to sleep.

When she awoke, it was 10 o'clock in the morning. Tony was sitting by the brightest window with a cup of coffee and a book. He had already swept the apartment, except for Laika's room, and had found nothing, so Laika felt she could talk freely. "Where's Joseph?" she asked.

"He took the cup and the knife up to the museum to see that friend of his. He was up pretty early—I don't think he slept too well last night. Kept tossing and turning." Tony shook his head. "I'm starting to think he has something against putting bullets into people."

"I'll try and pretend you're joking. He probably did save your life last night."

"I could've evaded that knife. Still, it helped. He proved himself. I don't feel as much at risk with him anymore."

"That's big of you. I don't think he's any more afraid than we are. He just doesn't like killing, that's all."

"When you're in the field, you don't have much choice in the matter."

"Not in the doing," said Laika, "but you have a choice in the *liking*. Do you like it, Tony?"

He met her gaze evenly. "No. I don't like it, Laika. But when I have to do it, I do it, and I don't even think about it. You don't like or dislike what you don't think about."

She nodded. "Joseph will be all right."

"I guess so," Tony said, standing up to get more coffee. "But he thinks too much."

Joseph came back at noon. He looked more pale than

usual, and didn't smile as Laika greeted him with, "So what's the news from the museum?"

"Umm . . . strange. The news is rather strange. David— this friend of mine?—is in antiquities, and when I showed him the cup, he hemmed and hawed, but came to the conclusion that it definitely *could* be first century A.D. If it's not, he said, then it's an extremely clever forgery. But he couldn't explain why anyone would make a forgery of such a . . . nondescript and plain cup.

"The box he dated to the thirteenth century, though the velvet inside is much later. The knife, he said, is from about the same time. He, uh, asked me where I got it, and I was pretty noncommittal. But he recognized the sign of the Knights Templar on the knife, and told me that most of the designs on the box were connected with the order as well.

"Then he said to me . . ." Joseph paused, and took a deep breath. Laika couldn't get over how uncomfortable he seemed. "He said, 'So are you going to try to sell this to the press as the Holy Grail?'"

"So McAndrews, or whoever he was," said Laika, trying to ignore the comment about the Grail, "might truly have been a Knight Templar?"

"They were supposed to have died out centuries ago," Joseph said. "But there were always stories of their survival. The most persistent story had them being connected to a Scottish Masonic lodge a few centuries ago."

"And it's a good bet that the eleven who died . . . and McAndrews . . . were all Scottish," said Laika.

Joseph nodded. "Things tie together even more. In some medieval documents, the Holy Grail is called the *Sangraal*, which can translate as *sang real*."

" 'Royal blood,' " said Tony. "The bloodline of Christ."

Joseph didn't respond. Instead, he sat down at his computer and glided the mouse over the pad, clicking several times. "I got up early this morning," he said, "and scanned the fingerprints we took from McAndrews onto the computer. Then I sent them to the *Sûreté* and asked them to do two things. One was to see if there were any other suspects captured in the attempted burglary where Robert Gunn was arrested. And if there were, to check their fingerprints against those I sent.'' Joseph read what was on the screen, and the corner of his mouth twisted in a bitter smile.

''There *was* another man,'' he said. ''Ewan McCullough. And the prints match. Perfectly.''

''You mean,'' Laika said, feeling a numbness start to creep up her back, ''that Kyle McAndrews—the man who died last night—burglarized that house back in 1907? *Ninety years ago?*''

''Yeah, unless you want to believe that the *Sûreté* made another 'mistake' like they supposedly did with Gunn.''

Laika shook her head. ''They didn't make any mistake.''

''There's something else,'' said Joseph. ''Something I didn't tell you before. The house that was burglarized? The Villa Bethania? I found out when I read the book. You remember the priest who found the documents in the pillar? The one who got mysteriously rich?

''That priest built and lived in the Villa Bethania. Gunn and McAndrews were trying to break into the house of the man who had discovered the bloodline secret.''

"**W**hy didn't you tell us?" said Laika. She could feel her jaw clench, and wanted more than anything to hit Joseph.

"I . . . I thought Tony would get on the conspiracy thing again. And that you'd go along with it. I thought it was crazy, just a waste of time, but now—"

"Now what?" asked Tony.

"Now I know it's not," Joseph said flatly.

Laika knew why his heart hadn't been in his skepticism of the night before. He had known more than they had, and what was worse, had kept it from them.

"Joseph," she said, "I warned you before about not backing us up. Last night you proved you could, at least with a weapon. But backing your team means more than that. It means sharing *everything* you know, and everything you suspect. You didn't do that. You withheld information, important information. Do you have any reason why I shouldn't immediately terminate your involvement in this mission?"

"Yes," he said instantly. "I do. I'm a skeptic, but I'm not unreasonably stubborn. I know I was wrong to keep information from you, but I did it for what I thought was the good of the mission. I was afraid of losing focus on the facts. But once I saw how the facts could fit together, I knew enough to do it and tell you about it." He paused, sat back in his chair, and interlaced his fingers. "I also think that I know what McAndrews might have been trying to say before he died. It occurred to me on the way back here this morning.''

"What?'' said Laika, still angry.

"It sounded like 'Andra.' But I think it might have been 'Andrea.' '' He put the stress on the second syllable.

"Andrea who?'' Laika asked.

"Johann Valentin Andrea. Remember the *Prieure de Sion*? The Priory of Zion?''

"The secret society that wanted to put the Merovingian bloodline back on the thrones of Europe,'' Tony said, sitting down at his computer and booting it up.

"Right. This Andrea was supposed to have been the head of the organization sometime during the seventeenth century. He wrote a lot of occult texts, and practically founded Rosicrucianism single-handedly, and Rosicrucianism ties right in to the Grail legends and the Knights Templar. It's just all too interconnected to be a series of coincidences.''

"Unless McAndrews didn't mean Johann Andrea in the first place,'' said Laika. "Maybe he meant a woman's name, or the French name André, or he was trying to say 'under,' or half a dozen other things.''

"Now you're trying too hard to be me,'' Joseph said with an apologetic smile. She had never seen him as diffident as he was now, and she could feel her anger recede as a result. "You may be right,'' he conceded, "but so many things point to, for want of a better phrase, a religious conspiracy, that it seems unlikely there's any other, less sensational explanation.''

"If you want to add fuel to that fire,'' said Tony, looking at his monitor, "here's another log. When I got up this morning, I did what you suggested, Laika, and put in a request for information on the Drummond Building. Guess who's owned it for the past seven years?''

"The Catholic church,'' Laika said.

"You got it. The Archdiocese of New York.''

Joseph grinned. "God bless 'em, they're everywhere. Look,'' he went on, warming to the topic, "I can't begin to explain the longevity angles here, how these two Scots could have lived to be over a hundred and look like they're thirty. But this whole bloodline plot is something that I *can* explain, something it doesn't take any faith in divinity to believe in. Like I said before, I believe in what I can see and understand, and I can believe in human passions. I can understand greed.''

"What do you mean?" Tony asked.

Joseph leaned forward and spoke with a sudden intensity. "I mean the lust for kingdoms and thrones and power. Look, I don't believe Jesus was divine, but I think there's plenty of evidence for an historical Jesus. The man existed, he wasn't mythical, though the stories that sprang up around him were. Since he existed, it's very possible that he could have fathered children, whether he survived his crucifixion or not. And those children could have had children of their own, and so on down the generations, for hundreds of years. And somebody kept track, okay? Somebody knew that these were Jesus's great-great-great-grandchildren. But maybe that was a secret that the church didn't want to get out.''

"All right," said Laika, "I can see why—the early church was fairly jealous of the competition. A descendant of Christ would have challenged their power.''

"So what do they do to the heir when they find him—or when he comes to claim his ancestor's kingdom?" said Joseph. "They imprison him.''

"I can't buy that," Tony said. "I mean, they'd have made him Pope or something. He was Christ's *descendant.*''

"No," Joseph insisted. "He was *Jesus's* descendant. The concept of Christ makes it necessary that Jesus was divine, and if he wasn't chaste, he sure as hell wasn't divine. Gods, or at least, a god like the Catholic church worshiped, didn't go around getting women pregnant. There's a descendant? Proof that Jesus was a man and not a god? Boom, there goes the church. So lock him up out of sight.''

"But for two thousand years, Joseph?" said Laika. "Why not just have him killed? Some of the early popes were pretty unscrupulous.''

"And some of the *later* ones weren't real charmers, either.

But how could they kill the descendant of Christ? The popes might have been infallible, but hey . . .'' Joseph laughed. ''. . . they didn't know *everything*. The ways of God, to those who believed in him, were always strange and inexplicable. Maybe there was a divine reason that Jesus spread his seed on earth. And were they going to risk eternal damnation by destroying the result? Not too likely. So they kept him alive, and maybe more than that, they kept the *line* alive.''

''What the hell are you saying?'' Tony said. ''That they *bred* him?''

''To keep the bloodline intact,'' Joseph said. ''It's certainly possible, and apparently it had to happen somehow, if the prisoner, who more than just *we* are looking for, is really alive somewhere. Why would the church fathers have wanted the bloodline of their Lord to die out? For all they knew, that could have been blasphemy or worse. So, yeah, I'm saying it's altogether possible that they found him a nice girl . . . maybe a nun, since they're supposed to be brides of Christ anyway—''

''This is *bullshit!*'' Tony said, turning away from Joseph and Laika and stalking to the window.

''All right, then,'' said Joseph, ''maybe it wasn't a nun. Or rather, *they* weren't nuns. This would have had to happen, after all, every thirty years or so for there to be a new generation.''

''This is . . . this is sick, Joseph, *perverse.*''

''Tony, maybe you're not aware of the things some of the popes did? One of them made a pact with the devil and was beaten to death by a husband who found him screwing his wife. Another one had six thousand people killed in a personal vendetta against a rival family. And Alexander the Sixth, who was one of the Borgias, would sell cardinalships, poison the new buyers, and sell them again! So you're telling me that people like that, with an unbridled lust for worldly power, couldn't have come up with a plot like this?''

''Sure, there were bad popes,'' Tony said, ''but that was centuries ago!''

''And centuries ago,'' said Joseph, ''was when this was

all put into place. Things like that become self-sustaining. It's altogether possible that the popes themselves might not have known about this for hundreds of years now."

"Joseph," Laika said slowly, "twenty-four hours ago, you would have said that this was all a huge theory, tied together by a dozen coincidences. What changed your mind?"

"I saw all the pieces, but I hadn't put them together. Now I have, and I think they all fit. It's like . . . if I tried to put together a jigsaw puzzle and all the pieces fit, and it made a picture of a duck, I wouldn't be stubborn enough to say that random chance produced that duck. And as far as I'm concerned, when I look at all these pieces together—the unknown captive, the two Knights Templar, the two-thousand-year-old wooden cup, the involvement of the church—and everything else, well, goddamn it, Laika, it looks like a duck, it waddles like a duck, and it quacks like a sonofabitch.

"So who am I to say it's a chicken?"

They talked for a long time, trying to fit in the other stray pieces, like Peder Holberg's sculpture and his fugue states, the cultists who wanted to find the unknown captive, and the old priest buried alive in the tomb. Tony suggested that Father Samuel might have tried to free the descendant (if that was who he truly was) and been punished by his subterranean imprisonment. That, however, did not explain the man's preternatural age.

They pondered, too, the flat black lead walls that had surrounded Father Samuel, and how the Peters tomb apparently had never been built to house any caskets. "Could it have originally been the place they housed this prisoner?" asked Laika, receiving shrugs and nods that replied, "Why not?" "But why make the walls out of lead?" she went on. "Is there any religious significance to lead?"

"Not that I know of," said Joseph. "They had lead in biblical times, of course, but as for any connection—Tony?"

He shook his head. "Nothing in Catholicism that I ever came across. It's about the heaviest metal, isn't it? So if they wanted to *really* lock somebody away, it would at least give the impression of entombment better than any other substance.''

Laika finished what seemed like her tenth cup of coffee and sat back with a sigh. ''We could go on like this for days. But I think the thing to do now is to get back to the warehouse, reassemble that sculpture, and find out where it's going to steer us next.

''The map is still the answer, though I'm damned if I can figure out what the question is.''

Chapter 45

*T*hey arrived at the warehouse by mid-afternoon and worked feverishly at putting the pieces of the puzzle into the proper order. Five hours later, Joseph switched off the torch, wiped the sweat from his forehead, and pronounced, "That's it. We're finished."

When they pushed away the steel ladders, they saw that the pattern of pipes and rods came together unmistakably at a central point nearly twenty-five feet above the floor of the warehouse. So many of the pipes met at the locus that it resembled a star, the pipes the beams of light radiating outward from the core.

"Jesus, I can't believe it," Joseph said. "If we'd had this at the beginning, this would've been our first stop. I mean, how can you ignore something like that? It anchors the whole thing."

"And now you can see," said Tony, "that the blast, or whatever it was, must have started from there. The pipes are in the worst shape, the rust is worse—look how red it is— shit, how did Guaraldi make a mistake like that?"

"Near exhaustion, "Laika said, "and the fact that putting this . . . monstrosity together was certainly more complex than anything he'd ever done before. And unfortunately, what we see here apparently also made sense in the way that Guaraldi looked at it."

"But it doesn't—not really," Joseph said. "It was chaos before, and now it's not. It has a center." He walked along its length, pointing. "See the relationship it has to the other two places we were at already? It triangulates here."

Laika followed the imaginary lines Joseph drew in the air. The new locus did seem to be the point of a triangle, the two points of whose base were made up of the locations of St. Stephen's Church and the abandoned subway station. "So is it a pattern?" she said. "Any three points will make a triangle, you know."

"A perfect isosceles?" Joseph asked. "*Look* at it!"

"I'm looking," said Laika, "but you're just eyeballing. It might not be anywhere near perfect. How long will it take for you to make the changes in the computer program so we can find the exact location in the city?"

"A few hours," Joseph answered.

"Then get to it instead of admiring this thing. It's a map, that's all, so let's go where it tells us to."

While Joseph tackled the computer, Laika and Tony spoke softly at the other end of the room. "Does it look like a perfect triangle to you?" she asked him.

"I kind of hate to say it, but yeah, it does. And with the rise from the floor up to that top point, you can just imagine a plane connecting all three points, and it looks like a giant wing, or something. Taking us right up to the top of . . . of what? The city? Some building?"

"But why those three points?"

Tony shook his head. "We can only guess. The prisoner might have been held in the crypt, and maybe it's possible that he—or an ancestor, if this other theory of ours is valid— was also held in the subway station—after it was abandoned, of course. If that follows, then maybe, just maybe, the current prisoner is being held in this new location, and that's why it's the locus of the map." He let out a self-deprecating laugh. "But that's one helluva lot of maybes."

"And if that's all true, then we have to assume that Peder Holberg either talked to this prisoner, who told him the locations where he was held, or . . . ?"

"The fugue states were when Holberg was being dictated to by this other mind. *'Doo-bee-doo-be, doo-bee-doo-bee. . . . ' ''*

Laika recognized the theme from *The Twilight Zone.* "Telepathy, huh? This thing just gets goofier and goofier. The religious conspiracy I can almost believe. It's farfetched, but possible. But *telepathy?*''

"What about Joseph's dream? You think that was just a coincidence, too? Or did whoever got into Holberg's head pay a visit later to Joseph's?"

"A few days ago I would've said it was a coincidence. Now I'm not so sure.''

"I've got it!" Joseph cried from the other end of the warehouse. Laika and Tony trotted toward him, and he went on. "It's a block off Broadway, just north of the financial district. It's a thirty-three-story building called the Weyandt Tower, built in the 1890s, pretty tall for its time. There are a couple of shops on the street, but the rest of the building—''

"Is vacant," Tony finished.

Joseph smiled. "And I bet you can even tell me who the owner of the building is.''

"The Archdiocese of New York?" Laika offered.

"Right again. May I suggest we pay the Weyandt Tower a visit?''

"Sure," said Laika. "But first we need to set a few things straight.''

Joseph tensed. "Like what?"

"Like what we're going to do if we get there and find a prisoner being held by the Roman Catholic Church. I don't think the Vatican has its own version of the Mossad, so I doubt if they're going to open up on us with Uzis, though I could be wrong. But if they do, are we going to fire back? Tony?''

"I wouldn't fire on priests, no. But there won't be any priests shooting at us. There may be somebody, but not priests.''

"What about nuns?" Joseph asked.

"Go to hell.''

"Who knows what the night may hold?"

Laika ignored the exchange. "Kidnaping, if that's the crime here, is a federal matter."

"What," said Tony, "you're suggesting we get the FBI in on this?"

"Just an observation. My point is that no matter what happens, who this person turns out to be, we have to maintain a low profile. A nonexistent one."

"So we free them and ride off into the night," said Joseph. "That shouldn't be difficult."

"It could be very difficult. I want to consider this evening's incursion as a scouting expedition. We'll try and discover exactly what the situation is. If we find we can take some sort of action, we may. But we're not going to go in expecting a firefight or anything more than a reconnaissance."

"We'll be armed?" Tony asked.

"Of course. I think we should be ready for anything." She looked at her watch. "It's 2300 hours now. I want to go in very late, at 0300. Let's go back to the apartment, get a little food, a little rest. We'll go back out at 0230."

Chapter 46

At 2:30 in the morning, Laika, Joseph, and Tony, fully armed, drove south toward the financial district of the city. There were still people on the streets of midtown, but when they got below 34th Street, the small crowds thinned and became nonexistent.

The area in which they found themselves, just north of streets which were among New York's busiest during the day, seemed in the early morning to be a no-man's land. The only thing moving was the occasional cab, or the steam rising through manhole covers like thin, insubstantial ghosts, scrawny, drug-raddled wraiths of the city. Here and there a coffee shop or a bar was open, but even the lights announcing their presence were low and subtle, speaking in soft voices of blue and purple neon. Inside the coffee shop windows, the brighter lights fought a losing battle against the darkness of the streets.

Because of the minimal traffic, all of them felt confident that they would easily spot any car trailing them. That lack of vigilance made them fail to notice the low red car that had been following them at a distance of three or four blocks shortly after they had left 72nd Street, or the van just behind it.

The three operatives finally pulled over to the curb a half block from the Weyandt Tower. It must have been imposing in its day, Laika thought. Even now, a hundred years after its erection, it dwarfed most of the structures in the vicinity.

It was at the end of a triangular block, and like the Flatiron Building, was the three-sided shape of the block it dominated, an enormous sharp-nosed wedge. In the mist which crept up from the Hudson and the East Rivers, Laika could nearly imagine the building as the hull of a great ship steaming through the night, leaving a wake of two streets as it glided into the current of the avenue ahead.

Except for the dim lights that shone inside the closed shops on the ground floor, the building was totally dark. As far up as they could see, the only lights in the windows were reflected from the city around it. The Weyandt Tower seemed a great body without a heart.

According to the scale of Peder Holberg's map, Joseph had estimated that whatever it was that Holberg was pointing out was located on or near the top floor of the building. "Any thoughts," Laika asked Tony, "as to how to get inside?"

"Not yet," he said, as he swung the car out into the street again.

"Not giving up already, are we?" Joseph said.

"This is recon," Tony said, "or did you forget already? I want to check out all the entrances, see if there's an interior courtyard that might be open. Not to park—too easy to get trapped that way—but to stay out of sight from the street."

"You weren't this picky in the Bronx," Joseph said.

"Better security in Manhattan than the Bronx, in case your finely attuned senses didn't pick that up. Ah, here we go. . . ."

Tony slowed the car. Ahead of them was a motor entrance covered by an iron gate. Tony drove past it as he looked at it carefully. "Looks good," Laika said. "Padlocked."

Tony nodded agreement. "Probably an underground garage put in later." He parked the car half a block away and they got out, locking all the doors.

They saw no one as they walked to the gate. Tony looked at the street, and up at the windows of the buildings on the other side, but if anyone was watching, they watched from the darkness. Finally he shrugged. "Let's do it," he said, and went to work, checking first for any sign of an alarm system. Finding none, he began to pick the lock.

Five minutes later, he shook his head in frustration. "This is one tough sonofabitch," he said, as he changed picks and tried again. Still another few minutes passed until Laika heard the sound of the heavy padlock opening. "I should get some locksmith's award for that one," Tony said, as he took it off the hasp. "Let's go."

The paved drive angled steeply downward, and Laika knew that it must lead to an underground garage. After a walk of forty feet and a descent that she estimated as fifteen feet, they came up against a wide garage door set into an old brick cellar wall. Tony opened the inset lock easily and raised the door just enough for them to get under it. Laika winced at the sound of it going up on its rollers.

They ducked under it and went into the dark garage, leaving the door open for an escape route. The garage had room for several dozen cars. At the far end they saw another ramp leading up, wide enough for only one vehicle. Laika thought it might come out somewhere on the other side of the building, though she couldn't remember seeing any exit there.

A van was parked near an elevator door. It was large and had no side windows except for those in front. Laika made a mental note of the New York license number, though it seemed to have been parked there for months. Dust had settled on the oil-stained floor all around it.

Tony shined his light on a door next to the elevator. In it was a small glass panel through which Laika could see stairs leading up. As best as she could determine, the stairs were at the narrow end of the building, where the two long outside walls met at the point of the wedge. "Let's go," she said softly, pushing open the unlocked door.

They walked slowly, their sneakered footsteps making no sound on the hard-surfaced stairs. They stopped every five flights for a few seconds' rest. A thirty-three-story hike wasn't bad, but Laika didn't want them to be winded when they reached the top floor, not knowing what might be waiting for them there.

"We can't be sure, can we," she whispered to Joseph on the twenty-fifth-floor landing, "that we want the thirty-third?"

Joseph shook his head, then pointed upward, circling his finger to indicate that their goal could be anywhere above them. "Thirty-two or thirty-three, I think," he whispered back, careful to use no word with a sibilant. Ss would carry through the echoing silence of the stairwell like a gunshot.

Laika nodded and continued to walk. They would enter the thirty-second floor. If there was nothing there, perhaps they could hear movement on the floor overhead.

Then a sound came to Laika's ears that made her stop. She could not tell where it had come from, but she didn't think it had been made by her party. The others stopped, too, and she listened for a moment but heard nothing more. Joseph and Tony looked questioningly at her, but she shook her head and continued to climb the stairs.

Ten floors below, James Winston continued to freeze. He didn't move and scarcely breathed, though it was hard to breathe quietly through a broken nose. He pressed the lens of his flashlight against his body, trying to ignore the pressure against his aching ribs, smothering its light for a long time, before he dared to let it shine between his fingers again and illuminate just enough of the stairs to let him see where he was walking.

Maybe he'd shine it a little more brightly. It had been too damn dark, which was why he'd tripped and fallen and rapped the flashlight against the stairs. But not too bright. If he could look up the narrow stairwell and see their lights high above, that meant that they could look down and see his, too. And he didn't want them to know he was coming. No, he didn't want them to know he was there until the very last minute, just before he shot them all.

James Winston had spent the past several weeks brooding, nurturing his grudges like a string of cancers. The list of sins against his righteous ass was long and unforgivable. First, Laika had blindsided him and beat on him; next, that goddamn dago had showed him up in the lobby of the apartment building; and finally, and worst of all, that bitch had pulled some karate shit on him in that parking lot—busted his nose and his jaw and four of his ribs before he even had a chance to defend himself. His ribs were still taped, his jaw was going to be wired for another two weeks, and his nose hurt like a sonofabitch.

On top of everything, his car had been stripped down to the chassis. He barely made it out of that shithole alive by finding a cop and giving him a story about how these guys had carjacked him in Manhattan, made him drive across to the Bronx, and then beaten the shit out of him. Then the insurance company went medieval on his ass, with three different investigators, and only one of them a brother, questioning him up and down, trying to find out if he was bullshitting them. And the goddamn *brother* was the one who said he was full of crap and here was why, and threatened to have him busted for filing a false report if he didn't withdraw his claim.

It was all that bitch Laika's fault. Her and her two white boyfriends. And now it was time for her to make it all up to him by dying.

He had gotten a sweet little piece from his old homeboy Pipe. It had cost an arm and a leg, but it was brand new, a Smith and Wesson .38 revolver with a big-ass barrel. James had told Pipe that he didn't want a revolver, he wanted an automatic, but Pipe had just shaken his head. "Automatic, my ass. Cops don't carry automatics, they carry revolvers, and you know why? 'Cause revolvers don't jam up on ya, James. Last thing you want is to just be about to smoke that bitch when that automatic jam up on ya. Shit man, the cops, they know...."

So he had taken the revolver, and he had to admit it was pretty nice. Made him feel like a cowboy when he carried it. Bought himself a harness for it, too; tucked it under his armpit just like Dirty Harry. Sure, it only had six shots, but if he couldn't take out three people with two bullets each, then he wasn't much of a man, was he?

But he *was* a man, and that was what he was going to prove to Laika Harris once and for all, and to her two pimps, too.

He had tried to follow them before, but had lost them most times. He didn't want to go back to the warehouse because there was too much open space there, no place to hide and sneak up on them. After all, trying to hide under that car had been a real disaster. But though he wouldn't admit it to himself, he just didn't want to go back to the place where he had gotten the shit kicked out of him.

Her apartment wouldn't work, either. There were people all around that neighborhood, even if he could get out of the building afterward without some asshole sticking his head out after he heard shots. No, James wanted to kill them, but he wanted to kill them and walk away, maybe even spend a little time gloating over them as they lay dying, spitting on them while they were still alive. He had had worse fantasies than this one, or more pleasant, depending on your point of view.

But this, Jesus, this was damn near perfect. He had been able to follow them easily through the nearly empty streets, even hanging back a good piece. And when they had tooled into the financial area, which was a ghost town after rush hour, he knew this was the time, and things just got better and better.

He had parked his new car (leased, and insured under a new carrier) two blocks from where their taillights had finally stopped. Then he'd followed them through the iron gate, waiting at the top of the ramp until their lights had vanished. He had held the lens of the flashlight in his fist, spreading his fingers enough for a few slashes of light to shine on the floor and show him the way.

He had walked right into the partially open garage door that way, bumping his nose and jarring his tender ribs before he saw the door itself. Cursing between his teeth, he crouched, trying to keep his torso from bending, and duck-walked under the door. Then he had followed them up the stairs, staying far below them.

Now he waited to see their lights begin to move again so that he could follow them to their deaths. He didn't know what the hell they were doing in this building, what the hell they'd been doing in that warehouse. And he didn't care.

He had them where he wanted them now. There didn't seem to be a soul but them in this whole building. Nobody would hear the shots, and nobody would hear that bitch scream as those bastards went down and she joined them. It was going to be mighty sweet.

James took a deep breath, wincing as the air pressed his lungs against his ribs, and started to climb the stairs again.

In the garage, now far below James and the three operatives, eight people dressed in dark colors spoke quietly together, their heads looking toward the floor. There was no visible light in the room, but each person wore night goggles that lit the garage with a pale, monochromatic light. They all carried weapons.

Finally one of them said, slightly louder than the others, "Amen," and raised his head. Then he looked intently at one of the others and said, "Got it?"

The other nodded, and the leader smiled. " 'Today,' " he said, " 'you will be with me in paradise.' " Then he headed for the stairs and pushed open the door. The group followed and noiselessly began to climb.

Chapter 47

*A*t the door stenciled "32," Laika paused and turned off her flashlight. Tony and Joseph did the same. She looked through the glass panel, but saw neither light nor motion. Tony examined the door frame and found no indication of any alarms, so they opened it. They entered a small vestibule that opened onto the hall.

It led straight down the center of the building. There were small, shallow offices on either side, but as the building widened, so did the offices. Dust coated the floor, and there were no footprints that Laika could see. Many of the doors were open, and most of those that were not had translucent glass panels through which dim light filtered in from the glow of the city outside. Laika discovered that there was easily enough light to show their way.

As they moved into the wider part of the wedge, the offices on either side grew into suites. They explored several and found them to be increasingly labyrinthine, one leading into another. By the time they reached the end of the hall, there were numerous side halls as well, going to left and right and having their own tributaries.

Laika gestured back toward the point of the wedge and they retraced their steps. But halfway back she thought she heard, directly above them, a dull rumbling noise, as of something heavy being moved on rollers. She held up a hand, and the others stopped and listened, too, nodding to show they heard.

302

There was someone in the building, after all, and on the floor above.

They moved more quickly now toward the stairs, and Laika turned on her light, pushed open the door, stepped onto the landing, and started to climb the last flight to the thirty-third floor.

James Winston turned off his flashlight, unthinkingly pressing against his gut so hard that he nearly yelped from the pain, but he choked it back just in time. The light had come like a flare through the glass pane of the door above him, and he sank to his knees on the landing where the stairs switchbacked between the thirty-first and thirty-second floors. He even put his head down so that his eyes wouldn't gleam.

If any of the three he figured were coming through that door shone his flashlight down at him, he'd be seen instantly, and then he'd have to shoot, and he didn't want to—not yet. He wanted to get them on *his* terms.

But they didn't shine their lights downward, or come that way. Instead, they went up the next flight, and he let a sigh of relief hiss slowly from between his clenched teeth. He waited until he heard the door above open softly, and then waited for another few minutes on the dark landing, his heart pounding so loud he thought he could hear it.

Laika trotted up the steps and looked through the glass panel in the door. Seeing only darkness, she opened it, and they stepped into the vestibule.

She listened intently and thought she heard the sound again, a low trundling noise. Beckoning to the others, she started down the hall. They looked to either side as they walked but saw only empty offices until they reached the wider part of the building.

There the hall started to brighten, and Laika saw that a light was on somewhere in one of the corridors to the left. She increased her speed, running silently down the carpeted hall, and eased her head around the corner. A short, straight hall lit by fluorescent overhead lights lay ahead of her, with several doors to either side and a strange panel at the end.

Laika put away her flashlight and took out her pistol, then stalked down the hall, Tony and Joseph at her flanks, both holding their weapons, checking each empty office as they passed. Finally, at the end of the corridor, they saw that the office on the right had been occupied. A floor lamp and a desk light shone on a twenty-foot-square room that held a couch, two easy chairs, a desk, and a coffee table, along with a mini-refrigerator. There were no windows. A coffeemaker sat on the desk, its red light glowing. Two nearly full mugs, still sending up plumes of steam, were on the coffee table, along with an Andrew Greeley paperback, several magazines, and a small Bible. A Walkman and headset were on the floor near the couch.

But what drew Laika's attention most was a metal panel mounted on the far wall. It was a foot square, and on it were four small red lightbulbs, one of which was blinking.

"Alarm," she said. "They knew we were coming."

A door at the far end of the room was slightly ajar, and she ran to it. At this point she didn't expect a fight. These people, whoever they were, had fled. They wanted to get away, not stand against intruders. Otherwise, the operatives would have been met with a hail of bullets. Still, she did not holster her weapon.

Beyond the door was another short corridor, dimly lit by inset ceiling lights. At the end were two doors, one ajar, the other closed. Laika pushed open the one that was ajar and found herself in a small room that was as dead as Father Samuel's tomb. The walls, floor, ceiling, and door were lined with lead, and the door frame had the same material around its edges, as if to make a seal when shut. The room was utterly empty.

Tony had already tried the other door, but found it locked. There was no keyhole. "Locked or barred from the other side," he said.

"Get it down," Laika said, and the three assaulted the door with their shoulders. Something in the frame cracked, and in another few seconds they threw it wide open. A dimly lit hall lay ahead, and from the grooves in the carpet it was obvious that whatever had been wheeled away was very heavy.

There was a noise ahead, a clanking sound as though another door had closed somewhere, and they ran thirty feet to where the corridor turned left. There, another twenty feet away, the corridor opened into a wider cul-de-sac. The far wall appeared to be decorative, covered with heavily textured plaster. There was no way out but the corridor down which they had come.

Laika heard a mechanical sound and put her ear to the plastered wall. "There's an elevator behind here." She jerked her head around to the others. "Christ, they're on their way down. . . ."

It was easy now. James just stuck his flashlight in his hip pocket and followed the lights. It was going perfectly. He'd get them in one of these narrow corridors and just blast away. Shit, there was no *way* he could miss.

He poked his head around the corner and looked into an office. The coffee sure smelled good. Maybe he'd have himself a cup on the way out to celebrate.

He edged his way into the short hall and saw an empty room ahead. They probably went through the kicked-down door. He had heard it splinter way back in the main hall.

James could hear voices ahead. It looked like they were after something, and if they were, they wouldn't expect anybody coming up on them from behind.

He stopped where the corridor turned left. He heard her voice, though he couldn't make out the words. Okay, she was there, it was time, goddamnit. He had thought a lot about what to say just before he opened up on her and had finally come up with something so simple and vicious that it would send her through the gates of hell totally pissed off.

So long, bitch.

He wanted the word that she hated so much to be the last thing she heard in this life.

James took a deep breath and cocked the pistol, wincing at the *click* it made. Though the sound of metal meeting metal was very soft, it sounded loud to James. But he steeled himself by thinking that the others couldn't have heard it. Then he stepped around the corner, his weapon still at his side, but ready to come up as soon as he saw his targets . . .

. . . And looked into the muzzles of three guns just as big as Christ and death pointing at him from less than fifteen feet away.

"*So long bi*—" was as far as he got before terror choked him.

Laika, Joseph, and Tony had just turned to run back down the hallway when they all heard the soft but unmistakable sound of a hammer being cocked. They instantly went into a three-man combat stance, aiming their weapons down toward the bend of the corridor. When James Winston suddenly appeared, his gun starting to come up, Laika knew that he saw death looking at him.

"Drop it!" she barked. She knew that Tony and Joseph were trained not to fire until the pistol in James's hand came above his waist. James was only two inches from dying.

She saw fear enter his face, and the gun tremble. This was the moment. He would either bring it up in panic or lower it all the way. If he panicked, he would die before he could get off a shot.

"Turn it around," she said more gently. "Hold it by the barrel. Hand it to us." James was crazier than most people she had known, but she thought even he wasn't crazy enough to pass up a chance of living.

She was right. The .38 slowly dropped to his side, and he reached over with his other hand, took it by the barrel, and held it out toward them.

Tony covered the distance in a second, never letting the muzzle of his gun leave the target of James's chest, and smoothly snatched the pistol from his hand. He shook his head as if at the man's stupidity, then grabbed him by the shoulder and flung him against the wall. "You," he said, "are one real dumbass."

"He's right, James," said Laika. "You *are* a dumbass."

"We've gotta get downstairs," Tony said, "and fast."

Laika knew what he meant. And she knew why James had come after them. The gun told her that. He had wanted to kill her, and probably Tony and Joseph, too, figuring they were her lovers, or some other bullshit.

She was just about to give Tony the nod to do what had to be done when James, as though realizing his fate, shook his head and backed away toward the turn in the corridor. As he stepped back, a shot rang out.

For a split second, Laika thought that Tony had shot James without an order. But then more shots followed, and Laika saw the bullets spitting into the wall next to James. He leapt toward Laika and the others, and she knew the gunfire was originating from the end of the corridor down which they had first come.

She threw her arm around the corner and opened up with her Jati-Matic, throwing half of her twenty-round clip down the corridor at their attackers. She whipped her head and arms back around the corner to safety as the firing from the other end ceased. "Great," she growled. "Now who the hell are *they?*"

"This is getting to be like a convention," Tony said.

"Friends of yours?" Laika asked James, but he shook his head.

"No . . . no, I came alone. . . ."

"How many, you think?" she asked Tony.

"From the sound of it, I'd guess six to eight. Semis and full. They're well equipped. But as long as we've got ammo, there's no way they can get down the corridor."

"And no way we can get up it," she added.

"What the hell . . . what the hell's goin' on, man?" James said. Laika was far from feeling amused, but she couldn't help but relish the fact that James was sweating like a pig and looked positively chalky.

"What's going on is that you stepped into the wrong place at the wrong time," Laika said.

"With the wrong people," Tony added. Joseph, Laika noticed, wasn't saying much, for a change, but he didn't look scared, just determined. "We gotta get out of here, Laika," Tony said. "Those people on the elevator are gonna be long gone by the time we get out of this, if we do."

"Well, what about the elevator?" asked Laika. "It's worth a try. Joseph, you stay here. They try to advance, fire a few shots to drive them back. James, you come with us."

James obeyed like a puppy dog, staying just ahead of them as she held him at gunpoint. When they reached the wall where they had heard the elevator, there was another burst of gunfire from the hall, but she saw Joseph swing his Uzi into the open and spray the hallway with bullets, and the silence fell again.

Laika kept her gun trained on James, while Tony covered the rough-textured wall with searching fingers. "There's got to be a catch here somewhere. . . ."

He found a small switch at waist level, under a decorative ridge at the right edge of the wall, where no one would come across it by accident. As soon as he pressed it, the panel slid into the wall to the right like a pocket door, revealing an elevator double door of brushed aluminum and a panel with one button.

Tony pushed it, but nothing happened. "Shit!" he said, and the word was punctuated by another blast of gunfire from the corridor. Laika heard Joseph shooting back. "They must've locked it down below."

"Can we open it?" Laika asked, then gestured with her gun. "James, help him."

Tony took a small tool from a pocket and jammed it between the elevator doors, opening it enough to get his fingers in. "Come *on*," he grunted to James, who did the same on the other side. "Pull, goddamnit!"

As the men increased the pressure on the doors, they slowly slid open until they reached the midway point. Then they flew all the way open, throwing James back against the wall and nearly tripping Tony, who kept his balance. Laika stepped to the entrance and looked in.

The counterweight was directly across the shaft, which told her the elevator itself was all the way at the bottom. Four feet ahead was the thick cable. There was no emergency ladder. There was nothing else at all but an open shaft thirty-three stories down.

"Could you get down?" Laika asked Tony. "On the cable?" She didn't know if it was possible, but thought it might be. It would be like climbing down a rope, but a slick one. It would take tremendous upper body strength, and she was strong, but not that strong.

Tony thought for a moment. "Maybe if I cut apart some holsters, use them to grip the cable, wrap a belt around them and hang on to that, I don't know. But that means leaving you two here—I can't do that."

"Bullshit you can't," Laika said, taking out a commando knife and slipping off the holster that housed her single action pistol. "Cover him."

Tony held his SIG on James while Laika stuck her pistol in her belt and cut apart the holster. "Score the inside surface," Tony said. "Give it more traction." Laika did as he'd asked, cutting hatches on the rough leather. Then she snaked her belt off her dark jeans.

"What about your shoes?" she said. "You've got to be able to grip the cable with your feet, too."

"Okay." Tony took off the holster that housed his .45 semi-automatic and jammed the pistol into his waistband alongside James's .38. "I feel like a walking gun shop," he said.

Laika cut the holster open, scoring the leather, and then ran to Joseph, who was reloading during a brief lull in the firefight. "I need your belt and holster for grips," she said. "Tony's going to go down the shaft."

"He'd rather die falling than getting shot?" Joseph said, taking off his belt, and his effort at banter relieved her. But then they both ducked involuntarily as another fusillade came from the end of the hall. Joseph waited until it had died down and then answered it with a rattling series of his own. "Just to let them know we're still here," he said with a smile.

Laika ran back to the elevator, where she performed the same operation on Joseph's holster and cut his belt into strips. Then she gave the whole mess to Tony, who tightly bound the holster leather around his shoes with the belt strips. When he was finished, he gave James's pistol to Laika and handed her his SIG.

"Take good care of her. I'll keep the .45, try and follow them when I get down. I'll come back when I can."

"Good luck," said Laika.

He patted his chest. "Hey, I got my St. Christopher medal. Who needs luck?"

Then he put one hand on the elevator doorway and reached out with the largest of the leather holsters for the cable. "Shit," he said. "I need both hands."

"Hold his waist," Laika told James. "He falls, you'd better go with him."

James gingerly stepped to the edge of the shaft next to Tony and put his arms around his waist. Tony leaned out over the abyss, wrapped the rough side of the holster around the cable, whipped the belt around it, and cinched it tight. At least the cable wasn't greasy. On the contrary, it seemed rough with rust. "You know," he said, "I have absolutely no idea if this is going to work or not."

"Leap of faith," said Laika softly.

Then Tony stepped into space, his leather-soled feet reaching for the cable.

Chapter 48

*H*e fell several feet before he found his footing. Clutching desperately at the belt around the cable, he scrambled frantically with his feet, afraid that he was going to plunge unchecked straight down thirty-three stories.

But the rough hide caught on the twisted cable, never stopping entirely, but slowing him enough so that by great pressure of hands, wrists, and legs, he was able to check his speed. Even so, it was terrifying to him, shooting downward in total darkness, unable to sense how quickly he was falling. It felt fast, too fast, so that he expected at any second to slam against the top of the elevator car as though he had been thrown by a giant fist.

But as the seconds passed and the expected impact did not come, his panic diminished slightly. Still, he could not relax for an instant, clutching the belt tightly with one hand, and holding onto the leather holster itself with the other, while pressing his feet tight against the cable. From above, he once again heard the sound of gunfire, and the thought came to him that even now the attackers might be storming down the corridor and around the corner, riddling Laika and Joseph with bullets.

Suddenly the palm of his hand on the holster started to burn, and he realized with horror that the leather was wearing through. In another two seconds, he began to feel his feet slipping, and knew that the leather on his shoes had burned through to the point where only the rubber of his athletic shoes was against the cable. They did not grip.

His feet went straight down, and the increased pressure ripped the skin from his left hand so that he could hold on no longer.

Then the belt in his right hand snapped.

He fell, trying to twist his body so that he could land on his side, and hit the top of the elevator car almost instantly.

The impact knocked the air out of him, but did not splatter him over the top of the car, as he had feared. He had been only twenty feet above the car when the leather pads had given out and had free-fallen only ten feet. He had hit his left arm on the cable bar, and from the pain suspected that he might have broken a bone in his wrist, but there was no time for concern about that.

In the darkness, he felt around the top of the car for an escape panel, and his hands soon clutched a lever. He pulled up hard and the panel yielded, clattering to the surface of the roof as light poured up from the opening.

Tony pulled his .45 from his waist and dropped down into the car. The switch was set to lock, but far worse for Laika and Joseph, the control panel had been pried open and the wires ripped out. There was no way to send the car back up for them.

Tony snarled a curse and stepped through the open elevator doors into a well-lit twenty-foot corridor with a closed door at the end. He ran down it and shoved open the door, his pistol up and ready.

The door opened on the same garage through which they had entered the building. At its far end, the van that had been parked there was roaring up the ramp to the street. Tony ran across the dirty concrete floor, following it up the ramp and out onto the street.

Damn it, he thought as he ran. If they'd only locked the gate behind them when they'd gone in, that idiot James wouldn't have gotten in, and maybe neither would have whoever had been shooting at them up above. But most of all, the van driver would have had to stop to unlock the gate.

Tony saw the van heading east, already a block away.

There was no way he could catch it on foot, not with so little traffic to slow it down.

He ran to the corner and waited at the red light for several seconds until a car stopped. It was an ancient and rusting Ford Pinto, but he had no time to shop. He yanked open the car door, shouted, "Move!" and pulled out the screaming driver. Then he climbed in and tore after the van, whose taillights he thought he saw now three blocks away, still heading toward the East River.

The Pinto labored and wheezed when he tried to push it, but by running red lights and stop signs he had closed the gap to two blocks. Then the van turned right and he lost it.

He made the turn, heading south, and was surprised to see no vehicles ahead of him. Thinking the van had started out going east and might have taken the next left to keep going that way, he slowed and looked down the block toward the river a half mile away, but saw only a car headed toward him.

Still, it seemed the best bet, so he swung the Pinto to the left anyway. No van suddenly appeared, nor did he spy it on any of the side streets he passed. Finally he drove down Old Slip, hoping to catch a glimpse of it, but found nothing.

Frustrated, he retraced his route, but could find no place where the van had pulled in to let him by. South and east, Tony thought. Where the hell could they have been going? There were no bridges south and east of the financial district . . .

But there were piers. Wondering how he could have been so stupid, he made a U-turn and drove back to the river. When he hit South Street, he went south on it, hugging the docks, and there, parked under a sickly yellow light at the end of a short pier, was the van. A small covered boat was already a hundred yards out in the East River, heading to Brooklyn or Bayonne or Staten Island or any point south.

"Shit!" Tony cried, as he drove down to the pier and then out onto it. He jumped out of the Pinto and ran to the end of the pier, hoping that he could make out something on the rapidly disappearing power boat. But he couldn't. Its running lights were the only thing visible, and from them he assumed that the boat was a twenty-footer, maybe more. He couldn't tell another thing.

He looked inside the van, but it was totally empty. Nothing under the seats or in the glove compartment or the storage wells. The license plate had been removed, and the serial number had been filed off.

Slamming the van doors, he got into the Pinto and quickly headed back toward the Weyandt Tower. Through the open window, he heard a siren sounding from the area from which he had come and wondered if it was a police car responding to his act of grand theft auto. But then he figured, hell, this was New York; there were always sirens.

When she saw Tony glide away down into the darkness of the elevator shaft, Laika considered shining her flashlight down on him, but then thought that might distract him more than help him. The point was made moot by another outburst of gunfire from the corridor.

She beckoned to James to get moving, and they rejoined Joseph, who had just fired off another short burst and was now reloading. "I hate to say this," he said, glancing up at her, "but I didn't bring enough ammo to continue this indefinitely. How's Tony doing?"

"He went down the shaft. I don't know if he made it."

"Oh, *that's* encouraging. Even if he did, he's no good to us at the moment, nor, I'm afraid, can we count on him in the near future. Any suggestions?"

Laika glanced at James. "You're not in on this—get the hell back to the elevator and wait there until I call you." James seemed so scared that he didn't give her any backtalk, not even a second look. He just nodded and went. Laika turned back to Joseph. "You don't have to tell me, I know he's got to die."

"We may all have to die," Joseph said, giving a fairly noble smile. "Though I'd prefer not to."

"You and me both."

"Who *are* those guys? The goths from the subway station?"

"The goths didn't have that kind of firepower. But the squad that attacked the goths did."

"Why would they help us then and try to waste us now?" Joseph asked.

"Don't know—maybe it's a new player entirely."

"Christ, how many we got in this game?" Joseph was quiet for a moment, then said, "The kid could be useful."

"Don't call him a kid," said Laika. "He's no kid."

"Okay, the *asshole* could be useful."

"That's more like it. What are you thinking, send him out?"

Joseph nodded. "With gun blazing."

"The thought had occurred to me, too. Maybe he'd get lucky and take out one or two before they got him. Fewer for us to deal with. Maybe improve our chances."

It was damned heartless, and the thought of doing it to somebody she had once thought she loved made Laika half sick. But James had planned to kill them, all of them. He had that sin against his soul, and also the sin of discovering them in action. To any of their superiors in the Company, that alone would have condemned him.

"You want me to handle it?" said Joseph, as if sensing her unease.

She shook her head. "I'll take care of—"

But her words were interrupted by another blast of gunfire from the hallway. This time she stepped past Joseph far enough to thrust the barrel of her Jati-Matic around the corner and open up on whoever was foolhardy enough to try and advance on them. The firing stopped.

"James!" Laika called, and the man appeared, looking, fittingly enough, as though he were about to get killed. "We're going to have to go out," she told him.

"Into that?" he said. "Are you crazy?"

"We'll run out of bullets eventually. We're low now. We stay here, we're dead. So here's the deal. We give you back your pistol, and we go out together, firing away. They're down at that end of the hall. We shoot straight down, we'll hit them. But the part you're not going to like is that you're going first.''

James's mouth fell open. "No way!"

"Now look, you bastard, this is the way it is. You came in here to kill us, you think we're going to turn our backs on you? This way, at least you've got a chance. You don't go along with this . . ." She put the muzzle of her Jati-Matic against his forehead. ". . . I kill you right now." She clicked the lever to single fire. "One shot, because I can't waste the ammo. Be a man. Make the call."

James had pressed his eyes shut when the cold metal kissed his flesh. Now he opened them. "All right, all right . . . I'll do it."

Laika pulled her gun away and set it back to automatic fire. Then she took out the .38 Tony had taken from James and handed it back to him barrel first. "Don't touch that trigger yet. Turn around and get in front of me . . . that's right. Right by the corner of the wall. They can't hit you there. Now, just keep holding it by the barrel. You grab the grip, you're dead. You turn around, you're dead."

"What . . . what do I do?"

His voice sounded so frightened that she almost felt sorry for him. But *almost* was the key word. "We wait until they shoot again, try to come down the hall. But this time we don't shoot back. They'll think we're out of bullets, and then their own firing will slacken. It may not stop, but it'll slow. Then I'll say go, and we go. Go out shooting. Advance two or three feet, fire your six straight down the hall, and then drop to the floor."

"Why . . . why can't I drop first?"

"Time. Surprise is all we've got. They'll be too surprised to react immediately. You'll have time to get your shots off, and so will we. Now. When the firing starts, take the gun by the grip and cock it, but don't turn around or I'll kill you. You got it?"

He didn't say anything, but she saw his head nod. When she glanced at Joseph, she saw that he was looking at her with a mixture of respect and something else, something that may have been a touch of revulsion. She didn't care; her job now was to get him and herself out alive, and she'd let a dozen James Winstons die to do that.

Two minutes later, the firing started again, sending bits of the wall flying into the air in tiny clouds of plaster. James winced, but didn't move otherwise, and Laika tensed, ready for what was to come. Neither she nor Joseph returned fire, and in a few more seconds their attackers' fire slowed to the point where they could hear stealthy footsteps advancing down the corridor toward them.

"*Now!*" she said softly, and prodded James in the back.

He ran out at an angle, flattened himself against the opposite wall, and fired his pistol down the corridor with his right hand. Laika remained where she was, behind the shelter of the protecting wall, her hand on Joseph's shoulder in case he had not seen through her subterfuge.

He had, and watched with her as Joseph, only four of his six shots fired, went down in an assault of lead that bit into his legs and side and head with titanic force, tearing away bits of flesh and droplets of blood that dappled their faces as they saw him die.

He was a dead man who could not fall down. The impact of the continuing hail of bullets pushed him back against the wall and held him there until the firing stopped. Then he slid slowly down the wall, his blind eyes open, leaving a trail of red on the bullet-pocked surface.

"You lied to that man," Joseph said softly, wiping the sprayed blood from his face.

"I'm CIA. I lie for a living."

He didn't speak for a moment. "Think we ought to toss a couple shots down there," he finally said, "let them know there's more than one of us, and we're not dead?"

"Maybe we ought to let them know something," she said. Then she called out: "Hey! We're still here, and we still have enough ammo to stand you off for a long time. If you came for us, then that's how it'll go. If you came for what *we* came for, you're too late, and so were we."

There was no reply. She looked at Joseph, and he looked at her and shrugged, as if to say, "What could it hurt?"

"Whoever he or she or . . . *it* is, they took it down on an elevator. We can't go down. They locked it. So it's *gone*, you understand? If it's what you wanted, then we both lose."

She waited, but still only silence came from down the hall.

"Do you hear me?" she called. "Talk to me, where are we here?"

Still, there was no answer.

"Shit," she muttered, and let herself slide down the wall until she was sitting on the floor. She looked at James, dead, but in much the same position, and wiped her forehead with her sleeve. "Okay," she said, loud enough for the unknown quantities at the end of the corridor to hear. "That's how we'll play, then. We'll be here."

"Just fire if you want us," Joseph added softly, and Laika had to smile in spite of herself. "Miserable situation," he said.

"I've come through worse. Tony could come back, help us out."

"Firing his way through half a dozen well-armed men."

"Well, if anyone could do it, I'd put my money on Tony." She thought for a minute. "Or maybe they'll get bored and leave."

"There is that," Joseph said, and Laika was glad to hear a small but sincere chuckle from him. "I feel like Butch Cassidy and the Sundance Kid."

"Shall we yell 'Shit' and jump down the elevator shaft?" she asked, the last word breaking apart into a giggle. She hoped Joseph didn't think she was cracking up, but she had resorted to humor before to get her through life-threatening situations. It was one of the glories of the human animal, she thought.

"Why not, Sundance?" Joseph answered. "We've already done the 'Who *are* those guys?' bit."

They sat for a long time, waiting for the next round of shooting to start. Laika walked back to the elevator and looked down the shaft. She thought she saw a small square of light at the bottom, but couldn't be sure. "I think Tony got out," she told Joseph when she rejoined him. "Looks like the escape door of the car's open."

"Maybe he'll come back, then, if he didn't get killed by whoever was running." Joseph shrugged. "He knows who's here. He might be able to come up behind them. And I don't think Tony would feel any hesitation about shooting them in the back."

They sat on the floor, leaning against the wall, waiting for something to happen. Laika looked at James's body, from which the blood was still running, puddling all around him as he sat dead on the floor.

To her surprise, she didn't feel a thing. Even though the dead man had shared her bed and lodged for a time in her heart, she felt nothing, not even regret that he had been stupid enough to follow them to his certain death—if not at the hands of their attackers, then at their own.

"The bastard is dead now," she said softly.

Joseph looked up. "What?"

"When I was a kid, I read James Bond novels," she said. "I guess that was what first got me interested in espionage. And at the end of one of them, I forget which, Bond discovers that this woman who was his lover was a double agent. And I don't remember whether he kills her or not, but I think the villain does it, and in the last line of the book, he's telling one of his colleagues that she was a double, and he says that, only he calls her the bitch. And it was just so goddamned ice cold. I always wondered what Bond was thinking. Was he just lying to himself?" She looked away from the corpse. "He used to call me a bitch. I didn't like that. I didn't like it any better than when James Bond called the dead girl that."

"*Casino Royale*," Joseph said. "Good book, shitty movie."

"Did you read them all, too?" Laika said.

"All the Flemings."

"Which were better, books or movies?"

"First three Connerys were better than the books, Mizh Moneypenny."

"Worst Bond?"

"Lazenby."

She shook her head. "Moore."

"At least Moore could act."

"He couldn't act *Bond*. And they gave him all those dopey special effects. And that Jaws guy."

"Wasn't *Moore's* fault. You like Dalton?"

"Liked Brosnan better."

"Just another pretty face." Laika nodded. "Best villain?"

"Goldfinger."

"Nope," Joseph said. "Has to be Rosa Klebb."

"Rosa *Who?*"

"Lotte Lenya in the movie."

"The knife-tipped shoes," Laika said. "I always hoped I'd be issued a pair of those."

"And speaking of villains, how long has it been since that bunch last fired at us?"

"About twelve minutes." She looked up, startled. "They're coming."

Joseph listened, and heard it, too . . . Soft footsteps coming slowly down the corridor. "Take them here, or. . . ." He jerked his head back toward the cul-de-sac by the elevator, where they could get on either side of the wall where it widened. Here, at the turn of the corridor, there was only room for one to make a stand.

Laika nodded and they slipped quietly back to the elevator. Laika took the right, Joseph the left, and they waited, their weapons pointing toward the turn, where their enemy would appear from the right.

Chapter 49

*T*hen they both heard a voice. "Laika? Joseph?"

"*Tony?*" Laika said, raising the muzzle of her weapon toward the ceiling as Tony Luciano appeared from around the corner. "Jesus!" she said, overjoyed to see him and not the half dozen shooters she had expected. She met him halfway down the corridor and slapped him genially on the arm, and then, unable to restrain herself, gave him a hug. Joseph grabbed his hand and pumped it.

"Ow, man, easy!" Tony said. He held up his hand to reveal a red and oozing spot where the cable had torn it. "I don't know why you're so glad to see me, anyway," Tony said. "I lost them."

"Yeah," said Joseph, "but you lost the gunmen, too. That's who we were expecting when you poked your head around the corner."

"What the hell happened here?" said Tony, looking at James's corpse. "No, maybe I shouldn't ask. There's another dead one at the end of the hall."

"Did you see our attackers on your way up?" Laika asked.

"Not a sign of them."

"They must've gone right after we talked to them. We should've tried that earlier," Joseph said, nodding at James's corpse. "He might still be alive." Then he looked at Laika's grim face. "Or not," he added softly. "So how did you make out? You said you lost them?"

Tony nodded glumly. "Stole a car and followed them, but they got away. Escaped in a boat down the East River. Not one damn piece of evidence in the van. Cops are all over the streets looking for the car I stole, so I just drove it down into the garage and came up the stairs again."

"Well," said Laika, "whoever was here is gone, and so are our attackers, so let's take some time to look around and find out what we can."

When they walked back into the corridor, they saw the body at the end of it. The man had been hit twice in the chest, and had probably died quickly. "Looks like James was a straight shooter at the end," Joseph said, kneeling next to the body.

"Search it," Laika ordered. "I'll take the office we came through. Tony, you check the rest of this suite—see what's around the corners and in the other rooms."

Before she went into the office, however, Laika more closely examined the boxlike cell in which she assumed the prisoner had been held. She ran a fingernail along the flat black surface of the wall and ascertained what she had first thought, that it was an unbroken plane of lead. The room must have weighed a ton. She examined the strips along the frame of the door. Although they might have been made of a hard rubber beneath, they were coated with lead as well. She searched for an air vent of some kind, but there was none. The room was a box, and when the door was closed, that box would be sealed airtight.

Next she went into the office. The magazines on the coffee table were the latest editions of *Time*, *National Geographic*, and *Entertainment Weekly*. The Bible was a King James version with no markings or name on it. The Greeley book looked as if it had been heavily read. Its spine was broken in a dozen places and the pages were dogeared in a dozen more.

She picked up the Walkman and opened it. A Natalie Cole cassette was inside. The tape box was nowhere to be seen. A box of coffee filters and a large can of Maxwell House coffee sat next to the coffee machine, whose red "on" button was still glowing.

The desk was empty. There was nothing in any of the drawers, not even the detritus of paper clips or broken pencil points or bits of torn paper. With the alarm system as further evidence, it seemed as though these people, whoever they were, expected to be raided, and had a contingency plan for just that occasion.

Laika turned as Tony came back into the room. "You know that panel we saw at the end of the big hall?" he said. "It covers the windows—it's set a few feet back from them so that from the outside the place just looks dark and empty. This whole thing isn't any too sophisticated, but it worked."

"What do you mean?"

"I mean they got away."

"Anything else in the other offices?"

"Not much. There's a cot in one close by, looks as though it's been used recently, but otherwise, not a thing in any of them. No filing cabinets, desks, chairs, *nada*. And no trace evidence to speak of."

Joseph came in from the hallway where the dead men lay. He was wiping blood off his hands with a handkerchief. There was a small book tucked under his arm. "Find anything?" asked Laika.

"Yes. There's a list of some sort, and what appears to be a coded message. They were both folded up in this." He took the book from under his arm and held it out spine first. It was slightly larger than a pack of cigarettes and bound in brown leatherette. Laika could read "Holy Bible" on the spine.

"Funny how these things keep cropping up," Joseph said. "There wasn't a bit of personal ID on the body—no wallet, keys, nothing. Even the labels had been cut from his clothing. It's almost like these people expected to get killed."

"How old was he?" Laika asked.

"Twenty-two, twenty-three. A suicide squad for Christ? I took a set of prints we can run."

"All right, then. We've stayed here long enough." Laika turned to go.

"So," said Tony, "we gonna let the police find out who he is? And the other one, too?"

She shook her head. "I think I know what'll happen after we leave. The police will never see the inside of this place—it would raise too many questions. The two bodies will disappear, and so will the lead cell. I don't think anyone will ever see that dead soldier . . . or James Winston again."

"I ought to remove his ID," said Tony. Laika nodded in agreement and Tony disappeared into the next room for several minutes, while Laika looked at the papers Joseph handed her.

The list had been made on four pieces of yellow legal paper and was now tattered, as if from having been carried about unprotected for a long time. The Latin words *Locus hominus aeterni* were written at the top, and there were six columns across the page. On the left of each column was a list of four-digit numbers. On the right was the name of a location. It began:

1204 Rome
1208 Venice
1217 Bologna
1223 Paris

It continued in this way for all four sheets, front and back. The last entry was "1996 NYC." She was just about to ask Joseph what he thought it meant when Tony returned.

"We can go," he said. "I've got all his ID."

"What about dental records?" Joseph asked. "And fingerprints. Is he on file anywhere?"

Tony looked at him darkly. "I said I got *all* his ID."

That was enough for Laika. She didn't want to think about what Tony had done, and she didn't want to guess what besides a wallet he might be carrying out in his pockets. "Then let's go," she said, and led the way out, down the stairs to the cellar garage and up the ramp.

Tony locked the garage door behind them, leaving the stolen Pinto in the darkness. He reattached the padlock to the iron gate as well, and they saw no one observing or following them as they walked through the streets to their car several blocks away.

As Tony drove them uptown, dawn was just beginning to brighten the strips of sky visible around the tops of the buildings. In the passing light from street lamps and signs, Laika continued to look at the list, holding it up for Joseph, who leaned over the backseat.

"It's headed *Locus hominus aeterni*," Laika said for Tony's benefit. "Then a list of dates and places. Europe first of all, and then, from the 1700s onward, all over the world."

"Ending here in 1996," Joseph said. "A couple years ago."

"What's the location for 1919?" Tony asked.

Laika found the date. "That's also New York City," she said.

"Want to bet that it was St. Stephen's Church?" said Tony.

"The implication?"

"That this is a list of the places where the prisoner was held over the years . . . hell, over the *centuries.*"

"You mean the prisoners, as in more than one," Laika said.

"You don't know Latin?" Tony asked, and Laika shook her head.

"German, French, Italian," Joseph said dryly, "but they never spoke Latin anywhere I was assigned."

"I learned it in Catholic school," Tony said. "And those words at the top of the list? They mean 'Place of the one who never dies.' " Laika watched Tony, but he kept his eyes straight ahead. "So. I say *the* prisoner. As in one."

"You think," Laika said slowly, "that this list refers to one person only? For nearly eight centuries?"

" 'The one who never dies,' " Tony repeated. "How does that make any sense otherwise?"

"The line," Joseph offered almost desperately. "The line never dies."

"*Hominus*. Singular. Not the line, not the many, not one in general—the *one*."

"We don't even know where this list came from," Laika said. "We don't know who those people were."

"They came for him," Tony said. "Like the cultists, only it wasn't them. These people were disciplined, ready. They were after him." He was silent for a moment. "I think they wanted to free him. The Bible suggests they were Christians. I think they wanted to free . . . *Him*."

Tony said the last word with so much reverence that it chilled Laika. It was impossible, unfathomable. "This paper," she said, "is all the evidence we have. That's a big conclusion to jump to on that basis."

"It's a *crazy* conclusion," said Joseph. "Jesus, Tony? You're saying that this prisoner is *Jesus*, the Christ himself, semi-mythical founder of the primary religion of the Western world? Uh-uh, no *way* can I believe that. That would mean—"

"That would *mean*," Tony said, "that all your cynicism was bullshit, that everything you've believed—or *dis*believed—over the years was false. What was it that Sherlock Holmes used to say? When you've eliminated the impossible, whatever remains, no matter how improbable, is the truth. And this truth means that your world's turned upside down, Joseph."

Joseph said nothing for a moment, but when he spoke, his voice was calm. "No, Tony. It means *yours* is. If Jesus didn't die, it might mean he's immortal, but it also means that he wasn't resurrected and lifted into Heaven. And unless I'm very much mistaken, it's *that* little miracle that's the pillar the Catholic church is based upon. You can't have it both ways—he had to be a mortal to die and be resurrected. But if he's *im*mortal, then he's not divine. Sorry."

Tony's cheeks reddened, his hands gripping the steering wheel tightly, and Laika saw the sudden panic and confusion in his eyes. "Okay," she said, trying to keep him from exploding, "this isn't a seminary. We're going to deal with facts here and nothing but. The list isn't the only thing we have—we've got the coded message, too."

She took it out and looked at it. It was on one sheet of paper, front and back, and consisted of numbers. It began: "250-17-4 19-2 293-4-3 26-8 29-10 7-30-2," and continued. Both sides were covered with the numbers, written in precise and tiny handwriting.

"It's a book code," Joseph said, leaning over her shoulder. '250-17-4' means page 250, line 17, the fourth word. Then '19-2' is line 19, second word. '293' starts with another page."

"So what's the book?" Laika asked. "That Bible?"

"I already checked. That Bible's double columned, so that makes the line numbering tricky, but I tried it several ways and just got gibberish. Besides, you'd never carry a book code message along with the book. No, I think the Bible was more a sign of devoutness than it was a code breaker." Joseph quickly looked over the paper. "Highest page number is 452, which means the book could have more pages but not fewer. Highest line number is 34, and highest word number's 14."

"What about the Greeley book?" Laika asked.

Joseph shook his head. "Not long enough." He sighed. "There are a whole lot of books in the world. I guess we should start checking what's common to . . . religious people, for want of a better word."

"There's something else we need to do first," Laika said, "and that's to return to the sculpture and see if there's any-place else it leads. We still don't know what happened to Peder Holberg. Then we'll disassemble it and destroy the plans. If we figured out where to go using it, other people will be able to as well."

"We can look again," said Joseph, "but I don't think there's going to be a damn thing that leads us anywhere else. And as for taking the time to destroy it, why? Even if somebody follows the map to the Weyandt Towers, there's nothing there now."

"We don't leave a trail," she replied. "We cover *all* our tracks, and that sculpture is one hell of a provocative piece of evidence. It'll be a lot more enigmatic as a pile of iron. Let's go. Now. To the warehouse."

Chapter 50

*T*he sun shone in through the windows as they crossed the bridge to the Bronx. It was going to be a warm day. Tony had cranked down his window, and the breeze stroked Laika's hair. It felt good, she thought, clean. She had been in too much darkness lately. She was ready for some light.

Four young kids were playing baseball in the parking lot, and Laika realized that school must be out by now. Summer was here, and she hadn't even noticed its coming. They parked, stepped out into the sunshine, and went up to the door.

It seemed undisturbed since they had last been there. Tony had started putting a thread near the bottom of the door after Laika had discovered the bug, and the thread was unbroken. They unlocked the locks and went inside.

When the bright overhead lights went on, Laika realized immediately that something had changed. For a moment she didn't know what it was, and then she saw that the iron itself was different. It seemed darker, as though the rust had fallen from it and it had resumed the previous deep black of wrought iron.

"What the hell. . . ." she heard Tony say, and followed him as he walked closer to the sculpture.

At the heart of the structure, where the explosion had torn and bent the iron, there was a substance on the dirty wooden floor. It looked like flaking rust that had fallen from the iron above. Mixed with it were small yellow shards, none more than a quarter inch wide. Though the powder was spread over a large area, Laika thought that if it were all swept up it would easily fit in one bucket, perhaps two at the most. On the one side, the powder had seemed to form itself into a very definite isosceles triangle whose short point seemed to indicate one of the walls.

Laika knelt and dipped her fingers in the powder. Where her hands were moist, the red particles clung to her flesh and seemed to melt at the contact, like remarkably tiny bits of ice. But she knew they were not ice. And the small fissures in the yellow fragments, like cells in a honeycomb, told her what they were.

"Rust?" Joseph said. "The rust came out of the metal? How the hell could that happen?"

Laika saw that Tony was kneeling, too. "I've seen too much of this to call it rust," he said. Then he gathered a thimbleful in his palm, spat on it, curled his fingers inward, and rubbed. His palms and fingertips gleamed a brighter red, the moisture working its alchemy.

"The powder—it's dried blood," he said. "And those little shards are bone fragments." He looked at Laika. "His blood tinted the iron."

"Wait a minute," Joseph said, now on his knees as well. "The blood was *in* the iron? And . . . and whose blood? That's crazy, how could it—"

"You know damn well whose blood," Tony said. "We'll type it, run a DNA test on it, but you know whose it's going to be."

"Peder Holberg," Laika said quietly. "He's here." She looked at the small, dry pond of brown dust. "Whatever's left of him was here all the time. In the iron." She looked at Tony, then at Joseph. "Who wants to put it all together? That's what we're here for, right? When you've eliminated the impossible, whatever remains, no matter how improbable. . . ."

"Even," said Tony, "if the truth is what we thought was impossible? I don't know what Holmes would've said about that. But I know what *I'll* say, if nobody else is willing to."

Tony straightened up and looked at the chaos of ironwork before them. "Peder Holberg built this," he said. "He built it when he was in what we'll call, for lack of a better term, a fugue state. A trance. And while he was in that trance, *something*—some entity, some voice, some intelligence— took over most of his mind. And it, and he, built *this.*" Tony wrapped a fist around a rod of iron.

"Holberg didn't understand what he was doing," he went on. "He had no idea why he was suffering these blackouts, where he was going, or why. When he came across the cultists in some club, he felt an affinity for them. Maybe somehow they just caught the psychic tail end of the messages this entity was sending to Holberg, and they misinterpreted them. It seems certain that their version of whoever he was is corrupted, somehow.

"But somehow, maybe through contact with the cultists, or maybe just over time, Holberg became aware of what he was doing, and maybe even caught a glimpse of the reason behind it."

"Which was?" asked Joseph in a voice heavy with irony.

"Which was to show where he was being held prisoner."

"If it had this power over Holberg," Joseph said, "then how come this critter didn't just tell *him* where he was at? Why go through the whole sculpture routine?"

"Because maybe he didn't want Holberg to free him, or knew that he wouldn't or couldn't. The purpose was to show somebody else. But then Holberg threw a monkey wrench into the works. He started building his bomb. He might not have realized what was guiding him, or he might have mistaken it for something evil."

"Instead of what, Jesus Christ?" Joseph said.

"I don't know. But he built the bomb, probably to destroy the sculpture, thinking that if he did that, he'd be free of this control. Guaraldi said that during the show Holberg had seemed distracted, as though he was hearing voices in his head. I suspect he actually was, and he went up to that store-room either to be alone, or to get the bomb and take it to the warehouse and blow the whole thing up. But he didn't get that far.''

Tony looked down at the red powder on the floor. ''Okay, maybe he did, in a way. But somehow the bomb went off. It didn't kill Holberg. Not there. Instead he was, what, *beamed* into the warehouse?''

'' 'Apported' is the proper term,'' Joseph said dryly. '' 'Beamed' sounds a little too *Star Trek.*''

''Fine, apported. But it was done with such force that the sculpture was shattered, and Holberg's body—blood, muscle, and bone—was blended with the iron, became one with it.''

''And you think that Jesus—if that's who this prisoner is—did that to somebody he had chosen to be his guide for the people who were looking for him? Not a very merciful savior, if you don't mind my saying so.''

''There could have been another force,'' said Tony, ''a force in opposition to . . . to the prisoner, that was trying to keep people from discovering his location.''

''An *eee*-vil force,'' intoned Joseph.

''Yeah,'' said Tony, nodding shortly. ''An evil force.''

''I'm not a subscriber to extremes of good and evil, Tony. I see political expedience in most situations where people tend to bring in those absolutist concepts. But although I may not buy everything you say . . . ,'' Joseph looked at the sculpture, at the layer of red dust, at the faces of his partners, ''. . . I don't have any better explanation right now. Not to say that there isn't one. Hell, there are a lot of possibilities.''

''Like what?'' Laika asked.

''Like maybe this entity, good, bad, or indifferent, wanted revenge for Holberg's bomb, or maybe Holberg was sacrificed by the thing, with his death being the final ingredient for whatever-the-hell purpose this thing was to have. And maybe Holberg even came up here on his own, sneaked out of his studio before the bomb even went off, and then whatever happened . . . happened.'' He shook his head and Laika saw agony in the small gesture. ''But whatever it was, I'm spooked by it. I don't like this shit. I've never seen a weirder assortment of circumstances and unexplained phenomena. I don't know. I feel like I don't know anything anymore."

Joseph took a small glassine envelope from his pocket and scooped up some of the dried blood. "But at least I know how to do a blood test." He sealed it and tucked it away. "Now, let's look at this gigantic piece of crap one more time before we tear it down."

After further examination, they concluded that there was nothing more to be learned from the sculpture. Then they turned their attention to the most recent anomaly, the triangle of blood. They investigated the area of the wall that the short point faced, but found nothing there. Then Joseph, thinking of a larger picture, took a compass reading. "It's pointing roughly west-southwest," he said.

"So what's there?" asked Tony.

Joseph shrugged. "Lots. Ohio, Kansas, Arizona, Hawaii, and it just keeps going."

"They went that-a-way," Laika said, but did not smile.

"Maybe," said Joseph.

She hissed in frustration. "I'm sick of 'maybes.' Tony, what's the fastest way to bring down this piece of shit?" She pointed at the sculpture.

"Small charges," he said, "placed in certain junctions. It'll collapse like a house of cards. I guarantee nobody will ever put it back together without the plans."

"Do it."

Laika rolled up the plans while Tony went out to the car to get what he needed. Joseph started to sweep up the earthly remains of what Laika was sure would be Peder Holberg, and she helped him after she put a rubber band around the plans, which she planned to burn later.

She paused at the triangle, trying to listen in the dead, dusty air for whatever it commanded, but heard nothing, and swept it up so that it lost its meaning, becoming only particles of dried blood, as devoid of significance as the brown dust was devoid of life.

They put the remnants in a cardboard box in which one of the computers had been transported. Laika had overestimated. Swept up, Peder Holberg's remains would have filled only half a bucket.

When Tony had the charges set, they went behind the wall that separated the anteroom from the warehouse. The noise of the explosions was surprisingly muted, but the clattering the iron made as the pieces fell was nearly deafening, and seemed to go on far longer than Laika would have guessed.

Tony had promised the truth. All that remained of Peder Holberg's work was a pile of iron bars and rods. The charges had actually done more damage than the original force that had battered the sculpture months before.

Using an exclusive Company program, they wiped the hard drives of the computers in the warehouse past recovery, and went back outside, where the sun was continuing to shine brightly. The boys who had been playing were gone.

By the time they'd reached the apartment, Laika had made her decision. She asked the others to sit down in the living room while she explained.

"I want to tell you," she said, "what I want to do with the report we send to Richard Skye. It won't be what really happened, because I don't trust Skye with that information. Because of the Company-issue bug in the warehouse and what MacAndrews said before he died, I don't think Skye is telling us everything he knows, or disclosing the real reasons for our assignments. And if he is indeed connected to the killings of the eleven men in Plattsburgh, that would be a flagrant violation of the CIA charter. That would also be multiple murder.

"Now, I know we've got little room to talk, since our very existence as a unit here is against that charter. And also, as you both know, my actions in withholding information would be considered gross insubordination, and possibly traitorous. Still, this is what I'm planning to do, but only if you both agree. If either of you disagrees, then you'll have to band together and both make the true report yourselves. At that point I'll be relieved of my assignment and turned over for a private judicial hearing within the Company.''

She looked at them, putting her life in their hands once again.

Chapter 51

A week later, Richard Skye looked out his window across the green treetops that surrounded Langley. He was frowning as he held the telephone to his ear and listened. But when he heard Mr. Stanley's voice in the earpiece, he smiled as broadly as he would have had the man been sitting across the desk from him.

"I'm afraid, sir," he said in a cloying voice, "that I have some discouraging news. I have a full report from the operatives, and despite all initial appearances of a positive link, the entire Holberg case seems to have a natural explanation. It seems Holberg was never in the room when the bomb went off, which accounts for the lack of human remains."

Skye winced as he listened to Mr. Stanley's response, and then tried to explain further. "Well, as it turns out, those witnesses who saw Holberg enter the storeroom seem to have been unreliable. There had been a good deal of drinking, as well as other illicit drug use. While they might have seen Holberg go into the room, they apparently didn't notice him coming out again after he had set the bomb to go off. . . .

"Why? An attempt at faking his own death, apparently. These supposed fugue states were merely a sign of mental distress, an inability to cope with his own success, from what his homosexual lover said. My people found the warehouse where Holberg had been working, and after he left his showing, he went up there and destroyed his final work of art.

The lover was later killed in an accident trying to restore it . . .

"No sir, Holberg is gone. My people traced his last whereabouts to a steamer heading back to Norway. But Holberg never arrived. I suspect his body is somewhere in the North Atlantic. It's only a short step from faking one's death to actually accomplishing it. . . .

"No, there appears to have been nothing paranormal connected with it at all. I had hoped our quarry might somehow be involved, but such was not the case. I'm sorry. . . .

"I certainly understand your disappointment, sir. Believe me, it's no greater than my own. I really thought this was a valid incident. After all, it had all the earmarks of—

"Yes sir, no, I'm sure I *don't* have to explain them to you, no indeed. But there *is* a new development, something I've never come across before. It's begun to draw some attention, and it is totally inexplicable. . . .

"Well, sir, it's a phenomenon that's taking place in the Southwest. Out in the desert."

Laika and her partners were supposed to be relaxing now. Skye had allowed them a week off before he would give them their next assignment. They went to movies, and Laika attended the opera. They ate long, lingering meals at good restaurants, and stayed up late into the night, talking about what had happened and about what might come, thinking about which book, of all the books in the world, might be the one to unlock the riddle of the code.

Now Laika lay in the darkness, music in her ears, and shuddered. She was listening to a recording made in the forties of Lauri-Volpi singing Verdi's *Otello*, calling out for "*sangue, sangue.*" *Blood, blood.*

She had seen enough blood.

She turned off the Discman, set the earphones on the bed table, and closed her eyes. But the pealing cry for blood remained in her head, making her think of the powdery remains of Peder Holberg, for the blood tests had proved it was him, and the torn, bullet-riddled body of James Winston.

Tears pooled in her eyes then, not at the thought of what he had become, but what he once was, a man who had laughed with her and loved her. A man she had loved, until something he'd buried away for love of her crept back out and possessed him.

And at the end, it had been Shakespeare's green-eyed monster of jealousy that had plagued James just as it had plagued Othello, the thought of white men sleeping with his woman. It had drawn James Winston to the Weyandt Tower and his death as surely as it had drawn Othello to his suicide in Desdemona's bedchamber. The only difference was that this time Desdemona was black as well. And alive, because she was stronger than Othello. Because it was her business to see through subterfuge.

But if that was the case, why couldn't she see any further into the secrets of this prisoner who'd escaped them? Was he, as Tony had suggested, actually Christ, living for millennia, or a descendant of Christ, the less fantastic premise in which she suspected Joseph believed?

Or was he someone else, someone completely different? What powers did he have? Why was he encased in lead? And if the Roman Catholic Church was holding him, why they? Was he evil? Or was he of such a great good that even the church could not permit his freedom? How did he threaten them?

What was he?

She had no answers, but she continued to look for them in her dreams.

Three days later, FBI agent Alan Phillips gave Quentin McIntyre the report he had been waiting for. "We found them—Luciano, Harris, and Stein. They were holed up for the past few months in an apartment in New York City. An agent who had seen the three photos just happened to spot them coming out of a movie theater late yesterday afternoon. Followed them to a restaurant, then to an apartment building on West 72nd Street."

McIntyre nodded eagerly. "Any idea what they've been up to?"

"Not yet. But whatever it was . . . ," Phillips paused uncomfortably, ". . . they seem to be done in New York."

"What? Why?"

"We lost them. The agent put a twenty-four on the building, but at three in the morning Luciano comes up in a car, the others come out the door with a lot of bags, throw them in the trunk, and they're off. The agent calls in a trace car soon as he sees they're heading out, but it's such quick notice that the only driver available was a real novice. Still, traffic was light that time of morning, so he was able to tail them through the city and the Holland Tunnel over to the New Jersey Turnpike. They caught Route 78 at Newark, and that's when they made our tail. They dry cleaned the kid, slipped off at the next exit, slammed through a business district. Luciano's a great driver—this kid didn't have a chance to stay on him."

"So which way were they headed when our agent lost them?" McIntyre asked.

West.

He was going west. Clad in darkness, sheathed in lead, still a captive.

The road he was on was made of iron. How fitting a trail for someone new to follow, he thought. He had nearly been freed. Nearly. What had happened in the process, at least *that* was good. The blood.

He regretted the loss of the artist. Those he could reach were becoming fewer on this world. People used their minds less—at least, that part of the mind he could touch. The world was too fast. There was too little time for meditation, introspection, those soft hours of thought when souls were open like petals.

Still, the artist had betrayed him. He knew as clearly as if he had read it in a book that he was planning to destroy the work he had had him create, the work that would guide his followers to him.

And that betrayal had infuriated him, enraged him so that the force burst from him, even through the lead, and did what it had done, made the artist one with his work, blended flesh and blood and iron until the place of imprisonment was found.

But then it was too late. The surge of power had weakened him, as it always did, and when he was being moved, when his captors were most vulnerable, he was, ironically, at his weakest. His powers were finite, even if his life was not.

No matter; there would be further opportunities. His strength would return. He would endure. He would inspire.

He could wait.

He had all the time in this world and the next.

Readers wishing to further investigate the reality of the paranormal will find much of worth in the following books: *The Encyclopedia of the Paranormal* edited by Gordon Stein, Ph. D.; *The New Age: Notes of a Fringe Watcher* by Martin Gardner; *An Encyclopedia of Claims, Frauds, and Hoaxes of the Occult and Supernatural* by James Randi; *The Demon-Haunted World* by Carl Sagan; and the publications of the Committee for the Scientific Investigation of Claims of the Paranormal (CSICOP) at *http://www.csicop.org*.

Zecharia Sitchin's
The Earth Chronicles